A Nightingale Sang

Sally Anderson

First published in 2013

ISBN-10: 1493515659
ISBN-13: 978-1493515653

CONTENTS

ACKNOWLEDGMENTS

This is a work of fiction, but I began this book by researching the events of World War Two to ensure that the period detail was as accurate as possible. Any errors are mine, but I am particularly indebted to the following authors and books: Juliet Gardiner *'Over Here': the GIs in Wartime Britain*, and *Wartime Britain 1939-1945*; Jenel Virden *Goodbye Piccadilly: British War Brides in America*; Stuart Hill *By Tank into Normandy*; Stephen E. Ambrose *Citizen Soldiers: From the Normandy Beaches to the Surrender of Germany*; Nicola Tyrer *Sisters In Arms: British Army Nurses tell their Story*; Lucilla Andrews *No Time For Romance*.

1. ARRIVAL

August 1943

Hampshire, England

Samantha Mitchell was halfway to the hospital when she first heard the faint hum that sounded like motor vehicles approaching. The wheels of her bicycle whirred beneath her and she could hear the familiar sounds of birds calling and of leaves rustling in the hedgerows and trees that lined the lane. But there was something else too. She was sure she could hear the slow, steady drone of distant engines drifting towards her on the breeze.

The day promised to be clear and bright, quite unlike the short gloomy days of the previous winter when the cold had seemed to add miles to her daily journey from her aunt's house to the town where she worked. It was a warm day at the end of August. The sort of day, it seemed to Sam, when it was hardly possible to believe there was a war on.

The breeze rushed past her and the ground rippled beneath her tyres as she approached the squat grey pillbox at the end of the lane. She slowed down as she drew level with it, then turned out onto the wider, smoother road that climbed steeply through woodland and then dropped away from the crest of the hill, twisting down towards the town.

The morning sunshine filtered through the overhanging branches of the trees, dappling the road. As she started up the incline, Sam could hear the rumble of motor engines growing louder, but there were still no vehicles in sight. She lowered her head and pushed hard on the pedals, her calves stinging as she toiled up the gradient.

All at once the countryside opened out in front of her. She trailed her foot along the ground and the bicycle shuddered to a halt. From where she'd arrived at the top of the hill she could see the long line of military vehicles that was curving up from the town below. Her stomach fluttered and the breath caught in her throat. *The Americans*, she thought. *So they're here at last.*

She had seen the rows of Nissen huts that had been erected in the parkland around Foley Manor, the elegant country mansion that stood in extensive grounds less than a mile away from her Aunt Leonora's house, and for the past few weeks the arrival of the Americans had been eagerly anticipated by Diana and Nancy, her closest friends. But although she'd known that they were coming, she'd never imagined anything like this. The road was choked with canvas-covered trucks and military Jeeps, gun-carriers and armoured vehicles, the like of which she'd never seen before.

The sun moved in and out behind a wisp of cloud as the snaking convoy steadily approached. Sam hesitated for a moment, considering what to do, then dismounted and wheeled the bicycle a few yards down the hill. The verge that fringed the road was all but buried under weeds and brambles, but she spotted an open patch of grass beneath a tree. It had rained the night before and the earth squelched beneath her feet as she manoeuvred the bicycle off the road.

The truck at the head of the convoy loomed gradually larger. Sam saw the white star emblazoned on its bonnet and then her eyes met those of the soldier who was driving. A broad grin stretched out across his face. She straightened her shoulders and braced herself, suddenly realising what was to come. The truck pulled away from her and through the rear opening in its canvas skin she caught sight of the American soldiers who were sitting along the benches in the back.

Almost at once, one of them lifted his head and pushed back his helmet to meet her gaze. His dark eyes widened and he scrambled to his feet. 'Hey, honey!' he cried. 'How about a date tonight?'

A loud wolf-whistle rang out above the din of the engines and the other soldiers rippled into life. They began laughing and calling out to her, and Sam felt the colour rushing to her cheeks.

The dark-eyed soldier leaned out from beneath the canvas skin, one hand placed theatrically over his heart. 'Don't be shy, beautiful - we won't hurt you!' He was still grinning widely as the back of the truck receded away, vanishing over the crest of the hill in a cloud of dust.

The other vehicles flowed slowly past, a steady stream of whistles and calls trailing out from behind them. It was impossible not to be flattered by all the attention, but as she watched from the roadside, Sam felt an ache near her heart. The soldiers were warm and friendly, young and handsome, but their carefree, youthful vitality only served to remind her of all she had lost.

Lieutenant Jack Webster rested one hand on the steering wheel of the Jeep and brushed the other thoughtfully over his chin. It was over three weeks since the troopship in which he'd crossed the Atlantic had pulled out of New York, and that was the last time he could remember having had a decent shower and a shave.

Bill Crawford, his friend and fellow officer, was travelling in the passenger seat next to him. They'd met at military camp in New Jersey and had already seen many long, hard months of training together.

'I could sure use a shave,' said Jack.

Bill glanced at him and smiled wryly. 'You and me both.'

Jack changed down a gear. They were travelling up a narrow, winding road flanked by rolling countryside and he could see the soldiers in the back of the truck in front of them lolling against each other and gazing out over the unfurling view. It had come as something of a surprise to him when he'd been told where they were to be posted. He'd expected to be sent to the deserts of North Africa and to go straight into active combat there along with the rest of his division. Instead, his unit had been given the task of setting up a base in England, where they were to prepare for the eventual opening of an Allied second front in Northern France. He remembered the feeling of frustration he'd had when his commanding officer had first given them their orders. He knew they'd been given an important job to do, but there was no telling how long it would be before they finally went into battle.

Bill shifted in the seat next to him and Jack gave him a sideways glance. 'Foley Manor shouldn't be too much further now. Another couple of miles or so, at the most.'

Bill nodded. 'Foley Manor,' he repeated thoughtfully. 'It sounds pretty impressive. I wonder what it'll be like.'

'Well, we should have more than enough space to accommodate all the men. We've been promised the whole place to ourselves. The house, the grounds - everything.'

'And what about the owners? Any idea what's happened to them?'

'No. All I know for sure is that the place was requisitioned weeks ago.'

Bill gave a short laugh. 'That should make us popular with the locals.'

The truck in front of them slowed to a crawl and Jack shifted down another gear.

Bill whistled softly, 'Say, will you take a look at that…'

Jack followed the direction of his gaze. A girl was standing off to their left by the roadside ahead of them, gripping tightly to the handlebars of the bicycle that was balanced by her side. She looked young, probably only about twenty, he thought, and she was wearing a faded cotton dress that skimmed her slim figure and billowed softly in the light morning breeze.

Catching sight of her, the soldiers in the truck in front started into life and he heard their barrage of wolf-whistles above the engine noise of the Jeep.

Jack noticed the proud lift of the girl's chin, but he saw too how her shoulders subtly tensed. His brows pulled together into a frown.

'I wish those guys would knock it off.'

Bill nodded. 'Still, I can't say as I blame them. She's a knockout.'

Sam slipped her starched white apron over her uniform and then adjusted her cap in the little square mirror that hung on the wall above her locker. She turned around and briefly contemplated the empty common room of the small cottage hospital where she worked. Shafts of morning sunlight slanted through the windows onto the polished wooden floor and the faded olive-coloured walls were decorated with government posters urging people to do their bit. Two mismatched, sagging sofas were strewn with cushions and a small coffee table was heaped with well-thumbed magazines.

Sam had been living with her Aunt Leonora and working at the hospital since the beginning of the year; she'd moved there after finishing her training at St Thomas's, one of the big London hospitals. She'd experienced at first hand the devastation of the Blitz, and seen the awful casualties, and she still wasn't entirely used to the relative quiet and tranquillity of her current surroundings.

She heard the sound of hurrying footsteps coming along the corridor outside and a moment later her friend Diana stepped through the doorway into the room. She was dressed as Sam was, in a blue nurse's uniform, and her thick brown hair was coiled into a roll beneath her cap. She was twenty-two, just a year older than Sam, and strikingly pretty with her dark eyes and pale skin. They'd been best friends ever since their school days when they'd sung together in the choir.

Diana's eyes darted across the room towards her. 'Did you see them?' she asked breathlessly, her face flushed with excitement.

Sam raised her brows. 'Did I see who?'

'The Yanks, of course, silly! Did you see them arriving?'

'I certainly did. Why do you think I'm so late? I had to wait for ages at the top of May Hill for their convoy to go past.'

'So you must have seen the way they looked! Have you ever seen so many handsome men in your life before?'

'You've been too long without seeing any men around at all,' said Sam, laughing, 'let alone any good-looking ones.'

'It's more than that. There was just something about them. An energy, a vitality…' Diana's cheeks flushed a little pinker. 'Don't tell me you didn't notice something special about them.'

'I noticed how bold and forward they were.'

'But you must have been pleased to see them.'

'I was, even though they did make me late for work. We could use a little help if we're ever going to win this war.'

Diana looked at her. Her forehead puckered into a frown and she crossed the room and flopped down into one of the sofas. 'It wouldn't be a crime for you to show a little interest in the opposite sex again, you know,' she said, sounding deflated. But then, almost immediately, her back straightened and she raised a hand to her mouth. 'I'm sorry, that was so thoughtless of me. I didn't mean – '

'I know you didn't.'

'I must have sounded dreadful.'

'Really, it doesn't matter.'

Diana studied Sam's face for a long moment, then sank back into the sofa again. Her large brown eyes grew sad and she sighed deeply. 'Sometimes it feels as if all we've ever known is this awful war. I'm so fed up of it all. Can't we allow ourselves to enjoy being young for once and have a little fun while the Americans are here? No one's saying it has to be anything serious.'

Sam felt a deep pang of guilt. If only for Diana's sake, she ought to have shown a bit more enthusiasm about the arrival of the Americans. After all, things hadn't been easy for her as far as men were concerned.

Sam's expression grew soft as she regarded her friend silently across the room. Diana's eyes were closed now and her head was tilted back against the cushions of the sofa. Until six months or so ago, she had been one of the happiest people Sam knew; she'd been in love with Sam's cousin, Leonora's eldest son Robert, and he had seemed to love her passionately in return. Then, out of the blue, it had all ended and Diana's whole world had come crashing down.

Robert and Diana had first met in the spring of 1939, just a few months before the outbreak of the war. It had been Sam herself who had first introduced them. It had been a lovely weekend in May, she remembered, and she and Diana had been visiting Leonora when Robert had turned up unexpectedly on a fleeting visit home from Cambridge. Sam could still vividly recall the moment she'd introduced them. It had been on the terrace at the back of the house and the garden had been flooded with sunshine. The attraction between Robert and Diana had been immediately obvious and it hadn't been long before they'd started seeing each other as often as they could.

With the outbreak of the war, Robert had joined up almost immediately, becoming a pilot in the RAF. Diana, meanwhile, had decided to become a nurse. After she'd completed her training in London, she'd applied for her job at the cottage hospital where they were now in order to be close to Robert whenever he was home on leave. Everyone had expected them to marry, but then, six months or so ago, Robert had suddenly and inexplicably brought the relationship to an end. It had all come as an enormous shock and Sam knew how deeply unhappy Diana had been ever since. Only the news that the Americans were coming had in any way lifted her spirits.

Sam crossed the room and sat down on the edge of the sofa next to Diana. 'I'm the one who should be saying sorry,' she said softly. 'Of course we should make the most of things while the Americans are here. It's about time we all had a little fun.'

Diana opened her eyes and looked at her. 'Do you really mean that?'

Sam nodded. 'Yes, I do. And from what I saw this morning, there certainly looked to be plenty of them to go around.' She tipped her head and smiled. 'Government Issue,' she mused. 'Isn't that what they call them?'

Diana's eyes grew soft. 'That's right,' she said wistfully. 'They call them GIs.'

Sam's aunt, Leonora Edwards, had spent the day collecting unwanted clothes with the Women's Voluntary Service and when Sam arrived home late that evening she was still wearing her uniform, a two piece suit of bottle-green tweed piped with red, and her greying auburn hair was pulled back into an elegant bun. She was fifty-three and had been a widow for five years, but although she missed her husband Charles, it wasn't something she allowed herself to dwell on. She'd been a VAD nurse during the Great War and she'd met Charles just afterwards. For twenty years her home and family had been the focus of her life and now, in middle age, she might have expected to be spending her time playing bridge or tending to her garden. Instead, the war had come along, bringing with it new opportunities for her organising abilities and stamina. She was thriving in the WVS and there was nothing she enjoyed more than organising afternoons of knitting and sewing so that the women of the town could make and mend for the troops. She was a practical, no-nonsense sort of woman, with a clear sense of the natural order of things. The arrival of the Americans that morning had come as something of a shock.

'I've never seen anything like it in my life before,' she told Sam. 'All that shouting and whistling! You'd think they'd come here for a holiday, not to fight a war.'

They were doing the dishes together after supper and Leonora was standing at the sink in front of the blacked out kitchen window. A few strands of hair had escaped from her bun and she tucked them back behind her ear with the tip of her finger, then pulled another plate from the sink and rested it on the draining board.

'I suppose they were in high spirits,' said Sam, thinking back to the enthusiastic wolf-whistles that had greeted her that morning, 'but they must have been relieved to have finally arrived. It can't have been easy for them, crossing the Atlantic and then travelling all the way down here from Liverpool.'

'But why did they have to come here?' complained Leonora. 'I'm sure we're going to be completely overrun.'

Sam picked up a plate from the draining board and wiped it absentmindedly with the worn tea towel she was holding. She knew that Leonora was probably right. Apart from the cinema and a few pubs, the town had very little to offer that was likely to entertain all the young men she'd seen arriving.

'And you should have seen how the girls in town were carrying on this morning,' continued Leonora. 'I don't think I've ever heard so much giggling and silliness in my life before. I do hope that none of you nurses were like it at the hospital.'

'Well, there was quite a bit of excitement,' admitted Sam, smiling. 'But I shouldn't worry - I'm sure that Matron won't stand for any nonsense.'

Leonora pursed her lips. 'I do hope that you're right, darling. But I'm afraid certain standards do seem to have slipped just recently. What about that other nurse? The one that Diana shares a house with.'

'Nancy?'

'Yes. She's always seemed rather flighty to me. I know that you'd never lose your head over an American soldier, but it's girls like her that I worry about.'

Sam felt a prickle of annoyance. She loved Leonora, and she felt sorry for her. Her husband had died before the war, Robert was risking his life every time that he went up in his plane, and her other son, David, was in the army and had been missing in action for almost two years. Despite all her troubles, she never showed the slightest trace of self-pity and she was dedicated to her work with the WVS. But sometimes her prejudices and schemes could really be exasperating.

Sam thought of Nancy's bright blonde hair and the cherry red lipstick that she loved to wear. She knew that it was partly her appearance that worried Leonora, but it was also a question of her background. Sam had only known Nancy since she'd first started working at the hospital at the beginning of the year, but she knew that both her parents had died when she was a child. A grandmother in Winchester had brought her up and the only other family she had to speak of was a brother, who was much older than she was.

'I'm sure that you don't need to worry on Nancy's account,' said Sam, treading carefully. 'She may not have had the same privileges as Diana and me, but she's got a heart of gold.'

Leonora paused from the washing up and studied her thoughtfully. 'I'm sorry, darling,' she said, after a moment. 'I didn't mean to upset you. You're probably right. I imagine you know her much better than I do.'

Sam smiled and nodded. Her vague feelings of irritation subsided and she regarded her aunt with faint surprise; it was unusual for her to admit that she might be wrong. Once she got an idea in her head, it was very difficult to make her change her mind.

Leonora stacked the last of the plates onto the draining board. 'Still,' she said, 'I do feel rather sorry for Sir Giles and Lady Olivia up at Foley Manor. I hear they've had to move into the old gardener's cottage at the edge of the estate, in order to make room for the Americans. Imagine having to give up one's home like that.'

'I'm sure it must be very difficult,' said Sam softly, 'but at least the Americans are going to help us now. It's what everyone's been praying for.'

Leonora looked at her thoughtfully again. 'I know I should be grateful, but I do find it all rather difficult. Let's just hope that they won't be here for very long, so that everything can get back to normal again as soon as possible.'

Sam nodded, but she said nothing.

Leonora smiled at her affectionately, then briskly pulled out the plug from the sink.

2. BEGINNINGS

It was a warm afternoon and sunshine flickered on the tall sash windows of Foley Manor. Jack walked up the broad sweep of stone steps in front of the house, went in through the pillared entrance and crossed the wide, flagstoned hallway to a set of open double doors. He paused on the threshold and looked around. The ballroom was panelled in oak and a glass chandelier hung from the centre of an ornately moulded ceiling. A few hard-backed chairs were scattered about, but otherwise the room was unfurnished. Bill Crawford was sitting just inside the doors with his legs stretched out on an empty, upturned crate. Jack had arranged to meet him there.

'How's it going, Bill? Been here long?'

Bill looked up from the orientation handbook he was reading. 'No, I only just got here.' He sat forward and laid the book down on the crate in front of him. 'What is it that's on your mind?'

Jack drew up a chair and sat down opposite him. 'You're not going to believe this, but the CO wants us to organise some kind of dance.'

'A dance?' Bill's voice was incredulous. 'But we only got here a week ago.'

Jack smiled. 'That's exactly what I said. But it seems that some of the men are already getting a little restless because of the lack of things to do around here and the CO's worried about having a lot of bored, resentful soldiers on his hands.'

Bill still looked baffled. 'I guess we can only keep them training and doing drills for so long, but it still seems kind of soon for a dance.'

'Well, there is more to it than just the welfare of the men,' explained Jack. 'The CO wants us to try and build a few bridges with the locals around here. He's already had a couple of calls from families worried about their girls socialising with soldiers they don't know. He thinks a dance

9

might help promote a little Anglo-American understanding.'

'And here was I thinking that we were over here to liberate Europe from the Nazis.'

Jack laughed. 'You said it, Bill. I didn't think this would be our job when we got over here. It seems a strange way to fight a war.'

Bill smiled wryly and then his gaze swept briefly round the room. 'So I take it that this dance you're planning is going to be in here?'

'That's right. That's why I asked you to meet me here. We'll need to get hold of a few flags and banners and fix up some sort of staging for the band. I was hoping you might have a few ideas.'

Bill pondered. 'It shouldn't be too difficult to spruce this place up a bit,' he said, glancing about again. 'Although a little more furniture might come in handy.'

'All the equipment we need is on its way. The way I see it, that's the least of our worries.'

'What do you mean?'

'A lot of young guys fighting over a handful of women, that's what I mean. How many women can there be in a town like this one? Not enough to go around, that's for sure. The army can send us all the supplies and equipment it wants, but there's one thing it can't ship us, and that's girls. There's bound to be trouble.'

'I guess you could be right about that.'

'You bet I'm right. There's going to be a lot of lonely, homesick GIs around here for the next few months, and it's going to get to be quite a headache.'

For a second Bill didn't answer, but then he casually raised his hands behind his head and leaned back in his chair. 'I guess I'm one of the lucky ones. I've got Maisie waiting for me back home.' He looked at Jack speculatively. 'Things could be a lot harder for you, though.'

Jack shrugged. 'You know I'm not planning on getting involved with anyone while we've got a war to fight.'

'Are you sure about that? From what I've seen so far, there seem to be quite a few pretty girls around.'

Jack shook his head.

Bill grinned. 'Don't tell me you haven't noticed. Remember that girl we saw at the top of the hill on the day we arrived? Well, if I were single -'

'I guess it's just as well that you aren't,' said Jack, cutting him off before he could elaborate. 'Otherwise I'd have you to add to my long list of problems.'

Bill's smile grew wider and Jack shook his head. Bill was still grinning as they got to their feet and headed out through the open doorway into the hall.

The glass in the door to the teashop was criss-crossed with wide, beige-coloured anti-blast tape. Sam looked in through it. She'd half expected to see the teashop crowded out with GIs, but apart from a couple of elderly ladies eating wedges of toast at a table opposite, the only other customers she could see were Diana and Nancy.

They were waiting for her at their favourite table in the large bay window that overlooked the park and their heads were almost touching as they laughed together over some shared piece of news. They looked very striking together. Nancy's blonde hair was swept up and fell in soft curls over her forehead, whilst Diana's dark hair fell loosely to her shoulders. The door rattled as Sam pushed it open and they lifted their heads and saw her.

She crossed the room to join them. It was a Friday afternoon and the first time since the arrival of the Americans that their days off had coincided, allowing the three of them to meet. Sam was pleased to see her friends and they greeted her warmly as she sat down between them. It was bright and warm in the homely teashop. Sunshine streamed in through the taped up bay window, splashing onto the sprigged cotton tablecloth that covered the table.

'We've already ordered,' said Diana. 'It's just tea and scones, though. They haven't got any cakes today, I'm afraid.'

A plump waitress in a black dress and white apron came over and set a battered-looking tray of tea things down on the table. She passed round the plates and cups and set the teapot between them, then left them again.

As they began exchanging their news, Diana poured out the tea. It wasn't long before she mentioned shyly that she and Nancy had met some Americans.

'I knew it wouldn't be long before you did,' laughed Sam, putting down her teacup. 'How did it happen?'

'We met them in the queue for the pictures last night,' explained Nancy. 'They just started talking to us. One thing led to another, and they insisted on buying our tickets.'

Sam raised her eyebrows fractionally. 'And you accepted?'

'It wasn't as bad as all that. They're a long way from home and they just wanted a little company, that's all.'

A smile still hovered around Sam's lips, but she saw that Nancy looked put out. 'I'm sorry,' she said, tilting her head a little. 'I was only teasing.'

Diana flushed. 'It was all very innocent and friendly,' she said. 'After the pictures they took us to The Fox for a drink. They looked after us all evening. Really, Sam, they were wonderful. Their manners were impeccable and they were such fun to be with. They were like a breath of fresh air.'

Sam looked at the faces of her friends and felt a pang of envy for their carefree enthusiasm for the new arrivals. With her obvious attractions, Nancy had always had admirers, but as far as Sam knew she'd never been in a serious relationship of any kind. Diana, on the other hand, had suffered enormous heartache because of Robert, and yet even she seemed to have managed to shake off her unhappiness now. Why couldn't things be so simple for Sam?

'I'm sure you'd like them if you met them,' said Nancy. 'Their names are Ed Walker and Chester Dawson. They're both sergeants and they come from the same town in California, so they're old friends. In spite of everything we've been led to believe about the Yanks, they both behaved like perfect gentlemen.'

Diana nodded. 'And they told us that there's going to be a dance at Foley Manor, a week on Saturday,' she told Sam excitedly. 'All the girls in town are going to be invited. Nancy and I are planning to go. You will come too, won't you?'

Sam looked at her in surprise. 'A week on Saturday? But isn't that your birthday? I thought we were all going to the pictures. We arranged to have the same night off weeks ago.'

Diana's eyes lit up. 'I know. Isn't that lucky? A dance will be a much nicer way to celebrate. Please say you'll come.'

Sam shook her head, but she felt helpless. She didn't want to go to a dance, but how could she disappoint Diana? 'I'm not sure,' she murmured. 'It's been such a long time…'

Nancy lowered her teacup and looked at her in a determined sort of way. 'That's exactly why you have to come,' she said firmly. 'You need to have a little fun for once. There'll be food and drink, and a band. Really, Sam, you must see that you can't possibly miss it.'

The following Saturday, Sam found herself clambering into the back of one of the canvas-skinned trucks that had pulled up in a row in the main town square. In spite of her reservations, she'd finally given in to Diana's coaxing and gone to the reception desk at the town hall, where a WVS lady who was a friend of her aunt's had added her to the guest list for the dance.

She sat down between Diana and Nancy on one of the benches that ran the length of the truck on either side. Other girls climbed in behind them, the noise level rising and the benches shuddering until there was room for no more. A soldier snapped shut the tailgate, the engine roared into life, and the truck moved off with a lurch to a chorus of giggles and screams.

Dusk was falling over Foley Manor when they pulled up on the sweep of drive in front of it. Sam jumped lightly down from the rear of the truck and looked around. A queue of girls already stood waiting on the wide stone steps leading up to the house. The Stars and Stripes fluttered above it and the laid-back sound of American music drifted out from inside on the cool evening breeze.

Diana touched her arm. 'You'll enjoy it once you're inside,' she whispered. 'Nancy and I will look after you, I promise.'

Sam smiled faintly. Now that she'd actually arrived, anxiety once more tugged at her heart.

Nancy giggled as a solider helped her down from the back of the truck. 'That was a rather bumpy ride,' she laughed, shaking out her blonde curls and smoothing down her skirt. 'Hardly the most glamorous way to travel.'

Diana laughed and Sam smiled, properly this time. Nancy's excitement was infectious and couldn't help but lift her mood. She brushed away her doubts and resolved to enjoy the evening. It was only a dance, after all.

The soldier ushered them away from the truck and its engine started up with a juddering sound. They watched as it pulled away into the fading light.

'Well, there's no escape now,' said Nancy, nodding after it. 'They won't be back for us until midnight.'

Their shoes crunched over the gravel as they made their way across the drive to join the queue of girls that was still forming on the steps. Sam looked up at the pillared entrance. The front door opened and the sound of music and laughter spilled out onto the night air. The knot of girls at the front of the line stepped into the light and then the door closed quickly behind them.

'It's a good job there's no air raid warden about,' said Nancy, as they joined the back of the queue.

Diana shivered next to her. 'I wish I'd brought my coat.'

The darkness was thickening, but the moon was out and the greyish outlines of the Nissen huts beside the house were still visible. 'I wonder what it's like living in those huts,' mused Sam. 'They don't look very comfortable, do they?'

Nancy made a face. 'They're certainly going to be cold when winter comes.'

Sam looked at her. 'Do you think they'll still be here then?'

'Yes,' said Nancy. 'At least, that's what Ed thinks.'

Ed. It was just two weeks since Nancy had met him, but already she seemed to be completely smitten. And Nancy wasn't the only one. All over town, or so it seemed to Sam, girls had fallen head over heels for men they barely knew. She peeked at Diana. Her dark eyes were fixed on the entrance to the house, but Sam could see them sparkling in anticipation of the evening that lay ahead. She knew that she'd been out with Chester at least twice more since their first meeting, but Sam was yet to be convinced that he was anything more than a passing fancy. Diana felt the weight of her gaze and turned her head and smiled. A swell of affection washed over Sam. As usual, she was worrying too much. It was Diana's birthday and Sam was just thankful that she wasn't sitting at home in her room by herself, pining over Robert.

They came to the front of the queue, the front door opened and they were swept into the house by the press of girls behind them.

The hallway was dominated by a broad staircase with gleaming banisters and Sam was immediately aware of the smell of polish and the freshly washed flag-stoned floor. Two GIs sat behind a trestle table to one side of the entrance, checking invitations. Girls in party dresses stood murmuring together in little groups and soldiers in smart, well-cut uniforms milled around them. At the back of the hallway were tall double doors, and the music they'd been able to hear outside was coming from the darkened room beyond.

Sam handed her invitation to one of the soldiers sitting behind the table. He looked at it briefly and checked for her name on a list. 'Welcome to the party, ma'am,' he said, lifting his gaze. He stared at her for a moment, almost as if he couldn't believe his eyes, and then gave a low, appreciative whistle. Diana gave him a hard look of disapproval and the soldier grinned. They moved off. 'You ladies have a good time, you hear,' his voice came after them.

The ballroom was already very busy. It was decked out in red, white and blue bunting and a huge banner saying *Welcome* had been draped above the curtained windows. At one end of the room, a row of soldiers was pressed up against a bar, waiting to be served, and at the other, a small band was playing on a raised wooden stage. People sat talking and drinking at circular tables and couples were up and dancing in the middle of the room.

Nancy gestured to Sam and Diana to follow her and they began weaving their way in the direction of the stage. Soldiers turned their heads and stepped aside to let them pass.

'Hey, girls, where've you been hiding?'

'Can I get you a drink?'

They ignored the friendly invitations, pressing on until they reached a small set of steps near the stage, the meeting point that Diana and Nancy had arranged with their dates.

Looking up at the stage, Sam saw that the soldiers in the band seemed no different to the other men in the room, and yet the music they were playing sounded surprisingly professional.

'Happy birthday, sweetheart,' said a voice behind her.

She turned around and saw a dark-haired soldier kiss Diana lightly on the cheek. He looked up and she saw that he had dark eyes, almost black, and smooth, naturally olive skin.

Diana turned, still laughing with pleasure at seeing him, and started to make introductions. 'Chester, I'd like you to meet my friend, Sam Mitchell. Sam, this is Chester. Chester Dawson.'

'It's good to make your acquaintance at last, Sam,' said Chester. 'Ed and I have heard a lot about you.'

'And this is Ed,' said Nancy, smiling up at the tall, lean-looking GI with sandy-coloured hair who was now standing beside her.

'How do you do?' murmured Sam, her gaze moving between the two grinning soldiers. 'It's so nice to meet you.'

The introductions made, a few moments of indecision followed. There was a vacant table close by and Ed pulled out two chairs, allowing Sam and Diana to sit down. He rounded the table and pulled out another chair for Nancy. Chester leaned in to speak to him, then headed off to fetch some drinks from the bar.

Ed sat down and Sam saw him shift his chair closer to Nancy's. He slipped his arm around her shoulders and whispered something into her ear. She realised, suddenly, that she was staring, and felt embarrassed. She fumbled with her handbag, unclasping it and pretending to check inside it for her lipstick and compact. Then she closed the bag again and folded her hands in her lap.

The band paused briefly, then struck up again, playing a different, much faster tune. Almost at once, Ed stood up and pushed back his chair, drawing Nancy to her feet.

'Will you ladies excuse us?' he asked, his gaze flickering across the table.

'Of course,' Diana assured him. 'You two go ahead, I'm sure we'll be fine.'

Sam watched as he steered Nancy onto the dance-floor and found them some space. He danced well, with quick, expert steps, and Nancy followed him fluently.

'Hey, girls, you sure look swell tonight.'

The voice spoke close beside her, making Sam jump. A blond-haired soldier was standing at her shoulder. He had a square-jawed, confident face and he was grinning broadly. He seemed to have materialised out of nowhere.

'You don't mind if I join you?' he said, pulling out the chair beside hers.

Diana's lips tightened. 'I'm afraid these seats are taken.'

'Well, then…' His smile faded, but only for a moment. His eyes fixed on Sam again. 'We can have a dance, though, can't we, beautiful?'

'I'm sorry, but I don't really feel like dancing.' Sam did her best to sound calm, but she was uncomfortably aware of the blood that was rushing to her cheeks. To her dismay, her blushing face only seemed to encourage him further.

'Say, come on, don't be shy. You English dames aren't usually like this. Just wait until you see the nylons and chocolate I can get you.'

'No,' she said, this time more firmly. 'No, thank you, I really don't care to dance - '

'Stow it, Brad.' Chester was there suddenly, with the drinks. 'Can't you see the lady just wants to spend a little time with her friends?'

Brad straightened his shoulders. Chester turned to face him and there was a moment's tension.

A slow smile spread across Brad's face. 'I guess you're right, Dawson. You know I didn't mean any harm.' His eyes slid to Sam's again. 'Never mind, beautiful. Maybe we can have that dance of ours a little later.'

Sam stared at him, stunned into a silence. He seemed impervious to the fact that she had already declined his invitation twice.

Brad eyed Chester one last time, then looked back at her again. He gave her a wink and turned on his heel, and she watched him disappear across the darkened room.

Jack drained the last of his beer and set down his empty glass on the smooth wooden surface of the bar. Looking around the room, he saw that there were more women at the dance than he'd anticipated. The men looked happy, he thought, and for the moment at least, there were no signs of any trouble. Anyway, even if anything did happen there that night, he was sure it wouldn't be anything that he couldn't handle.

'The guys seem to be having a good time,' said Bill, handing him another beer. 'There sure are some pretty girls here tonight.'

'Don't start that again, Bill. I've told you I'm not interested.'

'That doesn't mean you can't enjoy the view.'

A dark-haired girl in a yellow dress whirled around in front of them and the soldier dancing with her reached out to steady her. She gave a high-pitched laugh and took his hand, and then they were swallowed up again by the sea of dancers.

Jack raised an eyebrow. 'At least they all look to be pretty decent girls,' he admitted, in spite of himself. 'That system of invites you came up with certainly seems to have worked.'

Bill looked pleased. 'Yeah. In the end we asked the local WVS to check over the invitation list for us, to make sure we kept out any good-time girls. All the dames here have had official invitations from the CO.'

Jack studied his beer. 'You've done a good job, Bill,' he said. 'But like I said before - it sure seems a strange way to be fighting a war.'

The ballroom was warm and hazy with smoke. Ed's arm was draped along the back of Nancy's chair and they were deep in conversation, and Diana and Chester were murmuring quietly to each other. Sam sat with her chair turned at an angle away from the table, sipping her drink and listening to the music.

Her gaze trailed over the couples who were dancing. The men were wearing smart, well-tailored uniforms, quite unlike the rough, coarse uniforms and heavy boots that British soldiers had to make do with. The women looked shabbier than their partners did, in dresses that had seen better days, but they looked to have spent hours on their hair and make-up. Sam looked down and smoothed her skirt with her free hand. The dress she was wearing had been one of her favourites before the war, but it occurred to her now that what had suited a seventeen year old girl might not be the ideal outfit for a twenty-one year old woman. She thought how unsophisticated she must seem.

When she lifted her gaze again, she saw that Nancy was looking at her across the table with a curious expression. 'You haven't moved all evening,' she said in a gently reproving tone. 'Wouldn't you like to have a dance too?' Before Sam could frame her reply, she turned to Ed and added, 'You'd show her how it's done, wouldn't you?'

A glimmer of surprise showed in Ed's eyes, but his easy-going smile quickly surfaced again. 'Sure, I'd be delighted.'

Sam looked at them. 'Oh, I really don't think that I could...' She floundered. 'I mean, I think I'd be happier just sitting here and watching.'

But even as she spoke she could tell from Ed's expression that it was useless to resist. He brushed a loose curl of hair from Nancy's forehead. 'Don't go anywhere while I'm gone, you hear,' he told her. He kissed her on the cheek, then stood up and circled the table, taking Sam's hands and pulling her to her feet.

The dance-floor was thronging with people, but Ed found them a space. At first Sam had to concentrate hard to follow his practised steps, but her mind was soon lost to the quick beat of the throbbing music.

Suddenly, a lowered voice called out from behind her.

'Hey, baby, I thought you said you didn't dance.'

She spun round, swaying for a moment before regaining her balance, and was at once caught in Brad's cool blue gaze. He took a step forward and grasped her wrist, then looked at Ed sharply.

'I saw her first, Walker,' he said, in a menacing tone. 'You don't mind if I cut in here, do you?'

Jack set his glass down on the bar and watched for a moment as the two soldiers squared up to each other over the girl in the pale blue dress. He recognised her at once. She really was a knockout, he thought, remembering Bill's words when they'd seen her from the Jeep on the day they'd first arrived. Even the old-fashioned dress she was wearing couldn't conceal her slim, shapely figure, its lightweight fabric whispering over her neat curves and small waist. The hemline of the dress reached just below the knee, revealing long, slender legs that seemed to go on forever.

He checked his thoughts. She was undeniably beautiful, but what was that to him? Hadn't he promised himself not to get involved with anyone whilst there was a war to fight?

He considered the girl again. Even from this distance he could see that she didn't look happy. He knew that there was no point in letting things get out of hand.

'Is everything all right here, ma'am?'

Sam looked up into the questioning blue eyes of the American officer and felt a sense of grateful relief. 'Actually, I think I'd just like to sit down.'

He held her gaze for a moment and she felt his eyes appraising her behind his expression of concern. His gaze flickered over Ed and Brad and they sprang to attention.

'You heard the lady. Why don't you guys just give her a break?'

The officer was dark-haired and handsome, and, glancing at the insignia on his collar, Sam saw that he was a lieutenant. He motioned to the men to step away from her and spoke to them briefly. She didn't hear what was said, but it had the desired effect. Brad shifted his stance to face her again and mumbled an apology. The lieutenant gave him a nod of dismissal and he turned on his heel, slipping away across the dance-floor.

The lieutenant's eyes met hers again and she felt suddenly self-conscious, wondering if he'd been aware of the way that she'd been studying him. 'I'm sorry to have caused any trouble,' she said quickly, hopeful that in the darkness he wouldn't see her blushing.

His expression was inscrutable. 'No problem at all, ma'am,' he replied in a low, reassuring voice.

She felt the light pressure of Ed's hand in the small of her back. 'If you'll excuse us then, Lieutenant?'

The lieutenant glanced at Ed and nodded briefly, then looked back at her again. 'I hope you enjoy the rest of your evening, ma'am.'

She nodded. 'Thank you, I'm sure that I will.'

He acknowledged her words with a slight smile, and then he left them.

Reaching their table again, Sam saw that Diana's eyes were clouded with concern. 'Is everything okay?' she asked, her forehead furrowing.

'It was nothing,' Ed assured her, sliding into his seat next to Nancy. 'Just Bradley Hunt getting a little over eager, that's all.'

Sam nodded. 'I'm fine, really. Anyway, the lieutenant dealt with it and it's all over now.'

Diana seemed satisfied. She nestled back next to Chester, who ran his arm along the back of her chair. He swallowed a mouthful of beer, then began to tell them a story about a GI who'd gone up to London and got lost in the blackout. It was something that he'd heard on the wireless, and Sam felt grateful to him for having changed the subject. She listened for a few moments, but then her attention strayed to a group of soldiers that was gathering near the steps to the stage. There was a small commotion and for a few moments she wondered if there were going to be some sort trouble.

One of the soldiers was short and stocky with cropped brown hair. She watched him climb the steps, cross the stage, and position himself behind the standing microphone. He said something to the band leader behind him, then blinked into the spotlight and waited for the opening chords of the music. A hush fell across the room and he began to sing a love song in a deep, attractive voice.

They watched him all through the song and into the start of another. It was another ballad, but the murmur of conversation began to rise again.

'He's very good, isn't he?' said Diana.

Chester nodded. 'Some of the guys really know how to put over a song.'

Diana looked at Sam pointedly. 'Why don't you sing something for us too, Sam? It would be so lovely if you would.'

'You can sing?' Chester looked surprised.

'Yes,' admitted Sam, casting Diana a brief, reproachful glance. 'But Diana knows very well that it's a very long time since I have.'

'It isn't so very long,' said Diana. 'Remember all those solos you used to have to sing at school? You have such a beautiful voice, I'm sure everyone would love to hear you.' She smiled up at Chester. 'Do you think anyone would mind?'

Chester shook his head. 'One of the boys in the band is a buddy of mine,' he told Sam. 'I could take you up on stage to meet him, if you'd like.'

Ed gave her a nod of encouragement. 'It sure would be good to hear you.'

Sam hesitated. She didn't want to sing, but all their eyes were upon her and as she searched for an excuse it suddenly seemed to her as if there was no way out of it. She looked at Diana again. 'I suppose it is your birthday…' she murmured.

Diana smiled. 'It really would be a lovely present.'

Sam's gaze travelled over their expectant faces. 'Well, I'll sing, if you really want me to,' she sighed, giving in at last, 'but I'm afraid I'm rather rusty.'

'I told you she was really something,' murmured Bill.

He was standing at the bar beside Jack and they were both looking towards the stage, watching the girl who had stepped forward into the soft pool of light behind the microphone.

'I guess I've got to hand it to you,' Jack finally conceded. 'She sure is.'

A swell of anticipation seemed to run around the room. The girl dropped her gaze and closed her eyes, and for a brief moment Jack wondered if she were going to change her mind, but then the band played the opening bars of *I'll Be Seeing You* and she lifted her head and began to sing. The music was soft and sentimental, her voice pure and lovely, and the couples on the dance-floor pressed closer together, swaying gently to the romantic tune.

Bill drew a packet of cigarettes from the pocket of his jacket. 'It's a pity Ed Walker got there first,' he said, taking out a cigarette. 'Funny though, I thought he was dating a different girl. One of the nurses from the hospital.'

Jack glanced at him, wondering briefly if he might be right. He studied his glass for a moment, then took another long drink of his beer.

Sam gazed out over the room at the pale, upturned faces. The last notes of the music faded away and then, all at once, the sound of clapping and shouts for more rose up towards her from the crowd. Tears pricked behind her eyelids and all the sorrow she had suppressed for so long suddenly threatened to overwhelm her. She lowered her head and gave the briefest of bows, then retreated across the stage and down the steps, back to the safety of their table.

The band played one more song before the lights came up just after midnight and the dance finally ended. Sam said her goodbyes and left Diana and Nancy at the table to spend a few final minutes alone with their dates. She followed the moving crowd across the hallway, went out through the doorway into the chill of the evening, and paused at the top of the steps. She could hear the low murmur of voices interspersed with the sound of laughter, but it took a few moments for her eyes to get used to the darkness. The grey outlines gradually took shape and she picked her way down the weathered steps towards the waiting trucks, hugging herself against the cold night air.

3. RATIONS

'We've only got mutton left, I'm afraid, Miss Mitchell,' the lady behind the till in the butcher's told Sam.

'That'll be fine thank you, Mrs Cole,' said Sam, smiling. She handed over the ration books she was holding and then looked in her purse for some change.

She put the small parcel of meat into her bag and then went out into the street. She crossed the road, walked a little way, and then joined a short line of people waiting to be served at the grocer's. The woman in front of her was pushing a large, rather battered, cream-coloured pram and Sam smiled at the chubby-faced little girl who was sitting up in it and gurgling happily.

The queue gradually grew shorter, until at last she reached the front of it. She bought a tin of condensed milk, some powdered eggs and the small ration of tea and butter that she and Leonora were allowed. Then she left the shop and retraced her steps towards the town hall, where she'd left her bicycle propped up next to a wall. She loaded her shopping into the basket mounted on the front, then wheeled the bicycle out into the road.

Sam rode quickly along the high street and before long she was starting the slow climb up the hill towards home. It was hard work, but the day, though it was September, was fine, and there was a pleasant breeze. The countryside was green and beautiful and the hedgerows still full of colour, and she had a rare feeling of contentment as she cycled along.

Soon the ugly grey pillbox came into sight that marked the junction with the lane that led to The Elms. Sam turned into the lane and almost at once found herself in the path of an oncoming Jeep that seemed to be coming straight towards her. She heard the screech of brakes as she swerved across the road and then the bicycle buckled beneath her on the rough grassy surface of the verge. She felt the touch of cold metal against her skin and a flash of pain in her ankle before tumbling sideways into the grass.

The breath was completely knocked out of her. She turned onto her back and then lay motionless, her eyes closed. She heard the sound of the driver's feet as he jumped down from the Jeep and ran across the road.

'Are you okay?'

Sam opened her eyes. The sky was cloudless, a lovely clear blue. A man's voice. She turned her head. He was kneeling by her side, leaning over her. His dark hair was cut very short and she noticed how his smooth skin glowed with a light tan. She knew him, didn't she? Yes - wasn't he the lieutenant she'd encountered at the dance? Still feeling dazed, she slowly raised herself up onto her elbows. Then her mind registered what he'd said. 'I think so,' she murmured.

His gaze travelled over her body and then his eyes met hers again. He frowned. 'Are you sure?'

She nodded. He didn't look convinced, but he straightened up and held out his hand to help her. She shifted her weight to try to get up, but she immediately felt another sharp twinge in her ankle. She bit her lip and tried to hide how much it hurt, but she couldn't suppress a small gasp of pain.

His frown deepened. 'Where does it hurt?'

'My ankle...' she replied weakly.

He nodded. 'I'd better take a look.'

He knelt down at her feet and, with his hand supporting her ankle, carefully removed her shoe. She flinched slightly and he looked up and gave her a brief smile of encouragement. With one hand still supporting it, he began carefully moving her foot from side to side with the other, as if to see if there were anything broken. She bit her lip again, in anticipation of the pain to come, but his touch was unexpectedly gentle.

He sat back on his heels and rested his hands on his thighs. 'There's nothing broken,' he said. 'There'll be some bruising I expect, but you'll be fine. Next time just make sure you look where you're going. You could get yourself killed riding along like that.'

'Look where I'm going?' Sam stared at him in utter disbelief. 'You came hurtling along as if you owned the road and you tell me to look where I'm going?'

An unmistakable look of amusement flickered through his eyes.

She lifted her chin. 'I don't know why you think it's so funny. You said yourself that I might have been killed.'

'Hey, I'm sorry,' he said, holding up his hands in a gesture of mock surrender. 'You're right, it isn't funny.'

She glared at him angrily. 'It certainly isn't.'

He raised his eyebrows at her tone, but he didn't say anything. She felt the colour come into her cheeks and glanced awkwardly away.

'Look, why don't you tell me where you live?' he said, after a moment. 'The least I can do is get you home.'

His tone was conciliatory, but when her gaze met his again she saw that he was still finding it hard to restrain a smile. She felt another swell of anger and frustration. 'Don't worry about me, I'll manage...' It was then that she saw her shopping. The meat, the tin of milk, the powdered eggs, the tea, the butter - all their rations. All of it had spilled out from the basket on the front of her bicycle and lay scattered about on the ground behind him. Her gaze trawled over it in disbelief, and for a moment she couldn't speak.

He turned his head, following the direction of her gaze. 'It's just a little food,' he said dismissively. 'Don't worry about it. Just be glad that you're in one piece.'

'Just food?' Her voice was incredulous as her gaze snapped to his again. 'Have you any idea how long I spent queuing for that this morning?'

For a moment he looked completely at a loss. He shook his head, glanced briefly away, then met her gaze again. 'I'm sorry, I don't seem to be saying the right things here, do I? What would you say if I offered to get your things together and then take you home? How does that sound to you?'

His eyes were very blue and his expression was open and honest, and almost at once Sam felt her fury subsiding. Annoyed with herself, she lifted her chin. In spite of his evident charms, he was still in the wrong. She pursed her lips. "Well...' she began.

He got to his feet. 'Just give me a minute,' he told her. Another smile flickered across his face. 'Promise me that you won't go anywhere.'

He crossed the lane to the Jeep and delved in the back of it, retrieving his helmet. As Sam watched, he began gathering up the scattered shopping, using the upturned helmet as a receptacle to carry it in.

She looked down and scrutinized her ankle. Dark bruising was already beginning to appear. She reached out her hand and prodded it gingerly. It felt very tender and she knew that it would probably swell, getting worse before it got better. It would be days before she could walk on it properly again. She gave a heavy sigh, then raised her head again. The lieutenant had loaded her bicycle into the back of the Jeep and was brushing the dust off his hands as he came towards her.

He squatted by her side. 'Won't you tell me where you live?' he asked in a friendly voice. 'So that I can take you home?'

Sam hesitated, still unwilling to accept his help, but then his brows lifted fractionally and she felt a rush of awkwardness. 'I live with my aunt, along the lane here,' she explained quickly, motioning with her hand. 'It's about half a mile away. The house is called The Elms.'

The lieutenant glanced in the direction that she'd indicated, then looked back at her and nodded. A smile flickered across his face and he leaned towards her, pulling her into his arms and swinging her up from the grassy verge.

'Really, this isn't necessary,' blurted Sam. 'I'm sure I can manage.'

He shifted her weight in his arms. A smile still touched his lips and his eyes were soft and warm. 'I'm sorry, but there's no way you can walk with your ankle like it is,' he told her gently. 'Like it or not, you're going to have to let me help you.'

Her ankle throbbed painfully. Realising that he was right, Sam gave a little, reluctant, nod of assent and lifted her arms around his neck so that he could carry her more easily. As they started towards the Jeep, she was aware of the warm, tangy smell of his aftershave and even through the stiff fabric of his uniform she could feel the outline of his toned body. She felt herself blushing and kept her cheek against his jacket, so that he wouldn't see her face. It was a very long time since she'd been so close to a man.

The lieutenant gently lowered her down onto the passenger seat of the Jeep, then circled the front and climbed in behind the wheel. 'I'm afraid we haven't been properly introduced,' he said, shifting around to face her. He smiled and held out his hand. 'My name's Jack Webster.'

She looked back at him and nodded. 'And I'm Sam Mitchell,' she said, shaking his hand.

The corners of his eyes creased into another smile. 'It's a pleasure to meet you, Miss Mitchell.'

He turned the key in the ignition and waited until the motor caught, then began manoeuvring out into the lane.

The long gravel drive that led up to the house was shaded from the morning sunshine by the overhanging branches of the elm trees that grew on either side and which, Jack supposed, gave the house its name. As they drew up on the drive, he noticed the ivy that had spread untidily across the front brickwork of the house and he caught a glimpse of the peeling paint on the windowsills, but he could see that it had once been a fine home.

She must have heard the sound of the engine, because, almost at once, the front door opened and he saw a woman framed in the doorway. She stepped outside and came towards them. She looked about fifty, tall and slim, and smart-looking. The aunt, he assumed.

Jack climbed out of the Jeep, cutting across the woman's path. 'Good morning, ma'am.'

She looked past him at Sam, who was still sitting in the passenger seat, then glanced back at him sharply. 'Has something happened?'

'I'm afraid Miss Mitchell took a fall in the lane. She's sprained her ankle.'

'Don't worry, Aunt Leonora. I'm fine,' called Sam. 'There's nothing broken.' She made as if to get out of the Jeep. Her face puckered as she swung her feet to the ground and she immediately lifted her injured leg in pain.

Jack sprang forward and wrapped his arm around her waist to support her. 'I'm afraid there'll be no walking for you yet, Miss Mitchell,' he told her, looping his other arm beneath her knees and lifting her up. Her green eyes widened, but she looked up at him and nodded mutely.

The woman's lips tightened. 'Won't you please follow me?' she said crisply.

Jack was keenly aware of the warmth of Sam's body pressing against him beneath her light cotton dress as he carried her through the open front door and along the dim, narrow hallway inside the house. They came into a cluttered living room. A large sofa nestled behind a coffee table that was piled with books and newspapers and magazines, and there were several comfortable looking armchairs. Sunlight flooded into the room through tall French windows and a chaise longue upholstered in faded yellow silk had been placed at an angle in front of them, to take advantage of the view of the garden beyond. Side tables were laden with lamps and antiques, along with family photographs in silver frames.

Jack crossed the room and gently lowered Sam down onto the silk chaise longue. He waited a moment as she settled herself on the cushions. When she looked up and met his gaze, he noticed the smudge of colour that briefly touched her cheeks. 'Lieutenant, this is my aunt, Mrs Leonora Edwards,' she said quickly, gesturing to the woman behind him. 'And Aunt, this is Lieutenant Webster.'

He turned around and caught Leonora assessing him through narrowed eyes. She at once adjusted her expression and said smoothly, 'How do you do, Lieutenant? Thank you so much for your help.'

He smiled pleasantly. 'It was no trouble at all, ma'am.'

Jack let a few moments pass, then offered to fetch in the shopping from the Jeep. He left Leonora examining Sam's ankle and retraced his steps along the hallway alone. This time he noticed the faded paintwork on the walls and the threadbare rug that carpeted the floor. A black Bakerlite telephone rested on a small antique table near the front door. Next to the table was a pot umbrella-stand decorated with some kind of oriental pattern.

Outside, he unloaded the bicycle from the back of the Jeep and propped it up against a wall. He leaned in to retrieve his helmet from where he'd stowed it behind his seat. As he briefly checked its contents, his mind travelled back to his first taste of British food. He was sure he'd never forget the tough meat, boiled potatoes, and overcooked vegetables he'd been served the evening his troopship had arrived in Liverpool. He remembered how relieved he'd been to find that the food at the base was being shipped over directly from the States.

Leonora was waiting for him when he stepped back into the hallway. He handed her the helmet and assumed what he hoped was a suitably apologetic expression. 'I'm sorry, Mrs Edwards, but I'm afraid that's all there is.'

She emptied out the shopping onto the little table by the door. 'I'm sure we'll survive,' she said briskly, handing his helmet back to him. 'You see, Lieutenant, we've managed quite well by ourselves so far.'

A few minutes later, Jack was back in the Jeep, driving towards town. He couldn't help feeling that he'd just been dismissed.

Sam moved her foot slightly so that it rested more comfortably on the cushion below it. It was the day after the accident and she was lying on the chaise longue by the open French windows, fanning her face with a book.

Leonora came into the living room carrying a tray of homemade lemonade. She set the tray down on top of a pile of newspapers on the coffee table, then poured the lemonade and handed a glass to Sam.

'How are you feeling?' she asked kindly.

'A little better,' said Sam. The doctor had been that morning. He'd confirmed that there was nothing broken, but he'd told her that she needed to rest her ankle completely until all the pain had gone.

Leonora picked up a glass from the tray, smoothed the back of her skirt and sat down in an armchair. 'If only that American had been driving more slowly, then none of this would have happened,' she sighed.

'Perhaps it wasn't entirely his fault,' reflected Sam. 'I was in a bit of a dream when I came round that corner and with all the petrol rationing there is I'm not used to seeing many vehicles on the road.'

'He still should have been driving more slowly. I don't know what the roads are like where he comes from, but he ought to realise by now that these are just narrow country lanes.'

'They haven't been here long. I expect it's all taking a lot of getting used to.'

Leonora eyed Sam curiously over the top of her glass. 'It may be wrong of me, darling,' she said, after a moment, 'but you must know by now that I haven't really taken to these Americans. Whenever I see them they seem to be shouting or whistling or chewing gum. They don't even seem to know how to stand up properly. I saw two of them slouched against the wall in front of The George only this morning. They seem such brash young men, not at all like our own.'

Sam guessed that she was thinking about her sons, Robert and David, and felt a pang of sympathy. 'Yes, I suppose they are quite different.'

'And such showy uniforms!' said Leonora, encouraged. 'Have you noticed? Quite ridiculous if you ask me, not at all the sort of thing to go to war in.'

Sam restrained a smile. 'Those are just their dress uniforms that you've seen them in. They won't fight in those.'

Leonora drew in her chin and looked put out. 'Well, that's as maybe,' she said, 'but it does seem to me that they're having rather a good time of it here, whilst our boys are all away fighting.'

For a moment Sam didn't know quite what to say. She didn't want to upset Leonora, but nor did she want to be unfair to the Americans. 'They'll probably be asked to fight soon,' she said finally. 'They are here to help us, after all.'

'I suppose you may be right,' said Leonora, brushing a speck of something from her skirt. 'We'll just have to grin and bear it for a while and perhaps eventually everything will turn out for the best.'

It was cool and wet for the next couple of days and Sam was confined indoors, but by the end of the week the weather had improved again and although her ankle still hadn't fully recovered, she was able to put her weight on it and walk.

She looked out at the view through the open French windows. Leonora had gone into town to help with the WVS and she was alone in the house. A set of stone steps in front of the windows led down to a wide, flag-stoned terrace. The terrace was furnished with two faded wooden sun-loungers and a white-painted table with matching chairs, and beyond it a long strip of lawn was bounded at the bottom by a high, redbrick wall. Deep flowerbeds edged the terrace and lawn, but they'd been left to run wild for the last few summers, or had been given over to the growing of vegetables.

The garden was filled with light and in spite of its shabbiness looked invitingly lush and green beneath the blue of the sky. It was almost the end of September and Sam knew that this might be the last warm weather of the year. Moving cautiously on her ankle, she went out through the windows, down the steps and across the terrace to one of the sun-loungers. She dragged the lounger around so that it was facing the sun and eased herself down onto it. She lay back and stretched out her legs. In spite of everything, she thought to herself, it was still a beautiful world.

Half an hour later, she was still lying there, savouring the warmth of the sun, when she heard the sound of footsteps coming along the gravel path that skirted the side of the house. She thought vaguely that Leonora must have arrived home early.

'Good morning, Miss Mitchell,' said a man's voice.

Sam opened her eyes and raised herself up onto her elbows. Lieutenant Webster was standing off to her left, at the edge of the terrace. A few strands of hair fell across her forehead and she brushed them away. He looked impeccably smart in his officer's uniform, and he was carrying a brown cardboard box with *US Army* printed in large black letters along its side. His gaze strayed to her legs for a moment, and then his eyes met hers again.

'There was no answer when I knocked at the door so I decided to come look for you,' he explained. 'It's a beautiful day and I guessed you'd be out here.'

'Oh,' she said, still not quite understanding. 'I see.'

He stood without moving at the edge of the terrace and she began to feel uncomfortable beneath his unwavering gaze. She swung her legs off the lounger and sat up a little stiffly, pulling down the hem of her skirt as she did so. Seeing her movement, he seemed to recollect himself and started across the terrace towards her.

He placed the box down next to her on the lounger. 'I've brought you something,' he said. 'It's by way of apology for what happened to your rations the other day.'

He opened the lid and she looked inside. There were packets of sugar and coffee, cans of meat and tins of fruit. It was more food than Sam had seen together at once in a very long time. Her eyes shot to his again. 'It's very generous of you to bring all this, Lieutenant, but I couldn't possibly accept.'

He smiled. 'Sure you can. It's the least I can do, in the circumstances.'

He was standing close to her, his gaze fixed on hers. His eyes were very blue and this dark hair gleamed in the bright sunshine of the morning. She suddenly felt completely off balance. 'I really can't,' she mumbled. 'It's far too much. You see, my aunt...'

He shook his head. 'I'm sorry, but I won't take no for an answer.'

She looked at him. She knew how unwilling Leonora would be to accept anything from the Americans, but how could she explain that to him?

He waited a few moments, without speaking, then glanced at his watch. 'Well, I guess I'll be heading off then.'

'Oh, I'm so sorry, Lieutenant, please forgive me,' she said, feeling flustered at having forgotten her manners. 'Won't you sit down and stay for a few minutes?'

For a moment he looked uncertain, but then he drew up one of the garden chairs from around the table and sat down on it beside her. His gaze fell on the bruising that showed on her ankle. His brows pulled together. 'That still looks a little sore.'

Moving her knees slightly to one side, Sam looked down at her leg. 'Actually, it's much better. The doctor says it isn't anything very serious.'

He still looked uncomfortable. 'I should have been driving more slowly.

You could have been even more badly hurt.'

'You're not used to these lanes.'

'Maybe not, but that isn't any excuse. I'm sorry it happened.'

The sun went behind a puff of cloud and cast a brief shadow across the house. He smiled briefly and then his eyes released her and he looked out over the long stretch of garden beyond the terrace. 'You and your aunt must have your work cut out, looking after all this,' he remarked.

'I suppose we do,' she admitted, following his gaze. 'Leonora used to have a gardener, but he was called up at the beginning of the war. I believe he works in a munitions factory now. You should have seen the garden before the war, it was beautiful then.' She tipped her head and smiled at him. 'I suppose England must seem very shabby to you.'

He laughed. 'Well, I guess I've seen a few places that could use a lick of paint.'

'There is a war on you know.'

The voice came from the direction of the house and they both turned their heads. The French windows stood open and Leonora was standing at the top of the steps, her eyes fixed on Jack. 'Our factories haven't the time to make paint,' she told him brusquely. 'You see, they're making planes.'

Jack shot to his feet. 'I'm sorry, Mrs Edwards - '

She brushed off his apology with an impatient gesture. 'Our things may be shabby and worn, but we have nothing to be ashamed of. For four years now we've been fighting for our lives. The sooner you Americans realise that and knuckle down to helping us, the better.' She held his gaze for another long moment then threw Sam a quick, admonishing glance before turning away and stepping back into the house.

Jack stared after her. 'Me and my big mouth.'

'It isn't your fault, Lieutenant,' said Sam. He turned his head and she saw the hard expression that had come into his eyes. 'You see, the war's been very hard for my aunt,' she continued clumsily. 'Both her sons have been away fighting for over three years now, and that's been a great strain. Robert's a pilot in the RAF and David's in the army, somewhere out in the Far East. She hasn't heard from him since the fall of Singapore. Then you Americans appear -'

'I understand,' he said, interrupting. 'You don't need to explain any more. She must resent the fact that we're here now, instead of them.'

They sat for a moment without speaking. They heard the telephone ring, followed by the rise and fall of Leonora's voice as she answered it.

Jack shot a glance in the direction of the house and his expression hardened further. 'I've got to be going now,' he said, getting to his feet, 'but I'll pass by again in a couple of days to see how you're doing.'

'That really isn't necessary…'

'Maybe not. But I'd like to be sure you're okay.'

'Thank you,' murmured Sam, still feeling flustered. 'And thank you so much for the food. It was very kind of you to bring it.'

He relaxed a little. 'Like I said before, it was the least I could do.'

Jack left via the terrace, the way he had come. The garden wall was broken by an arched, wrought iron gateway smothered by a climbing rose. He went through it onto the gravel pathway that skirted the side of the house. When he was sure that he was out of sight he paused for a moment, marshalling his thoughts. He knew he should have got out of there sooner. He ought to have given her the food to make some amends for what had happened, and then gone. But he had found it impossible to leave.

He realised that he'd been undone the moment he'd first seen her lying there on the terrace. Framed by the bright sunshine, her beauty had been even more luminous than he remembered. He thought of the way she'd blushed beneath his gaze and sat up, demurely adjusting her dress as she did so. He knew that it was an image he wouldn't soon forget.

He strode along the pathway, crossed the drive and climbed into the Jeep. The hazy autumn sunshine flickered on the rich red brickwork of the house and it occurred to him that the building must have stood for at least a hundred years. He thought of the British, so proud of their Empire, and their old-fashioned, class-ridden traditions. Leonora Edwards was a prime example. Didn't she realise that they were there to help win the war? Impatiently, he turned the key in the ignition and shifted the engine into gear.

4. ATTRACTION

Sam stood gazing out of the kitchen window that overlooked the drive. It had rained overnight and the grass was still dewy, but the sun was now breaking through the cloud.

The kitchen clock ticked faintly on the wall next to her, but the rest of the house was closed up and silent. Leonora had got up early and gone down to the WI Hall in town. Sam knew that she would be there all day, helping to sort through the salvage that the WVS had been collecting for the war effort.

She turned away from the window and crossed the room. She sat down in the armchair by the dresser and rested her foot on the footstool in front of it. She pushed a cushion into the small of her back and studied her ankle for a moment. It was only a few days since the accident, but the bruising had faded and it probably wouldn't be more than a day or two before she could go back to work.

She felt suddenly very restless and got to her feet again. Knowing how much the hospital needed her, she didn't like spending so much time moping about at home. She adjusted and retied her dressing gown and then wandered across to the kitchen table. She picked up the small pile of unopened letters that lay on top of it and began idly looking through them.

It was then that Sam heard the noise of an engine and the sound of wheels turning on the gravel outside. She set down the letters and glanced up at the clock. It was after ten o'clock. How had it got so late? She went over to the window again and saw Jack making his way towards the house. His Jeep was parked on the drive behind him. He looked across and saw her through the window, signalling to her as he approached. She drew back in a sudden panic, wondering if it would still be possible to hide, but knowing at once that it was already too late.

She heard his knock and went quickly into the hall, plucking at her dressing gown and putting a hand to her hair as she went. She stood for a moment with her hand on the handle of the front door and then pulled it open.

Jack's eyes met hers. 'Good Morning, Miss Mitchell...' He looked surprised, then embarrassed. 'I hope I'm not disturbing you.'

Sam looked at him, aware of herself, breathless and flustered, and lifted a hand to her throat.

He took a step backwards and made as if to go. 'I'm sorry, I can see this isn't a good time.'

Her hand dropped back down to her side and she shook her head, suddenly filled with an instinctive need to save him from embarrassment. 'No, Lieutenant. Please don't go. It's very kind of you to drop by. I'd lost all track of time this morning, but I can soon get dressed.'

He hesitated.

'Please, do come in,' she insisted, moving aside to make room for him to come across the threshold. 'Really, it won't take me a minute to get changed.'

Jack stepped into the hallway and she shut the door behind him. He felt like an idiot for having come again, unannounced, but he knew he was being drawn to her like a moth to a flame. In the couple of days that had gone by since he'd last seen her, he hadn't been able to shake her from his thoughts, and when he'd found himself with a couple of hours to kill that morning he hadn't been able to resist getting into the Jeep and coming over to see how she was.

She took his hat and put it down on the little table by the front door. There was a door to the left of them, across the narrow hallway, and he followed her through it into a large, old-fashioned kitchen. There was a vase of fresh flowers on a scrubbed wooden table and a threadbare armchair by a heavy-looking dresser. Some of the paintwork looked a little chipped and faded, but everything seemed spotlessly clean.

Jack watched as Sam filled the kettle and put it on top of the stove. She shook out the match she'd used to light it with and dropped it into a little china pot, then turned around and met his gaze. Her face was still fresh with the glow of recent sleep and her dishevelled hair tumbled to her shoulders. He found himself smiling.

Her cheeks coloured and she glanced quickly at the kettle. 'If you wouldn't mind staying here, to see that it doesn't boil over...'

He nodded, composing his expression. 'Sure.'

Sam hovered for a moment by the stove, as if not quite decided, but then she moved across the room and put her hand to the door. 'I'll see you in a few minutes then,' she said, pausing to look back at him.

Jack nodded again. He waited until the door had closed behind her, then crossed over to the dresser and took down two cups from the shelves.

The cloud had thinned and the terrace behind the house was bathed in warm morning sunshine. Jack set down the tray of coffee things on the little white-painted table and looked out over the view. The garden sloped downwards to the high brick wall that enclosed it at the bottom, beyond which well-tended fields curved gently away into the distance.

He heard the sound of Sam's footfalls on the terrace behind him and turned around. Her light brown hair was tied back at the nape of her neck and she was wearing a short-sleeved, pale blue dress sprigged with dainty white flowers. Her gaze moved over the tray of coffee things.

Jack smiled. 'I went ahead and made some coffee. I hope you don't mind.'

'That was very kind of you,' she said.

Jack pulled out a chair for her and waited for her to be seated, then sat down himself at the other side of the table. He watched as she poured the coffee out into the pale china cups on the tray. He looked at her hands and noticed her slender fingers. Her nails were short, neatly cut and unpolished. She set the coffee pot aside, then glanced up at him, passing him one of the cups.

The coffee was hot and strong, just the way he liked it. He watched Sam lift her cup to her lips and blow on it gently. She took a sip and her brows lifted, and he laughed. 'I'd have made tea, if I'd known how.'

'Actually, it's very good. It's just been a very long time since I last tasted proper coffee.'

She said it lightly, without a trace of self-pity, but Jack was reminded of her distress on the day of the accident. He sat forward towards the table. 'Listen, Miss Mitchell - '.

'Sam,' she corrected him. 'Please call me Sam.'

He nodded. 'All right then, Sam. Listen, I still feel bad about what happened to your rations the other day. It sounds stupid, but I didn't realise quite how difficult things really were over here. If you ever need anything, you only have to ask. I'd be more than happy to help you in any way I can.'

Her forehead creased into a little frown. 'That's very kind of you, Lieutenant, but, you know, we've managed all right so far.'

Jack smiled. 'That sounds like your aunt talking.'

She dropped her gaze, and for a moment he thought that he might have offended her, but then he saw the smiled that hovered about her lips. He sat back in his chair and she raised her eyes to his again. 'I take it she isn't at home today,' he said, nodding towards the house.

'No, she isn't. She left early this morning. She's gone into town to do some work with the WVS.'

'I see.'

Sam tilted her head. 'You seem rather relieved.'

'I guess maybe I am. I didn't get the impression she was very taken with me last time we met.'

'She's rather proud and a little bit set in her ways, but I'm sure you'd like her, if you got to know her.'

It occurred to Jack how unlikely it was that he would ever learn to like a woman like Leonora Edwards, but the thought quickly disappeared from his mind. Sam was looking at him, her head still slightly tilted to one side. Her hair shimmered in the soft autumn sunshine and her skin looked creamy and pale. He felt a sudden, unexpected, urge to lean forward and cup her face and draw her mouth to his. But then the sun went behind a cloud and she moved in her chair, and the moment was lost.

Jack shifted in his seat and nodded towards the house again. 'Have you always lived here with her?'

The question sounded lame to him, but she tipped her head thoughtfully and gave no hint that she might have understood what had been going through his mind. 'I've only been living here since the beginning of the year, but this house is like a second home to me,' she said. 'Leonora's my mother's sister and we often visited in the holidays when I was growing up. My parents live in Hertfordshire.'

'Hertfordshire?'

She nodded. 'Yes, it's a county, north of London, about a hundred miles from here. My parents live in a village – my father's a doctor and my mother helps him at the surgery. I have two younger sisters, Penny and Grace, who were both still at school.'

'It must be difficult, being so far away from them all.'

'It is a little,' she confessed. 'But I can't complain really, a lot of families have been parted because of the war. At least living here I can be company for Leonora. It was lucky that I managed to get a job at the hospital in town. I'm a nurse, you see, and I spent three years training in London before I came down here.'

'London?' The idea surprised him. 'Wasn't that a little dangerous?'

She smiled. 'Well, I was there during the Blitz so I suppose it was. But we just had to get on with things and try not to think about the danger.' Her cheeks flushed slightly and she took another sip of her coffee. 'What about you, Lieutenant? You must also miss your family and your home.'

'Sure I do, but we've got a war to fight and I want to play my part. We can't let Hitler win this thing.'

Her gaze locked with his and her expression stilled. Her green eyes were soft and wide and he saw the look of sadness that briefly flickered through them. Her cheeks flushed more deeply and she glanced away.

A silence fell between them. Jack heard the faint whirring of a tractor starting up in one of the fields beyond the house and then Sam turned her head again and smiled. She offered him a fresh cup of coffee and steered the conversation to other things, asking him about life on the base and telling him about her routines at the hospital.

The cloud began to thicken and Jack glanced at his watch. Reluctantly, he picked up his cup and finished the last dregs of his coffee. 'I guess I'd better get going. They'll be starting to miss me back at the base.'

She nodded. 'Yes, of course.'

Jack waited for a moment as she arranged the coffee things on the tray, then followed her through the open French windows, into the living room and along the hall. She opened the front door for him and he stepped out onto the drive, his mind whirring. This couldn't be it, could it? Turning on the gravel to face her, all his resolve not to get involved with a woman suddenly slipped away. 'I'd like to see you again, Sam,' he told her. 'Sometime soon.'

Her cheeks flushed and he saw that he'd caught her unawares, but she gave a shy nod. 'Yes, I should like that,' she murmured.

'Are you free Saturday night? We could go to the movies. There's a new picture showing in town.'

'I'll be back at work on Saturday. I won't finish until seven.'

'Okay, I'll pick you up outside the hospital at seven-fifteen. We should still be able to catch a movie.'

With another shy nod, Sam closed the door gently behind him. Jack was smiling as he strode across the drive and climbed into the Jeep.

At five o'clock that afternoon, Diana arrived at The Elms for tea. Sam took her into the kitchen and put the kettle on. She spread some of Leonora's homemade gooseberry jam onto thinly cut slices of bread and poured out two cups of tea, then they went through to the living room, balancing their plates and cups, and settled themselves on the sofa together.

Sam listened as Diana described some of the little things that had been happening at the hospital. She felt distracted. Thoughts of Jack had been swirling in her mind all day and she had to force herself to concentrate. Most of Diana's news was about nurses who had started dating American soldiers. Sam considered telling her about her own date with Jack, but something in her held her back. She had never been very good at hiding things and she thought that Diana might notice something unusual in her demeanour, but as she listened to her speaking, she realised that Diana herself was preoccupied by something.

'Have you seen anything more of Chester lately?' Sam asked her.

Diana flushed slightly and nodded. 'I saw him last Saturday and he's taking me out again tomorrow night. He likes The Fox, so I expect we'll be going there.' She put her plate down on the coffee table and picked up her bag from the floor. 'Actually, he sent you these,' she said, fishing out a small packet. 'I told him about your accident and he thought that they might cheer you up.'

The packet crinkled as Diana handed it to Sam. Sealed inside a cellophane wrapper was a brand new pair of stockings.

Sam's eyes widened. 'Goodness, I can't remember the last time I had a new pair of these! How very sweet of him.'

'Haven't I been telling you how generous they are?'

'Well, it's a lovely surprise and I'm very touched. Please thank him for me, very much.'

Diana leaned forward to put down her bag. She half turned to say something, but then her forehead puckered and she looked away again.

Sam frowned. 'What is it, Diana? Is there anything wrong?'

Diana hesitated for a moment, then turned on the sofa and met Sam's gaze. 'I like Chester a lot, I really do. He's so easy to talk to and when we're together he makes me feel like the only woman in the world. But do you really think I should be seeing him?'

Sam looked at her. Her instincts told her that Chester wasn't right for her friend, but she wasn't sure that now was the time to voice her doubts. Diana had been through so much because of Robert. Perhaps all her new relationship needed was a little time.

Diana was studying her face carefully. 'You must know by now that I'm not the least bit in love with him.'

Sam smiled faintly. 'I know you're not. But these things take time. You've only known him a little while.'

'I know that. But I also know that I'll never be in love with him. Not properly. Not the way...' Diana's voice wobbled. 'Not the way I was with Robert.' Her lovely brown eyes misted with tears and she dabbed at them with the back of her hand. She smiled hesitantly. 'I don't suppose you know how he is?'

Sam looked at her uneasily. She knew that Leonora had received a letter from Robert the previous week, but in it he'd made no mention of Diana. But she couldn't tell her that, could she? There must still be some sort of hope. If only she could get to the bottom of things and find out what had really made Robert behave in the way that he had. She touched Diana gently on the shoulder. 'Have you really not heard anything from him at all?' she asked softly.

Diana shook her head. 'No, nothing for ages. Not since ...' She bit her lip, then said, 'Not since he threw me over.'

Sam felt an enormous rush of sympathy for her friend. 'I'm so sorry. I know how much you loved Robert, and I was always sure that he loved you too. I'll never understand why he behaved in the way he did, it seemed so very unlike him. I didn't understand it at the time and I still don't understand it now.'

Diana managed a small smile and gave a little nod. Then she leaned her head back against the cushions of the sofa and sighed deeply.

The following Saturday afternoon, Jack walked along the upstairs corridor of Foley Manor and turned through a door into the officers' mess.

'Say, you're looking all spruced up,' said Bill, looking up from the newspaper he was reading. 'What's the occasion?'

'I've got a date.'

'A date? Who with?'

'Sam Mitchell.'

Bill stared at him. 'The girl you tried to run down with the Jeep?'

'I didn't try to run her down.'

Bill whistled. 'You sure move fast. I thought you weren't interested in these English dames.'

'I'm not. I mean, I don't like all of them. Sam's different.'

'Is she now?'

Jack shook his head. 'For Pete's sake, Bill. It's only a date.'

The hospital was housed in a pleasant, single storey building set back from the main road on the edge of the town. It was seven-thirty before Sam finally emerged through the main entrance. She'd exchanged her uniform for her regular clothes and done her hair as quickly as she could, but it had taken her longer to get away than she'd expected.

Ahead of her, a stone drive formed a turning circle around a patch of lawn and then straightened out the short distance to the road between flowerbeds planted with rose bushes. GIs stood in little groups on the pavement beyond the entrance to the drive, chatting and smoking, and waiting, she supposed, for other nurses to come out.

She caught sight of Jack standing by himself to one side of the entrance. He motioned to her with his hand and watched her along the drive.

'It's good to see you,' he said, greeting her with a smile.

She smiled apologetically. 'I'm sorry I'm late. Matron gave me some extra jobs to do and I couldn't get away.'

'I hope she isn't working you too hard.'

Sam smiled again and shook her head. 'No, she isn't. It just feels good to be doing something useful again.'

They stood for a moment, considering what to do, and then Jack offered her his arm. Sam put her hand, lightly, in the crook of his elbow and they moved off together along the street. She felt the strength of his arm beneath her touch and the sensation unsettled her, but she knew that the Picture Palace wasn't far.

The lobby of the cinema was dark after the evening sunshine outside. Jack paid for their tickets at the counter, then they went in through padded doors at the rear of the lobby. They'd missed the organist's music, but the usherette who greeted them showed them to two empty seats near the front. As they sat down, the Pathé news came on. The Anglo-American invasion of Italy had begun at the beginning of September and the newsreel showed flickering black and white images of the fighting.

Sam peeked sideways at Jack. He sat motionless, but in the light from the screen she saw the straight line of his mouth and the faint line that had appeared between his brows. She looked away and the opening credits of the main feature began to roll. It was a Bob Hope comedy. She felt Jack shift his position and then run his arm along the back of her seat. She stared straight in front of her, but for a moment she saw nothing of the film. She felt hot, suddenly, and intensely aware of the clean, spicy smell of his aftershave. Her heart thudded quickly in her chest.

It was nine-thirty by the time they stepped out of the cinema again, and the sun was sinking in the sky. Other people came out through the doors behind them and Jack cupped Sam's elbow and they moved a few paces along the pavement to avoid the throng.

'Would you like to take a walk?' he asked, when the crush had subsided. 'I thought we could go to the park.'

She nodded and smiled. 'That sounds nice. It's a lovely evening.'

He crooked his elbow and she put her arm through his again. They walked along the high street and then turned a corner and went past the open door of a café selling fish-and-chips. They walked a little further, until the row of buildings came to an end and they saw the park. It was bounded by a row of arching trees behind a long, low brick wall. The railings had been removed to provide scrap-metal for the war effort and the top of the wall was pitted with holes.

They came to the park entrance. A pathway of pale gravel led between low walls of clipped hedge and there were lawns on either side.

The sun was low in the sky and the shadows were lengthening quickly between the trees. Other people were walking about. There were American soldiers with girls on their arms and older couples in civilian clothes. The air was heavy with the scent of freshly mown grass.

A middle-aged woman in a coral-coloured dress and matching hat came towards them on the arm of man in a pinstriped suit. Her gaze moved disapprovingly from Jack to Sam and then back to Jack again.

Jack tipped his hat. 'Good evening, ma'am.'

The woman gave him another, startled, look and then brushed past. He glanced briefly at Sam. Her eyes were fixed in front of her, but her cheeks were flushed.

After they'd been going for a few minutes, they arrived at a junction with another, narrower pathway that looped around a large, irregularly-shaped pond. They turned onto it and soon the people around them began to thin out. They came to a little arbour with a wooden bench and paused beside it. A few leaves had settled on the bench and Jack brushed them off so that they could both sit down.

Apart from the low hum of voices in the distance and the occasional splash from the water of the pond, for a few moments everywhere was very quiet and still. Then, suddenly the tranquillity was shattered by the sound of aircraft passing overhead. The noise built and when Jack turned his eyes upward he saw the dark outlines of heavy bombers silhouetted against the evening sky. The planes were Lancasters and the squadron was moving in formation, towards the south.

As the roar of the engines faded, he glanced sideways at Sam. She was sitting very still, locked in her own thoughts and looking towards the sky, her gaze following in the direction the planes had travelled.

He was reminded of everything she'd been through. 'What was it like?' he asked. 'The Blitz, I mean, what was it really like?'

She turned her head to look at him. Her face looked pale and serious in the fading light. Jack frowned, immediately regretting his question.

'I'm sorry if I've made you uncomfortable.'

Sam shook her head. 'You haven't, Lieutenant,' she said, smiling softly. 'I don't mind talking about it if you want me to. When the Blitz began I was in London working on a hospital ward, at the very beginning of my training. I can remember it all quite clearly. It was an afternoon in early autumn when the first bombers came and it was still daylight when they began dropping their bombs. I remember running to a window at the end of the ward and seeing the flames in the sky to the east. It wasn't long before the first casualties started coming in.' She paused briefly and a look of sadness came into her eyes. 'The Germans dropped thousands of bombs that autumn and winter, Lieutenant, but the more they attacked, the more determined people became not to give in.'

It occurred to Jack that no one could have guessed by looking at her lovely face that she had come so close to danger or witnessed so much suffering. A wave of protectiveness washed over him that disturbed him deeply.

Her expression changed suddenly and she drew away from him. 'Are you all right, Lieutenant?'

It was a moment before he could focus on what she'd said. 'Sure I am.

I was just thinking about everything you've been through.'

'It wasn't just me. Everyone's been through so much since the war began. I'm just grateful to still be alive.'

He couldn't take his eyes off her face. Her skin looked dusky in the falling light and he thought how beautiful she was. 'It's late and your aunt will be getting worried,' he said, keeping his voice as even as he could. 'It's time I took you home.'

They rose from the bench together. Sam brushed a leaf from her skirt. It was a narrow skirt that hugged the swell of her hips. Jack swiftly looked away.

They made their way back through the park the way they had come. Night was falling rapidly now and Jack walked quickly, conscious of Sam's soft, quick footsteps on the pathway beside him.

The Jeep was parked in a side street off the main town square. Jack put out his hand to help her as Sam climbed in. The movement was made awkward by the enveloping darkness and his palm brushed lightly against one of her legs. For a moment he felt the sheer, silky smoothness of her stocking. *Nylons!* he thought. Who the hell had given her those? He swiftly lifted his hand and stepped away.

Jack circled the Jeep and climbed in behind the wheel. He remembered seeing Sam with Ed Walker on the night of the dance. Hadn't Bill said that they were an item? He suddenly felt like a fool.

'Is anything wrong, Lieutenant?' asked Sam.

They were driving slowly in the direction of The Elms, along the narrow, unlit lane. Jack hadn't said a word to her since they'd left the town.

'Nothing's wrong,' he said, but she heard the tightness in his voice.

He braked sharply in front of the house and switched off the engine. The house was shadowy in the moonlight and around them everything was still. He sat for a moment, looking straight ahead, and then turned in his seat towards her.

'Do you mind if I ask you something? Something personal?'

He sounded almost angry and she felt perplexed. What had brought about this change in him?

'I don't think so. I suppose it depends what you want to ask.'

'Are you dating Ed Walker?'

'Ed?' Sam looked towards him, confused and not understanding. How had he got that idea? 'Why, no, I'm not. He's Nancy's boyfriend.'

Jack sat for a moment, without replying. His face was silhouetted against the dark of the sky and it was impossible to read his expression, but he seemed to be deliberating something. Turning away from her, he climbed down from the Jeep and she heard his footsteps on the gravel as he circled around to help her out.

Sam stepped down in front of him, the cloud lifted briefly from in front of the moon, and she saw his face clearly. His eyes searched hers for a moment and then he lifted his hand and touched her cheek. He slipped his arm around her waist and drew her towards his body, then bent his head and captured her mouth with his own.

His kiss was gentle at first, but then his mouth grew firmer, more insistent and she felt the fierce flood of his desire. His hands moved beneath her cardigan, pulling her closer, and for a brief moment all she cared about was the feel of his body pressing against hers, the taste of his warm lips, and the heady masculine scent of his skin, and her head started to spin with the awakening of desire. But then, just as suddenly, she was pushing him away. It wasn't right, not here, not yet, not now - she knew she wasn't ready.

'No,' she said, twisting away. 'No, please don't.'

'I'm sorry,' he murmured, stepping away from her. 'I shouldn't have done that. I was out of line.'

She lowered her head and turned away from him, her face on fire with shame. She ran across the drive towards the house, the gravel crunching loudly beneath her feet.

She fumbled in her bag for her keys, then wrenched open the front door and let it close heavily behind her. She laid her forehead against it. The wood felt cool and smooth. A tear rolled down her cheek and she brushed it away. How had she allowed things to go so far?

She heard the sound of the Jeep's engine starting up outside. It accelerated away into the distance, and then there was nothing left except the sound of silence.

5. ROBERT

The sweat was glistening on Jack's arms and his khaki vest was damp with effort. He was on a road march with a unit of men, the drill sergeant was shouting out instructions as they ran along the narrow country lane, and the men were chanting rhythmically in time with their feet.

They'd been training hard all summer. The men needed to be kept occupied otherwise they were liable to become ill-disciplined and hard to control, and the routines of training, drill and inspection helped to keep feelings of homesickness and boredom at bay. None of them knew what the army had planned for them. The order could come any day for them to be shipped away to the field of battle and they had to be combat ready at all times. It was the waiting that was the difficult part.

It was the middle of October and the leaves were turning, reminding Jack of the fall in New England where he was from, and he felt the strangeness of being so far from home all over again. As his feet pounded along the rain-drenched road, an image of Sam Mitchell came into his mind. The fields and lanes of Hampshire that he found so alien were part of her world. Could a relationship with her ever really work? She belonged here. He belonged thousands of miles away, somewhere else.

He'd kept away from her since that night when he'd lost his head and kissed her, but that didn't mean he could keep her out of his mind. He could still vividly recall the sweet taste of her soft lips, the deep curve of her waist beneath his hands, and her yielding response to his touch, which had driven him crazy with desire for more. But he also remembered the way she had pushed him away so decidedly.

Maybe he'd moved too fast. Maybe he'd forgotten in the heat of the moment how young and inexperienced she seemed. She wasn't like the sophisticated, confident women he'd always gone for back in the States, with their witty conversation and polished looks, but he felt powerfully drawn to her in a way he never had for any other woman, and the feeling disturbed him. From what she'd told him about nursing in London during the Blitz he knew she was a very courageous young woman, yet he felt a strong urge to protect her that he couldn't remember ever having felt for anyone in his life before.

He was breathing hard as they went up a hill. They'd come ten miles already and there were another ten to go. He began to chant out loud in time with the men, resolving as he did so that he would do everything in his power to overcome the deep, instinctive urges she'd stirred within him and keep his mind on the fight ahead. He had to remember that they had a job to do, and that was the only reason they were there.

Sam sat on the sofa in the living room reading through the letter that Leonora had received from Robert that morning. Leonora was sitting in an armchair by the fire, darning a sock.

Sam finished reading and put the letter down on the coffee table. Robert had sent a photograph with the letter, a recent one, and she picked it up by the edges and studied it. It had been taken in a studio and he was wearing his distinctive grey-blue RAF uniform. He was looking into the distance, off to the left, and he'd signed his name in the bottom corner with a flourish.

Leonora glanced up at her over the top of her glasses. 'He looks very handsome, don't you think?'

Sam nodded. 'Yes, very.'

'And he's got eight days' leave. It's going to be so wonderful to see him, it's been months since he's been home.'

Sam rose from the sofa and propped the photograph next to the clock on the mantelpiece. A fire spluttered weakly in the grate.

'And what do you think?' asked Leonora. 'Do you suppose you could get some time off and go up to London to meet him for a couple of days, as he suggests? You could use the flat in Kensington.'

Sam's forehead puckered. 'It's nice of him to suggest it, but don't you think he'd really rather spend time there with one of his friends?'

'I don't think so, darling. He wouldn't have suggested it if he did. You know how fond he is of you.'

'I really don't know if I'm up to it.'

Leonora stopped darning and took off her glasses. 'Really, Sam, isn't it time you had a change and did something different? You've been here more than eight months now without a proper break. You're still so young, you can't bury yourself here forever. It would be good for you to mix with a few young people of your own kind, even if only for a couple of days. I'm sure you'd be perfectly safe in London. There's hardly been any bombing just lately and you know that Robert would look after you.'

Sam nodded, but she said nothing. She leaned forward to pick up the poker by the fireplace and prodded with it at the fire. She didn't know if she could face going up to London; a trip there was likely to rake up painful memories from the past. On the other hand, it would be a golden opportunity to speak to Robert and to try and find out how he really felt about Diana. It probably wouldn't be easy to broach the subject, but if she had a couple of days with him alone then surely an opportunity would present itself. Diana was still seeing Chester and she hadn't mentioned Robert for weeks, but Sam was sure she knew where her friend's affections still truly lay.

'Robert so wants you to join him,' pressed Leonora. 'I can tell from his letter. Try to think of him.'

The fire sprang to life in the grate and Sam sat down on the sofa again. 'Perhaps you're right,' she conceded, looking over at Leonora. 'I'd love to join Robert in London if it means that much to him. I'm sure I could get a couple of days off from work if I asked Matron.'

Leonora smiled at her approvingly. She put her darning in the basket by her feet and went over to the painted wooden cupboard in the alcove by the fireplace. She searched inside it for a moment or two, then drew out a thin cardboard box from the bottom of a shelf.

Carrying the box in her hands, she sat down on the sofa next to Sam. 'I have a little surprise for you,' she murmured. She carefully removed the lid from the box and folded back the faded tissue paper that concealed its contents. Underneath was a length of silk the colour of the deep pink roses that bloomed in the summer in the garden outside.

Sam opened her eyes wide. Fabric for new clothes had been rationed for ages and she couldn't remember having seen anything so beautiful in a very long time. She reached out and stroked the silk tentatively with the tips of her fingers. 'Where on earth did you get it?' she breathed.

'I've had it for a long time. I've just been saving it for a rainy day.'

'It's so beautiful.'

'I thought we could get Mrs Mills to make up a dress for you for when you go up to London. You know what a genius she is.' Vera Mills was Leonora's dressmaker, and she had a small shop in the centre of town.

Sam drew back her hand and stared in astonishment at Leonora. 'But I couldn't possibly take this! You must have a dress made up in it for yourself.'

'It's just been sitting in that cupboard, going to waste. It isn't of any use to me. I'm far too old to be wearing this sort of colour.'

'But it wouldn't be fair. I really couldn't...'

Leonora smiled at her fondly. 'You're going to have a new gown to take up to London,' she said, gently but firmly. 'I've made up my mind, so there's no use arguing.'

She put the lid on the box and set it to one side. Piles of papers and magazines were heaped haphazardly on top of the coffee table in front of them. She leaned forward and began rifling through them. Watching her, Sam felt a surge of tenderness for her indefatigable aunt.

'Ah, here we are,' said Leonora at last, plucking out a magazine. 'I knew it was here somewhere.' It was a copy of *Vogue* and she held it up so that Sam could see its cover. 'My friend Mrs Forbes-Hamilton lent this to me just last week. I'm sure we'll find something suitable for Mrs Mills to copy from in here.' She smiled at Sam over the top of her glasses. 'We do want you to look fashionable when you're up in London, don't we?'

Less than two weeks later, Sam found herself standing with Leonora under the platform clock at the railway station at the edge of the town, waiting to board the London train. It was early in the morning and there was a mist hanging in the air, but the lights on the platform gave out a dim glow in the blackout.

'Robert's going to meet you in London, so there's nothing to worry about,' Leonora told her as they said their goodbyes.

A porter opened the door to the carriage and Sam stepped onto the train and made her way along the aisle of the carriage to find her seat in one of the compartments. Pleased to find that she would be travelling alone, she reached up to place her small suitcase on the luggage rack, then smoothed down the skirt of her tailored brown suit and sat down.

The sun began to come up and she felt an unexpected sense of excitement as the train pulled out of the station. It was only then that she realised quite how much she needed a break from the long demanding hours that she worked at the hospital. She'd had no trouble in getting the weekend off. She was a reliable worker and hadn't had an extra day off since she'd started working there, apart from that time in August when she'd hurt her ankle.

Unbidden, an image came into her mind, clear and sharp, of Jack kneeling over her beneath a vivid blue sky. Annoyed with herself, she looked out of the window. Why was she thinking about him again? She hadn't seen him for weeks, not since that night when he'd kissed her. It was abundantly clear that he'd lost all interest, and wasn't that for the best? She'd heard the other nurses gossiping at work about how several girls in town had already had their hearts broken by sweet-talking, easy-going GIs, whose natural warmth they'd mistakenly interpreted as love. Shaking herself out of her reverie, she opened her handbag and pulled out her book, then settled back in the seat to read.

There were problems on the line and the train pulled into Waterloo an hour later than expected. Sam stepped out of the carriage and joined the moving throng of passengers that was leaving the train. There were scores of people in the main concourse and everywhere she looked men in uniform were moving through the crowd, but after a few moments glancing around she spotted Robert standing beneath the central clock. He was holding a newspaper and smoking a cigarette. He turned his head and saw her and signalled to her with his hand.

As she came up to him, he dropped his cigarette and extinguished it with the sole of his shoe, then stepped forward to kiss her on the cheek.

'It's so good to see you, Sam,' he murmured.

'It's good to see you too, Robert.' She saw that he'd aged in the months since she'd last seen him. There were new creases in the corners of his eyes and there were even traces of grey in his light brown hair. 'I'm sorry I'm late.'

He smiled. 'Trains are never on time these days. I've had a coffee and read my paper, so you needn't worry. I just hope your journey wasn't too unpleasant. I'm grateful to you for coming.'

'I'm glad to be here,' she told him warmly. 'I'm looking forward to catching up.'

Robert took the suitcase out of her hand and they started across the concourse, making their way out of the station to the line of taxis that was waiting outside.

Half an hour later, their taxi pulled up outside the tall town house in Kensington that housed the flat that had been in their family since their grandfather had bought it twenty years earlier. They got out of the taxi, and for a few moments Sam stood looking up the steps at the front door while Robert paid the driver. Nothing seemed to have changed in that leafy street in all the time that had gone by since she'd last been there. She reflected on the seemingly random nature of the war the Germans had waged on London - a war that had left some streets completely obliterated and others, like this one, entirely untouched.

They went up the steps together and Robert opened the door with his key. The communal hallway had a door at the end that gave access to a shared back garden and an air-raid shelter. Ahead of them was a flight of tiled stairs with an iron banister. They climbed to the first floor and went through a door at the end of the landing.

No one had stayed there for several months and the flat smelled musty. The small, square-shaped hallway they had entered had several doors leading off it. There were two double bedrooms at the rear of the flat, a small kitchen and a bathroom, and a large living room with tall sash windows overlooking the street. Over the years, the flat had been used and enjoyed by all of their family. When Sam had been growing up, there'd been regular trips to London with her parents and sisters for shopping or meeting friends, or occasionally going to the theatre. Such trips had come to an abrupt end with the onset of the war, of course.

Sam took off her coat and hung it on a peg whilst Robert carried her suitcase into one of the bedrooms. He came out into the hall again and they went through to the kitchen together, where she filled the kettle and put it on the stove.

In the living room, two elegantly upholstered sofas faced each other in front of a marble fireplace and the walls were hung with a set of paintings depicting hunting scenes. Sam sat down on one of the sofas and Robert set the tray of tea things down on the coffee table between them. He went over to the gramophone, which sat on top of a mahogany cabinet, and put on a record.

'These things ought to be put into storage, for safe-keeping,' he said, glancing up at the antique mirror hanging above the fireplace. 'It would be a shame if it all got destroyed. I must speak to Mother about it.'

The sound of a jazz band filled the room. Robert turned the volume down low, then seated himself on the other sofa, opposite Sam. He quickly drained the cup of tea she'd poured for him, then fished in the pocket of his jacket and brought out his cigarettes. 'I suppose you must be wondering why I was so keen for you to join me here,' he said, opening the packet. 'It was good of you to come. I know how hard these things are for you still.'

Sam nodded. 'It's true, I did wonder. I'm sure you'd have had a better time with one of your friends.'

Robert smiled. 'Sometimes it's good to have a break from all that.' He held out the packet, offering her a cigarette, but she shook her head. 'I'm sorry, I was forgetting that you don't.' He put his hand in his pocket again and brought out his lighter. 'You don't mind if I do, do you?'

'No, not at all.'

He lit his cigarette and put away the lighter. 'To be honest with you, Sam, there's something I need to talk to you about.' He regarded her steadily, his face serious. 'You see, it's about Diana.'

'Diana?' Sam felt a thrill of hope, surprised and pleased that Robert had broached the subject of her friend himself.

His brows lifted. 'Does that surprise you so much? I suppose you thought it was all over.'

'I just know she hasn't heard from you in a while.'

'We did decide things weren't working,' he admitted. 'That is, I did at least. Diana was very cut up about it. I didn't want to hurt her, but I felt confused.' His blue eyes clouded over. 'Did you know that we'd talked about getting married?'

'No, not exactly, but I thought that you might have done.'

'Well, we had. But in the end I found I couldn't do it to her. I was afraid I would let her down by dying and leaving her with God knows what on her plate. It just didn't seem right.' He tapped his cigarette over the ashtray on the coffee table. 'Now I realise that I was wrong. Why shouldn't we have taken a shot at some sort of happiness, however brief? I still love her, Sam. Now more than ever.'

Sam felt a brief rush of delight, but then an unwelcome image came into her mind of Chester Dawson sitting beside Diana, his arm draped casually around her shoulders.

'What is it, Sam?' He had seen something in her expression. 'She hasn't found someone else has she?'

'I'm so sorry, Robert.'

'God, I've been such a fool.'

'I'm sure it isn't that serious…'

'Is it someone I know?'

Angry with herself for betraying her thoughts, Sam bit her lip. 'Actually, he's an American.'

Robert stared at her, and then said, in a tone of utter disbelief, 'A Yank?' He ground out his cigarette in the ashtray on the table. 'Mother did tell me about the American base at Foley Manor, but I didn't expect…' He shook his head. 'Diana and a Yank!'

Sam spoke quickly, the truth spilling out. 'I'm sure it's a shock for you, Robert, but Diana didn't think that you loved her anymore. It's a very long time since you were last in touch with her. You couldn't expect her to wait in case you changed your mind.'

He pushed his hand through his hair. 'I suppose I'm not being fair,' he said in a calmer voice. 'It's just a bit of a shock, that's all. How far do you think things have gone?'

'She's only known him for a few weeks,' said Sam, flushing. 'I'm sure she hasn't… I mean, she's not the kind of girl who would… do anything.'

'I'm sorry, I shouldn't have asked that,' said Robert swiftly, looking embarrassed. 'I just hope he's not shooting her a line. I've heard what these Yanks can be like, talking big about life in the States.'

'I'm sure it's nothing like that. But you don't know what it's been like at home. One minute the only men around were either old or infirm and the girls had to dance with each other if they wanted to dance at all, and the next thing we knew all these glamorous young Americans had arrived in town with nowhere to go and lots of money to spend. Some of the girls thought that Christmas had come.'

'Including Diana.'

'You know that she isn't like that,' said Sam softly. 'She was just lonely and she thought that you didn't love her anymore. Chester's been very kind to her.'

A muscle twitched in Robert's cheek. 'Chester,' he said glumly. 'That's his name is it?'

Sam nodded and then they both fell silent. Robert dug in his pocket again for his cigarettes, lit one up and began to smoke. The music from the gramophone turned to static and he went across to change the record.

'And what about you, Sam?' he asked her, over his shoulder. 'Have you got a Yank too?'

A vision of Jack flashed through her mind and she felt her cheeks grow warm. She shook her head quickly. 'No, Robert, I haven't.'

He studied her face for a long moment, then crossed the room and sat down on the arm of the sofa. 'Johnny wouldn't have wanted you to spend the rest of your life being unhappy, you know.'

Sam looked up at him and gave him a shaky smile. 'I know he wouldn't.'

He studied her face for another moment, drew on his cigarette one last time, then leaned forward and stubbed it out. 'Why don't we go out for a walk?' he suggested. 'Then, later on, I'll take you out somewhere special. Have you brought something pretty to wear?'

Sam smiled weakly again. 'Yes, I have. Your mother insisted I had a new dress to bring with me. I've no idea where she got the material, but you know how clever she can be.'

6. LONDON

It was drizzling with rain when the train pulled out of the station. Jack was sitting opposite Bill in the window seat of one of the small compartments of the carriage, heading out towards London on leave.

He thought back to his first railway journey in England. It had begun in Liverpool, the port of arrival for the troopship that had brought him from the States. England had seemed such a small country when he arrived. According to the handbook he had been issued with in Liverpool, it was hardly bigger than the state of Minnesota. He remembered how the train had clattered through the countryside that first night, stopping occasionally at dimly lit station platforms where women in uniform had handed out mugs of hot, sweet tea. It had been a cramped and uncomfortable journey and they'd seen nothing of the country as the blackout blinds had been pulled down. It had been more like being on the subway than on a train.

This morning was different. Although it was still drizzling, the mist had cleared and he was lounging comfortably in his seat, taking in the view of the green, undulating landscape of southern England.

'It's a mighty pretty country,' said Bill.

Jack nodded. 'It sure is.'

'Any idea where we are?'

Most of the station signs they had passed had been painted over. Others appeared to have been removed altogether in order to confuse any German invaders.

Jack looked at Bill and laughed. 'Your guess is as good as mine.'

Swollen barrage balloons drifted along the London skyline. It had stopped raining when they arrived, but the city looked damp and the cloud cover was still thick and heavy. Sandbagged doorways, heaped up piles of rubble, and the hollowed-out remains of bombed buildings slid past their windows as their taxi wove its way through the streets.

The pavements were full of people. There were drably dressed civilians amongst them, but most seemed to be service personnel, dressed in uniforms of khaki, blue or grey, and every shade in between. There were soldiers and airman and sailors on shore leave. They were smoking and talking and chatting to girls, or studying maps and looking up at buildings.

The taxi turned a corner and skirted the edge of a park, where Jack saw a group of GIs playing a game of baseball in the shadow of anti-aircraft guns. The streets grew wider and more elegant as they continued westwards.

They pulled up at the kerb outside the Red Cross Club for officers in Kensington, where they were to stay the night. Jack paid the driver and they carried their luggage inside. The plan was to spend the day walking the streets of the city and taking in the sights.

The evening light was fading when another taxi dropped them off on Shaftesbury Avenue, at the corner of Piccadilly. The Stars and Stripes fluttered in the breeze above a redbrick Victorian building with three tall, blacked-out, bay-fronted windows.

'So this is it,' said Bill, nodding towards the building. 'The famous Rainbow Corner Club.'

They went in through the entrance and came into a lobby. They stopped at the information desk, where a dark-haired receptionist welcomed them and directed them through a door to the dining room.

The room was large and smoky and crowded with American servicemen. They found a couple of empty seats and gave their order to an English waitress, who brought them hamburgers and coke. After they'd eaten, they went through to a recreation room. The room held pool tables and GIs sat around talking and smoking and playing cards. The strains of *Chattanooga-Choo-Choo* could be heard being pumped out from a jukebox in the corner.

They played a game of pool together and had another coke.

'I could use a real drink,' said Jack, as they started a second game.

Bill looked up from his shot. 'Yeah, me too. I didn't realise that this joint wasn't licensed. Captain Langdon told me about a place somewhere in Mayfair. A hotel with a bar and a place for dancing.'

Jack nodded. 'Sounds good to me. Any idea how we get there?'

'I know the name of it,' said Bill. 'I guess they'll be able to give us directions at reception.'

Outside the club, the street was shrouded in inky blackness. They waited in the doorway for a few moments for their eyes to get used to darkness, then began moving westwards, along Piccadilly.

'I wish I'd had the sense to bring a flashlight,' muttered Bill.

'Hello Yanks. Looking for a good time?'

The woman's voice came out of the darkness. The dim light of her torch touched briefly on their faces and then she turned it upon herself.

Jack caught a glimpse of her heavily made-up face before the faint beam swung downwards onto her slim legs and ankles. He cleared his throat. 'No thanks, honey. Not tonight.'

She melted away into the shadows and they moved off again, walking slowly. All about them now were tiny pools of light from shaded torches and they could hear the low buzz of voices as women bargained with passing soldiers.

The voices faded and they continued heading west. The streets were busy with pedestrians and there were taxis and other vehicles about. They saw the shadowy outlines of people going down into the Underground laden with bags and baskets, food and bedding. Above them the sky was starless, the moon completely hidden behind cloud. It seemed to Jack that the Germans were unlikely to attempt a raid on such a night.

They heard the sound of voices and laughter coming from the blacked-out windows of pubs and restaurants as they passed along the streets. The white helmet of an American MP showed up palely in the darkness and they stopped him to ask for directions.

The hotel was on a corner. It was old and built on a grand scale, and there were several Jeeps parked beside the pavement outside. They walked up to the entrance and pushed through the doors.

The lobby was bright after the darkness of the street. Velvety red sofas stood on a swirling carpet and an enormous chandelier hung from the centre of the ceiling. There was a reception desk with staff dressed in uniform behind it, and a wide staircase with thick mahogany banister rails. Facing them as they entered was a set of double doors, which briefly opened and shut to reveal a high-ceilinged ballroom and people dancing to a tuxedoed band that was playing the music of Glenn Miller. To their right was another set of doors and they crossed the lobby and went through them into the hotel lounge.

The room was softly lit and men and women in uniform and evening dress were seated around low, glass-topped tables. Jack led the way between the tables to the bar at the back of the room and they sat down on two high circular stools in front of it. Bill lit a cigarette and they ordered their drinks from an ageing bartender wearing an immaculately pressed black suit.

As they drank their beers, Jack examined the room. He saw that the women there looked smart; they were the most elegant he'd seen since arriving in England. He also noticed that although the atmosphere was more cosmopolitan than it had been at Rainbow Corner, the majority of the uniforms were still American.

Bill extinguished his cigarette. 'It's pretty quiet in here. Maybe we should go check out the band.'

Jack nodded. He put back his head and finished the last slug of his beer.

It was when they went out into the lobby that he saw her. She was laughing as she came in from the street, her eyes sparkled and her cheeks were flushed from the chill of the night air. She was wearing an evening dress of deep pink that perfectly complimented her pale complexion. Its folds enveloped her slim, shapely figure, emphasising the soft contours of her body. With her was a tall, fair Englishman wearing the distinctive blue uniform of an RAF officer. Seeing her with another man, Jack felt like he'd been punched in the stomach, and it stopped him dead in his tracks.

She turned her head and saw him, and for a brief moment she looked as if she couldn't believe her eyes. She stopped smiling, her body stilled and the pink tinge in her cheeks grew deeper.

She stepped towards him. 'Lieutenant Webster,' she said, her voice soft and breathless. 'I didn't know you were in London.'

'Sam.' He had to take a moment. 'Bill and I arrived this morning,' he said, forcing out the words. 'We're here on a forty-eight hour furlough.'

He saw the proud lift of her head as she waited for him to say something more.

'You gentlemen must be friends of Sam's,' said the pilot, speaking with a well-bred English accent.

Jack met his steady blue gaze. 'Yes, that's right, we are.'

The pilot extended his hand. 'How do you do? I'm Robert Edwards, Sam's cousin.'

Jack looked at him. Thinking back, he remembered she'd once told him that she had a cousin in the RAF. Why hadn't he thought of it before?

Refocusing, he saw that Robert was still waiting for him to speak. 'My name's Jack. Jack Webster. It's good to meet you.' He leaned forward to shake Robert's hand, then introduced him to Bill.

'What a coincidence, meeting you both here,' said Robert. 'Won't you join us for a drink?'

Sam was conscious of envious glances from some of the women when she entered the hotel lounge with the three handsome young officers.

There was an empty table close to the door. Robert stopped next to it and pulled out a chair. 'Why don't you wait here, Sam, while we get the drinks? Perhaps Lieutenant Webster will wait with you.'

Sam saw the tight line of Jack's mouth. 'I'm sure I'll be all right by myself for a moment,' she said primly, sitting down.

'Get me another beer will you?' said Jack, glancing at Bill as he sat down next to her.

'Sure.'

'Sherry, Sam?' asked Robert.

'Yes, please,' she said.

She folded her hands in her lap and stared down at them. Seeing Jack in the hotel lobby she'd been completely stunned, and even now she couldn't quite believe he was there. And he hadn't been at all happy to see her, she thought, judging by the look that had crossed his face and the few words that he'd spoken. She glanced up and was at once caught in his appraising blue gaze.

'How are you, Sam?'

He was looking at her steadily, but there was nothing in his expression now, no clue as to what he might be thinking.

'I'm fine, thank you,' she replied crisply.

'I've been meaning to call round and see you.'

Her chin rose fractionally. 'I haven't been expecting you.'

His lips twitched, as if he were fighting a smile. 'I know you haven't. But I should have called. I should have apologised for what happened that night. I was way out of line.'

Sam lifted her hands and rested them on the table. 'These things happen, Lieutenant. It really doesn't matter now.'

Jack reached out and she felt the warmth of his hand over hers and caught the faint scent of his aftershave. Her skin tingled disconcertingly.

'Yes, it does,' he said softly. 'I'm sorry. It shouldn't have happened that way.'

Before she could frame her reply, Sam saw Robert and Bill approaching the table behind him, carrying drinks. Her cheeks flushed and she pulled her hands quickly away.

The drinks were handed round and cigarettes were offered, then the men settled back in their chairs and began discussing the state of the war. The Americans asked Robert about his life in the RAF but they were able to draw little out of him except to learn that he'd survived the Battle of Britain and flew a Hurricane fighter plane. Listening to Robert speak, Sam felt proud of his loyalty to his comrades, and his unaffected modesty.

'I just feel privileged to be able to do my bit,' he said. 'We all feel the same, I'm sure.' It was clear that he wanted to change the subject. 'How are you finding the English weather? A bit damp, I expect.'

Bill gave a short laugh. 'It's taking a lot of getting used to. Our quarters are like an icebox in winter.'

Robert smiled. 'But I take it you're being well looked after?'

'We've had a real good welcome from everyone,' Bill told him. 'It can't be easy having us here, taking the place over.'

'You've come a long way to help us, Lieutenant Crawford,' said Sam. 'We're just grateful that you're here, ready to risk your lives for us.'

Jack sat back in his seat and studied her thoughtfully. 'I guess it's our war now, just as much as yours.'

The doors next to them opened and a couple came in from the lobby. The woman's face was flushed and the American captain she was with was looking down at her and laughing. Sam heard the opening bars of *Moonlight Serenade* coming from the ballroom behind them.

Jack glanced at the couple and then his gaze met Sam's again. 'Would you like to dance?' he asked.

His invitation caught her completely off guard. She pictured herself on a dance-floor with him, imagined the contours of his body pressing close to hers, and felt a swell of panic.

'No,' she said firmly. 'Thank you, but actually I'm feeling quite tired.'

Jack smiled, but his eyes released her. 'It is getting late.'

There was a brief silence and Robert looked between them. Sam could see him thinking things over, and she saw the look of understanding that came into his eyes. 'It isn't so very late, Sam,' he murmured.

The doors swung open and shut again as another couple went through them. The men's eyes were all upon her, curious and expectant, and Sam felt suddenly ridiculous. She stood up and pushed back her chair, and the three men rose to their feet.

Jack smiled at her encouragingly, putting out his hand for her to take.

The lights were soft and the music tender. Jack felt the curve of Sam's waist beneath his hand and the warmth of her body through the sensuous folds of silk. The air stirred around them as they moved and he caught the light perfume of her hair and skin.

He'd asked her to dance with him on a sudden impulse, without really thinking. Although sharply aware of her sitting next to him, he'd tried to avoid allowing his attention to stray in her direction and had concentrated instead on what Robert had been saying. But when he'd heard the music drifting through from the ballroom, he hadn't been able to resist.

The song ended and he withdrew gently from their embrace. When he looked down into her eyes, the expression in them was soft and vulnerable.

'Lieutenant,' she said. 'I'm sorry, Lieutenant... '

'Jack,' he corrected her. 'Call me Jack.'

'Jack,' she whispered. 'I'm sorry, Jack. I don't think I'm ready for this.'

He heard the anguish in her voice and a wave of protectiveness washed over him. 'Don't say anything,' he said softly. 'I'm not in any hurry.'

She shook her head. 'I can't do this,' she said, her words sounding choked. 'I'm so sorry.'

She twisted away from him and fled towards the open doors of the ballroom, but he was too quick for her and before she'd reached the hotel lobby he'd captured her by the wrist and stopped her.

He pulled her close and held her there. 'Don't run away from me,' he murmured, keeping his voice low and steady. 'I understand that you're not ready. I'm not going to hurt you. I don't know what it is you've been through, but I certainly don't intend making it any worse.'

It was quiet outside in the lobby. Sam sank down into the deep velvet cushions of a sofa, grateful that Jack seemed to understand that she needed a few minutes to gather herself before they returned to the others.

The chaos of her feelings both shocked and embarrassed her. For a little while, as they'd danced, everything around them had seemed to recede into the background and there'd been only him. But then the song had ended and the bubble had burst, and all the old memories had come suddenly, painfully, rushing back.

'If there's anything I can do...'

His voice interrupted her thoughts and she shook her head quickly. 'I'm all right. I'm sorry to have been so silly.'

There was a brief rise and fall in the music as the doors opened and closed behind them.

'You're sure you're okay?'

His face was still clouded with concern and she made an attempt at a smile. 'You must find my behaviour very strange, Lieutenant. You see, it's very difficult for me. It's hard to explain...' She broke off, struggling with what to say.

'Whatever it is, it's none of my business and you have nothing to explain. I'm just sorry to have upset you, that's all.' He looked at her seriously and his voice lowered. 'You know, sometimes I feel like I'm just a spectator to all of this, sent here for some reason I can't quite fathom. You've been in it since the very beginning. Maybe I won't understand any of it, not what people are going through, not how it makes them feel, not any of it, not until we actually go into battle.'

A shiver flashed down Sam's spine. She looked away, so that he wouldn't see the fear that she suddenly felt for him. 'None of us knows what lies ahead of us, Lieutenant,' she murmured.

A couple came in from the street through the doors in front of them, a British naval officer with a girl in a red dress on his arm. The girl was dark-haired and glamorously made up and the officer was carrying a small leather suitcase. They stopped by the reception desk and the officer spoke to woman behind it. The girl turned her head to look around the lobby and met Sam's gaze. She smiled and nodded briefly, then turned her attention to the officer again. Sam watched them laughing together as they made their way, hand in hand, up the thickly carpeted staircase.

'They sure look happy, don't they?'

Sam turned her head. Jack was smiling at her and all the gravity had lifted from his face.

She nodded. 'Yes. Yes, they do.'

'Look, I know maybe we haven't got off to the best start this evening, but this is my first time in London. Bill and I don't know anyone and it's a real stroke of luck that we've bumped into you and your cousin. Shall we just try to relax and enjoy ourselves a little?'

His look was open and friendly and all at once a weight seemed to lift and her head cleared. She nodded again. 'Yes, Lieutenant, you're quite right. I think that sounds like a very good idea indeed.'

'There's just one thing you could do for me though.' His voice was playful.

'Oh? What's that?'

'Promise me that you'll stop calling me Lieutenant.'

'Where are you two staying?' asked Bill.

It was after midnight and they were all standing in the lobby, preparing to leave. Sam adjusted the wrap that was draped around her shoulders. Through the open doors to the ballroom she could see the band packing away and there were people drifting past them, making for the street.

'We've got a flat in Kensington,' said Robert. 'We'll need to get a taxi.'

Bill nodded. 'That's the direction we're headed. Maybe we could share a cab.'

Outside, there was a crisp chill in the air from which the thin fabric of Sam's clothes offered little protection. She shivered and instinctively linked her arm through Jack's as they waited for their eyes to get used to the darkness.

'I'll never get used to this blackout,' said Bill. 'I can hardly see the sidewalk. I didn't think to bring a flashlight.'

Robert drew a torch from the pocket of his jacket. 'Don't worry, I know my way around. The queue for taxis is just along here. If you look hard you'll see the white lines they've painted along the kerb. Use those to guide you.'

Robert and Bill went in front, with Sam and Jack following a few paces behind them. She hadn't been thinking when she'd taken his arm, but now she felt glad of the warmth of his body next to hers, and his strong reassuring presence.

'I was in London when they first turned out the lights at the beginning of the war,' she told him. 'I was staying with my parents at the flat and we had just been to the theatre. It was quite eerie when they turned off the lights and we were all plunged into darkness. I wish you could see London all lit up. It's a beautiful city by night.'

'I'm sure it is,' he answered, through the darkness.

A bus passed them. The pavements were busy, but they went quickly because of the cold. Robert lifted the shaded beam of his torch from the kerb and Sam saw the long dark outline of the queue of people waiting at the taxi rank.

'You Brits love standing in line for everything,' said Bill, after they'd been waiting for a few minutes. 'If we went down the street a little we could get the first cab that came by before it got down here.'

Sam laughed. 'Well, I'm afraid you're in England now, Lieutenant Crawford and you'll just have to wait your turn...'

'What is it?' Jack was looking down at her, his face shadowy in the darkness.

'I thought I heard something...'

She put back her head and looked up, just as the air-raid siren began to wail and the criss-crossing beams of the searchlights illuminated the sky.

'We'd better head for the Underground,' said Robert quickly. 'It isn't far, but there's no time to lose.' He glanced down at Sam's dainty dancing shoes. 'Do you think you can manage it?'

She nodded. 'Don't worry, I'll be fine.'

They started moving along the pavement again, going swiftly. Sam held up her long dress to stop herself from tripping over its hem, but she still struggled to keep up with the men's long strides. She was aware of Jack slowing his pace to hers. At least they could see where they were going more easily now, thanks to the searchlights, she thought.

People came pouring out of the clubs and restaurants that were all about, hurrying for the safety of the Underground. There was the sound of a bomb exploding in the distance, to the east, amid the first sharp bursts of anti-aircraft fire, and she quickened her pace.

They reached the mouth of the Underground, where an air-raid warden was directing people down to the station. He blew his whistle. 'Quickly now please, the bombers will be overhead any minute.'

Sam heard the rumble of another explosion, which seemed closer this time. Jack pulled at her arm and together they dived down a long flight of steps, heading towards the safety of the platform below.

At the bottom of the steps, someone handed them a blanket and they began negotiating their way along the already crowded platform. Sam walked ahead of Jack, past the rows of huddled bodies. The electric lights blazed overhead and she saw that there were old people and children amongst them, as well as others like themselves wearing uniform and evening dress. People sat on mattresses and blankets, eating and smoking and playing cards. Some simply sat in silence, waiting for the raid to pass.

Robert and Bill stood waiting for them in a space at the front of the platform, next to the rails. Jack spread out the blanket on the floor and Sam sat down gratefully.

A family came along the platform and stood close to them, discussing where they should sit. The parents were carrying their sleeping children and Sam saw that they all wore nightwear beneath their coats. They were laden with blankets and cushions, and the man carried a basket of provisions. She was amazed at what they'd found time to bring with them and watched, fascinated, as they settled down beside her and carefully spread out their things.

The man glanced up and noticed her watching. 'All right, Miss? Like a cup of tea?'

She smiled at him and nodded. 'Yes, please, that would be wonderful.'

He produced a large thermos flask and poured out a cup of rather weak looking tea. 'It ain't much, but at least it's hot,' he said cheerfully as he handed her the enamel cup. 'We didn't have time to make sandwiches. We haven't had a raid like this in a long time, so we weren't as prepared as we used to be. I wonder what Jerry's up to tonight.' He paused and glanced up at Jack. 'Would you like a cup, officer? We've got plenty here.'

Sam smiled to herself when she saw the expression that crossed Jack's face and heard his polite refusal.

The lights dimmed for a moment and dust fell from the walls as the shock of an explosion reached them. The teacups rattled and the voices along the platform fell to a murmur.

'Let's have a song, shall we?'

A large, middle-aged woman dressed in a siren suit was seated to their right, a few rows along from them. Her words were greeted by a ripple of approval, and before long a loud rendition of *Roll out the Barrel* had begun, drowning out the bumps and bangs coming from above.

Looking along the platform, Jack was struck by the intense sense of camaraderie of the people sheltering there. How many times, he wondered, must these people have spent their nights underground like this? Yet they seemed to be full of spirit, determined to get through anything that was thrown at them and not be beaten.

The shrill cry of a woman near the entrance caught his attention. He saw a man staggering onto the platform with his hand clutched to his head. Jack could see that he was bleeding and he guessed that he must have been hit by flying glass. He looked disorientated and the woman beside him was shouting for a doctor. Jack heard the rustle of silk as Sam drew herself to her feet. For a fleeting instant her gaze met his, and then she began pushing her way along the platform in the direction of the couple. She moved quickly, determinedly, and instinctively he followed.

A warden was already speaking to the injured man when they reached him.

'I'm a nurse,' Sam told them. 'Can I help?'

The warden looked her over for a moment, then nodded and gestured for her to follow him. 'Come with me,' he said. 'There's a first aid post over here.'

The injured man was still shaking when he sat down on the chair at the first aid post. Sam opened the medical kit given to her by the warden. She bent over the man and began examining what lay beneath the stained handkerchief he'd been holding against his forehead.

As Jack watched her, he saw how much her demeanour had changed since earlier, when they'd sat together in the lobby of the hotel. She no longer seemed the vulnerable, uncertain girl she'd been then, and there was no confusion in her manner now. Her hair was dishevelled and her face a little smudged, but she was oblivious, completely engrossed in her task. He watched as she gently cleaned the wound and gave the man some morphine, then pulled a needle and thread from the first aid box.

'You're going to be fine,' she told the man gently, when she'd finished stitching his wound. 'Just rest there for a little while, and we'll see if we can find you some tea.'

Sam straightened up and adjusted her crumpled dress. She hoped it wasn't ruined, but if it was it didn't matter - the important thing was that she'd been able to help. She sensed Jack's eyes upon her and looked up at him.

'He'll be all right,' she said quickly, embarrassed by the scrutiny of his gaze. Looking past him, she saw Robert and Bill approaching along the platform.

'The raid's over,' said Robert, coming up to them. 'I think it's time we all got out of here and went home.'

Sam had been so absorbed in her task that she hadn't noticed that the thuds and shakes from above had gradually faded to nothing. She picked up the wrap she'd discarded whilst tending to the injured man and drew it around her shoulders.

She felt the pressure of Jack's hand on her elbow. 'Ready?' he asked.

Sam smiled and nodded.

They were amongst the first to leave the safety of the Underground and the streets outside were strangely quiet. They could see the outlines of fires blazing in the distance and hear the crackling of smaller fires nearby.

They began to walk, slowly at first, as they allowed their eyes to become accustomed to the darkness again. They came to a junction in the road and turned left. Above the row of houses that had come into view, they saw the tips of the flames of a fire burning in the street beyond. They carried on walking and within a few minutes they had turned right and were standing at the end of the blocked-off street. The windows had been blown out of one of the buildings along it and it was burning brightly. The air was thick with dust and debris and fragments of things from the building lay all about. A fire engine had pulled up next to blaze and the firemen had their hoses trained onto the flames.

'There's nothing we can do to help here,' said Robert, after they'd stood watching for a few minutes. 'Let's see if we can find a taxi.'

The road felt hot under the soles of Sam's thin shoes and she hoped that they wouldn't have to walk much further. Just as she was beginning to think that she couldn't carry on any longer, by some miracle they spotted the dark outline of a solitary taxi in the street ahead of them and Robert managed to flag it down.

She climbed into the rear of the taxi and sank down gratefully. The men climbed in beside her, Robert gave the directions to the driver, and the taxi pulled away.

7. OLD TIMES

'Do you really think she'll want to see me?' asked Robert.

They were on the train and he was sitting opposite Sam, smoking a cigarette. They had the compartment to themselves, but the train was travelling slowly and Sam knew it would be ages before they were home. She was looking out of the window, watching the countryside slide past, and felt tired after their late night and the tension of the raid.

'Yes, I'm sure she will,' she answered, turning her head to look at him.

His brow furrowed. 'She isn't in love with this Yank she's seeing?'

He looked young suddenly, worried and vulnerable. It was a look Sam hadn't seen since they were children.

'No, Robert, she isn't.'

'How can you be so sure?'

'I just know.'

He crushed his cigarette into the ashtray under the window, then fished in the packet for another one. 'I've only got a few days,' he told her seriously. 'I don't want to waste any time.'

He dipped his head to light his cigarette and Sam regarded him fondly. Just a few words of reassurance from her and his confidence seemed to have been fully restored. But it didn't surprise her. Ever since they were children he'd always had a strong sense of self-belief. Perhaps it was that that had kept him alive.

Robert looked up again and she smiled at him. 'I'll see Diana at work tomorrow,' she said. 'I should get a chance to speak to her then. If you want me to, I could ask her if she'd like to see you.'

Robert lowered his cigarette and shook his head. 'I can't wait that long, Sam. Tomorrow will be torture enough as it is. Why don't I meet both of you straight after work? We could go for a drink at The Fox.'

She looked at him in surprise. 'Both of us?'

He leaned forward, his expression earnest. 'You know it's been a long time since Diana last saw me. I'm sure she'd feel more comfortable if you were there too.'

'Are you really sure? I wouldn't want to play gooseberry all evening.'

'You wouldn't be.'

Sam could see that he was serious. She thought for a moment. 'I suppose you could meet us at Diana's house after work. Our shift should be over by six, but we'll need time to get ready. Why don't you pick us up at about seven?'

Robert sat back in his seat and nodded, satisfied. He drew on his cigarette. The train shuddered and rocked, then began to slow down.

'I liked them, you know,' said Robert

Sam tipped her head. 'Who?'

'Those friends of yours. The Americans.'

She flushed a little. 'Yes, they do seem very nice.'

'I wasn't expecting to. One hears so many things. None of it very good, I'm afraid, but I suppose it's just envy. The British army doesn't look after its soldiers quite so well.'

'They're certainly always very smartly turned out.'

'Lieutenant Webster particularly so.'

Sam flushed again, this time more deeply. 'I know what you're thinking, Robert, but there isn't anything - '

'Anything to be ashamed of?' He smiled at her. 'Of course there isn't. It's time you had a little happiness in your life again.'

She shook her head. 'It isn't like that…'

Robert leaned forward again. 'I meant what I said yesterday. Johnny wouldn't have wanted you to spend the rest of your life being unhappy, you know. How long has it been now? Nearly two years? Everyone knows how much you loved him, but we don't expect you to mourn him forever.'

A wave of emotion washed over Sam and for a moment she couldn't speak. The train had drawn up next to a station. Outside the window she saw a group of people waiting to get on. They looked shabby and careworn, their shoes down at heel. She heard a hiss of steam followed by the sound of the carriage door opening, and the people began to press towards it.

'There's something else, too,' said Robert. 'Something I perhaps should have told you before.'

Sam looked at him. 'Oh? What's that?'

The door of the compartment slid open and an older man in an ill-fitting grey suit looked in. 'Room for one more?' he asked cheerily.

Robert nodded. 'Yes, of course.'

The man stepped into the compartment and sat down next to Robert, then opened his newspaper and began to read. Robert opened his mouth to say something, then thought better of it.

'What was it that you were going to say?' asked Sam.

He shook his head. 'Nothing,' he said. He half-smiled. 'Nothing important.'

Diana and Nancy lodged together in a three storey Georgian house that backed onto the river, conveniently close to the centre of town. They rented the two rooms at the top of the house and had the use of the bathroom on the floor below.

The landlady was out when Sam and Diana arrived the following evening, and Nancy was at the hospital just starting her night shift, so the house was empty.

Sam followed Diana up the stairs and into her room. The walls were painted a shade of pale yellow and a large Turkish rug covered the floorboards. Clothes were scattered over the bed and cosmetics lay untidily across the top of the dressing table.

'Sorry,' said Diana, glancing about. 'I'd have tidied up if I'd known you were coming.'

Sam laughed. 'No, you wouldn't have,' she teased. 'Anyway, you know it doesn't matter.'

Diana sat on the bed and kicked off her shoes and Sam sat down on an armchair near the window that had once been a rich burgundy colour but which had now faded almost to pink. She'd changed into her regular clothes at the hospital and was wearing a cream-coloured jumper and a pair of slacks, but Diana was still dressed in her uniform.

Diana got up from the bed and began moving about the room. She went to the wardrobe and looked over her clothes for a moment, then drew out a red dress that Sam recognised as one of her favourites. She held it up to the light to inspect it, then hung it up on the outside of the wardrobe door.

She glanced across the room at Sam. 'You said he was coming at seven, didn't you?'

'Yes, that's right.'

Diana plucked at a loose thread hanging from the sleeve of the dress. 'How was he?' she asked shyly. 'I mean, do you think he'd changed at all?'

Realising that her friend was feeling apprehensive, Sam gave her a warm smile. 'He was just the same really,' she said reassuringly. 'He looked a little older, I suppose, but it was the first time that I'd seen him in ages.'

'But you say he was really keen to see me?'

'Seeing you again was all he talked about. He couldn't wait.'

Diana uncoiled her hair and shook it out, so that it tumbled in rich brown waves around her shoulders. 'His sudden change of heart seems a little strange, don't you think?' she mused. 'I mean, I'd have thought he might have written to me first.'

'Perhaps. But you know how Robert is, once he's made his mind up about something.'

'And he told you that he thought we deserved a chance at happiness?'

Sam nodded. 'Yes, that's what he said.'

Diana took the dress off its hanger. She held it against herself and considered her reflection in the mirror. Turning around again, she smiled at Sam uncertainly. 'You didn't say anything about the Americans did you? I mean, about Chester?'

Sam felt a flicker of guilt. 'I'm sorry, Diana,' she confessed. 'He asked me if you'd met anyone else and I'm afraid it did come out.'

Diana sighed deeply. 'I suppose it doesn't matter. It isn't as if it's been anything serious with Chester, so I don't suppose there's really anything for me to feel guilty about.'

'No,' said Sam. 'No, you haven't got anything to feel guilty about at all.'

Robert was waiting outside when they emerged from the house just after seven. He was standing with his back to them, smoking a cigarette, but he turned around at the sound of the front door closing. Sam noticed the blue open-necked shirt and the rather faded brown corduroy jacket he was wearing. It surprised her to see him dressed in civilian clothes, but she knew that as an officer he didn't have to wear uniform whilst he was on leave.

His hands dropped down by his sides when he saw Diana and he stood for a moment without speaking.

'Hello, Robert,' murmured Diana. 'It's nice to see you.'

He dropped his cigarette, extinguishing it with the sole of his shoe, and took a step forward. 'Hello, Diana,' he said, his voice sounding husky. 'It's been a long time.'

'Yes, it has, hasn't it?'

Sam looked down at her feet, wondering quite what she was doing there, unsure of what she could possibly say to make things easier for her cousin and her friend. She looked up again and saw that they were now smiling self-consciously at each other.

'I thought we might go down to The Fox,' said Robert. He put his hand to his hair, then let it drop again. 'That's if you'd like to.'

Diana nodded, still smiling. 'Yes, I think that would be very nice indeed.'

They started to walk. Robert moved alongside Diana, taking her arm in his, and Sam fell in step beside them.

The Fox was warm and welcoming and a fire burned invitingly in the large open fireplace. The pub was furnished with sturdy-looking tables and old oak chairs and the sheen of the wood took on a mellow glow in the firelight. There was a piano in one corner. Seeing it there, Sam thought back to evenings of singing and music in happier times.

They found the pub empty apart from two older men from the town who were standing by the bar. They recognised Robert when he walked in and greeted him warmly.

'It's good to see you, lad.'

'Let me buy you a drink.'

'Get a couple of pints in now, before the Yanks drink the place dry.'

'I can't imagine The Fox full of Yanks,' said Robert.

'The place will be heaving with them in half an hour. Here, get that down you,' said old Mr Matthews, handing Robert a dimpled glass full of beer. 'Now what would you ladies like?' he asked, turning to Sam and Diana.

Carrying their drinks in their hands, they crossed over to a table by the fire. Robert helped Sam and Diana off with their coats and they all sat down.

Sam took a sip of her sherry and looked about. Somehow, already, Robert had managed to smooth things over and it was as if he and Diana had never been apart. They were smiling and laughing together and looked once more like the happy young couple they had been before.

The pub began to fill up. The heavy wooden door on to the street kept opening and closing as people came in. A group of GIs arrived noisily. They joked with one another as they hung their greatcoats on a metal coat stand near the door, then went across to the bar and began ordering drinks. Sam heard the chinking of glasses from behind the bar and the sound of beer being poured. She gazed into the flickering fire and sipped her sherry and for a little while the buzz of voices faded into the background.

'Goddamn British can't be relied on. They ran away at Dunkirk, didn't they?'

She looked up. The voice had come from the table next to them. Four GIs were now seated around it and one of them was staring at Robert. She recognised him at once. He was Bradley Hunt, the soldier who had pestered her at the dance in the summer.

Brad drained his glass, then wiped his mouth. 'Hey buddy, are you too lily-livered to fight?' he asked loudly, still looking at Robert.

'Why don't you just simmer down a little, Brad?' Sam heard one of the men sitting with him say. 'We don't want any trouble.'

'Just look at him, hiding out in here with two women. Why isn't he in uniform? Leaving the job to us, I guess. Just like in the last war.'

Sam glanced at Robert. He looked calm. As she watched him, he put back his head and exhaled a ring of smoke.

'Hey, isn't that Chester Dawson's girl?' Another of the soldiers was looking at Diana.

Brad stood up and pushed back his chair. He glanced at his friends and straightened his jacket, then walked over and laid his hand on the table in front of Robert. He leaned over him. 'Say Limey, don't you realise that these are our girls now?'

Robert looked at him steadily. He lifted his glass and finished his drink, then calmly extinguished his cigarette in the ashtray in front of him. 'If you'll excuse me…'

Brad straightened up, allowing him to stand.

'Would you care to step outside?'

Brad lifted his jaw. 'Sure thing, buddy. I'll step anywhere you like.'

Diana jumped up from her chair and pulled at Robert's arm. 'Please Robert, don't. It isn't worth it.'

'Let me deal with this, Diana,' he told her softly. He gently prised her hand away, then took off his jacket and put it over the back of his chair. As he rolled back his sleeves, the noise in the pub fell to a murmur. Turning to Brad, he gestured towards the door. 'After you, soldier.'

The room fell quiet. Brad looked about him and a grin stretched out across his face. As he walked across the flag-stoned floor, soldiers stepped back to let him through like a sea parting. Robert followed behind him, his face determined, and Sam's heart began to race.

The door opened and Robert and Brad stepped out into the darkness. There was a swell of noise and the rest of the soldiers pushed after them, out onto the street, until only the locals were left behind.

Sam saw Mr Matthews coming over from the bar.

'The landlord's phoning the police,' he said in a loud whisper, putting his drink down on their table. 'Robert will be all right.'

Diana stood very still, looking dumbstruck, her eyes fixed on the door.

'Robert did use to box when he was up at Cambridge,' said Sam swiftly, searching for something to say that sounded the least bit reassuring.

Diana put her hand over her mouth, then sprang across the room to a window near the door, with Sam hurrying close behind her. They heard the sound of chanting soldiers coming from the street and Sam itched to peel back the blackout to see what was happening. She knew how dark it was outside and it occurred to her that the men wouldn't be able to see well enough to fight. But then there was an audible crack as a fist connected with something hard, and the whole street seemed to erupt with noise.

Jack took his foot off the gas as he approached the gated entrance to the base. An MP at the checkpoint was waving his hands and flagging him down. Jack pulled up beside him, leaving the Jeep's engine running.

The MP gave him at quick salute. 'We've had a call from The Fox. It looks like there might be some trouble in town between one of our guys and a Limey.'

Jack nodded. 'Well, you'd better get down there, Wilson. Hop on board. I'm headed that way myself.'

'What the hell is going on here?'

Sergeant Wilson directed the beam of his flashlight on the faces of the men and Jack stared incredulously at one of the figures swaying before him.

'Edwards?'

Wilson shot him a look of surprise. 'Do you know this man, Lieutenant?'

Brad wiped his bloodied nose with the back of his hand. 'He's a damn Limey coward.'

'Don't be an idiot,' Jack told him. 'This is Flight Lieutenant Edwards. He's a fighter pilot in the RAF. He was shooting down Nazis while you were still in high school.'

'Say, how were we to know?' said one of the other men. 'Why didn't you say something?'

Robert shrugged. 'You never asked.'

Jack looked at him through the darkness. 'I'm sorry if things here got a little out of hand.'

Brushing the dust off his shirt, Robert shook his head. He extended his hand to Brad and looked him in the eye. 'No hard feelings, I hope, solider,' he said.

Sam's mouth went dry when she saw Jack come into the pub with Robert. She was momentarily overcome by a flash memory of sitting next to him in the taxi, his strong body unsettlingly close to hers, but then someone put a hand on her arm to gain her attention.

'Miss Mitchell?'

It was Mr Matthews.

'Miss Mitchell, Ted and I were just wondering if you might favour us with a song. We thought it might help calm things down in here if we had a bit of music.'

Sam glanced over at the piano in the corner. An older, well-built man was settled in front of it. His face reddened when he saw her looking over at him.

'Do you really think it would help?'

Mr Matthews nodded. 'I'm sure it would. Ted over there will accompany you, but he's too embarrassed to ask you himself.'

Robert and Diana came up to them. Robert's clothes were a little dusty, but he seemed to have escaped any serious injury. Diana looked relieved, but her face was still flushed with nervous excitement. Sam saw Jack coming up behind her. He nodded when she briefly met his gaze.

'What is it, Sam?' asked Robert.

'Mr Matthews has asked me to sing.'

'Then why don't you? I'm sure everyone would love to hear you.'

'Well, I...' Sam's gaze moved over their expectant faces. She laughed, realising at once that there was no getting out of it. 'All right then, if I must.'

The pub was buzzing with people again and Mr Matthews ushered her between them to the corner of the room that held the piano. Glancing around the warm, smoke-filled room, she noticed that Jack had sat down at the table with Robert and Diana. He smiled at her when she met his gaze. She hesitated a moment, then bent to whisper the name of the song to Ted. She asked him to play *The White Cliffs of Dover*, which she knew to be one of Robert's favourite songs. Ted ran his hands over the keys, experimenting with a few chords, and the chattering voices fell to a murmur.

Sam rested her hand on top of the piano and spoke clearly, 'I'd like to sing this song for my dear, brave cousin, Robert.'

A ripple of approval ran around the room. Sam nodded briefly at Ted and he began to play. When the tune ended, there was a moment's silence, followed by loud applause and shouts for more. Sam blushed and gave a little bow, then Ted played the opening bars of *We'll Meet Again*.

The clapping and whistles of approval only ceased when Sam slipped back into her seat at the table next to Diana. A soldier settled down at the piano. He began to play a laid-back, American tune, and the noise level in the room began to rise again.

'I'd almost forgotten how lovely your voice was,' said Robert, handing Sam a glass of sherry. He lifted his glass. 'To Sam,' he said, 'and her beautiful singing.'

'To Sam,' said Jack.

She caught his gaze and her face flushed. 'Thank you,' she said, and then, changing the subject, added, 'I hope you'll promise not to get into any more fights, Robert. You scared us all half to death.'

Robert struck a match and lit his cigarette. He looked at Diana, his expression boyish. 'I'm sorry if I worried you. You know what an idiot I am.'

He held Diana's gaze for a long moment. Sam looked away, found that she was looking at Jack again and saw the smile that was playing about his lips, then glanced down at her hands.

Robert drew on the cigarette and sat back in his chair. 'Anyway, the good news is I shouldn't be getting into so many fights anymore.'

Sam raised her head to look at him. 'Whatever do you mean?'

'I mean I've been grounded.'

Diana stared at him. 'Grounded?'

Robert nodded. 'Yes, grounded. You see, I seem to have developed a problem with one of my ears and for some reason I can't seem to hear the operators over the radio anymore. I'm not happy about it, but they say it means I can't fly. It's just too risky. They want me to help train other pilots instead.'

'Oh, Robert,' said Diana quietly. Her expression softened and tears welled up in her eyes.

Robert leaned forward and put his hand over hers. He smiled a crooked smile. 'Why so sad? I thought my news would make you happy.'

Diana dabbed at her eyes with the back of her hand. 'Of course it makes me happy, it's just such a surprise that's all. So you won't be going out on any missions anymore? You won't be in any danger?'

Robert's face grew gentle. 'That's right,' he told her softly.

Sam glanced away and took a sip of her drink, aware of Robert whispering something else to Diana. After a few moments, he drew away from her and turned to Jack. 'It seems I'm going to be spending the rest of the war in a classroom, Lieutenant.'

Jack nodded. 'No one can say you haven't earned it, Edwards.'

'I'm so pleased for you, Robert,' said Sam, her eyes shining. 'Have you told your mother?'

'Yes, I spoke to her this morning. As you can no doubt imagine, she was delighted when I told her.' His gaze settled on Diana again. 'And, of course, it really does change so many things.'

'What do you think?' asked Diana. 'Do you like it?'

Sam looked up from the magazine she was studying. They were in the small dressmaking shop belonging to Vera Mills and Diana was standing on a low wooden chair in the middle of the room. She was dressed in a figure-hugging coat of pale blue crepe and Mrs Mills was kneeling at her feet, adjusting the hem.

Sam set the magazine down on the table in front of her. 'Oh, Diana, it's gorgeous,' she breathed.

'It's a Utility design, of course, but one by Hardy Amies. It is rather special, don't you think?'

Mrs Mills sat back on her heels and studied her work. 'You'll do,' she said. She stood up and helped Diana down from the chair.

Diana turned and studied her reflection in the mirror that hung on the wall at the back of the shop.

'You look lovely,' said Sam. 'Robert will be over the moon when he sees you in it.'

Diana's forehead puckered slightly. 'You don't think that he'll be disappointed that I'm not wearing a traditional white dress?'

'No, not at all. I'm sure he'll be absolutely delighted when he sees you in this.'

'I didn't have enough coupons for a long dress, even with those that you and Mummy gave to me. Anyway, I thought it was more sensible to have something I could wear again. Mrs Mills is making me a lovely hat to go with it.' Diana ran her hands over the soft fabric of the coat. 'It really doesn't matter what I wear,' she said quietly. 'I'm so happy. Robert loves me and that's the only thing that's important now.'

Robert had proposed to Diana the morning after they'd all been to The Fox together and a date for the wedding had been fixed for the beginning of December.

Diana took off the coat and handed it to Mrs Mills. 'Thank you so much,' she said. 'You've made a lovely job of it.'

'You're very welcome, dear. Everyone wants you and young Mr Edwards to have a lovely day.'

The shop bell jangled above their heads as Sam and Diana went out through the door. It was cold outside and the cloud was low in the sky. Sam drew on her gloves and put her hands in her pockets.

'Only another week to go now,' said Diana, linking arms with Sam as they moved off along the pavement, going in the direction of the teashop. 'Can you believe it?'

'No, not really,' smiled Sam.

'I spoke to Mummy last night. She and Daddy are still both disappointed that I'm not going back home to Sussex to be married, but she seemed a lot happier than when I first told her that the wedding would be here.'

'I suppose it's only natural to want one's daughter to be married from home.'

Diana nodded. 'But it would all be a lot more complicated if everyone had to take time off to travel down to Sussex from here. This way we can have more of our friends with us.'

'Well, I know that you've made Aunt Leonora very happy,' said Sam, smiling again. 'Just last night I heard her talking on the telephone to one of her friends. She was telling them about all the plans she was making and saying how lovely it was all going to be. But I do hope you don't think she's interfering too much.'

Diana laughed. 'She's being very sweet about it all. She's helped me with the invitations and she's booked the room at the back of The George for our reception.' She squeezed Sam's arm. 'I think it's all going to be just perfect.'

They walked slowly. The street was deserted, but then two GIs emerged abruptly from an alleyway, nearly bumping into them.

'Chester's been wonderful about it all,' said Diana, after the grinning soldiers had moved away.

Sam gave her a sideways glance. 'Has he?'

'I knew that you were wondering.'

'What did you tell him?'

'Only the truth. It wasn't easy, but he was very understanding. I think he always knew that our relationship wasn't serious. At least it gives him a chance to meet someone else now, if he wants to.'

The clouds had darkened and it had begun to drizzle. They came to the doorway of the teashop, pushed open the door and went inside.

8. A WEDDING

'You remember Julian, don't you Sam?' said Robert, coming into the living room. 'I'm sure you two have met once or twice before.'

Sam was standing at the window looking out over the bare winter garden. She turned around and saw the RAF officer who had come in with Robert. His wavy, light-blonde hair was smoothed back with Brylcreem and he was dressed as Robert was, in uniform. His skin was pale and lightly freckled and he had deep-set, greyish eyes. He looked familiar but she couldn't quite place him. When had she met him before? A drinks party in London at the beginning of the war perhaps?

She smiled at him. 'Yes, of course. Hello, Julian.'

He stepped forward and shook her hand. 'Delighted to see you again, Sam,' he said. She saw the look of recognition in his eyes. 'I was very sorry to hear...' He lowered his voice. 'It was bad luck about Johnny.'

She dropped her gaze. 'Yes, it was,' she murmured. 'Thank you.'

There was a short silence.

Robert glanced at his watch. 'You've got here just in time, Julian. The car will be here in a minute.' He smiled at Sam. 'Are you ready?'

She glanced down at her clothes and touched her hand to the string of pearls at her throat, a gift from her father when she'd turned eighteen. 'I hope so. These are the smartest clothes I have. Do you think I'll do?'

Robert laughed. 'I'm sorry, I wasn't thinking when I said that, was I? You look beautiful, as usual. The perfect bridesmaid.' He glanced at his friend. 'Don't you think so, Julian?'

Julian nodded. 'Perfect,' he agreed.

The door opened and Leonora walked into the room. She was wearing an elegant dress made of burgundy-coloured crepe and a small, neat hat with a matching ribbon. 'Are all of you ready to go?' she asked. 'The car's already on the drive, you know, and we don't want to be late.'

The winter sun moved in and out of cloud as the gleaming black car slid up to the kerb outside St Catherine's, the small Norman church on the outskirts of town. Sam climbed out onto the pavement in front of the lych-gate and watched for a moment with the others as the car moved off again. It slowly receded away along the road, heading into town to pick up Diana and her parents, Major and Mrs Howard, who had arrived from Sussex the previous evening.

Robert and Leonora went through the lych-gate together, with Sam and Julian following a few paces behind. Ahead of them, a stone pathway cut across the churchyard to the entrance to the church. They walked up the pathway and paused in front of the open doorway, which was flanked by holly bushes smothered with berries. It had been arranged that Sam would wait outside until Diana arrived, but Julian was unhappy about leaving her there by herself.

'It's rather cold out here,' he said. 'Wouldn't you be better off waiting inside with us?'

Sam smiled at him. 'Please don't worry. I'm sure it won't be long before Diana gets here.'

For a moment he regarded her with a cool, studied expression, but then he nodded. Sam watched him vanish into the gloom of the church, dipping his head to follow Robert and Leonora beneath the pale stone arch that curved above the entrance.

A layer of frost coated the churchyard and Sam pushed her hands into her coat pockets and stamped her feet to keep them warm. Guests had begun arriving. They came through the lych-gate, chatting and smiling, and made their way up the pathway towards her. Nodding polite greetings, they disappeared into the church.

Ed and Nancy appeared, strolling leisurely up the pathway together. Ed had his arm wrapped around Nancy's waist and Sam thought how wonderfully happy they looked.

'Hello, Sam,' said Nancy, giving her a warm smile and then kissing her on the cheek. 'Gosh, your face feels cold. Are you waiting out here for Diana?'

Sam smiled and nodded. 'Yes, I am. How was she this morning?'

'She was very happy and very excited. But she wasn't ready when Ed picked me up, so you might be waiting here a while.'

Ed put his arm around Nancy's waist again. 'It's a bride's prerogative to be late,' he grinned.

Nancy looked up at him, her eyes sparkling with fun. A few moments later they moved off again, their voices fading as they went into the church.

Smoke curled from the chimneys of the houses opposite and a bird hopped across the frosty ground in front of Sam. A Jeep came into view over the crest of the hill. As it descended the road towards the church, the figures in the front took shape. Jack was at the wheel and Bill Crawford was travelling in the passenger seat next to him. Diana had told her that Robert had invited them to the wedding, but Sam's heart still gave a little flutter.

The Jeep pulled up next to the kerb and the Americans climbed out. They were wearing double-breasted khaki greatcoats over their uniforms and looked smarter and more handsome than ever, almost like people from a film. Sam watched them come through the lych-gate and along the pathway.

'Good morning, Sam,' murmured Bill, tipping his hat. He nodded briefly to Jack, then ducked his head to go in through the doorway of the church.

'Is everything okay?' asked Jack, looking slightly puzzled.

Sam nodded, explaining quickly that she was waiting for Diana. 'She shouldn't be much longer now,' she said.

Jack's blue eyes flickered to the empty road. He said nothing, but he made no move to go.

A few moments later, the car reappeared carrying Diana and her parents. It came around a bend in the road, growing larger and then gliding smoothly up to the kerb.

'I think you need to go inside now, Jack,' said Sam, meeting his gaze. She flushed slightly, feeling self-conscious at saying his name again.

Jack smiled. 'I'll see you a little later then,' he said.

Jack followed Bill out through the doorway of the church. The bride and groom were already standing outside on the grass and a photographer was arranging a handful of guests behind them.

Bill drew a packet of cigarettes from the pocket of his greatcoat, then nodded in the direction of the group. 'It doesn't look as if they're going to be needing us for a while,' he remarked.

They considered what to do for a moment, then made their way across the churchyard and stationed themselves beneath the bare branches of an ancient horse-chestnut tree. Bill smoked his cigarette and they watched as the other guests came gradually drifting out from the church. Jack saw Leonora Edwards peering out into the weak winter sunshine. She stepped outside and Sam emerged through the doorway behind her.

He saw them pause on the pathway to watch some of the other guests forming into a group for the photographer. The sun moved out of a cloud and Sam touched her hand to her eyes to shield them. She wore her hair up, drawn away from her face and elaborately coiled at the back of her head. She was wearing a dark-coloured coat belted at the waist. He'd seen her take it off inside the church, revealing the outline of her figure beneath a cream silk blouse open at the throat and a slim-fitting brown tweed skirt that emphasised the curve of her waist and hips.

She turned her head to say something to her aunt. As she did so, she caught sight of him across the churchyard. She smiled and took a step forward, as if she were going to come over to speak to him, but then a tall, fair-haired RAF officer he hadn't seen before crossed her path and said something to gain her attention. She seemed to hesitate for a moment, but then she nodded to the officer and went with him to join the group of guests who were being photographed.

The wedding reception took place in one of the low-beamed, oak-panelled rooms of The George Hotel, an old coaching inn just off the main town square. The room seemed dark to Sam after the winter sunshine outside, but it was warm and welcoming.

It was to be a small gathering with no more than thirty or so guests. Robert and Diana had left the church ahead of everyone else and were standing near the doorway to greet people as they arrived. Next to them, glasses of sherry stood waiting on a small round table covered with a crisp white cloth.

Diana had taken off her coat, revealing a figure-skimming, matching blue dress. Sam kissed her on the cheek and told her how beautiful she looked. 'It was a lovely service,' she said. 'I'm so happy for you both.'

'Thank you,' said Robert, glancing proudly at Diana.

Diana's eyes shone brightly. 'Everything's perfect, isn't it?'

Robert handed Sam a glass of sherry. She saw that other guests were gathering in the doorway behind her and moved off, leaving Robert and Diana to welcome them.

At one end of the room a long trestle table was spread with a buffet and at the other end was a bar. Another table ran down the centre of the room, covered by a starched white tablecloth and set with silver cutlery and linen napkins. Bottles of wine stood at regular intervals along it.

Sam wandered across to the buffet table, sipping her sherry. There was a wedding cake hidden beneath a plaster casing that had been made to look like icing, and the hotel had provided plates of sandwiches and homemade pickles. To her surprise, she saw that there were also several generous platters of cold meats and three large cut-glass bowls of tinned fruit.

The babble of conversation and laughter grew louder as the room filled with guests. Looking around at their faces, it was clear to Sam that people were determined to enjoy themselves. It was a wedding, after all, war or no war.

Leonora came over to join her. Pulling on Sam's arm to take her to one side, she gestured with her chin across the room. Looking over in the direction that she'd indicated, Sam spotted Jack and Bill propped by the bar. They had tankards of beers in their hands and seemed to be deep in conversation. 'Why do you suppose Robert asked those men to come?' complained Leonora irritably. 'I saw them at the church, but I really didn't think they'd be coming here to the reception.'

'You know he met them when he was last on leave. He likes them.'

'Yes, but he hardly knows them and we haven't the least idea who their people are.' Leonora glared across at the Americans for a moment, but to Sam's relief they didn't seem to notice. 'Now Julian I can understand,' she went on. 'He wasn't always Robert's closest friend, but we've known the family for years. He seems to have turned into a delightful young man.' She dipped her head and lowered her voice. 'His father has an estate you know, not far from your parents' house. Julian will inherit it one day. He'll make someone a good husband, I'm sure.'

'Yes, I'm sure he will,' murmured Sam dutifully.

A woman came up to them. She was a friend of Leonora's and they began exchanging pleasantries. Sam stood listening for a little while, but then she saw Diana negotiating her way across the room and used her as an excuse to peel away.

'I think we have you to thank for this,' said Diana in a whisper, motioning to the buffet.

Sam's brows lifted. 'Whatever do you mean?'

'I've just been speaking to Lieutenant Webster. He brought the extra food as a wedding gift for Robert and me, and I wanted to thank him, but I'm sure he wouldn't have gone to so much trouble if it hadn't been for you.'

Sam looked at her, and Diana laughed. 'Don't look at me that way. I'm right, and you know it. I know you've been avoiding telling me about it, but I'm not a fool. I've seen the way he looks at you and I've seen you blushing when he does.' She glanced meaningfully over Sam's shoulder and added lightly, 'And it looks like you've got another new admirer as well.'

Sam turned her head and saw Julian Pennington a few paces away, chatting to Robert. She quickly averted her gaze and glared at Diana. 'But I've only just met him,' she hissed.

Diana chuckled. 'Come on, let me show you the cake,' she said, linking her arm through Sam's and steering her away. They rounded the table to the end and she leaned over and carefully lifted up the plaster casing that concealed the cake, briefly revealing the bare sponge beneath. Moisture darkened her large brown eyes. 'I know it isn't much, but I feel so touched when I think how generous everyone has been, saving up their meagre rations of butter and sugar for us over the past few weeks.'

'You mustn't worry, no one has minded,' said Sam, squeezing her arm. 'Everyone just wanted today to be as special as possible for you and Robert.'

A waiter came over to them and drew Diana away to speak to her about something. Sam glanced across the room and saw that Jack was still standing by the bar, talking to Bill. She watched them for a moment and then started across the room towards them, taking care as she went not to be drawn into conversation with any of the other guests.

Bill turned his head and saw her approaching. He murmured something to Jack and picked up his drink and moved away. It seemed to her that he was deliberately leaving them to have a few moments alone, just as he had done earlier, outside the church.

'Hello again,' said Jack. He nodded towards her empty glass. 'Can I get you another drink?'

'Oh, no,' she said, flushing a little. She put her glass down on the bar. 'That wasn't why I came over.'

'Oh?' He looked puzzled. 'Is there something I can do for you?'

'I just came over to say thank you.'

'To thank me? For what?'

'For the food. Diana's just told me about it, and I wanted to thank you.'

'The cookhouse could easily spare it. Think nothing of it.'

'But I'm sure everyone appreciates your kindness.'

He looked uncomfortable. 'I wish Diana hadn't said anything, I was just pleased to be able to help. Bill and I both feel privileged to be here. We didn't realise it would be such a private party.'

Sam glanced around the room. 'I suppose there aren't many here,' she reflected. 'And yet Robert always had so many friends. I don't think anyone was able to get any leave apart from Julian.' Her forehead furrowed and she added quietly, 'It's this war, you see.'

Jack straightened up. 'I'm sorry, Sam. I wasn't thinking - '

'Please don't apologise,' she interrupted, at once wishing that she hadn't embarrassed him. 'It's just the way things are and no one can change it. We just have to make the most of the people who are left to us.'

He held her in his gaze for a moment, thinking over her words, but he said nothing. Sam was aware of people chatting lightly in the background. All the guests seemed to have arrived now and the room was growing warmer.

Jack was still regarding her evenly. 'There's something I wanted to ask you,' he said.

'Yes?'

'We're planning on holding a Christmas party at the base for the local children around here. Their mothers and teachers are being invited too. It won't be anything swanky, but would you like to join us?'

Sam's heart fluttered. 'That sounds wonderful,' she said shyly. 'I'd love to come if I can.'

Jack nodded, looking pleased. He told her the date of the party and Sam thought quickly, hoping fervently that Matron would let her take the afternoon off.

A waiter came by collecting glasses on a tray. Julian appeared behind him. He glanced at Jack with obvious curiosity, then spoke briefly to Sam. 'I just came over to tell you we're going to be sitting down in a moment or two. Can I get you anything?'

'No, thank you, I'm fine,' she assured him. She quickly made the introductions. 'Jack, this is Julian Pennington, Robert's best man,' she said. 'And Julian, this is Jack Webster.'

Glancing at the insignia on Jack's collar, Julian nodded. 'So how are you finding it in England, Lieutenant Webster?' he asked.

Robert and Diana sat next to each other at the head of the table and Sam was placed between Diana's father and Julian. The Americans were further down, on the opposite side, and Sam noticed that Jack had been seated between two nurses.

Diana's father was an ex-Army officer, a Major who had served in the Great War, who was now a commander in the Sussex Home Guard. Sam had known him for years and he kept her entertained throughout the meal.

He glanced down the long table to where Jack and Bill were sitting. 'Of course, now that the Americans have joined us it won't be long until it's all over.'

'You really think so?'

'Yes, my dear, I do. It's just a question of time.' He sipped his wine and studied her thoughtfully. 'So now Robert and Diana have finally tied the knot, what about you? Tell me, is there any romance in the air?'

Just at that moment, Sam caught sight of Jack out of the corner of her eye. He was saying something to the girl next to him and she was smiling up into his eyes. She was a nurse who Sam didn't know very well, a girl called Anne. Sam quickly shook her head. 'No,' she said. 'No, there isn't anyone.'

The Major feigned astonishment. 'I just don't understand the young men these days.' He glanced past her then, at Julian. 'And what about you, Flight Lieutenant? Any wedding bells in the air?'

'I'm afraid not, Major Howard.'

'I see.' He looked between them thoughtfully. 'And you're staying the night, I presume,' he said, speaking to Julian again. 'Here at the hotel? Perhaps we could have a nightcap together. I'm sure my wife wouldn't mind.'

'I'm afraid I have to make the six o'clock train. I was only able to get a twenty-four hour pass and the CO was reluctant to give me that.'

'Got some sort of show on?'

Julian nodded.

'I see. Well, we know you can't tell us the details, but good luck, old boy.'

Something Robert said drew the Major's attention and he turned away.

Julian took a packet of cigarettes from the pocket of his jacket. 'You don't mind, do you?' he asked, glancing at Sam.

She shook her head. 'No, please go ahead.'

He bent his head over his lighter, then began to smoke. He moved an ashtray across from the centre of the table and placed it in front of him. 'Perhaps we could meet for dinner sometime,' he said, turning to her again. 'I'm often up in London, perhaps we could meet there.'

His invitation took Sam completely by surprise and she glanced awkwardly away. Jack came into her line of vision once again. He seemed to be laughing at something Anne had said and she saw that his face was alight with interest. Sam felt suddenly completely off balance. 'Yes,' she said, without turning her head. 'I don't get an awful lot of time off, but I'd like that.'

Jack looked up then, and caught her gaze. He smiled at her warmly and she immediately regretted her words to Julian. She took a sip of wine. It didn't matter, she told herself. She was hardly likely to find herself in London again for a very long time and Julian had probably only invited her out of politeness.

Julian exhaled a plume of smoke. 'I have your aunt's number. I'll give you a call when I'm next on leave.'

Sam noticed Leonora watching them from across the table and saw the look of satisfaction that had appeared on her face. Robert stood up and chinked his spoon against his glass to gain everyone's attention and Sam turned her gaze in his direction, listening attentively as he began his speech.

9. CHRISTMAS

It was just over two weeks since Diana and Robert's wedding and the afternoon of the children's Christmas party at Foley Manor. Sam had walked the mile there from home and she was dressed against the cold in a belted coat and woollen gloves, and a knitted hat and scarf, but even so her cheeks were glowing as she stood on the threshold to the ballroom looking in.

The room was warm and welcoming. Bunting had been draped beneath the ceiling and streamers rippled down the walls beneath swags of coloured balloons. Three long trestle tables were covered with paper tablecloths and set with plates and cutlery, and in the far corner of the room a Christmas tree heavily laden with twinkling lights reached almost to the ceiling.

Children from the town were seated around the tables and Sam could hear the snapping of crackers being pulled above the low buzz of their excited voices. Women were sitting and watching them from a row of hard wooden chairs that had been set out beneath the windows on the far side of the room. Other women were hanging their coats up on a metal rail by the door. Cups and saucers were stacked next to a metal urn on a table near the Christmas tree and a GI was arranging a plate of doughnuts next to them. Soldiers were moving between the tables, laughing and joking with the seated children.

'I'm glad you could make it,' said Jack, coming up to Sam from the hallway.

'I'm very glad to be here,' she said, turning to him and smiling. It was the first time that she'd seen him since the wedding and she felt the familiar fluttering in her stomach. 'It certainly looks like it's going to be a lot of fun. What can I do to help?'

'Everything's under control. I just want you to relax and enjoy yourself.'

'But I like to be useful.'

'I'm sure you do enough at the hospital. Let us look after you today.'

He looked determined. 'All right then,' she laughed. 'I'll try.'

She took off her hat and gloves and put them in her bag, then Jack helped her off with her coat and scarf and they went together to hang them up on the rail.

'Come with me,' he said, touching her elbow. 'I want to show you what there is for lunch.'

They went out into the hallway again and turned down a corridor. The sound of plates clattering came from an open doorway at the end and there was the smell of food cooking. They went in through the door and came into a large kitchen where soldiers in white tunics were busy preparing food. Pots and pans hung above a big wooden table in the centre of the room. The table was spread with platters of carved turkey and there were steaming dishes of mashed potato and bowls piled high with cranberries.

They moved further into the kitchen, out of the way of the GIs who had started coming from the ballroom to fetch the food for the children. Sam saw a soldier in a chef's hat carefully turning out a huge jelly onto a plate. The worktop in front of him was laden with cakes and blancmanges and bowls of sweets.

'It sure looks good, doesn't it?' said Jack.

'Where on earth did you get all those sweets?'

'The guys have been saving their candy for weeks.'

'That's very generous. How very kind of them.'

He smiled. 'I expect all this is making you hungry.'

'Well, yes,' she admitted, smiling too. 'Now that you mention it, it is a little.'

They went out of the kitchen, along the corridor and back to the ballroom, where the noise level had risen and the mood was lively. They crossed over to the table by the Christmas tree. Jack handed Sam a doughnut and a GI served them coffee from the urn.

As they stood to one side, drinking and eating, Sam looked about the room, her eyes shining as she soaked up the happy, welcoming atmosphere. The coffee was strong and hot, and the doughnut was sweeter than anything she'd tasted in a very long time.

As she finished her last mouthful, she glanced at Jack. His eyes were upon her and she felt a rush of awkwardness, wondering how long he'd been watching her.

He gave her a warm smile. 'Have you got any plans for Christmas?' he asked.

'Well, I'll be working on Christmas Day,' she told him. Her cheeks felt warm and she wished she was more adept at concealing her emotions. 'But it shouldn't be too bad as my shift finishes quite early. I'll be able to spend the evening at home with Leonora.'

'So it'll just be the two of you?'

'Yes, that's right. Robert's stationed in Somerset now and he'll be on duty over Christmas. Diana's got a few days off and she's going down to join him.'

'It must be tough on them, still not being able to set up home together.'

She nodded. 'It is hard, but I think that they're just grateful that Robert isn't flying missions anymore.'

He looked thoughtful. 'I guess they are.'

There was a moment's silence, then Sam tipped her head and asked him, 'What about you, Jack? Where will you be over Christmas?'

He smiled. 'I'll be here at the base. I'm on duty that day, too.'

'I expect it will be difficult for you all, so far from home,' she reflected, her gaze flickering over the soldiers who were moving about the room.

Jack nodded. 'Some of the younger guys are going to find it tough, that's for sure.' His gaze met hers again and he regarded her steadily. 'As a matter-of-fact, we're organising a dance on New Year's Eve, to help keep up morale. I was planning to ask you if you'd like to come.'

At her hesitant nod, he smiled. He seemed about to say something more, but just at that moment a ginger-haired soldier in a sergeant's uniform came over and hovered in front of them.

Jack looked at him. 'What can I do for you, Sergeant?'

'I'm sorry to interrupt, Lieutenant, but could I speak to you about something?'

Jack nodded. 'Sure.' He turned to Sam. 'That's if you'll excuse me for a moment?'

'Yes, of course.'

She watched him disappear into the hallway with the sergeant. Spotting an empty chair at the end of the row by the windows, she went over to sit down. She sipped the last of her coffee and watched the GIs going back and forth to the kitchen, bringing out the jellies and cakes and sweets, along with tall glass jugs of lemonade.

The children were finishing their puddings when Jack came back.

He frowned. 'I'm sorry about that. There was a last minute hitch.'

'Please don't worry. It's a lovely party and I've been enjoying myself. It's nice to see the children looking so happy.'

The ginger-haired sergeant suddenly reappeared. He stood for a moment, framed in the doorway, and called out across the room. 'Hey, you guys, Santa Claus is coming. Can you hear him?'

Everyone fell silent and Sam heard the faint sound of an engine as a Jeep drew up in front of the house. There were a few whoops of excitement and then chairs scraped against floorboards as the children jumped up and surged out into the hallway. A press of women and soldiers followed close behind them.

Sam stood with Jack at the top of the steps in front of the house. There was a bitter chill in the air, but the sky was vividly blue. A GI wearing a bright red suit and a long white beard sat in the back of the Jeep and two large sacks of brightly wrapped presents bulged next to him. Everyone else stood in a knot behind the Jeep, looking up at him. The children were at the front of the group, with the women and soldiers gathered close behind them. The GI got to his feet and stretched out his arms and there was a burst of laughter and cheering. He began handing down the parcels from the sacks and Sam saw that there seemed to be something for every child.

Her eyes were wide when she turned to Jack. 'Where did all those presents come from?'

He chuckled. 'Don't tell me you don't believe in Santa Claus?' His eyes filled with quiet pride. 'Some of the men have been making toys in the evenings,' he explained, 'and others asked their families to send things over from the States.'

'You've all been very generous,' she murmured.

'It was the least we could do. Some of these kids seem to have hardly had a childhood. We're just glad to have been able to do something to help.'

The last of the presents were handed out and the group behind the Jeep broke up and scattered. Women went inside to find their coats and then came out again, ushering their children towards the trucks that were waiting on the drive.

Jack went with Sam to fetch her coat. GIs were clearing the ballroom, picking up discarded paper hats and empty crackers, sweeping the floor and stacking chairs.

Outside, the sun was sinking quickly in the cloudless sky. The trucks started up and slowly moved off, and Sam saw the women and children wedged along the benches in the back. The children were muffled up against the cold, looking tired but happy, waving to the soldiers as they went by. Sam walked with Jack to his Jeep and he helped her in. Moments later, the engine started up and they moved off, following the trucks along the drive.

Sam walked briskly along the ward, her feet echoing on the bare wooden floorboards. It was Christmas Day and the young men who were convalescing at the hospital were in good spirits, in spite of everything they'd been through. Fires crackled in the grates at each end of the ward and the room was bright and warm.

A young sergeant was propped up against his pillow and Sam paused by the end of his bed.

'Merry Christmas, Nurse Mitchell.'

'Merry Christmas, Sergeant.'

'I think I'm in love.'

She went round to the side of the bed to adjust his blanket. 'Just try to get some rest,' she murmured.

She left the hospital just after three in the afternoon and by the time she got home it was almost dark. Leonora was in the living room building a fire. Sam called through to her to say she was home, then went upstairs to change her clothes.

She pulled off the sweater and trousers she'd worn beneath her coat to cycle home and hung them up in her wardrobe. She looked through her clothes and drew out a wine-coloured dress with a Peter Pan collar. She'd had it for years and some of the seams were worn, but she thought it would do. There would only be herself and Leonora there that evening.

She washed her face and hands in the hand basin in the corner of her room. The water felt icy. She towelled herself dry then slipped on her dress. She tidied her hair in the mirror above the dressing table and then took the string of pearls from her jewellery box and fastened it around her neck.

As Sam came down the stairs, she heard the sound of carols coming from the wireless in the living room. They hadn't bothered with a Christmas tree that year, but going through the door she saw that Leonora had trimmed the mantelpiece with candles and with holly from the garden. The fire burned brightly and there was a small pile of presents on a low table near the hearth.

Leonora was sitting in an armchair next to the fireplace. She smiled at Sam approvingly when she came into the room. 'You must be tired after your long day.'

'It was busy, but I quite enjoyed it.'

'Why don't you sit down and have a glass of sherry?'

A bottle and two glasses stood waiting on a tray and Leonora poured out the sherry. She handed Sam a glass and then settled back in the armchair. A log caught on the fire. It spluttered and burned fiercely, warming the room.

'It looks lovely in here,' said Sam.

Leonora beamed. 'Do you like it? I hoped that you would. I'm just sorry that there's only the two of us this year. I wish Robert had been able to get enough leave to come home, but at least Diana was able to get the time off to go down and be with him.'

Sam nodded. 'They seem very happy, don't they?'

'Yes, I'm so pleased for them. We just need to find someone for you now.'

'Why don't you undo Robert's parcel?' said Sam, steering the conversation away from herself. 'It's the one wrapped in blue isn't it?'

'Oh yes, how nice it looks. I wonder where he got the paper, it rather puts ours to shame.' Leonora carefully pulled open the wrapping. Inside the parcel was a bottle of Yardley perfume. 'Goodness me, what luxury!' she exclaimed. She studied the label for a moment and then cautiously unscrewed the bottle and dabbed a little of the lavender scent on her wrists and temples.

A news programme came on to the wireless and Leonora asked Sam to turn it off. 'I don't think we want to listen to that, do you?' she said. 'Not today.'

For a few minutes they continued unwrapping presents. Sam had a pair of bright blue mittens from Leonora and when she opened the parcel that her parents had sent, she found an oyster-coloured satin nightdress and a flower-shaped broach made out of small pieces of red felt that her mother had sewn together with tiny stitches.

'Oh,' said Leonora, as if remembering something, 'and there's this too.' She reached down to the side of her armchair and picked up a long rectangular box that had been hidden from Sam's view. It was wrapped in cream-coloured paper and on it was a large silver bow. 'Your American friend called by with it this morning.'

'Jack came here?'

'Yes.' Leonora pressed her lips together. 'But he didn't stay long.'

Sam set down her glass on the coffee table. Leonora handed her the parcel and she knelt down on the floor in front of the fireplace and lifted the lid of the box. Inside were layers of tissue paper and she pulled them back. There was coffee and tea, a slab of plain chocolate, two pairs of stockings and a bar of Eve toilet soap.

Leonora frowned. 'Well,' she said, unable to hide her disapproval.

'How very kind of him.'

'But is it appropriate, do you think?'

Sam put the lid back on the box. The clock ticked on the mantelpiece and there was the sound of paper rustling as Leonora smoothed out the wrapping and set it to one side. Sam knew it would all be carefully put away and saved, so that it could be used again the following year.

The fire spluttered in the grate and Leonora leaned over and prodded at it with the poker. She put on another log and the flames burst back into life.

Sam waited until she'd settled back in the armchair, then said quietly, 'The Americans are very generous people, you know. I wish you'd been at the children's party they organised, you'd have seen it then. They made sure that there was a present for every child.'

Leonora looked at her. 'I'm sure they can be generous when they want to be,' she said crisply. 'But don't you think it's rather insensitive the way some of them throw their money around? There's often nothing left for others to buy.'

Sam looked down at her hands and made no comment. She knew that there was little point in arguing.

Later, they ate a simple Christmas meal in the kitchen before returning to the living room to play cards and listen to the wireless again. By ten o'clock, the fire had died down to its last embers and they switched out the lights and went upstairs.

Leonora hovered beside Sam's door on the freezing cold landing. 'Have you heard anything from Julian?' she asked.

'No, nothing.' The truth was, she'd completely forgotten about him.

Leonora looked disappointed. 'Well, I'm sure he'll call you soon, I think he was really taken with you at Robert's wedding.' She gave Sam a peck on the cheek. 'Happy Christmas, darling. Sleep well. I'll see you in the morning.'

The door to her room clicked shut behind her and Sam leaned against it, tilting back her head and letting out a heavy sigh. She crossed over to the window and pulled back the corner of the blackout. It was a moonless night and the sky was devoid of stars. Shivering, she changed into her nightdress and quickly climbed into the cold bed. She lay still for a while, turning things over in her mind, and then, finally, she turned onto her side and drifted off to sleep.

10. NEW YEAR

The end of the year drew near and a sense of excitement and anticipation spread amongst the nurses at the hospital. Those who were going were looking forward to the dance at Foley Manor and were talking and dreaming of little else. Sam and Nancy had both managed to get the night off, but Diana had told Matron that she was more than happy to work on New Year's Eve. She explained to Sam privately that she didn't feel it was appropriate for her to go, now that she was married to Robert.

Sam hadn't seen Jack since the day of the children's party, but he kept drifting unexpectedly into her thoughts and she found herself making careful preparations for the dance. She took a dress to Mrs Mills to be altered. It was one she'd rarely worn, having never liked the colour, but Mrs Mills had transformed it almost overnight by dying it a dark midnight blue and lowering the neckline and edging it with a fold of satin. Sam realised that it had been a very long time since she'd felt quite so excited about anything.

The last day of the year finally dawned. Sam and Nancy worked the same shifts at the hospital during the day and by five o'clock they were walking through the blacked out streets to the house where Nancy lodged with Diana.

Nancy led the way up the narrow staircase to the top of the house. She searched in her bag for her key, opened the door and showed Sam into her room. She crossed to the window and drew the curtains, and Sam switched on the light.

The room was almost identical to Diana's apart from the colour of the walls, which were painted a dull shade of olive green. There was a single bed covered with a floral bedspread, a few mismatched pieces of bedroom furniture, and a dressing table strewn with jewellery and cosmetics.

Sam placed her small overnight bag on top of Nancy's bed and opened it up. Her dress lay folded on the top and she picked it up and shook it out.

Nancy opened the door of her wardrobe, took out a hanger and handed it to her. 'What did you tell your aunt about tonight?' she asked. 'I know she still doesn't approve of you mixing with the Yanks.'

Sam put her dress on the hanger and hung it up on the back of the bedroom door. 'I told her that I was spending the evening with you, but I didn't say anything about the dance. I felt guilty about not telling her exactly where we were going, but I couldn't face a row.'

Nancy looked sympathetic. 'I don't blame you. It's much easier for me, of course. I'm sure my brother will love Ed, when he finally gets to meet him.'

Sam smiled. 'Yes, I'm sure he will. Ed's lovely.'

Nancy turned away to switch on her wireless. The sound of a dance band filled the air and she hummed along to the tune. They began moving about the room, getting ready, and took it in turns to use the bathroom on the floor below. They sat side by side on a long stool in front of the dressing table, looking in the mirror to arrange their hair. Sam brushed hers out and parted it to one side, and Nancy piled her blonde curls on top of her head so that they fell loose over her forehead. They applied their make-up and carefully pulled on their stockings.

Sam slipped on her dress and shoes. Pinning on the felt broach that her mother had sent her for Christmas, she studied her reflection in Nancy's long mirror.

'Very sophisticated,' said Nancy, glancing over her shoulder.

Sam laughed. 'Not bad, I suppose, for a bit of make-do and mend.'

Nancy was wearing a square-shouldered, pearly grey dress trimmed with dark blue ribbon. 'You look lovely,' said Sam, turning towards her. 'I'm sure Ed will be delighted when he sees you.'

Nancy sighed. 'He's seen it before. Wouldn't it be wonderful to have something new?'

'Ed will be looking at you, not at your dress. Your hair looks gorgeous like that.'

'Do you like it?' said Nancy, looking pleased and putting her hand to the curls along her forehead. 'I saw how to do it in a magazine. I thought it would make a change.'

'It really suits you.'

They finished getting ready, then gathered their coats and bags, switched off the lights and went out into the street. They stood for a few seconds, allowing their eyes to get used to the darkness, then moved off in the direction of the town square, where they knew that the trucks would be waiting.

Sam and Nancy climbed the flight of wide stone steps in front of Foley Manor. The front door opened and the sound of a band playing greeted them as they stepped into the hallway. Girls were hanging their coats up on a rail. Two GIs were seated behind a table, checking invitations, and soldiers were welcoming their dates as they arrived and guiding them towards the ballroom.

Ed appeared from the sea of people, looking smart in his sergeant's uniform, his short sandy-hair smoothed and parted. He came forward towards them. 'Say, don't you two look lovely tonight.'

Nancy laughed. 'We haven't even taken our coats off yet.'

Ed grinned. 'Well, you still look good to me.'

They handed their invitations to the GIs at the table, then Ed helped them off with their coats and they went over to hang them up on the rail.

Sam looked about.

'Lieutenant Webster sends his apologies,' said Ed, seeing her glancing around the room. 'He's upstairs with Captain Langdon at the moment.' He put his arm around Nancy's shoulders. 'He'll be a few minutes. Why don't you come and have a drink with us while you're waiting?'

A burst of music came from the ballroom as the band struck up again.

'If you don't mind, I think I'll wait here for him,' said Sam.

'Are you sure you'll be okay on your own?'

'Yes, of course. You two go and enjoy yourselves.'

Ed looked sceptical, but he nodded. 'Well, I guess Lieutenant Webster shouldn't be too long.'

He put his arm around Nancy and they moved away across the hallway. The doors to the ballroom had been folded back and they paused briefly on the threshold, looking in. Ed murmured something into Nancy's ear, then they vanished into the darkened room

Sam crossed over to wait for Jack by the foot of the stairs. There was a picture on the wall depicting the English countryside. A man and woman in the foreground were dressed in old-fashioned clothes and powdered wigs. It was the sort of thing that she'd seen many times before, but something in the woman's expression caught her eye. As she studied it, she was aware of the babble of voices and laughter behind her and the slow beat of the music coming from the ballroom. Two soldiers came down the stairs and one of them whistled softly when he saw her.

'Don't even think about it, Dick,' she heard his companion say. 'That's Lieutenant Webster's girl.'

'Some guys have all the luck.'

They brushed past her. Sam continued studying the picture and pretended not to have heard.

A few moments later, she heard a movement and looked up. Jack had appeared on the landing and was starting down the stairs.

'I'm sorry to have kept you waiting,' he apologised, reaching her. 'I hope Walker explained.'

'Please don't worry, I haven't been here long.'

He gestured to the busy hallway. 'And these guys have left you alone?'

She smiled. 'Yes, they have.'

Jack's brows lifted. 'I'm surprised,' he said. 'Surprised, but glad to hear it.'

The ballroom sparkled with Christmas lights, but it was very smoky and it was packed with people. GIs were serving beer and punch from behind a makeshift bar and there was a table spread with food. At the other end of the room, a band was playing on a raised stage in front of a crowded dance-floor. People were sitting at round, softly lit tables, leaning in close to speak to each other over the noise of the music.

Jack cupped Sam's elbow and they started threading their way through the room, looking for somewhere to sit down. All the tables seemed to be occupied and when Sam peeked sideways at Jack she saw that a line had appeared between his brows. A group of soldiers with drinks in their hands parted to let them through and she caught sight of Bill Crawford sitting at a table near a blacked-out window. With him were a couple that Sam had never seen before, an American officer and a woman in a black dress with peroxide blonde hair.

Bill looked up and saw Jack and Sam making their way through the crowd. He smiled and lifted his hand, beckoning them over.

When they reached the table, Jack drew out a chair for her and bent to speak in her ear, 'Wait here, will you? Bill will look after you while I go and get us some drinks.'

Sam looked up at him and nodded.

Conversation was difficult over the noise of the music, but Sam gathered in fits and starts that the blonde woman's name was Pamela and the officer was a lieutenant called Henry Taylor, who came from Ohio. As Bill was explaining that Henry was visiting from an American base in Dorset, Jack came back carrying a beer and a glass of candy-coloured punch. He set the glasses down on the table and sat down in the vacant chair between the women.

The tempo of the music changed and the band began to play a fast dance number. The conversation petered out and they all turned to watch the couples who were dancing.

A couple were dancing more expertly than the rest. The girl's bright red dress flashed against the darkness of the room and her dark-haired partner moved effortlessly around her. The other dancers began to fall away, giving them space, until a ring of people had formed around them.

The soldier swung the girl up high and the pleated skirt of her dress lifted up, revealing a brief flash of her knickers and stocking tops, and there were shouts of approval from amongst the watching men. The tempo of the music seemed to quicken further and the circle of onlookers began clapping in time.

The girl spun around and the soldier lifted her into the air. She tipped backwards and opened her legs, landing astride his hips. He threw her into the air again and swung her down between his legs, just inches above the floor, so that her skirt flew up to her thighs.

There was a crash of cymbals and then the music stopped. The ring of onlookers cheered and soldiers began swarming around the girl who'd been dancing.

Henry laughed. 'They seem to be having a good time.' He squeezed Pamela's knee. 'Don't you think so, Pammy?'

Pamela arched an eyebrow, looking slightly bored, then gazed around the ballroom. Her handbag rested on the table in front of her and she opened the clasp and drew out a packet of cigarettes.

'We're staying at The George,' Henry told Sam. 'Do you know it?'

Sam noticed Jack stiffen almost imperceptibly. He shifted in his seat, picked up his glass and took a long swig of his beer.

She nodded. 'Yes, it's very nice. It's an old coaching inn. You should be very comfortable there.'

The band started up again. This time the music was even louder, making it almost impossible to talk. Henry lit Pamela's cigarette. He drew his chair up close to hers and ran his arm along the back of her seat, whispering in her ear from time to time. Jack shifted in his seat again, angling his body away from Henry and Pamela and resting his arm on the table, almost blocking them from Sam's view. Sam glanced at him and smiled slightly, then turned her attention to the dance-floor and the couples who were dancing.

The ballroom grew warmer and the men went to and fro to the bar, fetching more glasses of beer and punch. Then, at about quarter to midnight, the band leader moved behind the standing microphone in the middle of the stage. The people who were still sitting at tables got up and moved forward, and Jack and Sam went with them.

The crowd jostled as rows formed to face the stage. After a few minutes, the soldier looked at his watch and began counting down the final seconds of the year. 'Five, four, three, two, one... Happy New Year!' He lifted his arms towards the ceiling and there was an explosion of noise as everyone clapped and cheered.

Sam felt the press of Jack's body next to hers. Her skin tingled and she felt a sudden surge of optimism. It was the dawn of 1944 and perhaps the war would be over before the year was out.

The band began to play Auld Lang Syne. Hearing the opening chords, the press of people opened out, forming into a circle, their voices picking up the words of the familiar song. The noise level swelled as they reached the final verse and the last notes took a time to die away. Then there was another burst of clapping and cheering.

The band struck up again, playing a tune that was soft and sentimental. Jack turned to Sam and looked down into her eyes. 'Happy New Year,' he murmured. He bent towards her, his gaze dark with desire. Sam felt hot suddenly, but then he abruptly lifted his head and drew back. Her arm jolted as a soldier pushed past them with his arm around a girl.

Jack grasped Sam's wrist protectively. 'Let's get out of here,' he murmured in her ear.

Outside in the hallway, it was relatively quiet. Jack pushed open a panelled oak door near the foot of the staircase and stood aside to let Sam through.

They came into a library. Books lined the walls to the ceiling and there were three tall windows shrouded beneath heavy curtains. The back of the room lay in shadows, but a fire still burned in a large open fireplace and side lamps had been left illuminated by the room's previous occupants. Wing-back armchairs sat on either side of the fireplace and the small tables next to them were littered with American papers and magazines.

Jack produced a bottle of whiskey from a cupboard and showed the label to Sam. 'I'm afraid this is all there is,' he apologised.

Sam smiled. 'Don't worry, I don't want anything anyway. I've had plenty of punch.'

She sat down in one of the armchairs and Jack poured himself a glass of the whiskey. He put the bottle back in the cupboard then came over and stationed himself in front of the carved mantelpiece. 'I'm sorry that things seem to have got a little out of hand tonight,' he said, frowning.

'You don't have to apologise,' said Sam, looking back at him. 'I've enjoyed it.'

He shook his head and his frown deepened. 'I didn't know Henry Taylor was going to be here. I met him at training camp, back in the States. You wouldn't know it, but he's got a wife and a kid back home.'

Sam flushed. 'Please, Jack,' she murmured, 'it really wasn't your fault.'

He took a swig of the whiskey, then studied the top of the glass for a moment. 'You know, Sam, when I first came to England I wasn't expecting to meet anyone like you. I've tried to fight it, but you must know by now what I've begun to feel about you.' He lifted his gaze and his eyes met hers. 'There's something that's making you hold back from me. I know I told you once, that time in London, that you didn't need to explain...' His brows pulled together. 'There was someone else once, wasn't there?'

Sam's stomach flipped over. She nodded and her colour deepened. 'Yes, that's right, there was.'

A muscle tensed in his cheek. 'It must be very difficult.'

He fell silent and a gulf seemed to stretch out between them. It wasn't fair to lead him on any longer, Sam realised suddenly. It was time she told him about the past, however hard it might be for her to explain.

'His name was Johnny,' she told him in a quiet voice. 'He was a pilot in the RAF, like Robert, but he was killed just over two years ago now, in the autumn of 1941.'

Jack looked at her steadily. 'I'm sorry, Sam. Truly sorry.'

'I met him just before the war began,' she explained. 'It was August, and my parents had taken a house in Dorset for the summer. We'd been there a few days when Leonora and my cousins joined us. Robert was studying at Cambridge then, and he brought Johnny down with him. We spent the days swimming at the beach and walking along the cliffs around Lyme Regis. Johnny had just turned twenty and I was seventeen. I'd never met anyone like him before.'

She told Jack how, when the holiday had ended, all the men had decided to join up. David had gone into the army and Robert and Johnny had joined the RAF. 'We all saw a lot of each other that autumn and winter. People called it the Phoney War as nothing really seemed to be happening, not in England anyway. I started my nurse's training in London and I saw Johnny whenever we could manage it. He would take me out to dinner or we'd go to the Four Hundred, a nightclub in Leicester Square. He loved going there.

'Then, in August 1940, the Battle of Britain began and I saw nothing more of him until the end of September. The RAF was fighting from dawn until dusk to keep the German bombers at bay and we all saw the dogfights overhead. I used to watch the vapour trails as the fighter planes twisted and turned in the sky and I'd wonder if Johnny's Spitfire was up there with them.'

She paused. She had a strange sensation of weightlessness, a feeling of being outside of herself, listening to someone telling a story about something that had happened to someone else.

'Against all the odds, both Johnny and Robert came out of the battle unscathed - at least physically, that is. On the surface they were light-hearted about it all, but the strain was beginning to take its toll. Johnny and I saw each other whenever we could, but I knew that he was emotionally drained. The following year his missions changed. I never knew exactly what he was doing, of course, but I did know that instead of attacking bombers as they came over England, he was defending British bombers on raids over France.

'He was flying as an escort on a bombing raid when he was killed. Their mission was to destroy a German target in Northern France, but Johnny's plane was hit by some anti-aircraft fire and began losing height. He made it back to the coast of France but there was a machine gun positioned on the beach…' Her voice quivered. 'He was too low to bail out and his plane crashed into the sea.'

Jack's brow furrowed. 'And there's really no hope?'

A tear rolled down her face and she brushed it away. 'No, none, Robert was in the same convoy and he saw him go down. He saw everything.' She bit her lip. 'I know I should be over it by now,' she said, trying hard to keep her voice steady. 'So many people have stories like mine, I'm not the only one. I know we have to forget and move on in order to survive.'

He looked at her. 'Keep a stiff upper lip, you mean?' He shook his head. 'No, Sam, there's nothing wrong in feeling his loss the way that you do, nothing at all. Never be ashamed of showing how you feel.'

A log spluttered in the hearth. The door to the library opened abruptly and Bill appeared. As he came into the room he cast a quick glance at Sam. He nodded briefly, then turned to Jack. 'I thought you might be in here. I just came to warn you that the party's over and the trucks are on the drive.' He looked between them again, then vanished back through the doorway the way he had come.

Jack turned his head and met Sam's gaze squarely. 'I was planning on running you home.'

Sam rose from the chair. 'Actually, I'm staying with Nancy tonight,' she explained, flushing a little. 'I probably ought to go with her.'

He nodded. 'Okay, but I'd like to see you again soon.'

They heard the sound of voices and a gust of laughter coming from behind the door. People were spilling out from the ballroom and into the hallway.

Sam held his gaze and smiled shyly. 'I'd like that too.'

'I still don't have your number,' he smiled. 'Will you let me have it? Then I'll call you when I can.'

Jack found a pen and a scrap of paper on the library desk. Sam told him her aunt's telephone number and he jotted it down, then they went out into the hallway together and joined the sea of people making for the open front door.

11. REALITIES

Jack turned up the collar of his coat to shield his neck against the morning wind, pushed his hands deep inside his pockets and went down the front steps of Foley Manor.

There was smoke rising from the chimneys of the Nissen huts and soldiers were moving about on the duckboards between them. Across the drive, a sweep of lawn sloped away from the house, giving way to a large expanse of parkland, and Jack crossed over and started across the cold wet grass.

Row upon row of khaki-coloured tents stretched out towards a belt of woodland in the distance. No one was living in them yet, but they'd been erected over the previous week, ready to accommodate the new influx of men that was expected to start arriving any day soon. Ahead of him, Jack could see a cluster of soldiers pitching a tent at the end of a row. The canvas shape of the tent was laid out on the ground between them, and even at a distance he saw how gusts of wind kept catching it and puffing it out, hindering their progress.

The Nissen huts were difficult to heat properly and the men complained regularly about the cold and damp. He knew that the tents would be even worse, but the CO had told him that hundreds more men would be arriving over the next couple of months and there simply wasn't the time to build enough huts to accommodate them all. It was the end of February and they were building up to something serious now. He was sure that they would have left England before the spring was out.

Jack thrust his hands deeper into his pockets. He knew that the way things were going it was no time to be getting serious with a woman. He didn't know how much longer he'd be in England, or if he'd ever be coming back. But he couldn't help himself. He needed Sam, and he saw her as often as he could.

There was nowhere really private he could take her; nowhere that they could be completely alone. He'd heard that some of the men had been caught pitching tents in the woods and taking their girls there to be alone with them. For some of the guys, anywhere would do - dark alleyways, secluded fields, they didn't seem to care. He could understand what drove them to it, but he knew there was no way it was for him.

He'd been busy just lately. The weeks had flown by and he'd only managed to see Sam a handful of times since the New Year's party. He'd taken her to see a couple of movies and they'd been to The Fox a few times for a drink. Something had changed in her since that night and it was as if some of the weight she'd carried had been lifted, but he knew that emotionally she still held him at a distance. It bothered him, but he couldn't help but admire her sincerity and the great sense of loyalty she still felt to Johnny. He only wished he could take away all of her grief and make her truly happy again.

The soldiers were stretching out the guy ropes to the tent and pegging them down. When they saw him approaching, they finished off what they were doing, came to attention and saluted. He inspected their progress and then, once he was satisfied that they had everything under control, he began making his way back the way he had come. It began to drizzle and he felt the fine droplets of rainwater as they found their way inside his collar and onto the back of his neck.

As Jack crossed the drive towards the house, he heard a voice calling out to him. Lifting his head, he saw Ed Walker approaching. The cloud above was thickening fast and a sleeting wind was beginning to blow. Jack pushed up the collar of his coat and paused to wait

'What can I do for you, Sergeant?'

Ed saluted.

'Is it possible to talk to you about something, Lieutenant Webster?'

'Sure. Go ahead.'

'Can we go somewhere more private? It's kind of personal.'

Jack nodded. 'Whereabouts are you quartered?'

They walked side by side to one of the Nissen huts. The hut was constructed of curved corrugated-iron plates, bolted together above a concrete floor. Narrow beds flanked the walls, and in the centre of the hut was small iron stove with a table and chairs beside it. Clotheslines had been strung at intervals across the room and items of uniform dangled from them. Pin-ups of movie stars lined the walls and personal possessions were strewn across footlockers between the beds.

The hut felt damp and the smell of stale cigarette smoke lingered in the air. Jack shook the rain and sleet from his coat and hung it up on a peg, and then they both sat down at the table by the stove.

'So what is it that's bothering you, Walker?' asked Jack, without preamble.

Ed rubbed the back of his neck with his hand. 'Well, you see, Lieutenant Webster, it's like this…' He paused, then looked Jack straight in the eye. 'I'm thinking about getting married.'

Jack's brows lifted. 'Married?'

Ed nodded. 'Yes, sir. To Nancy.'

'It's the CO you should be speaking to, Walker, not me. He's the only one who can give permission for a soldier to get married.'

'I know that, but even so I thought you might be able to talk to him for me.'

'Me?'

'I thought you might be able to bring him round to my way of thinking. Being as how you're in a similar situation yourself.'

Jack looked at him hard. He shook his head and drew back from the table. 'I don't know what to say to you, Walker. It isn't going to be easy, that's for sure. You know how the CO views these things. He's worried that a wife's liable to distract a soldier's attention from the job he's got to do, and he thinks a guy's less likely to look out for his buddies if he's got a woman on his mind.'

'I know what the CO thinks, Lieutenant, but I promise you it won't be like that. When the time comes to fight, I don't intend on letting anybody down.'

'You're serious about this, aren't you?'

'I sure am serious. I love Nancy and I don't see why we shouldn't take a shot at marriage.'

'You know that you won't get any special living arrangements or any other privileges?'

'Yes, I know that.'

Neither of them spoke for a moment.

'Have you ever heard of ETO Circular 66?' asked Jack, breaking the silence again.

Ed looked puzzled. 'No. What's that?'

'Eisenhower's idea. It stipulates that soldiers can only marry with their commander's permission and after written notice of two months.'

'Two months?' Ed stared at him. 'And what would happen if we got married before that?'

'You could be court-martialled.'

'Just for getting married?'

'Yes.'

There was another silence.

'Look, Walker, I'll tell you what I'll do. I'll help you to get the necessary paperwork together if you want me to, but you'll need to inform the CO yourself in writing. He'll want to interview Nancy, too.'

'Interview Nancy? You're kidding, right?'

'I'm not kidding. It's all part of the procedure.'

Ed shook his head slowly. 'They sure don't want us getting married over here, do they?'

'Maybe not. But as I said before, I'm happy to give you a hand. The first thing you're going to need is an affidavit to say that you're not married already.'

The damp hut grew warmer as the heat from the iron stove permeated the air. Jack observed the concentration on Ed's face as he described in detail the paperwork that was required in order for him to get permission to marry Nancy. A few months ago he would have done his best to talk him out of it, but now he realised that these things weren't quite as simple as the army would like them to be.

12. MANOEUVRES

'Hello?'

Sam clutched the telephone receiver to her ear, trying to ignore the cold draught that whipped around her ankles in the icy hall.

'Sam, darling, it's Mother.'

'Mother, how lovely to hear you. How are you?'

'I'm fine.'

'And Daddy? And Penny and Grace? Are they all right?'

'Yes, they're fine.' The line crackled and her mother's voice grew faint. 'Darling, we might be cut off any minute, so I'll be brief. Can you meet me up at the flat next weekend? Do you think you could get a couple of days off?'

'Next weekend? Well, I could try.'

'I wish you would. I haven't seen you in such a long time and I think we need to talk.'

'Can Daddy manage without you?' called Sam over the worsening line.

'Of course he can. It's just for a weekend. Ring me on Wednesday and let me know if the hospital can spare you.'

'All right, I'll ask Matron tomorrow.'

'I'll have to go now, but I'll speak to you on Wednesday,' her mother called. 'Hopefully we'll have a better line then.'

'Goodbye, Mother.'

'Goodbye, darling. Give Leonora my love.'

The line crackled again, then went dead. Sam replaced the receiver. She went back into the living room to join Leonora, who sat knitting in an armchair by the fire.

'If you go to Selfridge's could you see if they've got any Coty powder?'

asked Nancy. 'I haven't seen any in the shops for ages and I'm completely out. Would you mind?'

'Not at all,' said Sam. 'What colour would you like?'

'Whatever they have. Something light, for the spring, if they have it, but anything would do. After all, beggars can't be choosers.'

Sam was sitting in the teashop with Nancy and Diana, at the table in the bay. The window was steamed up, but through it they could see the drifts of yellow daffodils that had come into bloom around the entrance to the park. All the tables in the teashop were occupied and people kept opening the door and coming in, then going out again, disappointed.

It was a Friday afternoon at the end of March. Sam had explained that she was taking the following weekend off to go up to London to meet her mother and they were discussing what she might see in the shops.

'I'll see if I can get any lipstick,' said Sam. 'I don't know about you two, but all I've got left are a few odd ends.'

'I'm down to scooping out the ends and melting them down,' said Diana. 'I saw how to do it in the Home Companion.'

Nancy chuckled. 'It's all getting a bit desperate, isn't it?'

Diana looked thoughtfully at Sam. 'I wonder what it is that your mother wants to talk to you about.'

'I don't know. It's been ages since I last saw her. Perhaps she just wants to catch up, she must have lots of news. I think Penny has met someone - an officer in the Suffolks.'

Diana looked astonished. 'But she's so young!'

'Actually, she's nearly eighteen now,' said Sam. 'And she's thinking of joining the Wrens.' She glanced between her friends and her eyes sparkled. 'Mother says that she likes the uniform.'

There was a moment's silence as her words sank in, and then all of them laughed. They were still smiling when the waitress came over with a heavy looking tray and set it down on the table. She passed round the tea things and served each of them a rather dry-looking scone.

'Actually, I have some news for you, too,' said Nancy, when the waitress had left them. She paused for a moment, her eyes shining, and then announced, 'Ed has asked me to marry him!'

'Marry him?' exclaimed Diana, lowering her teacup.

'Don't sound so surprised,' Nancy chided her softly. 'I thought you said that you liked him.'

'I'm sorry. I didn't mean it to sound like that. Ed's lovely and I'm very happy for you, of course. I just didn't know things had got quite so serious, that's all.'

Nancy nodded and her face brightened again.

Sam smiled at her warmly. 'I'm so pleased for you. Do you think it will be soon?'

Nancy explained about all the paperwork there was to fill out, and told them about the two-month wait there would be even after everything had been submitted to the relevant authorities. 'But Ed wants us to be married as soon as possible,' she said, 'so it shouldn't be too long after that.'

'California's so far away,' murmured Diana, looking troubled again. 'You know that we'll miss you terribly, don't you?'

Nancy reached over and squeezed Diana's hand. 'And I'll miss both of you as well.'

Diana smiled faintly, her eyes growing soft.

Nancy sat back in her chair. 'We mustn't worry about that yet,' she said, brushing away the unwelcome thought. 'None of us knows what the future holds. Ed and I love each other and he thinks we should make the most of whatever time we have. I just wish that there wasn't all of this awful bureaucracy. I've even got to be interviewed by his commanding officer.'

Diana looked at her. 'What on earth for?'

'To make sure I'm suitable to be the wife of an American, I suppose. And to see that I haven't got an ulterior motive for marrying him.'

'An ulterior motive?' said Sam. 'Whatever do you mean?'

'Oh, they seem to think that the only reason an English girl would want to marry a GI is because she sees him as a passport to the American dream.'

'That's rather arrogant, isn't it?' said Diana.

'I suppose it is when you think about it,' admitted Nancy. 'But it doesn't matter,' she added firmly. 'Ed and I love each other, and it's as simple as that. We don't care what anyone else thinks.'

Sam sipped her tea, then took a bite out of her scone. It was hard and dry and she coughed as she struggled to swallow it. 'Let's just hope that the food in America is as good as they say it is,' she said lightly. 'I think this scone has seen better days.'

As her friends continued chatting over Nancy's plans, Sam's thoughts drifted. She heard a church clock striking in the distance and her gaze wandered to the misty view of the park through the steamed up window.

She had been seeing Jack regularly since the party at New Year. In fact, they'd fallen into something of a routine. Once or twice a week, if they were lucky, he would pick her up from the hospital in the Jeep. It all depended on what he was doing at the base and on what her shifts allowed. The winter evenings had been cold and dark and he would help her into the Jeep and cover her legs with a khaki blanket. They would drive over to The Fox in the gloom and then spend a few precious hours there together.

Jack was easy to talk to, but they always spoke about little things and never dwelt on anything too serious. Sam loved being with him in the warm, welcoming atmosphere of the pub, and for a few short hours the war would be forgotten.

Afterwards, he would run her home in the Jeep. He would help her down and see her to the front door, and then he would take his leave of her. She would hear his footsteps on the gravel, retracing his steps to the Jeep, and feel an emptiness wash over her, never quite knowing when it would be that she would see him again. She'd hear the sound of the Jeep's engine starting up and listen until there was silence again, then, with a heavy heart, she would step inside the house.

Jack always carried himself impeccably and never once had he tried to kiss her again. In the weeks that had gone by since she'd told him about Johnny, it had been as if he felt he had to treat her gently, as if he were wearing kid gloves. Perhaps it was just her companionship that he needed, or perhaps he was afraid of hurting her. Whatever the reason, he made her no promises and they never talked about what might happen after the war.

Sam saw a truck rumbling past the window along the street outside. Hearing Nancy talking about the future, she'd made a show of being cheerful, but inside her heart had turned cold. Everything she had with Jack would inevitably come to an end. Over the past few weeks, she'd seen all the new soldiers and vehicles arriving from America - they held her up on her way to work almost daily. There were GIs everywhere, buying up everything that wasn't rationed, filling the pubs and crowding the streets. Everyone expected the invasion of Europe to come soon. It was clear that the Americans were building up to something important now. They had come across the Atlantic to fight and their stay in England couldn't last much longer now that spring was on its way.

Sam's throat constricted. The Americans would move out and Jack would go with them. She would have to say goodbye to him and after that she might never see him again.

The train to London was packed. Sam was sitting in a window seat, facing the rear of the train, in a compartment with five other people. She was dressed for the cold March winds in her warmest coat, worn belted over her brown suit and cream blouse. Her small suitcase sat on the luggage rack above her head. It contained a few clothes and toiletries, as well as her pink silk evening dress. Her mother had asked her to bring something special to wear, but had left her wondering the exact details of what she had planned.

Sitting opposite her was a British army officer. He was reading a newspaper but kept looking up from it and smiling, trying to catch her eye. She kept her eyes fixed on her own magazine and did her best to ignore him.

To her right sat a woman who looked to be in her thirties with a tired, puffy face. She was wearing a shabby tweed coat and her hair was tied up in a faded turban. Her little boy sat next to her, but he'd fallen asleep almost as soon as he'd sat down.

Opposite them, next to the officer, were two girls of about her own age, dressed in khaki uniform. From the badges on their hats and lapels she knew that they were army nurses. They were both dark-haired, but one wore her hair short and curly, whilst the other had her hair scraped back and knotted low at the neck. They were talking about the training they'd been doing and Sam guessed that they had yet to see active service.

She had thought about joining up herself, after she'd qualified, but civilian nurses had still been needed and the job had come up at the cottage hospital where Diana was already working. It was what she had needed at the time - a break from the horrors of London and the Blitz, and a chance to grieve quietly for Johnny. But she'd seen the posters that had recently been going up around the hospital, asking for volunteers for the Army Nursing Service.

A train rattled past on the other line and Sam turned her head and gazed out of the window. Perhaps that was what she should do. Perhaps she should join up.

London looked gloomy under a wintry sky. The mob of passengers descended the train and Sam negotiated her way along the platform with the moving crowd.

She queued for almost half an hour for a taxi, then watched the familiar streets slide past through its windows. She saw the sandbags piled up in doorways and the pedestrians hurrying by along the pavements, wrapped up against the cold.

Sam's mother, Elizabeth, was already waiting when she finally arrived at the flat. There were new streaks of grey in her lovely auburn hair, but she looked beautiful in a simple suit of pale grey with a string of pearls at her throat. She gave Sam a welcoming hug in the little square-shaped hallway. 'It's so lovely to see you, darling,' she said.

They spent half an hour or so at the flat, so that Sam could freshen up and tidy her hair, then they went down the stairs and out into the street. They caught a bus going to Piccadilly and got off outside the Ritz. They crossed the pavement and went in through the bomb-proofed doors of the hotel, where they found the lobby humming with people. A liveried doorman greeted them and motioned them through to the dining room.

They were seated at a small, linen-clad table. A waiter brought them a menu and they ordered tea and chose from a limited selection of cakes.

'Well, isn't this nice,' said Elizabeth, glancing approvingly around the room. 'I hadn't expected it to be so busy, but then I expect it's a very convenient place for people to meet, with it being so close to the centre of things.'

Sam smiled and nodded, and then they caught up on news about her father and sisters for a little while, until the waiter came back with their order. The cups and saucers were made of delicate porcelain and the cake was thinly sliced onto matching plates.

Elizabeth folded her hands beneath her chin. 'Now,' she said crisply, 'you know that I never like to pry into what you do, but what's this that Leonora tells me about you and an American lieutenant?'

Caught completely off guard by her mother's question, Sam coloured deeply. 'He's just a friend,' she murmured.

'A friend? But Leonora says you've been seeing rather a lot of him. There must be more to it than just friendship.'

'I suppose I have been seeing him quite a bit. I enjoy his company, that's all.'

Elizabeth frowned. 'Your father and I are worried about you. Do you think that his intentions are honourable? And even if they are, what would we do if you married him and went with him to live in America? We might never see you again.'

'Honestly, Mother, I like him a lot, but there's really no need for you to worry. We're just good friends and there's been no talk of marriage. I do wish that Leonora hadn't said anything about it.'

'She was just concerned. She thought we ought to know what was going on.'

'There's nothing going on.'

'But what about his family? Do you know who they are? And what does he do? Is he some sort of cowboy, like John Wayne?'

Sam smiled in spite of herself. 'He hasn't really told me very much about his family. I do know that they live in Massachusetts, and that he has a sister called Caroline. They have some sort of family business, which he hopes to join one day. At least that was what he was planning to do before he was drafted.'

'Drafted?'

'Called up.'

'You're certainly becoming familiar with their way of speaking.'

'There are a lot of Americans around. I've got used to some of their expressions. It doesn't mean anything.'

Elizabeth was silent.

'I'm sure you'd like Jack, if you met him,' said Sam firmly.

'Jack?'

'Yes, Jack. Jack Webster. He's a lovely man and I do like him very much, but we're not involved in the way that you think.'

Elizabeth drew back in her seat and looked at her. The anxiety fell away from her face and she reached across and squeezed Sam's hand. 'I'm so glad to hear it,' she breathed. 'You've no idea how worried I've been.'

Sam smiled faintly. She knew that she wasn't being entirely honest and she felt guilty. She longed to confide in her mother about everything, but it was all so complicated and she knew that if she tried to explain it would only make her worry even more. She bent her head and took a forkful of cake. As she did so, a man's shadow fell across their table.

'Well, this is an unexpected pleasure. Good afternoon ladies.'

Sam lifted her gaze and found herself looking into the pale grey eyes of Julian Pennington.

Elizabeth beamed at him. 'Why, how nice to see you, Julian.'

'Hello, Julian,' said Sam. This seemed too much of a coincidence. She glanced at her mother, wondering what she and Leonora had been up to. 'What are you doing here?' Elizabeth coughed and Sam realised how rude she must have sounded. 'I mean, it's just a bit of a surprise to see you, that's all,' she added quickly.

'Oh, I always come here when I'm in London on leave. One's bound to see someone one knows.'

Her mother smiled up at him again. 'Won't you join us for some tea?'

Julian drew up a chair from a vacant table next to them. More tea was ordered and brought to them on a tray. Julian told them about the journey he'd had up to London, on a train seemingly packed with Australian servicemen. Elizabeth asked him about his parents and he told them about the land girls who were now working on his father's estate.

There was a lull in the conversation and Julian bent his head to light a cigarette. As he put away his lighter, he looked at Sam speculatively. 'I don't suppose that you're free for dinner tonight, Miss Mitchell?'

'Well, actually I'm dining with Mother. We haven't seen each other in a very long time.'

'Oh, nonsense, Sam,' said Elizabeth brightly. 'Of course you must have dinner with Julian. We have a duty to keep up the morale of our boys.'

Sam shot her mother a glance, but she knew it would be bad manners to contradict her. She gave Julian a weak smile.

'So that's settled then,' said Elizabeth, sounding pleased. 'You know where we are, don't you, Julian? I'm sure you must have visited our flat in the past with Robert.'

Julian nodded. He exhaled a thin plume of smoke and fixed Sam with his gaze. 'Shall I pick you up at about eight?' he suggested.

'Yes, that would be lovely,' she murmured.

Extinguishing his cigarette, he rose to his feet. 'If you ladies will excuse me, I'll leave you in peace to enjoy your afternoon together. I'm sure you must have lots to catch up on.'

Sam watched the back of his retreating figure for a moment, then leaned in to their table. 'Mother,' she whispered.

Elizabeth silenced her with a glance. 'I don't want to hear any more about it. He's just the sort of young man you should be mixing with.

Leonora knows his family very well and I've met the Penningtons myself on a number of occasions.'

Sam pressed her lips together, smarting with resentment at having been out-manoeuvred by both her mother and her aunt.

13. FLOWERS

Julian took Sam out to dinner and then to a nightclub housed in a basement, somewhere in the West End of London. The doorman seemed to know Julian well and welcomed them warmly when they arrived.

They went down a narrow flight of stairs and entered a small lobby richly decorated in red velvet. Officers in uniform and women in evening dress were milling about, talking and smoking and checking coats in at a counter. The cloakroom attendant was a petite blonde girl in a slim-fitting black crepe dress. Julian helped Sam off with her coat and exchanged it with the girl for a pale yellow cloakroom ticket. He handed the ticket to Sam and she pushed it into her small satin evening bag.

The sound of a band playing could be heard coming through padded doors at the rear of the lobby. Sam touched a hand to her hair and Julian pushed open one of the doors, revealing a large, softly lit, smoky room. A tuxedoed band was playing on a semi-circular stage that jutted out over a reflective dance floor. People were sitting on luxuriously upholstered sofas and armchairs arranged around mahogany tables. Large chandeliers glittered above their heads and gilded standard lamps threw out soft cones of light towards the ceiling.

They crossed over to the bar. Behind an expanse of dark polished wood, a set of tall, gilt-edged mirrors reflected the long row of bottles lined up in front of them. Sam's gaze travelled briefly over the labels on the bottles. She settled on a gin and tonic and Julian gave their order to the barman.

Carrying their glasses in their hands, they went in search of somewhere to sit. Julian spotted a sofa near the dance-floor that had just been vacated and they started towards it. A fair-haired girl stepped across their path, almost spilling Julian's drink. Lifting her gaze to his, she batted her eyelashes and apologised profusely. As they moved off again, Sam peeked surreptitiously at Julian. He did look dashing in his uniform, she thought, and no doubt any other girl there that night would be delighted to have had him as her companion.

They sat down together on the velvety cushions of the comfortable sofa. Julian lounged back and lit a cigarette, but Sam sat forward on the edge of it, her back straight. She pushed the soles of her shoes into the deep pile of the burgundy carpet and looked down at her feet. She knew that she hadn't been very good company during dinner and felt guilty. Julian was a brave man who didn't deserve to be treated badly and she resolved to make a bit more of an effort. Picking up her glass, she sank back into the sofa and sipped her drink, her gaze travelling idly over the couples who were dancing. The music paused for a minute or two as the band was joined by a singer. More people went onto the shimmering dance-floor and another tune started up.

Julian drew on his cigarette. 'Would you care to dance?' he asked.

'Yes, I'd like that,' said Sam, working hard to make her voice sound enthusiastic.

Julian ushered her into a space, then rested his hand on her waist and pulled her close. His body felt lean and wiry and his skin smelled very cleanly, of soap. He steered her slowly around the room, following the rotation of the other dancers. Neither of them spoke. Sam avoided looking into his eyes and concentrated instead on the row of ribbons on his chest. The song came to an end, but the final notes of the music took a time to die away. He released her for a moment and they joined in with the gentle swell of applause that rippled around the room.

'They're a jolly good band,' said Julian, nodding to the stage.

Sam smiled. 'Yes, they are, aren't they?' she agreed politely.

The singer stood behind the microphone and they heard the opening chords of another song. Putting his cool cheek lightly against hers, Julian drew Sam into his arms and they moved off again. They stayed on the dance-floor through another two songs, but then the tempo changed and the music became livelier and he cupped her elbow and steered her back to their table.

As Sam sipped her gin and tonic, Julian drew a slim silver case from the pocket of his tunic and took out another cigarette. He dipped his head to light it, then regarded her appraisingly. 'You're a very beautiful woman,' he said. 'You do know that, don't you?'

'Thank you,' she murmured.

'You look stunning in that dress. It's good to see a girl not in uniform, much more feminine. Makes a chap realise what he's fighting for.'

Sam took a deep breath. There was no use in pretending any longer; she had to spell things out to him, before it got too late. 'I've really enjoyed your company this evening, Julian, but I wouldn't want you to get the wrong idea, you know.'

'I'm not getting the wrong idea. I like your loyalty to Johnny. There aren't many girls like you these days.'

Sam felt a stab of guilt. It had been Jack she'd been thinking about, not Johnny.

Julian frowned. 'Are you all right?'

She made an attempt at a smile, but she didn't say anything.

'I'm sorry, I shouldn't have mentioned his name. It doesn't do to talk too much about a chap who's bought it. The show must go on and all that.'

Sam leaned forward and set her empty glass down on the low table in front of them. 'I think I'd like to go home now,' she said softly.

'Home?' He sounded genuinely puzzled. 'But the night's young yet.'

'I'm sorry, I don't want to ruin your evening but I just don't feel up to this tonight. Couldn't you drop me off and then come back again, by yourself?'

He regarded her coolly for a long moment. 'Of course, if that's what you want,' he said at last. 'Although I'd enjoy it more if you stayed.'

Julian waited for another moment, but Sam said nothing. He stubbed out his cigarette in the ashtray on the table. She knew that he must be feeling annoyed, but he had too much self-possession to show it. He swallowed the last of his drink, then they both rose to their feet and started across the smoky room towards the exit.

'Roses? For me?'

Shafts of morning sunlight slanted in through the windows of the hospital reception. Sam had got back from London late the evening before and she was feeling tired, but she smiled as she looked down at the bouquet that the delivery boy was holding. It was a long time since she'd last seen quite such beautiful flowers.

The delivery boy nodded. 'Yes, Miss Mitchell, they're for you. I tried to deliver them to your house, but there was no one there. Mrs Doncaster, the florist, told me to try here.'

He handed her the bouquet. Sam thanked him and he doffed his cap and left her. Turning away from the entrance, she saw Matron coming towards her along the hallway.

'Ah, Nurse Mitchell,' she said briskly, 'I was wondering where you'd got to.'

'I'm sorry, Matron. A porter told me I was needed here. I came through and found these waiting for me.'

Matron gave the flowers a cursory glance. 'Well, they're very nice, I'm sure, but Mrs Hill needs to have her dressing changed. Find somewhere to put those and then come through to Ward Three straight away.'

'Yes, Matron.'

Matron strode off, the doors to the corridor swinging behind her. Sam hurried across the tiled floor of the reception to leave the flowers at the hospital desk. She noticed a small white envelope sitting amongst the blooms and pushed it hastily into the pocket of her apron, then raced through the doors in the direction of Ward Three.

Leonora was in the kitchen making supper when Sam arrived home that evening. A stew was simmering on the stove and when Sam came in through the door she was giving it a stir. Her face lit up when she saw the bouquet she was carrying. 'What lovely flowers!' she exclaimed. 'Whoever are they from?'

Sam laid the roses down carefully on the draining board by the sink. 'Julian Pennington sent them. They arrived at the hospital this morning.'

'From Julian? How wonderful! But then I could tell at Robert's wedding how much he liked you.' Leonora beamed with pleasure. Then she added innocently, 'I spoke to your mother this morning on the telephone and she mentioned that you'd met him in London whilst you were there.'

Sam nodded. 'Yes, it was quite a coincidence that he was at the Ritz when we were. He seemed to appear out of nowhere.'

'And he took you out to dinner, didn't he? And to a night club afterwards.'

'Yes, that's right.'

Leonora nodded, looking satisfied, reminding Sam for a moment of a cat who had been given a saucer of cream. She felt even more certain that her meeting with Julian had been anything but a coincidence. Leonora turned her attention back to the stew and Sam began moving about the room, busying herself with the flowers as she mulled things over. She got a vase out of the dresser and filled it with water, then took a sharp knife out of a drawer. She opened the paper in which the flowers were wrapped and began trimming the bottoms of the stems and placing them in the vase.

It had gone seven o'clock when they sat down to eat, but it was still light outside and through the kitchen window Sam could see the bank of brightly coloured crocuses and primroses that were heralding spring outside along the drive. She glanced across the table at Leonora. She didn't want to upset her, but she was determined to voice her concerns. She knew it wouldn't take much to get at the truth if she questioned her directly. It wasn't in Leonora's nature to lie.

'It really did seem rather a coincidence that Julian happened to be at the Ritz when Mother and I were there,' she remarked. 'I don't suppose that you and Mother would have had anything to do with it, would you?' she added, flushing.

Leonora looked across at her in surprise. Her cheeks reddened and she lowered her knife and fork. 'Well,' she began, sounding uncharacteristically flustered. She hesitated, then eyed Sam cautiously. 'Well, yes, I suppose to be truthful, actually we did,' she admitted. 'You see, Julian telephoned here a couple of weeks ago, whilst you were at work, and he gave me his number. I knew that you wouldn't go up to London just to see him, so I rang your mother and we worked out our little plan.'

'I thought it was something like that. And Julian was quite happy to go along with it, I suppose.'

'You mustn't blame him. I rang him up and explained that you were going up to London with your mother, and that you would probably have lunch at The Ritz. I told him that I was sure that you would like to have dinner with him, but that you were too shy to call him yourself.'

Sam pursed her lips. 'I see.'

'You're not too angry are you?' said Leonora, eyeing her pleadingly. 'He's such a nice young man. We thought it would be good for you to see him.'

Sam sighed deeply. 'I know that you and Mother only want what's best for me, but, really Aunt, you must see that you can't make me feel something for someone that I don't. I admit that Julian's a charming man. In fact, he's a complete gentleman. And for that reason alone I'm quite sure he doesn't deserve to be led on by anyone. I felt very awkward whilst I was with him and would very much rather that you didn't organise anything like that again.'

'But he's such a wonderful boy. He's so handsome and so brave. Surely you can see that? Perhaps it's just a question of giving it a bit of time.'

Sam shook her head. 'I don't expect you to understand why, but I could never feel anything more than affection for him.'

There was a short silence.

'It's still that American, isn't it?' said Leonora.

Sam lifted her chin a fraction. 'Perhaps it is. Would that matter so much?'

Leonora's lips pressed together into a line, but she said nothing.

'Why do you dislike the Americans quite so much?' asked Sam, feeling hurt. 'They're no different from other people, once you get to know them. Some of them are good, others are bad. It has nothing to do with where they come from.'

'I don't dislike them, and I know we need their help. But that doesn't mean that you girls have to go chasing after them.'

'I'm not chasing anyone.'

'No, darling, I know that. But some of the other ladies in the WVS have been talking.'

'About me?'

'No, not about you. Not exactly.'

'What have they been saying?'

Leonora ran her finger over a mark on the table. 'Some of the girls in town have been getting a bit of a reputation,' she murmured.

Sam bit her lip and nodded.

'With all of our own young men away it just doesn't seem right that you girls should be going out with these strangers,' said Leonora softly. 'It seems so disloyal. And you must realise that they'll be leaving here soon, and what will you do then? Do you really think that any of them will give a second thought to the girls they've met here once they've left?'

Sam glanced out of the window, Leonora's words still ringing in her ears. Her head began to throb and she suddenly felt completely emotionally drained.

Later on, when all the dinner things had been washed and put away, Leonora went upstairs and Sam sat down at the kitchen table again. She searched in her bag and brought out some papers that she'd tucked inside it at the hospital that afternoon. She smoothed them out on the table and began to read. It was recruitment information and an application form for the Army Nursing Service. She was halfway through reading the first page when she heard the sound of the telephone ringing in the hallway. Putting down the form, she got up and went to answer it

'Sam?'

It was Jack's voice. Sam straightened up, coming out of her daze. 'Yes, it's me.'

'Listen, I don't have long. I was just calling to let you know that I'm not going to be here for a couple of weeks.'

'Oh?' Her heart hammered quickly in her chest.

'I'm going away for a little while. Bill's coming too. I'm afraid I can't say any more. We're leaving in a few minutes, so I can't come over.'

Jack paused briefly and the line crackled, but Sam didn't say anything.

'I wanted you to know,' he said in a low voice.

'I understand,' she answered numbly, finding her voice again.

'Take care of yourself, Sam. I'll see you when I get back.'

'Yes, of course.'

The line went dead. She stared at the receiver, then slowly replaced it. It seemed as if all her hopes for some sort of future with Jack were turning to dust. She went back into the kitchen and sat down at the table. Tears pricked at her eyes as she began reading through the application form once more.

14. FOREIGN GIRLS

The weather began to change and by May the bluebells were coming into bloom.

The evening sunshine flickered on the mullioned windows of Foley Manor. Jack crossed the flag-stoned hallway and went out through the pillared entrance and down the steps to the line of vehicles that was parked on the drive.

He was smiling as he climbed into the Jeep. He'd been away on manoeuvres for almost a month and had only returned the evening before, but he'd managed to call Sam at the hospital that morning and had arranged to pick her up after she finished work. He turned the key in the ignition and the engine caught immediately. He turned the Jeep in a tight circle and moved off smoothly down the drive.

The roads were busier than usual, but less than ten minutes later he drew up outside the hospital. Looking along the drive, he saw Sam at once, picking her out easily from the nurses and soldiers who were moving about near the entrance. Her hair shimmered in the evening sunshine and she was wearing a fitted jacket over a dress that skimmed lightly over her curves. He jumped down from the Jeep and went to meet her.

The Fox smelled strongly of beer and cigarette smoke and it was packed with GIs. Jack hesitated in the doorway, wishing, not for the first time, that there were somewhere else that he could take her. He allowed Sam in through the doorway in front of him. Spotting an empty table by the fireplace, he cupped her elbow in the palm of his hand and began pushing his way through. Seeing the stripes on his sleeve, the soldiers parted, allowing them to pass, but he saw the way they looked at Sam and he read the envy in their faces.

Jack fetched a pint of beer and a glass of sherry from the bar and he and Sam sat at the table together, sipping their drinks. It felt good to see her after so many weeks. He couldn't tell her anything about where he'd been, but they talked about her day at the hospital and things that had been happening in the town.

Jack took a mouthful of beer. It was warm and frothy, completely different to the beer back home, but by now he'd grown accustomed to the taste. Sam lifted her glass and took a small sip of her sherry, then set it down on the smooth wooden table between them. She seemed anxious, he thought, and not quite herself.

'You're very quiet tonight,' he remarked.

Sam lifted her gaze and smiled distractedly. 'I suppose I am rather. I'm sorry.'

'Is there something on your mind?'

A faint line appeared between her brows. 'Actually, there is something I perhaps ought to speak to you about. I've been thinking about it for a while, but I haven't been quite sure how to tell you.'

'Oh? What's that?'

'I've applied to the Army Nursing Service. I've decided to join up.'

He put his glass on the table and looked at her. 'But I thought you enjoyed working at the hospital.'

'Yes, I do, but Matron says that the military are desperately short of nurses.'

Jack drew back in his chair. 'I don't like the sound of that, Sam. I can't say I like the thought of you being anywhere other than here when…' He trailed off. He knew he couldn't tell her exactly what was being planned. 'What I mean is, I just need to know that you're safe, whatever happens.'

'There's no need to worry, I'm sure things won't change for me that much. I'll probably just be posted to one of the military hospitals in the south of England.'

He saw from her expression that she was deadly serious. He shook his head. 'I still don't like it.'

'I'm sorry that you feel that way. But while you've been away, I've been thinking. I know you can't tell me any details about what's going on, but I'm not blind. I've seen all the new GIs arriving and all the new army vehicles that are on the roads. Something's going to happen, and it's going to happen soon, and I want to go where I can be most of help. I can't hide away here, not when I know I could be doing more.'

'I understand what you're saying, Sam, and I respect you for it, but that doesn't make it any easier for me. What about your aunt? What does she think about all of this?'

'Leonora understands my decision and she supports it. You know what a great believer she is in duty.'

She was looking at him steadily and he thought how fragile she seemed, and yet how determined. He felt suddenly powerless. 'So it's all settled then.'

'Well, I've made up my mind, if that's what you mean.' She took another sip of her drink. 'Nancy's applying to join as well,' she said. 'Did you know that she and Ed are thinking about getting married?'

He nodded. 'Walker spoke to me about it a few weeks ago.'

'Nancy says there's a lot of paperwork involved.'

'Yes, there is.'

'From what Nancy says, the United States Army doesn't seem very keen on its men marrying English girls.'

He moved uncomfortably. He hadn't anticipated this. 'No, I guess they don't encourage it.'

'Why not? Shouldn't people be allowed to follow their hearts?'

'These are difficult times. The army needs its men to concentrate on fighting and a man that's married might not do that so well.'

'But what about the men who were already married before they got here? Are they seen as a problem too?'

Jack frowned. 'Well, no,' he admitted, 'I don't suppose they are.'

She lifted her chin and he saw the smudges of pink that had come into her cheeks. 'So you're saying that it's just English girls that are the problem?'

'No, Sam, it isn't like that.'

'What is it like then?'

'When a man marries a foreign girl it can get complicated. The army doesn't want to be responsible for shipping thousands of women back to the States.'

She looked briefly about her, at the GIs crowding the pub, laughing and talking with their English dates. Her eyes met his again and he saw their look of rebuke. 'But I suppose it's all right for local girls to entertain Americans whilst they're on foreign soil.'

Her words hung between them for a long moment.

Why was she behaving this way? Jack asked himself. She knew what he felt for her, didn't she? His brows pulled together. Maybe she didn't. Maybe he needed to make his feelings clearer. 'It may not seem like it, Sam, but I agree with you. It seems to me that just because a man is asked to risk his life for his country he shouldn't have to give up the right to his own personal happiness.' He leaned in towards her. Lowering his voice, he said, 'You know that I'm crazy about you, don't you? You're different to anyone else I've ever met.'

'Different?' Her chin lifted again. 'Is that enough, do you think?'

'It isn't just that you're different. You must know how special I think you are. You're a beautiful, compassionate woman. I've never met anyone quite like you before.'

There was a short silence.

'I suppose you've known a lot of women.'

She said it coldly, and her words felt like a blow. It wasn't the reaction he'd been expecting. He drew back and for a moment he couldn't trust himself to speak.

'A few,' he said eventually. 'No more than my fair share.'

'You haven't got anyone special at home?'

'I wouldn't be here with you now if I had.'

She smiled crookedly. 'At least you Americans have brought some colour back into our lives.'

He looked at her and a muscle tightened in his jaw. 'Is that how you think of me? As just another American?'

'You are an American.'

'Why are you talking like this? Can't you see beyond this uniform and these circumstances? What I feel for you has nothing to do with the war. I'm not just looking for a good time with someone until we move out. I don't know what you've been thinking or what your aunt's been telling you, but I can honestly say that I've never felt this way for anyone in my life before.' He put back his head and drained the last of his beer, then set the glass down hard on the table. 'Maybe it's time I took you home.'

Jack turned his gaze away from her, immediately regretting the coldness in his voice. But couldn't she see that he meant what he said? He couldn't promise her anything; there was no way of knowing if he would ever be coming back. But he'd done nothing, said nothing that should make her doubt him the way she seemed to now. He hadn't seen her for weeks and he hadn't anticipated that the evening would turn out like this. Why was she putting up this wall between them and pushing him away?

He looked across at her again. She was staring down at her hands and her face was very flushed. She glanced up and caught his gaze and he saw the brief flash of vulnerability that flickered through her eyes. Suddenly he understood. She was trying to protect herself and that was why she was behaving this way. He suddenly realised that she was afraid.

It was a dark, starless night and Jack drove slowly in silence. He turned into the lane towards The Elms and Sam was aware of the Jeep slowing down as he abruptly changed down the gears and pulled over onto the grassy verge. He turned off the engine and the Jeep shuddered, then was quiet.

For a moment there was only the rustle of leaves outside, but then Sam heard the creak of leather as Jack turned in his seat. She could feel his eyes upon her but it was too dark to make out his face. 'I'm sorry about what I said earlier,' she breathed. 'You didn't deserve it.'

She felt the warmth of his hand on her arm through the thin sleeve of her jacket. 'I'm the one who should apologise,' he murmured huskily. 'After everything you've been through, I was pretty rough on you back there.'

Sam closed her eyes for a moment. The last month without him had been almost impossible to bear and her mind had wandered in all sorts of directions. Now she wanted to reach out to him and tell him how much she needed him and couldn't bear for him to go. But she knew that would be futile. She felt grateful for the darkness that enveloped them; she didn't want him to see the despair that must be written in her face.

He moved his thumb gently, caressing her arm. 'When I came to England I never expected to meet anyone like you.'

She felt the tears coming into her eyes and blinked them back.

'I'll be straight with you, Sam. When I first came over here I was determined not to get involved with anyone. I knew we had a war to fight and that the future was uncertain. But then I met you. I've willed myself to forget you, but it's no good - I'm sorry, but I can't.'

A chill had crept into the Jeep. His words danced through her mind and Sam suddenly felt sick. Everything is almost over, she thought. In a few weeks he will leave and after that I will never see him again.

'I'm very tired now,' she said, her voice trembling. 'Would you mind very much taking me home?'

There was a moment's silence. She heard him turning in his seat and the sound of the engine sparking into life. The headlights shone faintly into the greyness of the night. The Jeep jolted over the verge and then moved smoothly off along the lane.

15. A REVELATION

The sun shone again the following afternoon, but there was a cool easterly wind. Sam had arranged to meet Diana and Nancy at the teashop. She knew it would take a good half hour for her to walk into town, and she shrugged her coat on over her dress and cardigan before she left home.

Sam stood outside the door and looked in through the glass. The teashop was crowded out with GIs. Four of them were standing just inside the doorway, waiting to be seated. They were tall and broad-shouldered, and looked quite out of place in the cosy, low-beamed teashop with its little tables and sprigged tablecloths.

Diana was waiting at the table in the bay. Sam pushed open the door and the GIs in the doorway turned their heads. She heard a muted wolf-whistle, but they drew back, allowing her to pass. She felt their eyes following her as she negotiated her way across the room.

'Hello,' said Diana. 'It's nice to see you.'

Sam gave her a peck on the cheek. Taking off her coat, she hung it on the back of a chair and sat down. Through the window, they saw Nancy coming along the street outside, walking briskly, the sunlight catching her bright blonde hair. She turned her head and saw them, and waved.

A waitress came to the table to take their order. 'We've no cakes left at all, I'm afraid,' she told them, glancing about the crowded room. 'These Yanks have eaten every last crumb we had.'

'Oh, I see,' said Diana. 'We'll just have three teas then, please.'

The waitress jotted down the order on her pad, then turned away, almost bumping into Nancy. Her chair scraped against the wooden floor as she pulled it up to the table. 'It's like Little America in here,' she laughed, sliding into the seat. 'I wonder when they all arrived.'

The town seemed to be filled to bursting and they spent a few minutes discussing all the new convoys of men and equipment that they'd seen arriving over the past week or so. Nancy's forehead puckered. 'I suppose this means the second front will be opening soon,' she said vaguely, almost to herself. She touched a hand to her hair, as if to brush away the unwelcome thought. 'Well, that wasn't why I wanted to meet you two here, so don't let's think about that now.'

Intrigued by her words, Sam and Diana drew in closer to the table.

'Ed managed to get the necessary permission from his commanding officer and our special licence came through on Friday,' she told them, her eyes alight with excitement. 'I know it doesn't seem quite real, but we might even be married next week.'

There were a few moments of congratulations and laughter as Nancy told them the details of everything that had happened. Her face glowed with happiness. 'We're planning to get married somewhere near the sea. It's only half an hour to the coast from here by train, and we thought it would make it special. Ed's going to ask Chester to come as a witness.' She glanced awkwardly at Diana, but Diana didn't say anything. 'I was hoping that one of you might be able to come with us too,' she added. 'To be my bridesmaid.'

Sam nodded, wondering if Matron would give her the time off. She knew that Diana wouldn't want to go. It wouldn't be appropriate if Chester were going to be there.

'Have you thought about what you're going to wear?' asked Sam, changing the subject a little.

'No, I haven't.' Nancy's face clouded over for a moment. 'I haven't got enough coupons for a proper dress.'

'You can borrow my blue outfit, if you'd like to,' offered Diana. 'I haven't worn it since Robert and I were married and it's as good as new.'

'And I've got a few coupons you can have,' said Sam. 'Perhaps you could get something pretty for your wedding night.'

Nancy's eyes shone brightly as she smiled and thanked them, and not for the first time Sam felt a pang of envy for her easy, happy-go-lucky nature.

The waitress came across with the tray of tea things and spread them out on the table.

'Actually, I have some news as well,' said Diana shyly, reaching over to pick up the teapot and starting to pour out the tea.

'What is it, Diana?' asked Nancy. 'You're not...' Her eyes widened as understanding dawned.

Diana put down the teapot. 'Yes,' she said quietly. 'I'm going to have a baby.'

Nancy gave a squeal of delight and the people at the table next to them turned to look.

'Oh, Diana, how lovely,' breathed Sam. 'I'm so happy for you. I expect

Robert is over the moon.'

Diana waited for the people who were staring to turn away. 'Robert couldn't be happier,' she told them, her dark eyes growing soft. 'I thought we should wait until the war was over, but he said that he'd had enough of waiting.'

She told them that the baby was due in the autumn, probably in late October, and they began discussing her plans. Chairs scraped in the background as people got up to leave and others came in to take their tables. English and American accents mingled and the occasional clatter of china could be heard coming from the little kitchen at the back.

'And what about you, Sam?' asked Diana, pouring out more tea. 'Have you got any news for us too?'

'No, not really.'

'But what about Jack?' said Nancy. 'He's back, isn't he? Aren't you seeing him anymore?'

Sam flushed. 'Actually, I saw him last night. To be honest with you, we had a bit of a disagreement over something, but I think we're still friends.'

Nancy looked at her seriously. 'Well, to tell you the truth, I think you're really being rather silly. Anyone can see the way he feels about you. How will you feel if he gets sent overseas and you haven't done anything about it?'

'It isn't as simple as that. You know how my family feels about things.'

'This is your life we're talking about, not theirs. Who knows what's around the corner? You have to seize any chance of happiness while you can.'

Sam fiddled with her cup, but she said nothing.

'I think there's something I need to talk to you about,' said Diana. 'It's about Johnny, I'm afraid.'

There was a strange look in her eyes and Sam's heart gave a little lurch. 'Johnny? What about him?'

'I know how much you loved him and what I'm going to say might be very difficult to hear. You may not even want to believe it. But I'm your friend, so I have to say something. I know how much you've begun to feel about Jack and I think I know the real reason why you've been pushing him away. You feel that by loving him you're being disloyal to Johnny, don't you?'

Sam nodded. 'Yes, I suppose that is part of it.'

'Well, just recently I found out something that I think you should know. Even I didn't believe it when I first heard it, but Robert assures me that it's true. I'm really sorry to be the one to have to tell you this, but it seems that you weren't the only girl that Johnny was seeing before he died.'

Sam looked at her blankly and there was a moment's silence.

'I'm so very sorry, Sam, really I am,' said Diana quickly. 'Robert's sure that you were the most important one to him, but it seems that there were at least two others that he was seeing when he died.'

Sam shook her head. 'I don't believe it. I know he loved me, I just know it.'

'I'm not saying that he didn't.'

'Then why would he behave that way?'

'I don't know. Perhaps it was because he knew you were a nice girl, and a family friend. It seems that these others were not quite as nice as you were...' Diana hesitated, and then her expression grew very soft. 'Robert says that they were more... intimate.'

Sam felt as if she'd been hit by a blow. She couldn't believe what she was hearing - it couldn't possibly be true. She would have known, wouldn't she? But almost at once her mind filled with doubts. She thought back to the long separations, to the times she'd had to work late and hadn't been able to see him when he'd unexpectedly been given leave. Johnny had been a young man and death had hung over him like a shadow every day. Perhaps there'd been things he'd needed to experience, things she hadn't been able to give him herself.

Tears pricked at her eyes. 'But why didn't you tell me about any of this before?'

'I would have, if I'd known, but I only found out myself a few days ago. Robert thought you'd get over Johnny without ever needing to know. He thought it would only bring you more pain if you knew the truth. He did try to tell you once, I think, on your way back from London that time, but he found that he didn't quite know how. Then, when I was speaking to him on the telephone on Tuesday evening, he asked me how you were. I told him how I thought that you were falling in love with Jack, but that you didn't seem able to allow yourself to move on from Johnny, and that's when he told me what he knew.

'I've been trying to find the right moment to explain. I'm sorry to have told you here, like this, but I just had to tell you before it got too late. I couldn't watch you denying yourself the freedom to love someone else any longer. Johnny was basically a good, brave man, but he wasn't worthy of your undying devotion. I don't know if Jack is the right man for you, only you can know that, but I couldn't stand by and let you throw away a chance of happiness for the sake of Johnny's memory. You've been torturing yourself for far too long.'

Sam was aware of the clattering of crockery and the scraping of chairs against floorboards as a group of soldiers got up from a table to leave. The door to the teashop opened and she saw them adjusting their hats and laughing as they went out onto the street.

Diana squeezed her hand. 'Are you all right?'

Dragging her thoughts in order, Sam turned her head and nodded. 'Yes,

I'm fine. It's all a bit of a shock, that's all.'

'I'm so sorry.'

'I'm sure that everything you've told me is true. It all fits. And Robert has absolutely no reason to lie. It's just…' She broke off and glanced away, finding it difficult to voice her fears. 'I don't know if I'm strong enough to risk the pain of it all,' she said, meeting Diana's gaze again. 'To risk loving someone only to lose them again.'

Diana's face was soft with sympathy. 'You mustn't think like that.'

Sam answered her with a shaky smile. She picked up her cup and took another sip of her tea, but it had gone quite cold.

16. A SHOCK

It was well after eleven when Sam emerged from the rear entrance of the hospital the following evening. There was no moon that night and the darkness was all encompassing. She blinked into the blackness and fished in her bag for her torch. The shaded bulb gave out a dim cone of light and she trained it in front of her and began to pick her way along the pathway. There was no one else about and the only sound came from the clicking of her heels against the flagstones. Her feet ached after her long shift and she wasn't sure where she was going to find the energy to cycle home.

She saw the dark outline of the bicycle racks against the hospital wall. She fumbled in her bag again and drew out her key, then took off her gloves and leaned over to put the key in the padlock. It wouldn't turn. She straightened up and put her gloves in her coat pocket, then tried again. She worked the key in the lock and at last it gave.

Sam heard the scuff of boots on the flagstones behind her. She made to turn, but then a powerful set of arms gripped her from behind. Her torch clattered to the ground and she was engulfed in darkness. A man's weight met hers and he twisted her around making her stumble backwards. The hard stone of the hospital wall pushed up against her and she felt the rough skin of his palm clamping firmly against her mouth. His face came nearer, unbearably close, and she smelled the stench of alcohol on his breath.

He pulled at her clothes. Her coat fell to the ground and she heard a dreadful ripping sound as he tore open the front of her blouse. He pushed his free hand inside, groping at her breasts, and her heart began to beat wildly. He was strong and heavy and there was nothing she could do to stop him. Then, abruptly, he moved his hand away and grasped her skirt, wrenching it up above the tops of her stockings with a quick, sharp movement.

He groped roughly at the naked flesh of her thigh and pulled her closer against the swelling in his groin. He uttered a low, sickening groan of desire and Sam's panic was replaced with a sudden surge of burning anger and she bit down hard on to his hand. He yelled out in pain. For a brief moment his hold on her mouth relaxed and she seized her chance to break free from his grip and scream for help as loudly as she could. He slapped her hard across the face but the next moment he was gone, a dark shadow retreating swiftly into the night.

The effort of defending herself had been exhausting and Sam stumbled in the darkness, groping for something to hold on to, before sinking down onto the ground. Then, after a few, long, frightening moments, she heard someone coming quickly along the path.

'Hey, what's going on there?'

The porter's voice cut through the fog of her confusion. Feeling shocked and ashamed at the state in which he would find her, she forced herself up onto her feet again. She smeared away her tears and drew her cardigan tightly across the torn opening of her blouse, shielding her eyes when he drew near and the soft light of his torch touched her face.

'I'm all right,' she whispered.

'Nurse Mitchell!' His face was pale and shadowy in the darkness and she couldn't see his expression, but his voice was full of concern. 'Whatever has happened?'

'There was a man... '

The porter flashed his torch over the grass. 'Which way did he go?'

'I don't know,' she mumbled miserably.

She felt the warmth of his hand on her arm. 'Let me take you inside, Nurse Mitchell. I can see that you've had rather a shock.'

Sam lifted the mug of steaming liquid to her lips and tried to blank out everything apart from the sweet smell of the cocoa. They'd wrapped her in a blanket and seated her on one of the well-worn sofas in the common room. Through the slightly open door, she could hear Matron murmuring with the policeman who'd arrived half an hour earlier and who'd carefully recorded her account of the attack in his notebook. She knew there was no chance now of them finding her assailant and she just wanted to go home.

'Where is she?'

The familiar voice came from the corridor outside. The door swung open and Jack stood for a moment framed in the doorway, looking in, as if not quite believing what he saw.

Everything around her seemed suddenly muted. She watched as he came towards her across the room. He knelt in front of her and gently uncurled her fingers, taking the mug from her hand and placing it on the table, before taking her hands in his own. A wave of relief crashed over her. He was there, and she hadn't been certain he would come.

Jack lifted a hand and traced the tips of his fingers over the side of her face that was still stinging from her attacker's blow. His gaze travelled downwards and then stopped. She saw the tightening of his jaw. Looking down, she realised that the blanket she was wrapped in had dropped open and he was staring at the torn opening of her blouse beneath her cardigan.

His eyes narrowed and his expression stilled. 'What the hell did he do to you?'

'It's not as bad as it looks,' she whispered. 'He didn't...' She dropped her gaze and shook her head, unable to find the right words to explain.

There was a moment of quiet as he caught her meaning. She lifted her head and saw the look of relief that briefly flickered in his eyes, before being rapidly replaced by an expression of raw fury. He inhaled sharply, then got to his feet and began pacing the room.

The intensity of his reaction both shocked and frightened her. 'Please, Jack, I'm all right, really I am. I'm just a little shaken that's all.'

He turned to face her, the rage still flaring in his eyes. 'My God, Sam, if anything ever happened to you...'

She swallowed hard, realising in a rush how much she needed to tell him. It was all suddenly so clear to her. Of course the future was uncertain; no one could know what lay ahead. But what if her attacker had succeeded? What if he had raped her and denied her the joy of giving herself for the first time to the man who she was sure now that she loved? Nancy was right. They had to seize any chance of happiness while they still could.

Matron's voice sounded from the doorway to the room. 'Can I talk to you for a moment, Lieutenant Webster?'

Jack hesitated, then looked at Sam.

She managed a small smile. 'I'll be all right.'

'I won't be long,' he promised her.

A few minutes later he was back in the common room again, helping her on with her coat.

Jack drove as quickly as he could along the unlit roads and drew up sharply in front of The Elms. Sam's hand was trembling when he caught it in his and helped her down from the Jeep. She huddled against him, shivering, and he wrapped an arm around her, ushering her gently across the gravel. They paused by the front door and she fumbled in her bag for her key for a moment, but then the door was flung open and Leonora appeared in the darkness and swept her into the house.

In the light of the kitchen, Jack could see the dark smudges that were beginning to appear beneath Sam's eyes. She shrugged off her coat and sank down into the sagging armchair by the dresser. He watched as Leonora filled a kettle and put it onto the stove. Someone from the hospital had called her to let her know what had happened and she looked pale and tired and had clearly been worrying herself sick whilst she'd been waiting for him to bring Sam home.

The faint mark from a blow was still visible on the side of Sam's face and he was painfully aware of the torn opening of her blouse that she'd tried so hard to hide from him. He felt angry. Angry with the man who'd attacked her and angry with himself for not having been there to defend her. He knew that if he'd caught the man who'd touched her, he would have been capable of killing him with his bare hands. He couldn't remember ever before having felt such an elemental rage.

The kettle whistled and Leonora poured some of the boiling water into a teapot, swilled it round and tipped it into the sink. Jack looked at his watch and saw that it was long after midnight.

'I think Sam needs to get some rest now, Mrs Edwards.'

Leonora stopped what she was doing and swung around, her eyes blazing. 'I'm sure I know what's best for my niece, Lieutenant. You Americans have done enough damage this evening and I really don't need your advice.'

He felt like he'd just taken a punch.

'There's no doubt in my mind that it was an American who attacked Sam tonight,' went on Leonora, her voice quivering with revulsion. 'The sooner you've all gone, the better it will be for all of us.'

For a moment Jack was stunned into silence, but he saw Sam lift her chin. 'Please, Aunt,' she said in a tired voice. 'I've no idea who it was that attacked me tonight. Please don't treat Jack this way.'

Leonora ignored her. 'I think you know my feelings, Lieutenant Webster.'

Sam lifted her gaze to his for a moment and he saw the look of appeal that had come into her eyes. 'You're just not being fair,' she said, looking across the kitchen at Leonora again. 'Americans are individuals, just like us, every one of them with unique qualities and feelings. I want you to stop behaving so badly towards Jack. You know what I feel for him.'

Almost immediately, colour flooded her face. He realised that she'd said more than she'd intended to and he stared at her. At last, after all this time, there was an acknowledgement of her true feelings for him.

She bit her lip and glanced up at him shyly. 'Thank you so much for coming to the hospital and bringing me home. I don't know what I'd have done without you.'

He searched her face. It had taken every last shred of his self-control to stay away from her since the evening he'd taken her to The Fox, when she'd made it clear that being near to him only caused her pain. Now, suddenly, everything about her seemed to have changed.

He looked at Leonora warily. There wasn't the remotest possibility of her giving them any time alone. 'I'd better go now,' he said, turning to Sam and keeping his voice steady. 'You need to get some rest and I don't want to cause any trouble.' He had another gruelling schedule of training and manoeuvres lined up over the next few days and he knew that it would be virtually impossible for him to see her before the weekend. 'I'm pretty tied up for the rest of the week, but I could pass by again and see you on Saturday.'

Leonora shot him an indignant glance. 'I really don't think -'

'Please, Aunt,' said Sam, turning her head and looking across the room to silence her. Her gaze met his again and he saw the look of regret that had come into her eyes. 'Ed and Nancy are getting married on Saturday. I've promised to be Nancy's bridesmaid, and I have to go down to the coast with them.'

Jack thought things through for a moment before he answered. 'Don't worry,' he told her. 'I'll work something out.' His eyes flickered to Leonora. 'Good night, Mrs Edwards,' he said, allowing a hard edge to come into his voice. 'Don't worry; I'll see myself out.'

17. THE COAST

'I'm so excited for you,' whispered Sam, giving Nancy's hand an affectionate squeeze.

They were pressed tightly together in the small double seat in the back of the Jeep. Ed was sitting up front next to Jack, who was driving, and they were hurtling southwards towards the coast. The countryside sped past them. The verges that bordered the roads were thick with tall cow parsley and the hedgerows dense with leaves.

Sam was wearing a light summer dress and a pale pink cardigan, with a matching silk scarf tied in a knot beneath her chin. She tilted her head back to feel the sun on her face. The sky was a beautiful, cloudless blue and the day was full of promise.

'I couldn't believe it when Ed said that Jack had offered to drive us all down to the coast for the wedding,' said Nancy. 'This is all thanks to you, you know.'

Sam turned her head slightly to meet her gaze. 'There's no need to thank me. I wanted to get away somewhere too, after everything that's happened.'

Nancy's forehead furrowed. 'Have they caught him yet?'

Sam shook her head. 'No, they haven't. Unfortunately, I don't think that they're likely to now. Everything happened so fast and it was so dark, there's no way that I could identify him even if they did. I just hope that he doesn't attack anyone else.'

'Do you really think he was an American?'

'I don't know. He seemed to be in uniform, but I didn't hear him speak. It really could have been anyone.'

'I'm so sorry, Sam.'

'Oh, it did rattle me a bit, but I'm fine now.' She didn't want to spoil Nancy's day by telling her how shaken up she really was. 'Let's just enjoy today, shall we? I know it's going to be very special. How does it feel to be the future Mrs Walker?'

'Wonderful,' smiled Nancy, 'absolutely wonderful.'

They turned down a twisting road and passed through a hamlet of thatched stone houses. They travelled between open fields for a few miles, then trees closed in around them, making a tunnel of dappled shade. The road climbed and they emerged from the tunnel, coming out onto the crest of a hill. The countryside sloped away towards the coast and they caught their first sight of the sea.

A seaside town sprawled behind the outline of the bay and the traffic thickened as they descended the road towards it. They drove along a wide, cobbled street lined with rows of buildings painted in seaside colours. They passed the stuccoed façade of a hotel called The Royal and turned into the entrance next to it. They pulled up in the car park beside another Jeep and they all got out and stretched their legs and the men unloaded the luggage.

Inside the hotel, the lobby was busy with people. Potted palms stood in pots on a velvety carpet and receptionists were greeting guests from behind the polished expanse of a wide wooden desk. On the other side of the room, opposite the reception desk, wing-back armchairs surrounded a row of small mahogany tables. One of the tables had just been vacated by two British naval officers and they started towards it. Sam and Nancy sat down in the empty chairs to wait with the luggage and Jack and Ed went over to check in at the desk.

There seemed to be men and women in service uniform of every description. Sam watched them coming and going, through the main doors and up and down the central staircase at the back of the lobby. Three young army officers blocked her view of the reception at first, but presently they stepped away and she saw Jack and Ed talking to a fair-haired girl behind the desk. There was an exchange of words between Ed and the girl, her cheeks flushed and she shook her head. Ed spoke briefly to Jack, who nodded, and then the girl turned and drew something out from the wooden pigeonholes that were hanging from the wall behind her.

'They don't look very happy, do they?' said Nancy, following Sam's gaze. 'I wonder what the matter is.'

When the men came back from the desk, Ed was carrying two sets of keys with large wooden tags. He set them down on the table and rubbed a hand over the back of his neck. 'You're not going to believe this, but there's been some kind of mix up,' he said. 'I called ahead and booked two singles and a double, but the receptionist over there says all they have left is two doubles.'

There was a moment's silence as his words sank in.

'It shouldn't be a problem,' said Jack, glancing at Sam. 'I'm sure I can find somewhere else to stay. I saw plenty of places when we were on our way in.'

Sam nodded briefly and Nancy gave Ed a reassuring smile.

Ed looked relieved. 'Listen,' he said, his tone brightening. 'We haven't got much time. It's already nine-thirty and we have to be at the town hall by eleven. Why don't we take our bags up to the two rooms we have and then sort this out later? You girls could use one room to get ready, and we could use the other.' He looked at Jack. 'That's if that's all okay with you, Lieutenant.'

Jack nodded. 'I guess you're the one in charge today, Walker.'

The men picked up the bags and started across the lobby and Sam and Nancy followed behind them. They climbed the stairs to the first floor and turned along a corridor. There were pictures and mirrors on the walls and to one side of the passage was a row of panelled wooden doors. As they came up to a door, Ed checked the number on one of the keys. He unlocked the door and pushed it open, then stepped aside to allow the others through.

The room was more simply furnished than Sam had expected, but it looked clean and comfortable and through an open door she glimpsed a private bathroom. A large double bed was covered with a pink candlewick bedspread and there was a wooden wardrobe, with a matching dressing table near the window. The room was fresh and light and she could smell the sea through the large sash window that had been pushed slightly open.

Having arranged for them all to meet downstairs again at ten-thirty, the men departed. Sam and Nancy lifted their small suitcases onto the bed and clicked them open. Nancy held up the blue dress that Diana had lent her and shook it out and Sam pulled out her cream silk blouse and a lightweight, two-piece suit. It was a little tired looking, but the fit was neat.

They dressed carefully, then tidied their hair and touched up their make-up. Sam applied a dab of lipstick in the mirror above the dressing table and then pulled on her white cotton gloves. There was a cautious knock at the door and she went across to open it.

Ed was standing in the corridor, holding a small posy of white lily-of-the-valley. He held them out. 'Would you give Nancy these?' he said. 'I thought maybe she'd like them.'

'Of course,' said Sam, smiling at him and taking the flowers from his hand. 'We're almost ready.'

The wedding ceremony was brief and simple. Jack and Sam were the only witnesses, but watching them as they took their vows, Sam was sure that nothing could have clouded Ed and Nancy's happiness that day.

By one o'clock they were back at the Royal again, having lunch in the hotel's sun lounge. They sat in deep wicker chairs and ate small cutlets of pork with new potatoes, followed by trifle, and drank a bottle of champagne. Afterwards, a waiter set a tray of coffee on the table between them. They lounged back in the chairs and the conversation flowed easily.

It was three o'clock when they rose from the table again. They went out into the lobby and Jack checked at reception to see if another room had become available, but the girl he spoke to behind the desk simply shook her head.

They stood about for a minute or two, considering what to do. Jack suggested that Sam wait downstairs for a few minutes whilst he and the others went upstairs to sort out the bags and rooms.

Nancy looped her arm through Ed's and glanced at Sam. 'Well, I suppose we'll see you in the morning...' She blushed and Ed's eyes fixed on a point on the carpet in front of him.

'Yes, of course,' said Sam at once. 'I'll see you then.'

They started across the lobby, with Jack following a few paces behind them. Sam sat down at a table in one of the wing-back armchairs and watched until they had reached the head of the stairs and vanished along the corridor. The table was near a window and she saw the people who were strolling by on the pavement outside, enjoying the warm afternoon sunshine. Most were in uniform, and beyond them, across the street, sandbags were piled near doorways and some of the houses had been boarded up. She tried to imagine how different it must have all looked in peacetime.

A group of sailors came noisily along the street and she emerged from her thoughts. One of them saw her through the window and paused to smile and wink. She flushed and turned her head away, and saw Jack coming towards her across the intricately patterned carpet of the lobby. His gaze travelled to the window. The sailor saw him coming. His eyes twinkled and he gave Sam another wink, then moved off with his friends.

'It's lucky I wasn't gone any longer,' smiled Jack. 'I was hoping you'd be safe here on your own for a few minutes, but I guess I was wrong.' He glanced out of the window again. 'It still looks beautiful out there. Would you like to take a walk?'

Sam nodded and gave him an answering smile. 'Yes,' she said. 'That would be lovely.'

Outside the hotel, they paused on the pavement for a moment, looking up and down the cobbled street, then moved off in the direction of the sea. At the bottom of the street, they turned west along a promenade, separated by white-painted railings from the beach below it. Faded red-and-white-striped deckchairs were ranged in rows in front of the railings and people were sunning themselves and talking and reading newspapers. The high-pitched calling of gulls could be heard overhead and there was sound of waves gently breaking against the shore.

They strolled across to the railings and looked out towards the sea. A sleek grey battleship was cutting through the glittering waters towards the horizon and tangled coils of barbed wire glinted in the sunshine on the sand below them.

'Everything went well this morning,' said Jack, after a moment.

Sam turned her head and met his gaze. 'Yes,' she said. 'They both seemed very happy.'

A stray lock of hair blew across her cheek and he caught it gently and tucked it back into place. He studied her face for a moment, his eyes serious. He put his arm around her waist and drew her close, leaning down and drawing her mouth to his. His lips touched hers and she closed her eyes and a shiver of pleasure rippled slowly down her spine.

When at last he released her, they moved off again, walking slowly and Sam felt his fingers brush against hers as he reached down and captured her hand in his.

They walked hand in hand along the promenade until they reached the harbour. They stood for a while looking out over the fishing boats that were bobbing up and down on the incoming tide, and at the bay curving away from them. Then they started walking back again, the way they had come.

A row of shops was set back from the promenade. There was a kiosk selling postcards and cigarettes and a café with chequered tablecloths on tables outside. People were talking and smoking and enjoying the late afternoon sun.

They walked a little further, coming to a corner and the entrance to a small hotel. Piles of sandbags were stacked outside and balconies faced outwards towards the sea.

'I need to think about finding myself a room for the night,' said Jack, steering her towards the entrance.

It was a moment before his words sank in, but then Sam broke away from him and came to a stop. 'No,' she said, flushing as she glanced up at the peeling paintwork of the hotel's façade. 'No, you don't need to find another room.'

He waited for her eyes to meet his again. 'Are you sure that's what you really want?'

'Yes,' she said shyly. 'Don't you?'

Her eyes were filled with trust for him and he felt a sudden keen sense of responsibility. But he was twenty-seven years old and about to go to war. How could he deny himself now, after all these months of waiting?

He gently touched her cheek. 'You must know what I want by now,' he murmured. 'But I don't want to ask you to do anything that you're going to regret.'

She dipped her head, then met his gaze again. 'No, Jack, I'm not.'

He returned the soft smile she gave him, then took her hand in his and they moved off along the promenade once more, out of the shadow of the hotel.

It was six-thirty when they arrived back at The Royal, and the hotel was busy with people again. Two sets of double doors had been opened up at the rear of the lobby and couples stood waiting to go into the dining room through one of them. Through the other, Jack glimpsed people drinking cocktails at a bar.

Sam waited for him as he got the key from reception and then they climbed the stairs together and started along the corridor.

The room was hot inside and he went over to the window and prised it open, allowing in the sound of the gulls and the fresh sea smell. He threw the keys onto the kidney-shaped dressing table beneath the window. Sam was still standing by the door and he looked across at her. Her face was pale and he saw her eyes touch briefly on the bed.

'It isn't too late,' he said. 'Just say the word and I'll get another room.'

She caught his gaze and tipped her head. 'Actually, I was just thinking that I was feeling rather hungry.'

The tension he'd been feeling suddenly lifted. 'Well, I guess it has been a while since lunch,' he laughed. 'Let's freshen up a little and then go down. I could use something to eat myself.'

As they waited to be seated at the door of the hotel dining room, Sam smiled inwardly at the way Jack drew the eyes of the women coming out.

A grey-haired waiter in a plum-coloured jacket came to greet them. He handed them each a leather-bound menu and led them to a table in an alcove at the back of the room. It was set with starched white table linen and silver cutlery and a single candle in a crystal holder flickered softly in the centre.

Sam studied her menu briefly before closing it and looking up. She noticed the faint creases that had appeared around Jack's eyes as he frowned over the limited choices available. She smiled to herself again. She knew what he thought about British food.

'I guess we'll just have to take a chance on the fish,' he said, setting down his menu.

'I'm sure it'll be delicious.'

He raised an eyebrow.

'You look sceptical,' she said.

His mouth twitched. 'I am.'

The waiter came back again and they both composed their expressions and Jack gave him their order. A few minutes later, he returned with the wine and poured some out into Jack's glass. Jack tasted it, then nodded, and the waiter filled up their glasses.

When they were alone again, Sam lifted her glass and took a sip. The liquid sparkled in the candlelight.

Jack was watching her, his expression thoughtful. 'One day, I'll take you someplace special, back home. Then you'll know what good food really tastes like.'

His words caught Sam unawares. He'd never before suggested that she might one day go to America, and she wondered if he realised the implications of what he'd said.

'Yes,' she said, keeping her voice light. 'I'll look forward to that.'

Their food arrived on a small wooden trolley and the waiter served it with a flourish. After he'd left them, Sam stared for a moment at the insipid fish and boiled vegetables that were now lying on her plate. She looked up, meeting Jack's gaze. His brows lifted and they both laughed.

They drank coffee after the meal. The dining room began to empty and they went through to the bar in the other room. People were sitting at tables and talking together and a neat-looking man with a thin moustache was picking out a gentle tune on a piano positioned next to a small wooden dance-floor.

There was a splutter of applause as the tune ended. The pianist nodded and then started up again, this time playing a slow dance number.

A few couples were already up and dancing and Jack took Sam's hand and guided her across to join them. He drew her close and they moved slowly. Feeling the strong lines of his body pressing against hers, her skin tingled. Her mind went back to all the times they'd danced together before, when she'd suppressed and denied the warm, instinctive responses of her own body to his.

The music faded away and he released her. His eyes held hers for a moment. He didn't speak, but he took her by the hand again and led her to the door.

The lobby was empty apart from a few men who were sitting at tables by themselves, drinking and reading newspapers. A red-haired receptionist stood behind the desk and she looked up as they crossed towards the stairs.

'Lieutenant Webster?'

Jack turned. 'Yes?'

'There's just been a call for you, Sir, from a Lieutenant Crawford. He asked if you could ring him back. He said it was important.'

Sam saw Jack hesitate, but then he took the key to their room from his pocket and pressed it into her hand. 'I'll see you upstairs in a few minutes,' he told her, keeping his voice soft and low. 'This shouldn't take too long.'

The door creaked softly on its hinges as Jack closed it behind him. The room was dark apart from the glimmer of light that escaped from the bathroom door, which had been left slightly ajar. In the shadows, he noticed the clothes she'd been wearing lying haphazardly over the arm of a chair and he could hear the sound of running water coming from the bathroom.

'I'll just be a minute,' Sam called faintly through the door.

Jack turned on one of the pink-shaded bedside lights, then removed his jacket and boots and loosened his necktie. He lay down on the bed, clasped his hands behind his head and closed his eyes.

He heard a movement and his eyes flickered open again. Sam was standing by the door, silhouetted by the soft light from the bathroom behind her. She was wearing a satin nightdress that reached down to her ankles and her hair was pinned up loosely, a few strands curling softly around her face. The flimsy fabric of her nightdress couldn't conceal the exquisite body that lay beneath. His gaze travelled slowly down, over the curve of her breasts and the swell of her hips, and then his eyes met hers again.

She smiled hesitantly. He rose from the bed and moved towards her, his gaze locked with hers. He slipped his arms around her and drew her close. The clinging satin was cool to the touch but he could feel the heat of her body beneath and he was aware of the scent of her light perfume. He bent his lips to hers, kissing her gently, then drew away for a second. Her face was very close, her eyes wide, her cheeks flushed. He moved his hand over the curving line of her body, then kissed her again, harder this time.

Jack swung her around and guided her backwards towards the bed, kissing her fiercely on her face and neck. Sam's head began to swim and she pulled at his clothes, pulling off his tie and plucking at the buttons of his shirt. He lifted her onto the bed and she lay back against the pillow. He traced more hungry kisses along her neck and throat, then drew away from her, pulling off his shirt and discarding it onto the floor.

She reached up and gently moved her fingers across his chest. He shuddered beneath her touch and stopped her hand with his. They were both still for a moment. She saw his dog tags glittering in the half-light, a grim reminder of why he was really there. Then he lifted her hand to his lips and kissed her fingertips.

Keeping his eyes fixed on hers, he eased himself up from the bed. He unbuckled his belt and began unbuttoning the waistband of his trousers.

His body was toned and muscular, his honey-toned skin smooth and taut.

He lay down next to her, supported by his elbow, and ran his hand over her satin-clad body. He reached down and lifted the hem of her nightdress. The fabric rippled as he traced his hand along her naked thigh. She raised her body and lifted her arms and the nightdress fell away into a pool beside the bed.

She lay back and he moved over her, supporting himself by his arms and looking down at her for a long, exquisite moment. With a shy smile she lifted her hand and tangled her fingers in the chain around his neck, then pulled him down gently until his mouth melded with hers once more.

18. AFTERMATH

Jack woke early the next morning, just as the soft light of morning was starting to creep into the room.

He could feel the warmth of Sam's body lying next to him and hear her soft, regular breathing, and knew she was still asleep. He turned his head a little and looked at her. She was curled on one side, facing him, and her skin looked smooth and rosy against the stark whiteness of the sheets. Watching her, he remembered the soft yielding sweetness of her body and the unexpected passion of her responses the night before. Then he felt an intense stab of guilt. Making love to her had been everything he'd dreamed of and more, but he knew that he shouldn't have allowed it to happen.

He jaw clenched and he stared up at the dull ceiling of the room, his mind turning over the events of the previous day. Everything seemed suddenly, startlingly, clear, and he cursed himself for his weakness at having given in to his desire. There were more things at stake than his need for her and he should never have forgotten that. Any day now he would be going into action and he knew the chances were that he wouldn't be coming back. What if she fell pregnant with his child? What would happen to her then? How could he look after her, protect her like he would want to, if he were dead? In the cold light of day he could see that he'd been selfish and weak and he hated himself for it. He'd thought himself a better man than that.

Trying hard not to wake her, he carefully pushed back the sheets and eased himself up into a sitting position. He stilled for a moment, aware of the creaking of the bed, and as his gaze travelled around the simply furnished hotel room his mood sank further. He knew that a woman like Sam deserved more, much more. What had possessed him to take advantage of her in a place like this?

He glanced down at her again, checking that she was still asleep. In the soft light of the morning she looked more beautiful than ever and for a moment he ached to touch her. He had to force himself to look away. He knew that for both their sakes he needed to be strong.

Still being careful not to disturb her, he swung his legs off the bed and then leaned over and picked up his wristwatch from the bedside table. It was six in the morning. He got to his feet and started towards the bathroom, gathering up his clothes as he went.

Sam opened her eyes as the room filled with light. She lay for a moment without moving, then lifted her head and saw Jack standing near the window, drawing back the curtains. She pushed herself up onto her elbows, still not quite awake.

'Good morning,' she breathed, smiling sleepily.

He turned to face her and it was then that her mind registered that he'd already washed and shaved and that his body was once again hidden inside the smooth lines of his uniform. She watched as he placed the key to their room on top of the dressing table in front of the window.

A line appeared between his brows. 'Good morning, Sam.'

Hearing an unexpected strain in his voice, she suddenly felt wide-awake. What was wrong with him? Why did he look so tense? And why was he standing there, fully dressed, with the whole expanse of the room between them? He looked back at her, without speaking, and she was aware of her own nakedness beneath his gaze. She pulled up the bedclothes around her. Her action made him flinch and he abruptly averted his gaze.

The silence between them dragged on. He turned and started towards the door. Seeing him put his hand to its handle, she bit her lip. Surely he wasn't going to leave her there, all by herself?

'I'm going downstairs to look for Walker,' he told her, in a matter-of-fact voice. He paused, as if waiting for her to reply, but for a moment she felt too choked to speak. 'I'll meet you in the dining room for breakfast in an hour.'

'All right,' she said, somehow finding her voice again. 'I'll be down in a little while.'

She heard the sound of his fading footsteps as he moved along the corridor outside. Completely bewildered, for a few moments she didn't move. But then, suddenly, the force of his actions hit her and the questions began crowding into her mind. She sat up and pushed one of the pillows into the small of her back. Could it be that he was already regretting having made love to her? When she thought of his tenderness the night before it didn't seem possible, but then, what did she really know about men? She'd been wrong about Johnny, hadn't she?

She pushed off the sheets and climbed out of the bed. Seeing her nightdress lying on the floor where it had been discarded, she bent down to pick it up. Holding it up against her body, she thought of the way Jack had looked at her when he'd first seen her wearing it and how beautiful she'd felt beneath his admiring gaze. She remembered the feel of his hands on her body and let out a little sigh. Was it really possible that he thought that their night together had been a mistake?

She went into the bathroom and washed her face. She looked into the mirror above the basin. Her hair spilled to her shoulders and her eyes stared back at her beneath her dark lashes. With trembling hands, she picked up her hairbrush and began brushing her hair. She knew that by spending the night with Jack she'd acted more honestly than she ever had in her life before, but she wondered now if she'd been completely deceived. GIs were seducing girls like her every day, all over England. They were notorious for it. Perhaps she'd been nothing more than a distraction for Jack, just as her aunt had always said.

She put a hand to her hair and pushed the brush into her toiletry bag. She looked into the mirror again and her pride flared.

It was just after noon when Jack pulled up outside the house where Nancy rented her rooms. He drove off, leaving Ed and Nancy standing on the pavement outside, and it took a while for him to find a place where he and Sam could be completely alone. He came to a deserted track that led between two fields and turned onto it. The track was rough and dusty and the Jeep jolted along it until it petered out in front of a wooden stile.

He turned off the engine and sat for moment, struck by the peace and quiet of the place. Sam sat rigidly in the passenger seat next to him, looking firmly ahead, her hands folded. She'd hardly said a word to him since breakfast and he couldn't blame her for that, not after the way he'd behaved.

'Sam?' he said quietly.

She turned her head slowly and looked at him. 'Yes?'

'I just want you to know how sorry I am about what happened last night.'

Jack saw the colour that briefly touched her cheeks and neck and felt another stab of guilt. His words had embarrassed her and he didn't want her to feel ashamed; he was the one who had been at fault.

She lifted her chin. 'Sorry for what?'

'About last night. It shouldn't have happened, not there, not like that. We should have waited.'

'Waited?' This time her voice was incredulous and her face coloured again, more deeply. 'Why should we have waited?' she said bitterly. 'Johnny and I waited, and where did that get us? We never knew each other, not as a man and woman should.'

He stared at her. He'd suspected it, but he hadn't been sure. 'You'd never slept with anyone before?'

As soon as the inappropriate question came out of his mouth he regretted it, but there was no taking it back.

Her eyes were on him, shocked and disbelieving. Then, suddenly, they began to blaze. 'How can you ask me that?' she demanded in a voice quivering with anger. 'Do you think that I go to bed with American soldiers every day of the week?'

He put his hand on her arm, 'Sam, I'm sorry…'

She shook him off. 'Please don't keep saying that.'

'I just thought that maybe you and Johnny had -'

'Well, you thought wrong!'

Twisting abruptly away from him, she jumped down from the Jeep onto the dusty track and began to run. Swearing under his breath at his own stupidity, Jack jumped down and headed after her. She tripped on a stone and stumbled, but he caught her around the waist before she fell. Her body was trembling and he pulled her into his arms, reproaching himself all over again.

She lifted her head and tried to pull away. 'Please let me go.'

'No, I won't let you go. Not until you've listened to what I have to say.'

Her eyes flashed up to his. 'I don't want to listen. Why are you being like this? Did last night mean nothing to you?'

'Last night meant everything to me, that's just the problem. Any day now I'm going to be leaving this place and I don't know if I'm ever going to be coming back. I hate myself for taking advantage of you the way I did. I should have let you alone so that you could find another guy, someone who could look after you when I won't be able to.'

She looked up at him, searching his face, and her body stilled in his arms. He raised his hand to her hair and gently pushed away a strand that fallen across her forehead. Clouds were gathering to the west. The sky was darkening and the temperature was dropping. She shivered and laid her head against his shoulder. His jaw tensed. He'd been weak, and he knew it. It was time he got her home.

19. SEPARATION

Sam walked towards the large hospital building. Sandbags guarded its entrance against bomb-blast and she could see nurses in their distinctive grey and scarlet uniforms going in and out. It was a military hospital just outside Southampton and her orders to report there had come through the previous week. She'd thought long and hard about her decision to join up, but she still felt a little nervous as she approached the reception desk in the main hall.

'Good morning,' said the young woman who was sitting behind the desk. She was wearing a white cotton blouse beneath a dark suit and her thick dark hair was pulled away from her face in an elaborate wave. 'Can I help you?'

'My name's Samantha Mitchell and I'm here to see Matron Wilcox.'

'I see.' The receptionist picked up the receiver of the telephone in front of her and dialled a number. 'Just one moment please.'

A few minutes later a probationary nurse in a starchy uniform arrived to collect her from the hall. Sam followed her up a broad staircase and along a wide, sparklingly clean corridor that smelled strongly of disinfectant. The young nurse left her seated on a hard wooden chair outside the closed door of the matron's office.

Ten minutes passed. A doctor hurried by, glancing up and down at the notes on his clipboard, oblivious to her presence. She felt the butterflies in her stomach and folded her hands together in her lap.

She hadn't seen Jack since he'd dropped her off at home after that awful morning. By a horrible coincidence, no soldiers had been allowed off the base at Foley Manor in the two weeks since, and no civilians had been allowed onto it. It was terrible to think that that was the way they would part, perhaps never to see each other again, but at least her decision to join the Army Nursing Service had given her something to think about and focus on other than him. She knew she couldn't bear the idea of remaining behind when the Americans finally pulled out for good.

At last the door of the office opened and a plump, efficient-looking woman in a tight-fitting grey dress stepped out. She looked to be in her late forties and she wore a starched white collar and veil.

Sam rose to her feet. 'Good morning.'

The matron examined her closely through her round, wire-rimmed glasses, then smiled and held out her hand. 'I'm Matron Wilcox. I'm so sorry to have kept you waiting.'

The office was small and peaceful. A square of sunlight criss-crossed by the shadows of anti-blast tape illuminated a polished wooden floor. A large mahogany desk occupied a space beneath the only window and a mound of papers was stacked on top of it.

Matron Wilcox seated herself behind the desk, then gestured towards the high-backed chair on the other side. 'Won't you sit down?'

'Thank you,' said Sam. She smoothed down her skirt and perched on the edge of the chair, keeping her back straight.

Matron Wilcox took two sheets of paper from the top of a pile and placed them down on the desk in front of her. Sam waited as she glanced briefly through their contents. 'So you're Samantha Mitchell?' she said, looking up.

'Yes, that's right.'

'Matron Baxter has written to me about you. I'm pleased to say that she praises you very highly both in terms of your abilities as a nurse and in terms of your character. I have to tell you that we value character very highly here, probably more than anything else in fact. We believe that nurses are born, not made.'

She paused and studied Sam's face for a moment, and Sam thought guiltily of her night with Jack. What would Matron Wilcox make of her character if she knew about that?

'Now tell me, what makes you want to join the military? Aren't you happy where you are?'

'I'm very happy, but I've been qualified as a fully registered nurse for over a year and I feel I could do more to help the war effort by joining the Army Nursing Service. Matron told us that you were looking for volunteers and that's why I'm here.'

'And how would you feel if I told you that if you join us you will have to administer care in frontline positions, close to the field of battle?'

'I didn't realise that there were nurses working so far forward.'

'Does that put you off?'

Sam hesitated, but only for a moment. 'No, it doesn't, not at all.'

Matron Wilcox nodded. 'We've found it best to have nurses as far forward as possible, not least because the morale of the men is so much improved the moment they see them. And the primary aim of military nursing is to get the injured men back into the thick of the fighting as quickly as possible. The nearer we are to the front, the more easily that is achieved. But the work will be tough and demanding, like nothing you have ever experienced before. Hundreds of wounded men will pass through the field hospitals every day and you'll see terrible injuries. Do you think you could cope with that?'

Sam didn't shrink beneath her intense, probing gaze. 'Yes, I think I could. I want to go where my skills are most needed. If I could help save just one man's life - '

'Good,' said Matron Wilcox briskly, cutting her off before she could elaborate. 'There simply isn't room for anyone who can't take it. When you're in uniform, everyone expects everything of you and you have to be ready for any sacrifice.' She put the papers back on the pile. 'You'll need to sign some things now in the office next door and then in a few days' time you'll receive a letter notifying you of when and where you are expected to report for duty.'

She stood up and pushed back her chair, and Sam realised that the interview was over. They went out into the corridor and she extended her hand. 'Glad to have you with us, Nurse Mitchell.'

The marshalling camp occupied several acres of land a few miles north of Southampton. Lines of barbed wire fence circled the perimeter and perfect lines of green army tents stretched out as far as the eye could see.

It was still early in the morning when they arrived in the Jeep. Jack was behind the wheel and Bill was riding in the passenger seat beside him. He shifted down a gear and they pulled up behind the line of vehicles waiting at one of the security gates.

It was late May, but the clouds were thick and low and the sky was grey. Jack watched the soldiers in battledress moving about between the tents. He knew that thousands of men were gathering at the camp from all over southern England, ready for D-Day. If all went to plan, in only a few days' time they would be going into battle against the Germans and all the months of preparation and training would finally to be put to the test.

He hoped he'd be good enough for the task that lay ahead. It wasn't going to be easy, that was for sure. He knew that the Germans would throw every weapon they possessed at them to drive them off the beaches where they were to land. But he believed in himself and in the other men in his outfit and he was determined to do his best.

The line of vehicles in front of them gradually grew shorter. A sergeant checked their papers and motioned them through the gates and then they went in search of the tent in which they were to be quartered.

A few hours later, Jack lay stretched out on his bunk. He'd been trying to write a letter to Sam, but it wasn't proving to be easy, and the letter lay abandoned on the top of the locker next to him. He clasped his hands behind his head and closed his eyes for a moment.

He bitterly regretted how they had parted. The orders to move out had arrived without warning the day after they'd returned from the coast and he'd had no alternative but to leave without seeing her again. He knew that he'd left her feeling ashamed and confused and he fervently wished he'd had another chance to explain. But there were no telephones in the camp and no one was allowed to leave; they were, in effect, completely cut off from the outside world.

Jack opened his eyes and reached over to pick up the letter again. Flipping through it, he realised the inadequacy of what he had written. He sat up and swung his legs off the bunk, then screwed the paper up into a ball and tossed it into the waste paper basket at the foot of his bed. He took a fresh sheet and began again. He wrote a few lines telling her that he hoped she was safe and well, and promising that he would come back for her if he could.

He put down the pen and folded the letter into an envelope. As he wrote out her address, he felt the futility of writing to her all over again. The success of the invasion depended on complete secrecy and no mail would leave the camp until after they'd pulled out. He pushed the letter into the pocket of his jacket and lay back on the bunk. He knew that if he were to survive he had to put her out of his mind and concentrate solely on the job that lay ahead.

'How do you do?'

The girl was wearing slippers and a pair of short-sleeved cotton pyjamas, and her dark eyes were warm and friendly. She was sturdily built and had a round face surrounded by a mass of dark, very wiry hair. 'I'm Alice Thorpe-Jones,' she told Sam. 'We've been expecting you.'

They were standing in a large attic room that had been converted into a dormitory. A row of narrow metal beds ran along the length of it on either side. Between each bed was an upturned wooden crate that served as a locker or dressing table or the like.

Sam followed Alice across the bare floorboards of the room.

'This bed's free,' she said, lifting Sam's suitcase onto the crate beside it.

'Thank you.'

'You got here just in time. Lights-out in half an hour I'm afraid. Have you come far?'

'Not really, but the train I was on was delayed for hours. I didn't think I was going to make it.'

'And it was jammed with troops I expect. I don't suppose you managed to get anything to eat on the way.'

'I had a few sandwiches with me.'

Alice looked sympathetic. 'Breakfast's at seven. Did you manage to get a look around downstairs? The dining room's on the ground floor at the back.'

Sam shook her head. 'No, I didn't. I was told to come straight up here and get some sleep.'

'Don't worry, I'll show you around tomorrow and you'll soon get used to everything. It's a beautiful place. Belongs to a Lord something-or-other who's lent it to the army for the duration. Gorgeous grounds teaming with rose bushes and herbaceous borders, I'm sure you know the sort of thing. And it's actually all very relaxed at the moment. We're on standby, of course, and could get mobilised at any moment, but there aren't any patients to look after and it's been weeks since we've had any drills or lectures.'

'Lectures?'

Alice looked surprised. 'Yes. Haven't you had any with your unit?'

Sam shook her head again. 'I've only just joined up and this is the first unit I've been assigned to. I was told I'd missed some of the training, but they didn't think that it would matter. They said I'd pick it up quickly enough.' She saw Alice raise an eyebrow and hesitated. 'Have you been training for a long time?'

'Golly,' said Alice, laughing good-naturedly. 'We've only been in Scotland all winter!'

'Oh,' said Sam, somewhat taken aback, 'I see.'

Alice flopped down on the bed next to hers, then kicked off her slippers and drew her knees up in front of her. 'Look, Sam, you might find this all a bit of a shock at first. Being a nurse in the army is quite a bit different to being an ordinary nurse. There's all that saluting for one thing - a bit over the top, I'd say. You'll soon get used to it, though. Just be sure to do everything in a brisk, orderly fashion and you'll be fine. And remember that most of the girls here are young and newly qualified. There aren't many who've had any experience of nursing on the frontline.'

Sam nodded, thinking back to her years of training at the hospital in London. Her matron there had been fierce and she could still vividly recall the harsh regime of the nurses' home where she'd lived. She could only hope that the strict discipline she'd endured there would help her cope with whatever challenges that lay ahead.

She slipped between the cool sheets of her bed just as the lights went out. She lay awake in the darkened room, listening to the soft murmuring of the other girls, and a sensation of unreality washed over her. She had no idea of where she was going, or if or when she'd ever see her family and friends again.

Jack was glad that the waiting was over. For him that had seemed the hardest part. It was almost a relief to be sitting in the convoy of vehicles heading in the direction of Southampton and their embarkation point. If all went to plan, by the end of the day his unit would be assembling aboard a transport ship, ready to leave for the beaches of Normandy.

The CO had called his officers into his tent the previous evening and briefed them about their part in the operation. It had been a hot and humid night, heightening further the sense of tension and anticipation that was in the air, and Jack had slept fitfully.

Now, despite his lack of sleep, he felt alert and awake. It wasn't that he was unafraid; only a fool would be that. But he felt calm, ready after all the long months of waiting and preparation for whatever fate had in store.

The road was choked with vehicles carrying men and material and the convoy was barely crawling along. He knew that it would take hours to reach the docks and he was glad of Bill's company in the Jeep. At the beginning of the journey they'd joked together and made light-hearted conversation, but as they'd driven through the countryside they'd noticed the tanks and trucks hidden amongst the woods and trees and the huge mounds of equipment waiting to be transported across the Channel, and they'd fallen silent.

The traffic had thickened even further by the time they reached the outskirts of Southampton late in the afternoon. They turned a corner and came into a street that led between the remains of bombed-out houses. A truck stalled ahead of them and they came to a standstill beside a short terrace of houses that had somehow survived the Luftwaffe's bombs.

A knot of women stood on the pavement outside one of the houses. Jack wondered how long they'd been there, watching the column of vehicles as it rolled slowly by. They seemed strangely silent, oblivious to the children that ran around at their feet, grimy-faced and full of life, and he thought how tired they looked, worn out by the war and hard domestic toil. But sitting there in the sunshine, he began to sense that the women's minds weren't on their own troubles, but on those of the men they were so quietly observing.

A stout, middle-aged woman in a faded floral apron emerged from the house next to them and came up to the Jeep. She was carrying a wooden tray laden with plates of sandwiches and glasses of homemade lemonade. They helped themselves when she held out the tray, quickly draining their glasses and handing them back.

'Thank you, ma'am,' said Jack.

'Thank you,' said Bill. 'That sure tasted good.'

She nodded at them approvingly. 'Good luck,' she said, as she stepped away. 'Take care of yourselves.'

The other women had scattered and were now walking to and fro between the stationary vehicles that were staggered along the street, offering food and drink to the soldiers. There was a kind of togetherness between the British and the GIs that Jack had never seen before. A muscle tensed in his cheek. He wondered if he would ever see England or Sam again.

20. NORMANDY

So this is it, thought Sam to herself. *My last view of Southampton.*

The moon was full and bright that night and from where she was standing on the deck of the ship she could see quite clearly the jagged outline of the bombed city she was leaving behind.

She was standing near a lifeboat, next to Alice, amongst a group of thirty or so nurses, listening to a naval officer explain the layout of the ship and the details of their crossing. They were destined for northern France and the ship would be travelling overnight, under the escort of destroyers.

A sailor dressed in overalls emerged from a hatch to their left, from a floor below, and stepped towards them. He distracted the officer, who broke off from what he was saying and looked at him sharply. The sailor said something and the officer looked down at his notes.

The nurses had been standing in silence, but now some of them glanced around and began to talk in surreptitious whispers. Sam's gaze travelled over the deck to the glistening surface of the sea and the shadowy outlines of the other vessels that packed the harbour. It was a warm night in the middle of July. The sea was calm and the deck hardly moved beneath her feet.

The rough felt of the khaki uniform she was wearing was still stiff and she lifted her hand and adjusted the collar of her shirt where it chaffed her neck. The tin hat and full battledress with which they'd all been issued had come of something of a surprise. She knew that the trousers, gaiters and boots that they were wearing were practical and necessary, but they were hardly very feminine. She wondered what Jack would think if he could see her in her new uniform.

She felt for his letter in the top pocket of her jacket. The few lines he'd managed to write to her had been heavily censored, but she was sure he must be amongst the tens of thousands of men who'd landed in France since the beginning of June. It occurred to her that it would be harder than ever for his letters to reach her once they arrived in Normandy, and she felt a twinge of anxiety in her chest.

Alice smiled at her, her face shadowy in the moonlight. 'Are you all right?' she asked, in a whisper.

'Yes, just a bit nervous, that's all. Aren't you?'

Alice nodded. 'It's jolly exciting though, isn't it?'

The officer scanned the rows of nurses in front of him and silence descended again. He told them that their cabins were ready and that the sailor would escort them below.

They followed the sailor through the hatch and down a flight of metal steps into a narrow grey passageway. Sam walked behind Alice, ducking her head to avoid the pipes that jutted out across the ceiling and along the walls.

The cabin that they'd been allocated was small and cramped. There were two bunks on either side of a central aisle and a tiny porthole in the wall opposite. Sam stepped over the sill of the doorway and put her small kitbag down on one of the bottom bunks. Alice had chosen the bunk above, and two other nurses clattered into the cabin behind them.

'It's a good job we haven't brought much,' said Alice wryly, glancing about. The big tin trunks containing most of their luggage had been sent on ahead of them.

Sam smiled at her. She took off her helmet and smoothed her hair. Putting the helmet down next to her bag, she glanced round the cabin for a mirror. Her brows lifted when she saw that there wasn't one.

The sailor had told them that there was a canteen on the starboard side of the ship that would be serving food until midnight. They consulted the map of the ship hanging next to the door and stepped out into the passageway again. As they made their way along it, they could hear the clanking of chains and the creaking of the ship. There was the sound of doors being opened and closed and the low murmur of masculine voices preparing for the voyage.

Finding their bearings proved easier than Sam had imagined and they soon heard the chatter of nurses coming from beyond an open door. They ducked their heads and stepped over the threshold.

The canteen was brightly lit and furnished with simple metal tables and chairs. Three sailors wearing white aprons were serving food from a counter at the back and a queue of nurses had already formed in front of it.

The meal consisted of potatoes and a simple stew. Sitting down at a table next to Alice, Sam felt a strange mixture of fear and excitement and wondered if her stomach would be able to accept any food.

She heard the rumble of engines coming from below. The floor beneath them began to vibrate and she realised with a start that the ship had begun to move. There was a brief silence, and then the room was filled by a burst of chatter and laughter.

Alice chuckled. 'It looks like we're on our way. There's no going back now.'

Later on, after midnight, Sam lay on her bunk looking up into the darkness of the cabin, listening to the vibrations of the ship. She could hear the clattering of feet on the decks above and the rustling of the other women in their bunks. Her boots stood on the floor next to her, but otherwise she remained fully clothed. Her tin helmet was slung around her neck and rested on her chest, just as they'd been instructed. She lay awake for a while, thinking about the strangeness of it all, but then the motion of the ship began to soothe her and she fell into a deep sleep.

Sam leaned against the ship's rail next to Alice. Ahead of them lay the coast of France, shrouded under a hazy mist.

It was just after dawn. A sailor had knocked loudly on the door of their cabin to wake them and they'd come straight up onto the deck. They hadn't been able to wash or change, but Sam felt unexpectedly awake and excited.

She looked along at the flotilla of vessels that had accompanied them across the Channel, bringing reinforcements of men, weapons and vehicles to the front. The flotilla lay at anchor, stretched out across the bay, and a destroyer was pounding its guns in the direction of the coast. She could hear the rumble of distant explosions mingled with the faint thrum of aeroplanes passing high overhead.

Gazing in the direction of the shore, she tried to imagine what it had been like for the first wave of troops as they'd approached the beaches on D-Day. She wondered how many men had been killed as they'd jumped into the sea from their landing craft and faced the German mines and machine guns that had guarded the shore. She shivered at the thought that Jack and his men would have been amongst them. At least she had his letter in her pocket and knew that he'd somehow managed to survive those first few terrible days.

The order reached them to go below and collect their things. Back in the cabin once more, Sam slipped a white armband that carried the Red Cross insignia over the sleeve of her jacket, adjusted the strap of her tin helmet beneath her chin and tugged her kitbag over her shoulder.

A flat-bottomed landing craft took them to the shore, shuddering to a halt at the bottom of the beach. As they waited for the front ramp to be lowered, Sam could hear the thud of bombs falling and the echo of gunfire in the distance, but she was also intensely aware of the gentle sound of waves breaking on the sand and the tangy smell of the sea.

No one said a word as the ramp was lowered, revealing a wide, sandy beach backed by high dunes and the burnt out shells of houses, shops and cafes. The clattering of their boots turned to soft thuds as they walked down the metal ramp and stepped onto the sands.

The nurses gathered together on the beach and a British army officer strode to greet them.

'Welcome to Normandy, ladies,' he said cheerfully. 'I hope you've had a pleasant journey.'

He briefly scanned their faces and then nodded towards the road beyond the dunes where two trucks stood waiting. Sam saw another officer poised next to them. He was holding a clipboard and looking over in their direction.

'The trucks are ready for you,' said the officer in front of them. 'Lieutenant Jones will assign you to your destinations.'

'Please be seated, ladies.'

The small, grey-haired woman dressed in khaki uniform viewed the rows of nurses standing to attention in front of her with a small smile. She waited for them all to sit down before continuing.

'My name is Sister MacDonald and you will all report to me,' she told them. 'As your commanding officer I should like to welcome you to Normandy. Many of you have experience of working in the front lines before, in Italy and North Africa. To those who are new to the challenge, welcome. You are greatly needed here and the work you will do will save countless lives. Tomorrow we expect our first convoy of wounded, so without further ado, I will pass you over to Sister Williams, who will detail you to your tasks.'

Sam was sitting next to Alice in the back row of three lines of folding chairs that had been laid out in the nurses' mess tent. They were in a tented field hospital situated in a large orchard somewhere along the main road that ran between the cities of Bayeux and Caen. It didn't seem important that they didn't know its exact location; they were just glad to have arrived at last. The journey in the trucks had been slow and uncomfortable, along narrow lanes bordered by high, dense hedgerows.

She felt very tired, but she knew that they still had important work to do before she would be able to get any rest. She listened in silence with the other nurses to Sister Williams' instructions.

An hour later, Sam and Alice left the mess tent with a group of other nurses and an orderly accompanied them across an expanse of rutted field. Ahead of them, three large tents had been erected to serve as wards. They followed the orderly into one of them through a canvas doorway.

An aisle of duckboards had been laid down the centre of a canvas floor, broken in places by the thick wooden poles that supported the tent. Near the doorway by which they'd come in, a dozen or so large wooden crates sat waiting. A selection of folding tables and collapsible beds was leaning next to them.

Sam and Alice lifted the lid off one of the crates. Inside, they found medical equipment that had been carefully wrapped in oiled paper and tightly packed. They unfolded a small table and placed it next to the crate, then set about unpacking the supplies.

It took the nurses hours to unload all of the crates. The light began to dim inside the tent and they lit hurricane lamps and suspended them from the tent supports. They stacked empty boxes to use as shelves for medicines and bandages, and then they made up the collapsible beds.

When they'd finished, they extinguished the hurricane lamps they'd been working by and stepped out of the tent into the blackening night. They stood for a few moments to get used to the gloom, but they could barely see the ground in front of them.

Sam and Alice picked their way carefully along, side by side, trying hard to avoid the rabbit holes and the ropes and pegs that were hidden in the darkness. Somehow they found their way to the vague grey shape of the tent in which they'd been quartered.

Lighting the lamp inside, Sam's gaze fell on the folding canvas bath tucked away in one corner. She smiled inwardly, wondering if she'd ever get a chance to use it. Tonight they would have to make do with their canvas wash stand and the bucket of cold water next to it. The tent was almost as small as the cabin on the ship. There were two narrow beds beneath the eaves, covered by rough army blankets, and she sank down into one of them. Every inch of her body ached. It had been a day, she thought, unlike any other she'd ever known.

Jack shifted his position in the ditch, trying to get comfortable, knowing how much he needed to get some sleep. It was the height of summer and the nights were short, and there never seemed to be enough time to rest between the long days of hard fighting. He'd do anything for a good wash and a shave, he thought, brushing his hand across his stubble. That, and a decent place to sleep.

He stretched out his legs, trying hard not to disturb the other men. He could see the shadowy outline of a hedge looming in front of him and he was aware of the sweet, damp smell of its leaves and of the grass beneath him. In the distance he could hear shells falling and the occasional burst of faint gunfire, but they were sounds he had grown used to and as yet they were far enough away not to worry him.

He began to relax, his mind emptying slowly of the bloody images of the day, and he thought only of Sam. He pictured her standing in the dusky light of the hotel bedroom, her hair loosely coiled about her head and her satin nightdress skimming the soft feminine curves of her body. He inhaled deeply, grateful that the memory of their one night of passion was still so vivid and sustaining.

Although deep down he still believed that he'd wronged her, as time had passed he'd found it more and more difficult to regret the night that they'd spent together. Surrounded by so much death and destruction, he'd begun to see things differently and he knew he would savour the memory of their night together for however long he got to live.

It seemed impossible that he would survive for long. The fighting was tough, far tougher than he'd expected, and the battle for Normandy was progressing slowly, hedgerow by hedgerow.

He lay still, his body tense. He knew that the enemy couldn't be far away. So this was the reality of combat. He thought back to the long months of training that he and his men had been through. The army had done its best to prepare them, but there was nothing that could have taught them what it would be like to lie helpless in a ditch waiting for another day of ugly warfare.

21. ARMY NURSE

A bugle sounded.

Sam looked up from her breakfast at the scrubbed trestle table outside the mess tent. An army ambulance was turning in between the high hedgerows at the entrance to the field. She grasped her tin cup and took a last sip of tea, sprang up from the bench and sprinted across the mud towards the tented wards.

Two more ambulances followed in behind the first, drawing up in a row. Orderlies began lifting out the stretchers and taking them inside one of the wards, and Sam slipped in through the canvas door behind them.

A soldier lay on a stretcher on a set of trestles. He was still wearing his dirty green uniform and a distinctive yellow tag was tied to one of the buttonholes of his jacket. His arm was wrapped in a stained bandage that was fraying at the edges. Sam picked up the tag to see what his injuries were and how much morphine he'd received to relieve his pain. No wonder he was so groggy, she thought, when she saw how much he'd been given by the medic who'd rescued him from the battlefield.

A steady stream of casualties flowed into the ward as the day wore on, their faces pale and their uniforms torn and stained and mottled with blood. Sam was aware of the constant sound of planes overhead and explosions in the distance but she didn't allow it to distract her. She moved from bed to bed, washing faces and cleaning wounds, and administering morphine and penicillin. It was a shock to see so many wounded men, but she knew that she couldn't afford the luxury of tears.

Late in the afternoon, a young sergeant was brought in and carried to an empty bed. The dressing covering his stomach was splattered with mud. Sam moved her trolley of supplies next to him and leaned over to peel back his dressing. She did it as gently as she could but he still cried out in pain. She straightened up and saw that his face was completely drained of colour.

A doctor was speaking to another nurse beside the adjacent bed. He was a good-looking, fair-haired man in his early thirties, and he wore a captain's uniform beneath his white coat.

'Excuse me, Dr Willoughby?'

He turned around at the sound of her voice and bent to examine the sergeant. He had stopped crying out and was lying motionless on the bed.

'Give him some more morphine,' said Dr Willoughby quietly, meeting her gaze.

She nodded at him, registering the expression in his eyes. She knew then that there was nothing they could do but try to relieve the man's suffering in what were sure to be his final few hours.

It was very late by the time Sam got back to her tent. The hurricane lamp glowed softly and Alice was lying on her bunk curled up on her side. Her eyes were closed and she seemed to be sleeping soundly.

Sam sat down on the edge of her bed. As she pulled the boots off her aching feet, she noticed a bundle of letters sitting on the little table between the beds. She paused for a moment, then slowly set her boots down next to each other beneath her bed and leaned over to pick them up. Her fingers trembled as she quickly searched through them. She saw by the handwriting there were several from her parents and from Leonora, as well as two from Diana. It was the first mail she'd received since arriving in Normandy and that, she calculated quickly, was well over three weeks ago now.

She found Jack's letter at the bottom of the pile. She set the other letters on the table again, unopened, and carefully prised it open. She unfolded the single sheet of paper she found inside and began to read. He wrote that he was in one piece and that she shouldn't worry. He said that he missed her and that she was always in his thoughts.

She sighed as she lay back on the bunk with the letter in her hand. It wasn't much. She was beginning to realise that he wasn't a natural letter writer. But anything was better than nothing. Looking at the date and postmark on the envelope, she saw that it had been redirected from England and she worked out that it had taken well over two weeks to reach her. She briefly closed her eyes. Anything might have happened since he'd written it, she thought.

Clutching the letter against her, she lay still for a while, listening to the low rumble of planes passing high overhead and the sound of Alice's soft, regular breathing. Opening her eyes again, she sat up and carefully refolded the thin sheet of paper on which the letter was written. She slipped it back into the envelope, then tucked the envelope into the top pocket of her jacket. She drew herself to her feet and stretched her legs, then began moving quietly about the tent and getting ready for bed, taking care not to disturb Alice.

Machine gun fire was ripping across the field.

Jack jumped up from the ground and sprinted for cover. 'Get down,' he yelled to the men behind him. He dived into a shell hole and lay flat on his stomach. Cautiously, he lifted his head just high enough to see out of his hiding place. He'd seen too many men killed out of sheer carelessness and he wasn't about to take any unnecessary chances. Through the trees in front of him, he could see flashes of grey-green uniform and hear orders being shouted in German. His order had been to take his platoon across the field and attack the enemy position ahead.

Three men had jumped into the shell hole next to him. 'Okay, let's get out of here,' he told them. 'Follow me.'

Within seconds they had crawled to a gap in the hedge that bounded the field. Straightening up, but keeping their heads low, they carefully edged their way along the outside of the hedge, to get as close as possible to the German position. They tossed their grenades, waited for the explosions that followed, and then opened fire. Jack yelled for the other men still lying in the field to attack and he watched through billowing smoke as the surviving Germans abandoned their position and started running for their lives.

'Did you get any letters yesterday?' asked Alice.

She was sitting on her bunk, trying to get the tangles out of her unruly hair with a brush. She was holding a curling strand in front of her eyes and frowning as she worked hard to remove a knot.

Sam was lying on top of the bunk on the other side of the tent. 'Yes, one or two,' she replied, without moving, feeling exhausted after another gruelling ten-hour shift. 'Did you?'

'A couple from Geoffrey.'

Sam knew that Geoffrey was Alice's boyfriend. He was in England, working for British Intelligence.

'Is he all right?'

'Oh, yes,' said Alice breezily. 'He's still cracking codes or something. It's all terribly important and very hush-hush.'

They were both silent for a moment, and it occurred to Sam how little they really knew about each other's lives. Home was a distant memory and all they seemed to have time to think about was work.

'Have you known him for long?'

'Oh, forever,' said Alice. 'He's an old family friend, you know how these things are. He's nearly thirty-two, so he's quite a bit older than I am. We're planning to get married, after the war ends.' She looked at Sam from beneath her fringe. 'What about you? You've never said. Have you got someone special?'

Sam hesitated for a moment, then thought how good it would be to have someone to confide in. 'Yes,' she said, turning her head slightly to meet Alice's gaze. 'Yes, actually there is someone.'

'Someone nice?'

'Yes, very.'

'Well, aren't you going to tell me a bit about him? Or is that terribly hush-hush too?'

'He's an American lieutenant,' Sam told her shyly.

'A Yank?' Alice's brows shot up and she put down her hairbrush. 'I wasn't expecting that. I had you down as being with some dashing English officer. You know, one of those public school types.'

Sam smiled. 'Actually, I think that's what my family would like for me.'

Alice studied her face for a moment, then began brushing her hair again. 'Where did you meet him?'

'There was an American base near the hospital where I used to work.'

'I see.' Alice looked thoughtful. 'And I suppose he's terribly handsome,' she mused.

'Yes, he is.'

Alice nodded. 'Well, just don't tell Dr Willoughby about him.'

Sam sat up on her elbow and looked at Alice. 'Whatever do you mean?'

'I've seen him looking at you.'

'When?'

'Oh, on the wards, and in the mess tent, at breakfast. I think he's taken a shine to you.'

'I'm sure you must be mistaken,' said Sam, still looking baffled.

'You're just too modest to notice. I think that's part of what he likes about you.' Alice smiled. 'Just look at you, Sam. You're so beautiful. I'm sure you have men falling head over heels in love with you wherever you go.'

The following morning, the sound of aircraft approaching from the north woke them just after dawn. When they emerged from the tent, the low hum of the planes had grown to a steady roar.

Sam lifted her eyes upward and saw the sky full of bombers overhead. The sun was coming up and there was hardly any cloud. It was the perfect day for a bombing raid.

Alice gazed into the distance, towards the south. 'They're heading for Caen,' she said, in a quiet voice. 'Monty must mean business today.'

Sam shivered. She knew that the city was heavily defended by the Germans and that the fighting there was likely to be hard and bloody. She heard the thunder of guns in the distance and the drumbeat of bombs falling to the ground as the planes emptied their loads.

22. BELGIUM

Sam moved along the row of beds in the tented ward. It was late in the afternoon and most of the patients were dozing. She stopped to check the temperature of a young corporal who looked a little feverish. Finding it to be normal, she smoothed down his sheets and then glanced at her watch. Her long shift was nearly over, her feet were sore and she was ready to get some rest.

Half an hour later, she emerged from the tent after her final round. Outside, the sky was overcast. She'd been aware of the sound of rain falling on the tent's canvas walls for most of the day and she saw that the ground had become a sea of sticky mud. It wasn't an unusual sight. The summer they'd spent at the field hospital had been unseasonably cold and over the weeks she'd grown accustomed to the monotony of the mud and the wet and the rain. She allowed the canvas door to fall back into place behind her, then bent her head against the drizzle and began moving along the duckboards that linked the long row of tents.

'Sam!' Alice was hurrying towards her from the nurses' mess, her boots splashing along the sodden boards. 'You'll never guess,' she cried, her eyes alight with excitement. 'The Americans have reached Paris!'

Sam stopped in her tracks and stared at her in amazement. She knew that the Allies had broken through the German line of defence at the beginning of August and since then had been rapidly pursuing the retreating German armies across France towards the Rhine, but she couldn't believe that they'd already reached Paris.

'Honestly, it's true,' laughed Alice. 'We've just heard it on the wireless. They liberated Paris this morning!'

A renewed sense of purpose spread through the hospital over the next few weeks. There were no new convoys of wounded and the beds emptied as the remaining patients were taken away in ambulances, ready to be shipped home. The nurses worked hard packing equipment into crates ready for transportation and orderlies took down and packed up the hospital tents.

The morning of departure dawned. Sam took one last look around at the muddy field they were leaving behind, then climbed into the back of the canvas-skinned truck and sat down on one of the benches, next to Alice.

The truck swayed and jolted across the churned up soil of the field, went out through the opening between the high hedgerows, and turned along a narrow twisting lane. It was early in the morning and there was a distinct chill in the air, but there were patches of blue in the sky.

They travelled through tiny villages with ancient churches and clusters of half-timbered houses. The cloud lifted almost completely, leaving only a haze. They came to a road lined with the rusting shells of abandoned cars and burnt out vehicles, and the naked stumps of trees. After a while, they crossed a bridge and entered the rubble-choked streets of Caen. Where there should have been shops and houses, there were mounds of shattered masonry and blackened bricks. Tank tracks had ripped up the streets and the earth was riddled with bomb craters. It seemed impossible that anyone could have survived such devastation and as she gazed out over the ruins from the back of the truck, Sam felt a chill pass through her.

They left the city behind them, moving forward behind the advancing armies, and Sam fell asleep for a while, lulled by the jolting motion of the truck. When she woke again, late in the afternoon, the countryside had changed. Hazy sunshine shimmered on fields of wheat and the roads were crowded with trucks carrying soldiers and vehicles towing artillery. The journey became smoother, along good roads, and they passed through towns and villages that seemed to have been barely touched by the battles that had raged only weeks before. Motorcycles and Jeeps sped past them. Sam thought of the enemy beating its rapid and hasty retreat eastwards towards Germany, with the Allies close behind them, and her spirits rose. Perhaps Hitler would surrender now, and the war might be over before the year was out.

By nightfall they'd crossed the border into Belgium. They passed through a forest of conifers and pines. A breeze stirred the tops of the trees, rustling the branches. When they emerged from the forest, they turned onto a long drive flanked by formal gardens that were landscaped with fountains and low hedges. They pulled up on a wide forecourt at the side of another truck and the driver cut the engine.

Sam and Alice eased their backs and stretched out their legs, then climbed stiffly out of the back of the truck.

A chateau built of white stone gleamed in the greying light. It was large and evenly proportioned, with two long wings flanked by circular towers radiating off a central, three storey section. Tall windows gave onto the drive and gardens and some of them stood open. The murmur of voices drifted out and the dark outlines of doctors and nurses could be seen moving about inside.

The chateau was being used as a temporary hospital and, for the foreseeable future at least, it was to be Sam and Alice's new home. They were allocated a room with whitewashed walls that smelled of lavender, on the first floor of the west wing. Two metal beds were covered with clean white quilts. There was a large wardrobe, a basin in one corner, and a long mirror in a wooden frame.

They set down their bags near the door and Alice went to the window and pushed open the shutters. Stars sparkled in the sky. 'Well, this is more like it,' she said, smiling over at Sam.

Sam looked around the room and nodded. It all seemed a world away from everything they'd known in Normandy.

They took turns to wash in the little metal basin and then climbed into their narrow beds. Within moments, they were asleep.

The hospital was stirring when they went down for breakfast early the next morning. After they'd eaten, Sister MacDonald assigned them to their wards. By eight o'clock, a new convoy of wounded soldiers had arrived on the forecourt outside.

Autumn gradually faded into winter, but still the war dragged on. The Allied assault on Arnhem failed and the Germans dug themselves in behind the Siegfried Line, the line of defence that ran the length of the German border in the west.

'I don't understand why they jolly well don't just surrender,' complained Alice, late one December afternoon. 'Surely they can see that they can't win now. What on earth is Hitler trying to achieve by holding out like this?'

They were rolling bandages at a dressing station in front of a window. Sam's gaze travelled over the bleak winter landscape outside. 'Well, everyone knows that he's a madman,' she said, turning to Alice again. A strand of her hair had worked itself loose and she tucked it back inside her starched white cap. 'I don't suppose he'll ever give in, at least not whilst there are still soldiers ready to fight for him. And now that they're defending their homeland, the Germans will probably fight harder than ever.'

Sam had been vaguely looking forward to Christmas, but her spirits had sunk at the news that the enemy had managed to assemble its armies and launch a huge counterattack in the forests of the Ardennes. She knew that the Allied lines of defence had been broken and that there were American troops trapped in the path of the Germans.

She felt a familiar ache of anxiety in the pit of her stomach. Her work was demanding and gave her little time to mope, but her feelings for Jack burned undimmed. She yearned for him as she lay in her narrow bed at night, looking up into the darkness, and he was the first thing she thought about when she woke up in the mornings.

The hospital had been notified to expect a heavy influx of casualties in the coming weeks, as the Allies resisted the German counterattack. Sam looked out of the window again and her eyes blurred with tears. Where was he? she wondered. Was he still safe? Willing herself to be strong, she blinked back the tears and picked up another strip of bandage and began coiling it tightly into a roll.

The top two storeys of the house had been blown away, but Jack guessed he would find shelter somewhere in the rooms below. It was bitterly cold and snowing and he knew that he had to find somewhere dry to spend the night.

He went into the shell of the house and down a flight of dank stone stairs that opened out into a cellar below. The air was thick with brick dust and cigarette smoke and it took a moment for his eyes to adjust to the gloom. The floor was covered with a sprinkling of straw and soldiers sat about smoking and playing cards. Others lay quietly beneath khaki blankets, trying to get some sleep. He smelled the aroma of coffee rising from a steaming pot on a battered metal stove and heard the sound of a swing band playing coming from the radio next to it. After three nights in a foxhole, he felt like he'd just entered the best hotel in Boston.

He found a space against one of the roughly hewn walls of the cellar and sat down with his legs drawn up in front of him. He drew a small bundle of letters from the inside pocket of his jacket and fingered their edges thoughtfully. He tilted his head back and closed his eyes, visualising her in his mind. Although it was months since he'd last seen her, he still remembered every exquisite detail. More than anything else, he was sure it was the memory of her that had kept him alive.

Sam glanced at the little card that was tied to the buttonhole of the soldier's jacket. Seeing that he'd been shot in the leg, she gently lifted the blanket that had been draped over him and examined the wound. The grimy leg of his trousers had been ripped open and the wound had been packed with a compress to stop the bleeding. She knew immediately that he would need an operation to remove the bullet that was lodged inside his calf.

She fetched a bowl of warm water and a roll of cotton wool, then removed the blanket and began to clean the skin around the wound as gently as she could. The soldier made no response, but she paused briefly to study his face. She'd recognised him as soon as she'd seen the orderlies carrying his stretcher into the ward.

The following afternoon she stood next to his bed and watched over him as he came round from his operation. He blinked into the light for a few moments and then he turned his head and saw her.

His brow furrowed. 'Sam?'

She smiled at him. 'Yes, Bill. It's me.'

The look of confusion lingered on his face. 'But how…?'

'Don't try to speak' she said gently. 'The doctors have removed the bullet and you're going to be fine, but you need to rest.'

The wound had been infected and she thought that there was still a chance that he might lose his leg, but she couldn't tell him that, not yet. She leaned over to smooth down his sheets. When she straightened up, she saw Dr Willoughby coming down the ward.

'Is everything all right here, Nurse Mitchell?' he asked, pausing at the foot of the bed.

'Yes, Doctor, everything's fine.'

She made as if to move away, but Bill's hand flew to her wrist. 'Stay here a minute, won't you, Sam?'

Dr Willoughby lifted his brows. 'Do you know this man?'

Sam nodded. 'Yes, I do. We met in England.'

'I see.' Dr Willoughby briefly adjusted the papers on the clipboard he was carrying. 'Well, you know he'll get the best possible care here,' he said in a brisk voice. 'The penicillin he's getting will soon clear up the infection he has in his leg. The bullet missed his bone and I'm sure he'll be back on his feet in no time.'

Dr Willoughby moved off. Sam waited as his retreating figure disappeared through the door at the end of the ward, then her eyes settled on Bill again. He still looked pale, but he was alert now.

He scrutinised her face. 'I can't believe you're here, so close to the field of battle. It just doesn't seem right.'

She flushed. 'It isn't right that any of us should have to be here,' she said, glancing down and rearranging his blanket.

When she raised her head again, she saw that he was smiling faintly. 'Jack's doing fine. You do know that, don't you?'

'When did you last see him?' she asked, in a trembling voice.

'Yesterday. He was the guy that dragged me out of there and put me in the ambulance.'

Sam nodded. Tears misted her soft green eyes, but for a moment she couldn't speak.

23. A SURPRISE

January was a gloomy month. Casualties poured into the hospital from the battle that raged in the Ardennes and the doctors and nurses were rushed off their feet. The days were cold and short and passed swiftly by. Sam was in a constant state of anxiety about Jack, but she was far too busy to have time to mope.

Bill recovered quickly, just as Dr Willoughby had anticipated, and with the aid of crutches he was soon mobile again. The stream of wounded flooding into the hospital meant that his bed was needed for other patients and he hadn't been there for more than a week when it was decided that he was well enough to be sent elsewhere to convalesce. Sam was pleased to see him back on his feet so quickly, but she knew that his speedy recovery would mean that it wouldn't be long before he was sent back to the front and into the path of danger again. It was with mixed feelings that she said goodbye to him and waved him off in the back of a truck early one bitterly cold morning.

The weeks went by. News reached them at the hospital that the Allies had closed the bulge and defeated the German counterattack and as February arrived, the flow of casualties began to ebb.

One morning when the wards were quiet, Sister MacDonald asked Sam to go to one of the storerooms and take an inventory of medical supplies. A supply truck was due at the hospital the following day. Sam saw clouds scudding across the sky through the windows as she tapped along the ground-floor corridor with a clipboard in her hand

Coming to the end of the corridor, she opened the door to the storeroom and stepped inside. She switched on the light and looked around, briefly assessing the stock that remained. Shelves lined the room from floor to ceiling and propped near the door was a small wooden ladder. She moved the ladder further into the room, unfolded it and climbed up to the middle rung. Balancing her clipboard on the uppermost shelf, she began carefully counting the jars of medicine in front of her.

'Sam?'

It was Alice's voice, calling to her from the doorway.

'Just a moment, Alice,' replied Sam vaguely, without turning her head. 'I'm just counting…'

'But Sam, there's an American captain here to see you.'

'A captain?'

Sam looked around, but Alice had gone. A figure appeared from the corridor beyond and her legs felt suddenly weak.

'Jack?' she whispered.

He stood for a moment, framed in the doorway, silhouetted in the weak shaft of sunlight coming from a window behind him. His eyes locked with hers and she caught her breath. He looked raw and masculine, with a new ruggedness about his face.

A smile touched his lips, but he didn't say anything, and his eyes didn't leave hers in the moment it took him to reach the ladder. His hands were warm and strong as they went about her waist. He lifted her down and drew her into his arms, bringing her close to his body and bending his head as he did so. At last, after so many months of waiting, Sam felt the warmth of his lips against her own and an exquisite sensation of joy exploded around her heart.

'Nurse Mitchell?' said a voice.

Sam's eyes darted across the room and she sprang apart from Jack. Sister MacDonald was standing in the doorway. 'Yes, Sister?' she blurted, snapping to attention.

Sister MacDonald's intense blue gaze moved over them unflinchingly. Sam peeked at Jack. His mouthed twitched at the corners and she dipped her head. She drew in a breath, hoping fiercely that he wasn't going to laugh.

'I assume you must be a close friend of Nurse Mitchell's, Captain?' said Sister MacDonald.

'Yes, ma'am,' answered Jack. His voice sounded serious and Sam risked raising her head again.

'And how long is it since you last saw her?'

'A little over eight months.'

'I see. And I take it that you're now on leave?'

'Yes, ma'am, that's correct. My company's been given a few days' Rest and Recuperation. We've been stationed at a camp a few miles east of here since yesterday. I got a twenty-four hour pass from my CO and came over as quickly as I could.'

'But how did you know she was here?'

'A friend of mine told me. He received treatment for a leg wound here, but he's been back with the unit for a couple of weeks.'

There was the sound of footsteps scuffling along the corridor outside as someone hurried past. Sister MacDonald looked at Jack steadily. 'Well, I'm sure that Nurse Mitchell has more than earned a rest after all these months,' she remarked. 'I hear that Brussels is very popular at the moment, so perhaps you might consider taking her there.' She smiled faintly and then her eyes briefly found Sam's. 'I'll expect you back here first thing in the morning, Nurse Mitchell,' she said briskly.

'Yes, of course,' mumbled Sam.

Sister MacDonald nodded. 'Good day to you both,' she said, glancing between them again. She turned on her heel, stepping away from the doorway and vanishing along the corridor, out of sight.

Sam left Jack waiting in the hallway and raced upstairs to her room. She shut the door and looked into the mirror. Her khaki blouse was buttoned to her neck and tucked primly in at her waist. She wished she had something prettier to put on, but all she'd been permitted to bring over from England was her uniform. Anyway, she thought, even if she did have something nice to wear, how could she possibly wear a dress with her clumpy shoes?

She found her small kitbag lying in the bottom of the wardrobe and hastily pushed a few things into it. She brushed her hair and secured it with a clip at the nape of her neck, then put on a dab of lipstick. She plucked her drab looking overcoat from a peg by the door and pulled it on, knotting the belt tightly. The coat was a couple of sizes too big for her and the fabric bunched around her shoulders. She frowned into the mirror again and touched her hair, then pulled on her gloves and picked up her bag. The door clicked to behind her and she raced along the first floor corridor and hurried down the stairs.

Jack was standing by a window in the hallway, looking out over the chateau gardens. Sam's shoes tapped across the marble floor and he turned around. His gaze flickered over her coat as she came towards him.

A smile played about his lips as he shouldered her kitbag and tucked her arm through the crook of his elbow. 'How in the world you made it through this battle zone I'll never know,' he murmured in her ear. 'But I sure am glad to see you.'

Outside, the air was cold and damp and swirling with sleet. Jack helped Sam up into the passenger seat of the Jeep and covered her legs with a blanket. He climbed in beside her, the engine caught, and they set off smoothly down the drive.

It had stopped sleeting when they reached Brussels, but the sky was still heavy with cloud. They turned into a side street and drew up outside a narrow building, several storeys high. Tall windows and wrought iron balconies faced the road beneath an ornately shaped roof and there was a blue canopy over the entrance advertising the name of the hotel.

They went inside to book a room. They were told by the receptionist that there was nothing available until the middle of the afternoon, so they left their bags behind the desk, then came out into the street again. They started towards the centre of the city, walking along pavements crowded with servicemen and passing rows of tall town houses with stuccoed facades.

The street they were following opened up into the main square. They strolled around for a while, soaking up the atmosphere and admiring the elaborately decorated guild houses and the majestic beauty of the gothic town hall. They turned into another street, lined with shops and perfumeries, restaurants and bars. Trams swayed and rattled by.

A woman stepped out through a shop doorway, nearly bumping into Sam. She was very stylishly dressed in a grey, square-shouldered jacket with a matching narrow skirt and a fox stole scarf. Her dark, almond-shaped eyes flashed wide and she cast a critical glance at Sam's overcoat. Sam lifted her chin. The woman brushed past her, her hips swaying suggestively as she moved away along the street.

Elegantly dressed mannequins filled the shop window and Sam's eyes were drawn to a red dress with a sweetheart neckline and softly pleated skirt.

'I think you'd look good in that, don't you?' smiled Jack, following the direction of her gaze.

Inside, the shop was fitted out with polished wooden shelves and a middle-aged man with a thin, brilliantined moustache stood waiting behind a counter. His gaze swept appraisingly over Jack's uniform before he greeted them.

'*Bonjour* Captain, *Bonjour Mademoiselle*,' he said, clapping his hands together in front of him. 'How may I be of assistance?'

'The lady here would like to try on a dress.'

'*Oui*. Yes, of course. Would *Mademoiselle* care to show me which one?'

Sam pointed out the dress that she'd seen in the window and the shopkeeper went over to a rail and brought out one in her size. He showed her to a small fitting room hidden behind a heavy brocade curtain at the back of the shop. She was aware of him casting his eyes over her uniform as she took off her coat and hung it up on a peg.

He wrinkled his nose when he caught sight of her footwear. 'I will find you some shoes and some stockings perhaps, no?'

'Yes, please,' she answered gratefully.

Sam took off her uniform and folded it over a chair, then stepped carefully into the dress. She plucked at the bodice and waistband and smoothed down the skirt. The woollen fabric was so fine that it felt like wearing silk. She looked into the mirror and saw how well the soft, berry red suited her complexion and how the cut of the dress flattered her curves. Behind her, in the reflection, she noticed the pair of matching, high-heeled shoes that the shopkeeper had pushed beneath the curtain. There was a little stool next to the mirror and she sat down and slipped them on.

She pulled back the curtain of the fitting room. Jack was standing with his back to her, looking out through the shop window at the street beyond. She came forward across the floorboards and he turned around. His eyes wandered down her body and lingered for a moment on her legs, and then he lifted his head and held her gaze.

The hotel room was large and comfortably furnished. There was an intricately carved mahogany wardrobe, a matching dressing table, two chairs upholstered in embroidered silk, and a big bed dressed with crisp white sheets and a velvet bedspread. A tall, sumptuously swagged window looked out over the street and a panelled wooden door stood slightly ajar, revealing a private bathroom.

Jack put their bags down next to the bed, then looked around. He glanced at Sam. 'So what do you think?'

'It's perfect,' she breathed.

Jack opened the door to the bathroom more fully. Blue and white delft tiles covered the walls to the ceiling and there was a big, ivory-coloured cast-iron bath. Everything sparkled and looked spotlessly clean. Sam gazed wistfully at the bath for a moment and then looked up at Jack. His mouth curved into a smile and he seemed to know exactly what she was thinking.

Her forehead puckered a little. 'You wouldn't mind, would you?'

His smile deepened and he shook his head. 'Go ahead and take a bath, if you want. There are a couple more things I need to do anyhow.' He kissed her lightly on the lips. 'Don't go anywhere. I'll be back before you know it.'

Sam sighed with pleasure as she slipped her body into the hot, silky water and sank down amongst the bubbles. She'd pinned up her hair and now she rested her head on the smooth curve at the end of the bath. The heat of the water touched her shoulders and began to wash away the aches and pains of the past few months. She lay motionless for a while, then began tracing rivulets of foam along her arms with the sweet smelling lavender soap that the hotel had provided.

She heard the door of their room click softly shut as Jack returned from the street.

'How's it going in there?' he called, through the slightly open door.

'It's absolutely wonderful,' she laughed.

She sank further down into the water to enjoy the caress of its warmth, then lifted one of her legs and began running the soap along it with her hands.

'I hope you're doing all that for me.'

Jack was standing in the doorway, naked down to his waist. He looked fit and lean, his muscles tightly honed by the exertions of battle. Instinctively, Sam sat up and crossed her arms over her chest.

His gaze held hers. 'Please don't be ashamed,' he murmured.

24. BRUSSELS

For a long, lingering moment, Sam didn't move, but then she slowly unfolded her arms and lowered them down into the water.

Jack walked with bare feet across the cool tiles of the bathroom floor and knelt down by the side of the bath, his eyes never once leaving her face. She lay still and quiet as his gaze moved over her body, travelling down past her neck and resting for a moment on the curve of her breasts, then moving on to where her pale skin disappeared beneath the rippling water.

He reached out and lightly traced the outline of her neck and shoulder with his hand. 'I want you, Sam,' he said softly. 'I want you like I've never wanted anyone or anything in my life before. I just don't want to hurt you. I need to know that I can keep you safe, whatever happens. And that won't be possible until this thing is finally over.'

'Please don't think like that,' she whispered. 'Let's just make the most of what we have now. None of us knows what tomorrow will bring. Whatever happens, I will always treasure our time together. I've never regretted what happened last May, and I'll never regret being here with you now.'

'You really mean that? You've never had any second thoughts?'

'No, never. It was the most wonderful night of my life.'

He studied her face for a long moment. She smiled shyly, and as he looked back at her a feeling of calm flowed through him and his tension ebbed away.

Soft, white towels had been folded onto a shelf above the bath. Jack eased himself up onto his feet again, reached for a towel, and held it open. The water rippled softly as Sam rose gracefully before him and he stepped forward and gently wrapped the towel around her body.

They went into the bedroom and lay down on the bed together. Jack had closed the curtains and the room was intimate in the half-light of the late afternoon. He ran his fingers lightly over Sam's skin. He felt her tremble slightly beneath his touch and stilled his hand. Her eyes looked soft and wide and he saw the trust she had in him. For eight long months she'd been nothing but a memory and now she was here, warm and alive, and more beautiful even than he remembered. Suddenly, nothing that had come before or that lay in front of him seemed important any longer. The long days of fighting and nights without sleep seemed to fade away in his memory, and there was only her.

Afterwards, they lay silently in the darkness for a while.

Jack raised himself up on his elbow and kissed Sam's shoulder. 'I hate to the ruin the mood,' he whispered, 'but are you hungry?'

Sam laughed. 'Well, now that you mention it, actually I'm ravenous.'

She bathed quickly again, emerging from the bathroom swathed in another towel. She felt Jack's eyes upon her as she crossed the room and sat down on the padded stool in front of the dressing table. She watched in the mirror as he moved behind her and then gently lifted her hair to kiss the nape of her neck. Her body tingled with renewed desire at the feel of his warm lips against her skin and she briefly closed her eyes. But then she opened them again and gave a little shake of her head.

He paused and looked at her through the reflection in the glass. 'I'm sorry,' he murmured. 'But you must know how hard you are for a guy to resist.' He kissed her shoulder then straightened up. 'Anyhow,' he said, in a different, playful, voice, 'aren't you going to ask me about my little shopping trip earlier?'

He crossed over to the bed and sat down on the edge of it. A towel was wrapped around his waist and the muscles of his upper body rippled as he leaned down to draw something out from beneath the bed.

The flat rectangular package was wrapped in crisp brown paper and had a red ribbon across it, tied in a bow. He laid it on the dressing table in front of her and her eyes widened.

'Aren't you going to open it?' laughed Jack, seeing her expression.

Sam carefully undid the bow and lifted off the lid. Inside was a layer of tissue paper. She opened it out and found a matching set of silk underwear, the colour of cream.

'I hope it fits. The guy in the shop said it was about your size.'

'I think it should,' she said, looking at the label. She gazed up at him for a moment. 'It's lovely. Much too lovely.'

'It's only what you deserve. You've been going without pretty things for much too long. I'm just glad I can finally do something about it.'

She ran the tips of her fingers over the silk.

'Don't I get to see you in it?'

She gave him a mock serious look. 'I think you might have to wait.'

'It's a pity,' he said, laughing again, 'but I guess you're right. We need to get going if we want to get anything to eat tonight.'

The bathroom door closed behind him. Sam finished doing her hair and make-up and then tried on the delicately embroidered underwear. It fitted her like a glove and the fabric felt light and sensuous against her skin. After months of wearing nothing but khaki, it was a pleasure to put on something so beautiful and so feminine. She carefully pulled on her stockings and stepped into the high-heeled shoes, then slipped on her dress

She was struggling to pull the back zip all the way up when the bathroom door opened and Jack reappeared. He'd freshened up and was fully dressed in his uniform once more. He saw her struggling and came across the room to help her.

'Allow me,' he said, moving behind her.

He pulled the zip easily into place. Sam straightened the dress with the palms of her hands and then turned around to face him.

'Thank you,' she smiled.

'You're welcome.'

'I can't remember when I last had so many new things.'

'You should have everything that money can buy. When all of this is over, I intend on spoiling you in every way I can.'

'Let's just enjoy tonight, shall we?' she said faintly, unable to allow herself to hope for anything more. The war was still far from over and anything could happen before it finally came to an end.

He stood behind her and helped her on with her coat. 'We should have fixed you up with something a little nicer than this,' he said, drawing her around to face him. He carefully fastened up each of the buttons and then tied the belt around her waist. He lifted the collar, then paused for a moment, and stroked the rough fabric beneath his thumbs. 'Still, I kind of like you in this,' he said playfully. 'I'll be the only one who knows what's underneath.'

Outside the hotel, the sun had set and the night was very cold. The pavements were full of soldiers and the atmosphere seemed to be brimming with excitement. Sam linked her arm through Jack's and they passed along the cobbled streets, following the direction of the crowd.

They came into the main town square, passing cafés and bars that were already crowded with revellers, and turned into an alleyway. Music seeped out through a doorway and there was the sign of a restaurant above it.

'One of the guys told me about this place,' said Jack. 'He said it was good.'

They went in through the entrance and climbed a narrow flight of stairs, going through another door into a burst of light. They came into a warm and smoky restaurant that was panelled in wood, with faded yellow walls above a dado rail. Men in uniform and a scattering of women sat at plain wooden tables and a low babble of English, Dutch and French filled the room. High, circular stools stood in front of a well-stocked bar and a dark-haired woman of about forty was draped against a battered piano, singing mournfully in French.

They were seated at an empty table and a waiter, dressed almost completely in black apart from the small white apron that was stretched around his waist, came over to take their order. His English was perfect and Sam wondered briefly if he'd spoken German equally well to his customers before the liberation. But perhaps she was being unfair. He could easily have been a member of the Belgian Resistance.

When the food arrived they ate hungrily, famished after their long day. They shared a bottle of wine, sipping it slowly and listening to the music.

The last bars of a song faded away and was followed by muted applause from the audience. The singer said something to the pianist and then sauntered over to the bar and sat down on one of the circular stools. A man with a moustache offered her a cigarette. He lit it for her and she began smoking lazily.

Sam noticed an American sergeant at the table next to theirs. He'd been sitting and drinking with his friends, but now she saw him getting to his feet. He stubbed out his cigarette in the ashtray on the table in front of him, then strolled over to the corner of the room that held the piano. The pianist vacated his seat, allowing the sergeant to sit down. Pushing back the sleeves of his jacket, he ran his fingers expertly along the keys. People turned their heads to look at him, and a murmur of approval rippled around the room.

Jack's gaze met Sam's through the soft candlelight that flickered in the middle of their table.

'I'd love to hear you sing again,' he murmured.

Jack watched as Sam made her way across the restaurant towards the piano, her hips swaying as she negotiated the uneven floorboards in her high-heeled shoes. He'd been across and spoken to the sergeant, who'd consented to his request to let Sam sing in a soft, southern drawl.

The song she had chosen was *A Nightingale Sang in Berkeley Square*, and her lovely voice moved effortlessly through it. She seemed to have come alive in the few short hours he'd been with her since that morning, and he'd have given anything to stay with her, keeping her happy and safe. But it just wasn't possible. Tomorrow morning he would have to take her back to the hospital and then report back to his unit. The war still needed to be won and nobody could be certain of what lay ahead of them.

Jack picked up his glass and drained the last of his wine, then set the glass back down on the table.

25. PARTING

Sam stood close to the hotel window, looking out over the skyline of the city. The night was clear and the sky was bright with stars.

She heard the click of the door as Jack pushed it to, and the sound of his footfalls as he crossed the room. He slid his arms gently around her waist and she felt the warmth of his body against hers as he drew her against him. She turned her head a little, so that her forehead pressed lightly against his jaw, then closed her eyes.

When she woke the next morning, Sam found herself still lying in the loose circle of Jack's arms. Careful not to disturb him, she rolled slowly onto her back and looked up at the elaborately carved ceiling above her. Her body ached, but it was a sweet, glorious ache and she had no regrets. Being with Jack again had made her feel completely alive.

She turned her head and her eyes travelled down over his body, admiring the smooth olive tones of his skin in the soft morning light. She knew he must be exhausted and she didn't want to wake him. She wondered how many nights he'd spent in the open during his long months of fighting, exposed to the cold night air. At times, it had been frightening for her at the field hospital in Normandy, and they'd sometimes come within the range of enemy fire. But compared to what Jack and the other men on the battlefields had been through, it was nothing. She could only try to imagine what it had been like for them, fighting their way across Europe, hedgerow by hedgerow, field by field and street by street.

As she gazed at Jack and thought about everything he'd been through, Sam's eyes grew soft. She slowly lifted her hand, reaching out and touching his chest with the tips of her fingers.

Jack opened his eyes and caught Sam's wrist in his hand. For a fraction of a second he wondered where he was, but then, remembering, he rolled over and pulled her into his arms.

'Good morning,' he whispered. 'Did you sleep well?'

He pulled her a little closer, remembering the night before and the unimaginable pleasure of being with her again. It felt good to be there, on that soft, comfortable bed, with her warm body nestled next to his. A world away from the long nights he'd spent outside on the frozen ground during months of hard, relentless fighting.

He glanced half-heartedly at the clock by the side of the bed. He knew that they had to get up. He had to take her back to the hospital and get back to the camp before he was declared AWOL.

'Sam,' he said, putting his lips against her hair.

'Umm…' she murmured, pressing herself even closer against him.

He groaned inwardly.

'I'm sorry, Sam, but we need to get up. I've got to get you back to the hospital.'

She stirred again, raising her head to look at his face. She lifted a hand and traced the tips of her fingers across his jaw. She kissed him lightly on the lips, then smiled sadly.

'I suppose you're right.'

She rose gracefully from the bed, pulling a sheet around her body to hide her nakedness, and Jack eased himself up onto his elbows to watch her. The crisp white sheet was draped tantalisingly over her feminine curves, revealing only the pale skin of her arms and back, and her hair tumbled to her shoulders. Watching her was like an exquisite torture, a memory that he knew would stay with him throughout the long and lonely nights that still lay ahead of him.

She paused by the bathroom door, glancing back at him and smiling sweetly, then vanished through the doorway, gently closing the door behind her.

It was Jack's idea that they have breakfast at the café just opposite their hotel. They sat at a little table next to a window, drinking coffee and eating waffles with syrup, watching the people wrapped up against the cold passing along the frosty street outside. It was still very early and the winter sun was low in the sky.

'There's something I need to talk to you about,' said Jack, when they'd finished eating. 'Something important.'

Sam watched as he pushed their plates to one side and then drew a small, green, gilt-edged box from the inside pocket of his jacket. Her heart gave a little leap. He opened the lid and she saw the ring. It was a simple gold band set with an emerald and two diamonds.

'What do you think?' he said. 'Do you like it?'

She looked up and met his gaze. 'It's beautiful,' she whispered.

'I know it's a lot to ask of you. I still don't know if I'm going to get out of this thing alive. But supposing I'm lucky, supposing I do...' He leaned forward and took her hands in his. 'I think you know by now that if I come out of this in one piece, then you're the woman I want to spend the rest of my life with. Will you marry me, Sam?'

Her expression stilled and it was a moment before she was sure that she'd really caught his meaning.

His brow furrowed. 'Sam?'

'Yes,' she said, the words coming tumbling out at last. 'Yes, of course I'll marry you.'

He took the ring from the box and slipped it onto her ring finger. 'I know it isn't much, but it was the best I could do yesterday. One day I'll get you something much better, I promise.'

'It's perfect. It's the most beautiful ring I've ever seen.'

'You really like it?'

'I love it,' she said, quite unable to hide her joy.

'I don't know how long it's going to be before I see you again. Are you sure you can wait?'

'Yes, Jack, I'm quite sure,' she laughed.

Satisfied, he smiled and nodded, but she noted with pleasure the fleeting look of relief that ran through his eyes.

They only had a short time left before they had to leave, and they spent it talking over the practicalities of their engagement. Sam explained that she wasn't intending to return to Hampshire to live with her aunt when the war finally ended, and she wrote down her parents' address in Hertfordshire on the back of a scrap of paper that the waiter found for them.

Jack lifted the flap of his jacket pocket and slipped the paper inside. 'Don't worry,' he told her seriously, 'I'll find you, wherever you are.'

An hour later, they drew up on the forecourt in front of the hospital. It was very cold and the sleet was beginning to turn to light snow. Jack cut the engine, then jumped down from the Jeep and leaned in to pick up Sam's kitbag from behind his seat. He hitched the kitbag onto his shoulder, then circled round the back of the Jeep to the passenger side, putting his hand beneath Sam's elbow to help her down

He held her in his arms, his cheek against the top of her head, feeling the warmth coming from her body and inhaling the light, familiar scent of her skin and hair. He thought grimly of everything they still had to overcome before they could be together again. There was the war to get through, and even afterwards there would be hurdles and heartache to face.

Dragging his thoughts in order, he pressed his lips against her forehead. He would do everything in his power to make their relationship work if he was lucky enough to survive. In the meantime, all he had to do was stay alive.

'I'm sorry,' he murmured against her hair. 'I don't want to leave you, but I have to go.'

Sam stared numbly after the Jeep as Jack manoeuvred it in a wide arch and then accelerated away along the drive.

She'd held back her tears as they'd said their final farewell, not wanting him to see her cry, but now they came freely, rolling silently down her flushed cheeks as she watched the Jeep disappear out of sight. She hoisted the kitbag over her shoulder and trudged up the steps, pushing through the doors and into the warmth of the hallway.

The hospital was busy as usual, with doctors and nurses and orderlies all going about their daily routines. A soldier went by on a trolley pushed by a porter and Sister MacDonald came up behind them.

'Is everything all right, Nurse Mitchell?' she asked, seeing Sam by the doorway and pausing to speak to her.

'Yes, Sister,' said Sam, giving her a watery smile.

'Don't cry, dear,' said Sister MacDonald kindly. She fished in her pocket and pressed a clean white handkerchief into Sam's hand. 'Come and sit in my office for a moment.'

Sam followed her across the hallway. Inside the office, a makeshift desk almost filled the whitewashed room. Sister MacDonald sat down behind the desk and Sam perched on the wooden chair in front of it.

'Didn't you have a very good time?'

Sam dabbed the handkerchief at the corners of her eyes and smiled a crooked smile. 'Actually, it was wonderful.'

Sister MacDonald studied her thoughtfully. 'I expect you're wondering why I let you go with him.'

Sam looked at her and nodded. 'Yes,' she said, after a moment. 'Yes, I suppose I did find it rather strange.'

'Well, you see, dear, I wasn't always the old spinster you see now. I know what it's like to be young and in love.'

Sam gazed at her, thinking that it was hard to imagine such an efficient, matter-of-fact woman as Sister MacDonald ever having been like that.

'I was a young nurse stationed in Belgium once, just as you are now. I was here during the last war, and I too fell in love with an army officer. He was a captain, just like your American.' A distant look came into her eyes and for a brief moment Sam thought she caught a glimpse of the passion she'd felt all those years before, 'Sadly,' she said, her voice faltering just a little, 'he was killed at the battle of Passchendaele in 1917.' She looked at Sam again and her expression changed. Her back straightened and she shuffled one of the piles of papers stacked in front of her on the desk.

26. PEACE

It took a day to travel through Belgium and cross the Channel and Sam arrived in Dover in the early hours of a damp June morning.

The train to London was packed with soldiers and sailors and service personnel returning from Europe and she watched the platform pull away from her from a crowded compartment at the back of the train. The journey was slow and uncomfortable but the mood was good and no one seemed to mind. Sam settled back in her seat and watched the dull green countryside unfolding outside the window beneath a murky sky, secure in the knowledge that every bump and jolt of the train was taking her closer to home.

It was well over a month since the Germans had surrendered and the war in Europe had finally come to an end. Sam remembered the overwhelming feeling of relief she'd felt on the day that the news had reached them. At first she hadn't quite been able to believe that there was to be no more shooting or killing, and no more bombs. But the beds of the hospital had gradually emptied and she'd come to accept that peace had really come at last.

By the time she reached London the rain had stopped, but the day was still damp and grey. From the windows of her taxi she watched men in drab demob suits and women in utilitarian clothing and low-heeled shoes passing along the pavements of the bombed out streets. The taxi driver caught her eye in the rear view mirror and began to talk, pointing out landmarks that had been lost and buildings that were under repair. She let his words wash over her, nodding occasionally, or smiling her assent. He was proud, she thought, and he had every right to be. The air-raids were over and London had survived.

The taxi worked its way northwards and she asked the driver to set her down outside a café near Liverpool Street Station. She ate a lunch of boiled meat and vegetables, and then walked the rest of the way to the station where she caught a train bound for Hertfordshire in the middle of the afternoon. She fell asleep on the train but the guard woke her brusquely before she missed her stop.

The platform was empty. She'd written to her parents to let them know that she was coming, but she supposed that the letter might not have arrived. She walked out of the station, pausing briefly on the threshold just as the sun burst forth from behind the departing cloud. The road curved away from the village and she began to walk the half-mile towards home.

Sam stood at the bottom of the drive looking up at the house. Rambling roses drooped over the high walls on either side of the gated entrance. The air was filled with their perfume and there were petals at her feet.

Apart from the weathered paintwork around its windows, the house was just as she remembered it. Red-brick and ivy-clad, it stood at an oblique angle at the top of a gently sloping incline, so that the windows along its side had a view down the drive. A long garden was laid to lawn in front of the house, but from where she was standing it was almost entirely hidden from view by a long screen of glossy-leaved rhododendron bushes.

Sam could see her father's small black Austin parked on the turning circle in front of the house. She knew that he would be somewhere inside, preparing to go down to his surgery to see his evening patients.

She went forward through the open gate and began walking towards the house. Through the study window that overlooked the drive, she caught sight of a man in a tweed jacket pottering about in front of a desk laden with papers. He had his back towards her, but she recognised at once the tall, well-built figure of her father. Seeing him there, after so many months, brought a lump to her throat and she felt the tears pricking at her eyes.

Her mother appeared round the corner of the house, wearing a wide-brimmed summer hat and gardening clothes. She looked up and saw Sam, and stopped abruptly. The battered wooden trug she was carrying slid to the ground and she called into the house through an open window. Her father lowered the paper he was reading and lifted his head. He came across the room and signalled to Sam through the glass. She waved back at him, then ran the remainder of the way up the drive.

Sam slept well after her long, exhausting day of travelling. She woke up early the following morning, feeling refreshed. She pulled open the faded pink curtains that hung at the tall sash window of her bedroom and looked out over the garden and the rolling green countryside beyond. The sky was blue, almost cloudless, and everywhere looked peaceful.

She straightened the curtains and moved away from the window, wandering across the room. She ran her hand slowly along the end of her big brass bedstead and then sat down on the edge of the mattress. The bed had once belonged to her grandparents, but it had been hers since her grandmother had passed away when she had just turned fifteen. The brass was slightly tarnished now, but the mattress on the bed was high and springy.

She perched on the bed, examining the room, thinking how incredibly familiar everything seemed, yet at the same time how utterly strange. The mahogany dressing table in front of the window was another family heirloom and the few cosmetics and brushes she still possessed were arranged neatly across it. A small set of bookshelves held books and photograph albums saved from her childhood. Jutting out at the end of a shelf was the spine of a leather diary that she'd once kept at school. Three pale watercolours depicting oriental women dressed in kimonos lined the wall above the bookshelves, and she could still vividly recall the pre-war shopping trip to London with her mother when she'd chosen them.

A lamp with a pink tasselled shade sat on the small table next to the bed and next to it was a photograph of Sam and her sisters, taken years before. She picked it up and leaned back on the bed, holding it out at arm's length to study it. It had been taken in a studio. Sam was on the left of the picture, dressed in her school uniform, Penny was seated on a high-backed wooden chair in the middle, and Grace, who looked to have been about ten years old at the time, was standing at her shoulder, her fair hair in pigtails and her face freckled by the sun. They were all smiling towards the camera.

Sam traced her fingertips over the glass in front of the photograph, thinking how carefree and innocent they all looked, and how much the war had changed things for them all. Penny had joined the Wrens, then married a young British army officer after a whirlwind romance and gone with him when he'd been posted to Scotland in the spring. Grace, meanwhile, was seventeen now and in her last year at school. Sam had expected to find her at home for the holidays but instead she was away in Cornwall, staying with the family of her best friend, and it wasn't certain when she would be home. Sam's forehead creased. Even if Grace had been at home, she reflected sadly, it had been so long since they'd last met, they would have hardly known one another.

She heard her parents moving about in the room next to hers and sat up slowly and placed the photograph back on the bedside table. She eased herself up off the mattress and went across to her dressing table and sat down on the stool in front of it. Her velvet-covered jewellery box looked worn and faded. She carefully lifted its lid and drew out the ring she'd placed there the evening before. She held it for a moment in the palm of her hand and then slipped it onto her finger. She gazed at it for another moment, then picked up one of the polished silver brushes that lay on the table and began brushing her hair in the mirror above.

There was a small terrace off the back of the house and Sam and her parents had breakfast there in the sunshine. The air was heavy with the perfume of roses and the grass was still coated with a fine layer of morning dew. There were eggs from the hens Elizabeth now kept at the bottom of the garden, along with coffee and toast.

They talked all through breakfast. Sam's father, William, said that although the war in Europe had ended, rationing was affecting people harder than ever. He was touched by the way his patients still insisted on giving him gifts of food. Elizabeth explained that Mrs Jackson, the housekeeper, had been given the day off to go and visit her son, Robbie, who was convalescing in a sanatorium near St Albans. He'd been badly wounded in Italy but it was hoped that it wouldn't be too long before he'd be able to come home.

They were finishing their coffee when the telephone rang. William pushed back his chair and went inside to answer it. Sam heard the low rise and fall of his voice from the hallway, followed by the click of the receiver.

He came back outside. 'I'm sorry, Sam,' he said. 'I was hoping to either cancel my appointments or ask Dr Fraser to take them for me and spend the morning here with you, but something's come up, I'm afraid. Rather an emergency, I think.'

'Please don't worry, Daddy. I quite understand. Actually, I was wondering if I could be any help to you myself, at the surgery. I haven't got any plans and it looks as if I'm going to be at a loose end for a while.'

He smiled at her fondly. 'I think you've earned a bit of a rest, don't you? Take it easy for a while and try to catch up with some of your friends.' He touched Elizabeth's shoulder and bent to kiss her on the cheek. 'I'm sorry, darling, but I shan't be back for lunch.'

He left them sitting at the table together, eating their toast. Sam heard the sound of the Austin starting up and moving off down the drive. Then for a moment everything was quiet.

Her mother finished her coffee and folded her napkin. Glancing at Sam's hand, she remarked, 'That ring I see you're wearing, is it special? I'm sure that I didn't see you wearing it last night.'

Sam stretched out her fingers and looked at the ring. The weight of it did feel strange. 'I was wearing it on a chain around my neck, for safekeeping,' she explained. 'We weren't allowed to wear any jewellery when I was working, but now that I'm home I thought that I'd put it on.'

'But where did you get it? It isn't one that I've seen before. And you shouldn't wear it on that finger, you know, not unless you want people to think that you're engaged.'

There was a short silence.

'You aren't engaged, are you?'

Sam's cheeks flushed. 'Actually, Mother, there is something that I need to talk to you about.' She explained as briefly as possible how Jack had somehow managed to track her down at the hospital in Belgium. She told Elizabeth shyly that he'd asked her to marry him.

'But why didn't you write to us about any of this? You never mentioned anything in any of your letters.'

'I didn't want to worry you; everything seemed so uncertain. I thought it would be better to wait until I got home.' She drew in her chin. 'I do love him, Mother. Very much.'

For a second Elizabeth didn't answer, but then she said, 'You know that all I want is for you to be happy, but you're very young to be so certain.'

'I'm twenty-three,' said Sam softly. 'That really isn't so young. Penny's only just turned twenty and she's already married. Besides, you were only nineteen yourself when you married Daddy.'

'But that was very different. I'd known him since we were children. You know that your grandparents had all been friends for many years before that.'

'Things are different now, Mother. The war's changed everything.'

Elizabeth pursed her lips. 'Has it really, do you think? Once you start seeing a few people I think you'll see that everything is getting back to normal now and things aren't really so very different to the way they were before.' She paused, then added, 'And you do realise that this really isn't the correct way of doing things, don't you?'

'Yes, I do know that. I'm sorry that you and Daddy haven't been introduced to Jack yet, but I'm sure that you'll like him when you meet him.'

Neither of them spoke for a moment.

'You say that all of this happened in February?' said Elizabeth.

'Yes, that's right.'

'And have you seen him since?'

'No, but he's written me letters.'

Elizabeth frowned. 'I see. And how long is it since you last got one?'

'It has been a little while,' admitted Sam. 'The last one arrived at the hospital just after VE Day.'

'But that's almost six weeks ago now!'

'That doesn't mean anything. You know how erratic the post can be. Sometimes it takes a long time for his letters to reach me, and when they do come they all arrive at once.'

'Darling, I don't mean to be unkind, but are you sure that he's going to come back here for you, now that the war is almost over? He was probably lonely while he was stationed here and needed some company. Don't you think that he'll go back to America now and marry one of his own people?'

Sam's stomach fluttered. Her mother's words were unbearably close to thoughts that had been nagging at the back of her mind over the past few weeks, and she didn't want to hear them. Now that the war in Europe had ended, Jack's thoughts would naturally turn to his home and to the family and friends he'd left behind before he'd ever met her. Perhaps he would never come for her and what would she do then? She bit her lip and didn't say anything. She spread out her fingers and looked down at the ring again.

'I'm sorry if I've upset you,' murmured Elizabeth.

Sam glanced up at her. 'Do you think that Daddy noticed my ring?' she asked quietly.

'Not yet, I don't think. But I'm sure that he will do if you keep on wearing it. Why don't you put it back on the chain around your neck? You don't want to upset him, do you? If your captain comes, he can ask your father's permission properly. In the meantime you can stay here quietly and get some rest. You do look rather tired and thin and I'm sure that you wouldn't want any man seeing you like that.' Elizabeth picked up the pot of coffee sitting on the table between them and poured Sam another cup. 'After breakfast, I'll take you down to look at the garden,' she said brightly. 'The delphiniums are doing wonderfully well.'

The weather continued to be good for the next few days and Sam began to settle down into her new routines. In spite of her concerns about the future, she was determined to be strong and not to give in to self-pity. She wore her ring on the chain around her neck, so as not to upset her mother, and kept her feelings for Jack to herself. The war still wasn't over. The fighting continued in the Pacific and she reminded herself every day to be grateful that Jack was still in Germany, where peace now reigned.

She continued to rise early, as she had done in her nursing days, and spent the mornings pottering in the garden with her mother, helping in the large vegetable plot next to the hen house at the bottom of the garden, or tending the flowerbeds Elizabeth had somehow managed to keep going in spite of the war. The June borders looked magnificent, the tall, delicate heads of the delphiniums rising gracefully above the mass of pink, white and blue petals of the plants below.

In the afternoons, Sam liked to go off on walks by herself. She went along pathways that wound through wooded hills and across fields of tawny-coloured crops. Everything seemed incredibly quiet and peaceful, and she gradually found herself beginning to unwind.

She arrived home after a long walk one such afternoon to see a red two-seater sports car parked in front of the house. The French windows to the west-facing sitting room stood open. She felt a thrill of hope and hurried forward, stepping through the windows and going into the house.

Inside, she found a man standing with his back towards her, looking up at the painting that hung over the mantelpiece of the fireplace. Hearing her footsteps, he turned around. It was Julian Pennington. He'd exchanged his uniform for a pair of light flannel trousers and an open-necked shirt, but apart from the clothes he was wearing, he hardly seemed to have changed at all.

'Sam, my dear,' he said, his face breaking into a smile. 'How very good it is to see you.'

'Julian,' she said, working hard to contain the disappointment she was feeling. 'How nice to see you, too.'

The door to the living room opened and her mother came through carrying a tea tray.

'Allow me,' said Julian, taking a step towards her

'It's quite all right, thank you, Julian,' said Elizabeth. 'I can manage quite well.' She set the tray down on the low table in front of the sofa and then motioned for them to sit down. She handed out the tea things. 'Would you excuse me for a few minutes?' she asked, her gaze flitting between them. 'Mrs Jackson wants to speak to me about something, but it shouldn't take long.'

A moment later she was gone. Sam took a sip of her tea and turned to Julian. 'It really is very nice to see you,' she said, her composure completely regained. 'Have you seen anything of Robert recently?'

'I caught up with him in London a few weeks ago. He seemed to be in very good spirits.'

'Is he? I'm so glad to hear it. It's over a year since I last saw him. I haven't seen Diana for ages either, but I've spoken to her on the telephone since I got home. She says little Peter is doing well.'

'How old is he now?'

'About six months, I think.'

Julian regarded her thoughtfully for a moment. 'It's a good time to be starting a family,' he remarked.

He was looking at her with an odd expression and Sam wondered at its meaning. It was a very long time since she'd last seen him, she thought, and surely he must have met someone else whilst she'd been away. He couldn't possibly be still hoping for anything from her.

She smiled at him pleasantly. 'Have you any plans, now that the war is over?'

'Well, father's getting on, of course, and there's the estate to run, but I thought I'd take a break until the end of the summer before I make a start with that.'

'Will you be going to the coast?' She remembered Julian once telling her that his family had a cottage in Norfolk.

'Possibly.' His gaze was fixed on her face, as if he were trying to gauge her reaction. 'It all depends how things go.'

'Well, I hope you have a lovely time whatever you decide to do,' she said smoothly. 'I'm sure you deserve a rest.'

'As I'm sure you do, too,' he smiled. 'How long is it that you've been home? Just a week or so, isn't it?'

'It'll be two weeks tomorrow.'

'I expect it's all taking a bit of getting used to.'

'It is rather,' she admitted. 'I've been taking orders and been busy for so long, it seems very strange to be at home again without very much to do.'

'You've just got to give it a little time.'

'That's exactly what my mother says.'

He nodded. 'She's right, you know. You deserve a break after everything I hear you've been through. I'm sure there aren't many other girls who have done as much as you have over these past few years.'

'Everyone has had to do their bit.'

'Yes, but I don't know of any other girls who came quite so close to the fighting.'

'Perhaps not, but I felt it was my duty to go.'

He didn't respond, but he continued looking at her curiously. Sam lowered her gaze and took a sip of her tea, then glanced out through the window. The evening shadows were lengthening outside.

She heard the sound of the door to the living room opening. Her mother peered in for a moment, then stepped through the doorway. Julian's teacup rattled as he put it down on the table in front of them and got to his feet as Elizabeth entered the room.

'I'm so sorry to have deserted you both, but Mrs Jackson delayed me for longer than I was expecting,' said Elizabeth. 'I hope you two have been all right without me.' She shot Sam a swift, meaningful glance.

'Sam has been delightful company,' said Julian gallantly. He glanced at the clock on the mantelpiece. 'However, I'd better start making tracks as I do have rather a pressing engagement this evening with one of the chaps I used to fly with.'

'What a shame,' said Elizabeth, sounding disappointed. 'But you will call on us again soon, won't you, Julian?' she added, quickly gathering herself and mustering a smile. 'It's so good to have you young people home again.'

Julian nodded. 'Yes, of course, Mrs Mitchell. It would be my pleasure.'

Outside, the front of the house lay in shadows. Sam stood with Julian next to the car. He drew out a cigarette and struck a match to light it, then drew on it briefly. 'It's been marvellous to see you again, Sam,' he told her. 'I'm so glad that you're home again, safe and sound.' Exhaling a thin plume of smoke, he pulled open the driver's door. 'I'll drop by again tomorrow and take you out for a spin, if you'd like.'

Sam smiled faintly. 'Goodbye, Julian,' she said.

She watched him get into the car and close the door. The engine roared into life and he sped away down the drive.

27. RETURN

The hotel bedroom was simply furnished. There was a narrow metal bed, a wooden chair and table, a wardrobe and a small chest of drawers. Jack laid his kitbag on the table, then took off the jacket of his uniform and hung it over the back of the chair. The room was small and stuffy and he prised open the window a few inches to let in some air. Outside, the street-lamps glowed and the sky was studded with stars. He looked out at the street for a moment then closed the curtains that hung limply from a thin wooden rail.

Jack sat down on the bed and the mattress groaned beneath him. He knew that he was in for an uncomfortable night, but he doubted whether there was anywhere now that he wouldn't be able to sleep. He pulled off his boots and unbuttoned his shirt, then lay back and listened to the sounds drifting in from the night. He heard the light sound of a woman's laughter and a well-bred English voice hailing a cab, followed by the low rumble of a double-decker bus passing by along the street below.

He had arrived in London late that afternoon, after travelling up by train from Dover. The familiar countryside had gradually unfurled through the window of his compartment, punctuated now and then by tranquil villages with pubs and teashops and low thatched cottages.

It felt good to be back in England again after so many long months on mainland Europe constantly on the move, but he knew that he wasn't going to be there for long. The CO had granted him a seven-day pass and once that was up he would be obliged to return to Germany. There was no telling how long it might be before he eventually got shipped back to the States. He might even get sent to the Pacific, where the war raged on and there was still no sign of a Japanese surrender. But for the moment all of that lay in the future and the war seemed far away. He had a week of freedom and, if everything worked out as he hoped, tomorrow he would see Sam again.

It was almost five months since he'd last seen her, but the agony of their parting still echoed in his mind. The memory of the brief hours they'd spent together in Brussels had sustained him as his unit had moved eastwards with the rest of the Allied forces. He'd been camped in a field in southern Germany the night victory in Europe finally came. He remembered the smell of the earth as he'd stretched out on the cool grass and gazed up into the night sky, watching shells exploding like fireworks in the darkness, in celebration of the peace that had come at last

Jack rolled over on the bed and picked up his watch from the table. In just a few short hours he would be with Sam. He'd written her a brief letter from Germany to let her know that he was coming, but he knew he himself would probably arrive long before it did. He imagined her surprise when she saw him again. She was living with her parents now, so things might be a little awkward at first, but he prided himself that he'd soon be able to win their trust and approval. All it would take was a little time.

Jack noticed the deep scent of roses as he stood for a moment at the foot of the driveway, looking up at the house. It was a substantial, well-proportioned building, with dark patches of ivy clinging to its walls. Mature trees surrounded what looked to be a large garden, but his view of it was obscured by a row of glossy-leaved bushes to his left.

The afternoon sunshine glinted off the two cars that were parked at the top of the drive, a small red sports car and a little black Austin. The sight of the sports car surprised him. It was a young man's car, and it struck him as a little unexpected to see it parked outside the home of a middle-aged couple and their three daughters. Thinking it over, he guessed it must belong to the boyfriend of one of Sam's sisters.

Jack went forward through the open gate and started up the driveway. His view of the garden opened up and he saw the table spread with tea things that had been laid out on the lawn. Two figures stood next to it. A man and a woman. Time froze for a moment and Jack felt his heart lurch, as if all the air had been punched from his lungs.

The couple before him were locked in a passionate embrace. He could only see the woman from behind and the man's hands cupped her head as he kissed her. She was wearing a pale blue dress that fluttered lightly in the afternoon breeze, her head was tilted back and her hair fell loosely around her shoulders. Jack knew at once that the woman was Sam.

He felt too stunned, for a moment, even to move. Still reeling, he took a step backwards so that he was once again hidden from view. He glanced up at the house. As far as he could tell, he hadn't been seen. He considered his options for a moment, then turned around on the driveway and began heading back in the direction he had come.

For a few seconds Sam was overcome by the sheer force of his kiss, but then a surge of indignation rose up inside her. She struggled free of his grasp and stepped away from him, angrily batting away his hands as he reached for her again.

'Julian!'

He stepped backwards and she saw his brief look of confusion and surprise. She realised that he'd been expecting a completely different reaction.

She flushed deeply. 'Julian, I'm sorry if I've in any way misled you, but my feelings for you... Well, they really aren't what you seem to think they are.'

It took him a moment to gather himself, but then he said calmly, 'I'm sorry. I should have given you more time.'

The ease with which he composed himself only served to infuriate Sam further. 'Really, I can assure you that it isn't a question of time. There's something that I should have told you before. I only didn't because I promised Mother that I wouldn't. You see, the fact is I'm engaged.'

He regarded her coolly. 'To that American, I suppose.'

'Yes, that's right. To Jack.'

He nodded, but he showed no emotion. There was a moment's silence and then he gestured with his chin to her hand. 'I see you aren't wearing a ring.'

'Well, no, I'm not, but you see he hasn't spoken to my father yet...' she trailed off, her cheeks burning.

Julian's face grew thoughtful. He drew a slim cigarette case from the pocket of his jacket, took out a cigarette and tapped it on the case. 'So you're saying it's nothing official.'

Sam lifted her chin. 'Nevertheless, I am engaged.'

Julian struck a match and lit the cigarette, drew on it and began to smoke. He smiled faintly. 'What would you say if I told you that I was thinking of asking to marry you myself?'

'But we hardly know one another!'

'Oh, come now, we know enough, don't you think? You're a very beautiful woman and from the moment I saw you at Robert and Diana's wedding I knew that we might have a future. Everything about us fits. We know the same people and I'm sure that if you were to give it some time you'd see how much we make sense together. It's all a question of background.'

'And what about love?' she blurted. 'Doesn't that come into it?'

'That would come in time. I'm sure you must realise that I'd make you a very good husband. I'd look after you, and I'd do it very well.'

She shook her head. 'I'm sorry, Julian, but it just isn't enough.'

For a long moment his cool, grey eyes looked steadily into hers. Then he studied the tip of his cigarette. 'Are you really sure he's coming back?'

'I don't think you have any right to ask me that,' she answered, her eyes flashing with indignation.

'You don't think it's any of my business?'

'No, I don't.'

The sun went behind a cloud and there was a short, brittle silence.

He looked at her coolly again. 'I think that you're making a big mistake.'

'Perhaps I am. I like you, Julian, and I'd like us to remain friends, but I'm afraid that for me it can never go further than that.'

A muscle twitched in his cheek. He drew on his cigarette one last time, then ground it out in an ashtray on the table. He held out his hand. 'Goodbye, Sam,' he said, in a formal voice. 'I wish you luck.'

'Goodbye, Julian,' she replied stiffly.

They shook hands briefly and then he turned and left her. Sam's legs felt suddenly weak. She crossed the lawn a few paces to the garden table and sank down into one of the deep wicker chairs beside it.

She watched as Julian climbed in behind the steering wheel of his car, then accelerated away down the drive. As the dust settled behind it, her father emerged from the house. He put his hands to his hips and cast his gaze down the drive for a moment, then came down the garden towards her.

'I thought Julian left in rather a hurry,' he said, coming up to the table. 'Was there anything wrong?'

'No, nothing, Daddy. Nothing at all.'

'Are you sure, darling? You look a little upset.'

She bit her lip. 'Well, he did say that he was thinking about asking me to marry him.'

'That seems a strange way for a man to propose.'

He had raised an eyebrow, and Sam smiled weakly. 'Yes, it was rather.'

William folded his arms across his chest, looping his hands over the leather elbow patches on his tweed jacket. 'And do you love him?'

She shook her head.

'Well then, I don't think you should give it any more thought. Julian doesn't strike me as the type of man who would take these things to heart. He'll probably have forgotten all about it by tomorrow. And even if he were serious about it, it would be very wrong of you to marry a man you don't love.'

Her father was looking at her kindly and Sam felt comforted. 'Actually, Daddy, there's something I've meaning to tell you,' she began. She broke off and dipped her head, not quite sure how to explain.

'About that American, you mean?'

She lifted her head in surprise. 'Yes. Has Mother told you about him?'

'No, not exactly. But although she does her best to hide these things from me, I probably know more than I should. Is it really very serious?'

'He's asked me to marry him.'

'And you've accepted?'

Sam nodded. 'Yes. But I know that he'd want to speak to you first.'

'Before it becomes official, you mean?' he answered, sounding amused. 'I thought that the war had changed all that.'

Her brows lifted. 'So you mean you don't mind?'

'The only thing I mind about is your happiness. I don't want you to go away from us, of course, but after everything you've been through these past few years I think you've earned the right to choose who you love.'

Sam felt choked, suddenly, and her eyes blurred with tears.

William drew a handkerchief out of his jacket pocket and handed it to her. 'Don't worry so much, darling. If you follow your heart I'm sure that everything will work out for the best. For the moment, the only thing you can do is wait.'

Sam dabbed her eyes with the handkerchief. The sun came out from behind a puff of cloud and a bird hopped across the lawn.

Her father glanced at his watch. 'I'm sorry, but I have some work I need to finish. Are you coming back up to the house or shall I ask Mrs Jackson to bring you out more tea?'

'I think I'd rather stay here for a few minutes.'

He smiled. 'Well, it is a lovely afternoon.'

He leaned over and kissed her lightly on the top of her head, and then he left her.

Jack followed the dusty lane back towards the village. He rounded a bend and came to the gated opening of a field. Wheat shimmered in the summer sunshine, giving way to a hedgerow and a belt of trees in the distance, and leaves stirred in the afternoon breeze. He rested his arms on top of the gate. It was peaceful there, and he'd come to appreciate tranquillity.

Seeing Sam in the arms of another man, Jack had felt like he'd been punched in the stomach, but as he stood by the gate looking out over the field, gradually his head began to clear. She couldn't have been back in England much more than a month, he reasoned, not long enough for her to have formed any kind of meaningful relationship with another man. He hadn't seen her since February, it was true, but there'd never been anything in her letters, no hint to suggest that she might have met someone else. There had to be some sort of rational explanation for what he'd seen, and he knew that sooner or later he'd have to go back and find out.

A cloud passed in front of the sun and for a moment a shadow fell across the field, turning the wheat a dull gold. Jack mulled over what he'd seen. He thought of the tall, redbrick house, the garden with its borders full of flowers, even the table on the lawn set with tea things. It was the home to which everything about her seemed to belong. He suddenly felt acutely aware of something; something that had been nagging at the back of his mind from the very beginning. If things worked out and she came to the States, he would be taking her away from everything she'd ever known. Did he really have that right? England had been on its knees, it was true, but someday it would recover, and Sam could have a good life here, in the world she knew and loved.

The sound of a car rapidly approaching shook him out of his reverie. He heard it slow to take the bend and turned his head as it came into view. He recognised the red sports car he'd seen earlier, and realised that he knew the man at its wheel. For a brief moment Jack had a clear view of the expression of anger on his rival's face, then the car accelerated away, leaving a billowing cloud of dust in its wake. Understanding dawned and a slow smile spread out across Jack's face.

Sam undid the chain around her neck, then slid off the ring and held it in the palm of her hand for a moment, before slipping it carefully on to her finger. It seemed to her, when she thought about it later, that it was as if in doing so she had somehow cast a spell, for when she raised her head again, Jack had appeared.

He was looking back at her from where he was standing, at the top of the drive. She gave a little gasp and sprang up from the chair, darting across the lawn towards him.

The hands that cupped her face were soldier's hands, roughened and hardened by the war. But it was a touch she had dreamed of night after night and her skin tingled with pleasure at the feel of it. He looked down searchingly into her eyes and then his mouth was hard on hers. His hands moved over her, tangling in her hair and then pulling her close, and his every move seemed wonderfully, achingly familiar.

They slowly withdrew from their embrace, then walked hand in hand across the drive and in through the open front door of the house.

28. A PICNIC

They were following a pathway that skirted the top of a field and then descended through a wood. Jack carried the basket of food she'd prepared, and Sam walked in front of him carrying a large, rolled up tartan rug. The brambles that edged the path reached up to her waist and she picked her way carefully along.

After they'd been going for a few minutes, the ground levelled out and the pathway opened up into a clearing that was dappled in sunlight. Sam spread out the rug on the grass and Jack set down the basket. He lay down on the rug, then pulled at his tie and closed his eyes. She regarded him lovingly for a moment. He had spoken to her father about marrying her the evening before and he had given them his blessing, and even her mother had seemed to like him. It was months since she had felt so happy.

She knelt in front of the basket and lifted its lid. There were two apples, a couple of hard-boiled eggs and a few sandwiches. Her brows knitted together. It wasn't much. She turned her head to look at Jack again.

'Would you like anything to eat?'

Jack's eyes opened and he shook his head, but a faint smile played about his lips. He reached out and caught her wrist with his hand, drawing her down next to him on the rug. Being careful not to crush her, he raised himself up onto his knees and straddled her body.

He looked down into her eyes for a long moment, then bent his head and kissed her gently on the mouth. His hair brushed her cheek as his lips moved softly down her jaw line to her neck. As he did so, he slid his hand beneath her dress. His touch was warm and strong as he ran it slowly along her naked thigh and Sam's heart began to beat more quickly.

Abruptly, Jack's body stilled. His hand stopped and he eased away from her. For a short second, she saw the conflict raging in his eyes, and then he rolled away from her, onto his back.

Sam lay still for a moment, bewildered. She sat up on her elbow and looked down into his face. 'What is it Jack? Is there something wrong?'

'I'm sorry,' he answered gruffly, turning his head to meet her gaze. 'If we'd carried on like that, there's no way I could have stopped.'

His voice quivered with restraint and Sam gave a little nod. She wanted to reach out and touch him, but she didn't want to make it any harder for him than it already was. He turned his head and briefly looked up at the sky, then closed his eyes again. The leaves rustled in the undergrowth that edged the clearing. There was nobody about, but Sam could hear the noise of farm machinery humming in the distance.

'I wish there was somewhere we could go,' she said eventually.

Jack opened his eyes again. 'I know how you feel,' he murmured. 'A part of me wishes that too, very much.' Turning on the rug, he reached out and lightly caressed her arm. 'But I've met your parents now and I have your reputation to think of.'

He said it in a joking sort of way, but she could tell that he was serious. Her forehead furrowed and she eased herself up off her elbow.

'There's something I need to talk to you about,' he said. His tone had changed again and now his voice sounded serious. He sat up next to her, drawing his knees up in front of him and resting his arms against them. 'You see, it's like this…' He hesitated and his forehead creased. 'I know we settled things with your parents last night, but I don't think that we should get married. That is, not yet, at least.'

She stared at him and the colour went out of her face.

'Don't worry, I'm still crazy about you, you must know that.' He touched his hand to her cheek and smiled. 'But I've been thinking. The war isn't over yet and my unit might even be sent out to the Pacific, to fight the Japs. When this thing is finally over I want you to come to the States and see how you like it, before you commit yourself to spending a lifetime there with me. I want you to be my wife, but I also want to be sure that living so far from home is going to be right for you.'

Sam dropped her gaze. It took a moment for her to absorb what he was saying.

Jack's eyes were soft when she looked up at him again. 'You're going to be leaving behind so much,' he told her in a quiet voice. 'I see that now, in a way I probably should have seen before. You'll be thousands of miles away from your family and from everything you've ever known, and it won't be just a trip, it'll be forever.' He looked away into the distance. 'I'll be taking you away from everything that matters to you and I don't know if I have that right.'

'But you're what matters to me now,' she whispered.

He turned his head to look at her again. 'You don't know how glad it makes me feel to hear you say that.'

'And yet you really think we should wait?'

He nodded, his face still serious. 'Yes, I do. It'll be difficult, I know, but it'll be worth it, you'll see. And it shouldn't take too long. I'll book you a passage and send for you as soon as this is all over. The way things are going, it may be a lot less time than you think, and then we'll have our whole lives ahead of us.'

Sam smiled at him weakly. She didn't want to wait, but she also didn't want to force him into doing something that he didn't want to. She wondered for a moment if he were beginning to have misgivings about marrying her. But if he were, then why was he even there? After all, he didn't have to be; he could have waited until the war had ended and gone home directly from Germany, without even giving her a second thought. Their whole relationship seemed to have consisted of long periods of waiting punctuated by difficult goodbyes, but they weren't the only couple to have been affected that way by the war.

Sam drew her knees to her chin and wrapped her arms around them. 'Perhaps you're right,' she murmured, careful to hide the doubts that had been tumbling through her mind.

He brushed his hand lightly against her cheek. 'Everything will work out for the best, Sam,' he told her softly. 'It won't be long until we're together again, you'll see.'

Puffs of cloud scudded across the sky from the west. They sat quietly for a while, sharing the food from the hamper, then stretched out on the rug again, talking over the future and gazing up at the sky.

The shadows were lengthening across the grass when they finally got to their feet and brushed down their clothes. Sam shook out the rug and Jack helped her to fold it. She placed it carefully on top of the basket and then they left the clearing and started back along the pathway through the wood, retracing their steps the way they had come.

Elizabeth came flying out of the house when she saw them approaching through a window. 'Such wonderful news!' she called out breathlessly. 'The Japanese have surrendered and the war is finally over. Come inside and listen to the wireless. They've been talking about it all afternoon.'

Sam's gaze met Jack's. They exchanged an astonished glance and then he reached for her hand and they ran together up the drive.

29. WAITING

Sam stared at the grainy photograph on the front of the newspaper. It showed the image of a ship entering a harbour and she could just make out the smiles on the faces of the women who were standing on its deck and waving towards the shore. The Statue of Liberty rose up in the distance behind them.

She stood in front of the little kiosk for a moment, scanning the article beneath the picture, but then a whistle sounded and she looked up. The clock above the platform showed ten to twelve and if the train arrived on time she knew that she only had a few more minutes to wait. It was the beginning of February and outside the station London was bathed in weak winter sunshine, but the platform lay in shade and there was a chill wind blowing in along the track. Sam shivered beneath her coat and hugged herself to keep warm.

Ten minutes later, the train arrived, pulling up beside the platform with a loud hiss of steam. The doors sprang open and passengers began spilling out. Sam caught sight of Diana stepping down from a carriage near the back of the train. She saw her pause briefly to pull on her gloves, then lift her head to look along the platform. She spotted Sam straight away and lifted her arm to wave, and Sam started along the platform towards her

'How lovely it is to see you,' breathed Diana, smiling with pleasure.

She was smartly dressed in a tailored coat and her dark hair was elaborately coiled beneath a plum-coloured hat. She seemed more sophisticated than Sam remembered, but she was, after all, now a married woman with an eighteen-month-old son.

'It's lovely to see you, too,' murmured Sam.

They decided to have lunch in a restaurant Diana knew of, at the end of a small side street off Piccadilly. It was already starting to fill up when they arrived. Some of the upholstery looked rather shabby and faded, but the atmosphere was warm and welcoming. They sat down at a vacant table by the window and an elderly waiter handed them each a leather-bound menu. He returned a few minutes later to take their order.

As they waited for the food to arrive, they began catching up on some of their news. Sam's cousin, David, had been found barely alive in a Japanese camp for prisoners of war the previous autumn and they talked about how he was getting on at the sanatorium near Southampton, where he was still recuperating.

Robert and Diana had moved in with Leonora at The Elms. It wasn't ideal and they were looking for a house of their own, but Diana said that it was all working out surprisingly well. She showed Sam a photograph of baby Peter. 'He's gorgeous, even if he can be a little monkey sometimes,' she said, glowing with pleasure. 'He and Robert are keeping me very busy.'

Sam smiled at the photograph, glad to see how much Diana seemed to be enjoying being a wife and mother.

The food arrived and Diana tucked the photograph back inside her bag. They'd ordered beef with gravy and vegetables. The meal was a simple one, but it tasted good. After they'd eaten, the waiter cleared the table and they ordered a pot of tea.

'Have you heard anything lately from Jack?' asked Diana, when the waiter had left them.

Sam thought of the flimsy sheets of airmail paper covered in his careful, masculine handwriting that sat folded into envelopes in the drawer of her dressing table at home. She'd read the letters over countless times, until she knew virtually every word they contained.

'He still writes to me every week, and I spoke to him on the telephone at Christmas. He often sends us presents, usually parcels of food and toiletries or that sort of thing, but to be honest he doesn't say an awful lot about his feelings. It sometimes feels like very little to go on.'

'Men are never very good at expressing themselves in letters,' smiled Diana. 'You must remember what Robert was like.'

Sam's forehead puckered. 'When I look back, I don't remember him ever actually telling me that he loved me. He often said that he was crazy about me, but do you think that really amounts to the same thing?'

'I'm sure that he loves you. He obviously hasn't forgotten about you or he wouldn't keep writing to you, would he?'

'I suppose you're right, but it feels like we've been waiting for ages. I haven't seen him since last August and that's nearly six months ago now. It's much longer than either of us ever expected.'

Diana leaned forward and folded her arms across the edge of the table. There was a trace of concern in her eyes. 'But surely you must have a date for your crossing by now?'

Sam shook her head. 'It isn't that easy. Jack tried to find a private crossing for me so that I could go over in the autumn, but we didn't have any luck. Even now, there are hardly any commercial ships going to America and the waiting lists for those that are going are still huge. The United States Army has just started providing ships to transport British war brides to America, and he's decided to try and find a space for me on one of those.' She explained briefly about all the forms there were to fill in and about all paperwork involved. 'The problem now is that I'm only a fiancée, and not a bride. Jack has heard that the U.S. Congress is talking about passing some sort of special law to allow the fiancées of former GIs into America on special visas. We'll probably have to wait for that to go through before I'll be able to get a passage.'

Diana nodded sympathetically. 'It does seem to be taking a very long time. I didn't realise quite how difficult it all was.'

The waiter arrived with their tea. Sam poured it out and then handed Diana a cup. 'I shouldn't complain really though, should I?' she said, in a brighter voice. 'Jack and I have both been lucky enough to come out of the war unscathed and sooner or later we should be together again. Since we first met we seem to have spent more time apart than we have done together, but we're not the only ones. There are probably thousands of people like us who've been affected this way by the war.'

'That's a good way of looking at things,' said Diana encouragingly. She took a sip of her tea. 'How are your parents feeling about it all?'

'Mother doesn't like it, as I'm sure you can imagine,' said Sam. 'I think Daddy must be disappointed too, but at least he's being supportive about it.' Through the window, she saw a couple strolling past along the pavement. They were wrapped up in coats and scarves and their collars were turned up against the cold. A double-decker bus rattled by and she looked at Diana again. 'Do you know how Nancy's getting on?' she asked. 'I haven't heard anything from her at all since Christmas. Is she still living with her brother and his wife in Devon?' She knew that Ed had been wounded in Germany, just before the war ended, but he'd made a full recovery and had been transported back to the States.

'She's never been very good at writing, has she?' said Diana. 'I've spoken to her a few times on the telephone and she seems happy enough. I think she's met a few new friends through one of those American Red Cross clubs for GI brides, like the one that you wrote to me about.'

The clubs had sprung up all over the country since the end of the war, and Sam had joined the one in Hertford. 'It seems that there are dozens of other girls like Nancy and me,' she sighed. 'All of us in love with American servicemen and still stranded here in England.' She explained to Diana how the club met every other week and how speakers came to tell them about what to expect when they got to America. 'Last week, a Red Cross lady came to give us a talk about all the new language we might have to learn. Did you know that chips are called fries over there? And a pavement is a sidewalk? And if you want me to, I can sing all the verses to The Star Spangled Banner.'

Diana laughed. 'I'm sure everything will work out for you soon,' she said kindly.

'Actually, I did see something just this morning that gave me a bit of hope. It was while I was waiting for you at the station.'

'Oh? What was that?'

'I saw an article on the front page of a newspaper saying that the first ship transporting war brides had just arrived in New York. There was a photograph showing it pulling into the harbour.'

Diana smiled. 'Well, there you are then. I'm sure that it won't be long now.'

30. JOURNEY

The days lengthened as winter turned to spring. Crocuses and daffodils appeared beneath the hedgerows, trees blossomed, and the rhododendrons along the drive came into bloom. As summer arrived, newspapers and magazines reported regularly on the ships of war brides that were arriving in America, but there was still no news of a passage for Sam. She lived from day to day, biding her time, trying to keep herself busy and not let her mind dwell on what seemed like endless months of waiting. She helped out at her father's surgery three days a week, and spent as much time as she could with her mother on the other days, helping her in the garden and around the house. They made the occasional trip to London together, to meet family or friends, or to go shopping or see a play, but for the most part they lived quietly. Sam closed in on herself, and the arrival of Jack's letters and her trips to the club for GI brides in Hertford on Thursday evenings became the highlights of her weeks.

It was the middle of July when the letter finally arrived. Her parents were up and dressed and having their breakfast out on the terrace behind the house when Sam got downstairs and saw the official looking envelope lying on the mat. She picked it up with trembling hands. Sunshine streamed in through the window by the door, making patterns on the walls. Her heart thudded as she carefully opened the envelope and drew out the letter it contained.

Arrangements are now being made for your passage to the United States and you should immediately prepare yourself to travel on very short notice.

For a moment, the words danced in front of Sam's eyes and her head felt light. She breathed deeply to steady herself, then looked down at the page again and continued to read.

The letter said that she was to report to an embarkation camp at a place called Tidworth in ten days' time in order to finish all the necessary immigration processing. The United States Army was running the camp and she would be provided with all the food and medical attention she required. To reach the barracks, she was to travel to Waterloo station and then board a special train. No friends or family were allowed to take the train with her, but American soldiers would meet it at the other end and assist her with her baggage. After that a bus would take her on the final leg of her journey to Tidworth. Once all the processing was complete, the letter concluded, she could expect to sail from Southampton sometime at the beginning of August. A list of all the documentation she was to bring with her was detailed on a separate sheet.

Her parents were still sitting at the table eating their breakfast when she went outside. Her father looked up at her and smiled. 'Good morning, darling. We've saved you some toast.' He saw the expression on her face, then glanced at the sheets of paper she held in her hand. 'What is it, Sam?' he asked, frowning. 'You look a little pale. Is there anything wrong?'

She shook her head and bit her lip. 'No, there's nothing wrong.'

'What is it then?'

'The letter I've been waiting for has arrived. I'm to leave for America at the end of the month.'

Elizabeth shot her a glance. 'Surely not so soon?'

Sam's forehead furrowed. 'It's been a very long time, Mother,' she said gently, 'you know that.' She sat down at the table and handed the letter to her father. He flattened out the creases, adjusted his glasses and began to read.

Elizabeth watched him anxiously as he looked through the pages. Sam took a piece of toast and spread it thinly with jam. There were flower tubs on the terrace and the garden looked lovely in the sunshine.

William looked up over the top of his glasses. 'Well, at least it looks like they know what they're doing.'

'So you're really intending to go,' murmured Elizabeth.

'You know this is what Sam wants, Elizabeth,' said William. 'She's been waiting a very long time for this to happen. We mustn't make it any harder for her than it already is.'

'I do find it very difficult.'

William smiled. 'We have to accept that she's in love with Captain Webster,' he said, in a firm, quiet voice. 'This is Sam's life we're talking about, not ours. It was torn apart by the war and I think she's earned the right to choose for herself what she does with it, now that the world is at peace. She didn't choose to fall in love with a foreigner, but it's happened and we, as her parents, must learn to make the best of it.'

'But America is so far away,' sighed Elizabeth. 'How will we be able to help her if she needs us? She may as well be going to the moon...'

William reached over and patted her hand. 'It isn't as far as you think.

Once things are back to normal and commercial flights are re-established, I'm sure we'll be able to visit. It isn't as if we haven't the means with which to do it.'

'And what if it doesn't work out? What will she do then?'

'Well, if that happens, and I don't for one moment think that it will, then we'll send her a ticket so that she can come back here to us.'

Sam shot her father a grateful look, then gently placed her hand on her mother's arm. 'This is my chance for happiness,' she said. 'You must know that I'm going to miss all of you desperately, but I have to take it.'

The main concourse of the station was thronging with people. Voices echoed beneath the huge steel-girded roof and Sam could hear the sound of whistles blowing and the hissing of steam as trains pulled in and out from the station. She was walking in silence beside her parents. Her father had asked a porter for directions to the correct platform and they were crossing the concourse towards it. A lump came into her throat and she tried not to think about how hard it was going to be when the time finally came for them to part.

A queue had formed by the barrier and women dressed in travelling clothes stood waiting to go onto the platform. Some of them seemed to be there on their own, but most were with their families. Bags and suitcases were piled onto trolleys between them, babies cried fretfully and small children clung tightly to their mothers' hands.

The train was already waiting on the tracks when they stepped through the barrier. American GIs were helping women with their luggage and families stood together in little groups, saying their last goodbyes.

Sam fought back her tears as she pressed her cheek against the tweed collar of her father's jacket and sank into his tight embrace. Her heart thudded quickly in her chest, drowning out everything else, and she was only vaguely aware of the sound of a girl sobbing in the background.

William gently released her and looked down into her face. 'We'll miss you, my darling,' he said, 'but we wish you joy and happiness in your new life in America. Your captain seems like a decent man and I'm sure he'll take good care of you, but remember that we'll always be here, if you ever need us.'

'I know you will,' murmured Sam, her voice wobbling a little, in spite of her determination to be strong. 'I just wish that things hadn't happened like this and we could all stay together, in one place.'

William kissed her on the forehead. 'Things don't always work out just the way we'd like them to.'

Sam's smile was shaky as she turned to embrace Elizabeth one last time. 'I love you, Mother. I'm going to miss you terribly.'

'Be happy,' whispered Elizabeth, her voice choked.

As Sam picked up her suitcase and stepped away from them, everything around her seemed to become a blur. As if in a dream, she climbed onto the train and moved along the carriage. Somehow, she found a space near a window and stowed her suitcase in the luggage rack above it. As she sank down on the upholstered seat, a guard blew his whistle, jolting her back to the moment. Her parents saw her and came close to the window and they walked along with the train as it started moving along the platform. The train gathered speed and they stopped, but Sam leaned close to the window and kept her eyes upon them as the platform receded away. After a few more moments, the train exited the station, and her parents disappeared out of sight.

Tidworth camp looked bleak, even in the summer sunshine. The landscape was deserted apart from several rows of austere-looking, rectangular huts that stretched out across the plain and the only trees were a few spindly conifers at the top of a hill in the distance.

'Good afternoon, ladies. Welcome to Tidworth.'

The American officer was holding a clipboard and the women faced him in rows in front of a grey, utilitarian building. They stood silent and expectant, coats and jackets buttoned up and headscarves blowing in the breeze. The officer smiled at them briefly, then began calling out from a list of names and telling them where they were to be billeted.

The next few days proved to be busy ones and gave them little time to dwell on the enormity of what they were doing. There were physical examinations, documents were checked and baggage was put through customs. The days passed quickly until finally the morning of departure dawned. A bus collected them from Tidworth in the early hours of the morning and they arrived at the dockside as dawn was breaking.

The ship seemed huge, far bigger than anything Sam had been expecting. It loomed up out of the water, outlined sharply by the pale blue of the early morning sky. She climbed down from the bus and stretched her legs, then collected her small battered suitcase from one of the soldiers unloading the luggage from the compartment at the back.

A wide gangplank rose from the quayside to an open hatch in the side of the ship. Women and children were pressing towards it. Seagulls hovered overhead and the sound of a brass band playing *Sentimental Journey* could be heard above the murmuring voices of the crowd.

Sam gripped the handrail and made her way up the gangplank. A Red Cross woman was waiting just inside the hatch. She checked Sam's name off a list and directed her along a passageway, giving her a friendly smile and wishing her a pleasant trip. At the end of the passageway, a metal staircase climbed to the deck of the ship. Sam followed the line of women in front of her, their shoes clattering as they clambered up the staircase. Coming out onto the deck, she saw that a row of women was forming against the ship's rail and she made her way across to join them. She gazed towards the shore at the sprawling city behind the docks and the dull green countryside beyond, locked in her own thoughts, aware of the deck gradually filling up behind her.

The engines started up and Sam watched as the gangplank was slowly lifted away from the quay. The band struck up again, playing *There'll Always Be an England*, and a lump came to her throat. The ship glided away from the dockside and she took a last, lingering look at the land she was leaving behind, then swung her gaze out to sea, unable to watch any longer. The water in the harbour looked peaceful. Beyond it, the sea sparkled in the sunshine and stretched out smoothly towards the horizon.

31. A LONG DAY

Sam heard the sound of footsteps tramping along the corridor outside the cabin. A woman's voice called out someone's name and there was a burst of chatter and laughter. A door opened and shut, and then the corridor was quiet again.

She looked at her reflection in the small mirror on the wall above her bunk and studied her face carefully from different angles. It was almost a year now since she'd last seen Jack and she felt a pang of apprehension, wondering how much he would find her changed. Pulling her thoughts together, she examined the scant contents of her make-up bag. She looked into the mirror again and dusted a little powder over her face and applied the last remains of her dusky-coloured lipstick.

A voice came over the Tannoy system, making her start. They had been at sea for nine days and now, very early in the morning, they were drawing close to land. The voice over the Tannoy issued a few final instructions to the crew, then faded out again.

Sam carefully secured her identity card to one of the buttons of her jacket, then rose from the bunk and smoothed out the wrinkles in her skirt. Her suitcase was propped next to the cabin door, packed and ready to go. She picked it up, then opened the door and stepped into the corridor outside.

Out on the deck, Sam leaned against the ship's rail, looking towards the shore. The floodlit Statue of Liberty rose up imposingly from the dark water in front of them, and thousands of specks of light illuminated the distinctive skyline of New York. As she gazed towards the city, a feeling of unreality washed over her. For months this had all been nothing but a dream and she could hardly believe that she was really there.

The morning light turned greyish as the sun rose over the sea behind them. The artificial lights faded and the outline of the city gradually took shape. The ship cut smoothly through the calm waters of the harbour, throwing up a white spume of wave around its bows.

As the ship manoeuvred towards the dockside ahead of them, Sam looked along at the line of women leaning against the rail. They were calling and waving towards the shore, their skirts billowing and their identity cards flapping in the cool morning breeze. People packed the dockside, their faces turned upwards towards the approaching ship. Men waited alone or in family groups, scanning the women on the deck, pointing occasionally and waving, cupping their hands to their mouths and shouting greetings that were lost on the wind and impossible to hear. Sam's gaze travelled over them, searching vainly for Jack.

The engines were shut down and the ship slowly glided up to the harbour wall. Gulls shrieked and circled overhead. A gangplank was hoisted up to the side of the ship and a message came over the Tannoy system, announcing to the women that it was time to disembark. Sam cast one more glance over the figures on the dockside below, then picked up her suitcase and turned away, following the direction of the moving crowd.

She descended the metal stairway and joined the queue of women forming along the passageway. The Red Cross woman who had welcomed her aboard stood by the open hatch, clipboard in hand, speaking to a fair-haired girl who was poised to leave the ship. The air was filled with nervous chatter. The girl in front of Sam opened her handbag and drew out her documents. Her fingers tightened around them and when she looked up again, Sam saw the moisture that brightened her eyes. Sam summoned an encouraging smile, but she felt too choked herself to speak.

The queue dwindled, until Sam reached the front of it. She told the Red Cross woman her name and she looked down at her clipboard and checked her off the list.

'Good luck, Miss Mitchell,' said the woman, giving her a friendly smile. 'I hope you've enjoyed your trip.'

Sam somehow found her voice again. 'Yes, thank you, I have.'

She smiled at the woman distractedly, ducked to avoid hitting her head on the rim of the hatch, and stepped out onto the top of the gangplank. The crowd ebbed and flowed around the bottom of it, held back by a ring of sailors, and a sea of expectant faces was lifted towards her. Her heart began to thump. So this was it. The moment she'd been waiting for, for so very long, had finally arrived. She gripped her suitcase firmly and took a deep breath, then started down the gangplank towards the dockside below.

She hesitated at the bottom, her heart still pounding, and a figure stepped forward from the crowd. The sailors pulled apart, allowing her through to meet him, and the weight of her suitcase was lifted from her hand.

'Hello, Sam,' he murmured.

She stood in front of him mutely, finding it difficult almost to breathe. Never before had she seen him in his civilian clothes, and he looked like a stranger in his dark, expensively tailored suit and tie, and crisp white shirt. A devastatingly handsome stranger, it was true, but nevertheless a stranger. Her forehead puckered and she lifted her hand to her throat, wondering what he must think of her in her shabby jacket with its flapping label and her few scraps of make-up. She thought self-consciously of her hair, matted by the wind as she'd stood on the deck.

But then, somehow, he had folded her into his arms and his mouth was on hers, warm and tender, and her heart filled with so much love that she thought that she would burst.

Sam caught her first glimpse of the house through the trees. They had collected her trunk from Customs and crossed New York by taxi, then travelled northwards by rail. A gleaming black, chauffeur-driven car had picked them up from the train station and she was now sitting her in the back seat next to Jack, gazing out of the window and watching the unfamiliar countryside slide past.

Just before the car turned off the main highway, she saw two rows of tall windows glinting in the bright sunshine of the late afternoon. They went along a driveway with avenues of trees on either side, and then the house came into full view. Beyond it, a well-manicured lawn sloped away into the distance towards the sea. The car swept up to a set of wide stone steps in front of the house and glided smoothly to a stop.

The chauffeur opened the door for her and she stepped out from the car. He opened the boot and set her dusty suitcase and battered trunk onto the smoothly raked gravel drive. Sam looked up at the house as Jack spoke to him briefly about what to do with the bags.

The chauffeur picked up the suitcase and carried it up the steps, and Jack touched her elbow. 'Feeling nervous?' he asked, his eyes smiling.

She nodded. 'Just a little.

'There's nothing to worry about. My parents can't wait to meet you and I know for certain that they're going to love you.'

Sam's throat went dry. The day had been overwhelming enough already and she felt a swell of panic at the thought of meeting his parents and sister. She'd hoped to have had the chance to arrange her hair and freshen up her make-up before she was introduced to them, but clearly that wasn't going to be the case. She glanced down at her faded brown suit, which was much too warm in the humid heat, and her practical, low-heeled shoes.

It was a relief, at least, to enter the relative coolness of the house. They came into a large hallway dominated by a central staircase with curving banisters. A large vase of freshly cut flowers stood on a highly-polished pedestal table. To one side, a door stood slightly open and through it she caught a glimpse of a spacious, comfortably furnished living room that was bathed in sunshine.

She heard the sound of light footsteps approaching and the door opened fully, revealing a slim woman who looked to be in her fifties. She was expensively dressed in a simply tailored, ivory-coloured dress and her dark, greying hair was elegantly arranged. The family resemblance was strong and Sam knew at once that she must be Jack's mother. She gave Sam a welcoming smile and came across the hallway with her hands outstretched.

'Mother, this is Sam,' said Jack, by way of introduction, 'and Sam, this is my mother, Martha.'

Martha took Sam's hands in hers and then drew back to look at her.

'How do you do, Mrs Webster,' said Sam shyly.

'Oh, please, I insist that you call me Martha. After all, we're going to be family soon.'

Sam smiled, and Martha's gaze swept over her again. 'How lovely to have you here at last, my dear. You certainly are as beautiful as he told us. Your photographs really don't do you justice. Did you have a good trip?'

'Yes, very good, thank you,' answered Sam, flushing.

'And what time did you arrive in New York?'

'Five o'clock this morning.'

Martha looked sympathetic. 'You must be very tired. Jack's sister, Caroline, will be here in a moment. She wants to show you to your room.'

Sam heard the sound of footsteps coming from the living room again and a girl of about her own age appeared in the doorway. Her dark, shoulder-length hair was damp, and she was wearing a bright red swimsuit beneath a white towelling robe.

'I was wondering what had become of you, Caroline,' said Martha. 'Come and say hello to Sam.'

Caroline came a few steps forward and held out her hand. 'Hi, Sam,' she said, 'I hope you had a good journey.'

The words were welcoming, but Sam noticed the little smile of disdain that played about her lips and was acutely conscious once again of the dowdiness of her own appearance. Determined to retain her composure, she lifted her chin fractionally and shook Caroline's proffered hand. 'It's very nice to meet you too,' she said politely.

Jack touched her elbow. 'I'll let Caroline show you to your room. Dad's still at the office in town, but he'll be here to meet you later. Do you think you'll be feeling up to it?'

Martha smiled. 'We're dining at eight.'

Sam's gaze met Jack's. 'I'll be fine,' she assured him, not wanting to let him down. 'I'm looking forward to it.'

A wide corridor ran all the way along the upper floor of the house, with bedrooms and bathrooms leading off it. Caroline showed Sam into one of the tastefully furnished rooms. There was a picture of a yacht on the wall and a vase of pink roses on the dressing table by the window.

'My room is just across the way,' said Caroline, casting a critical glance at the battered luggage that had been placed by the bed. 'And the bathroom's the next door along.'

'Thank you.'

Caroline smiled faintly. 'I'll see you at dinner, then. Make yourself at home.'

Caroline closed the door behind her and Sam went across to one of the windows and looked out. The bedroom had a commanding view of the garden behind the house and she saw that French windows opened out from the ground floor rooms onto a large terrace set with a swimming pool. The terrace gave way to the lawn, and sea was just visible in the distance, a dark ribbon of water edging the clear blue sky of the late afternoon.

A gentle breeze lifted the sheer curtains that hung at the window, carrying the scent of roses into the room. The delicate perfume reminded Sam of home and tears sprang into her eyes. She wondered what Jack's mother and sister really thought of her, and it hit her suddenly that from now on they would play a very large part in her life.

She sniffed and brushed back her tears, impatient with herself. She knew that she was being silly and after coming so far she needed to be strong and do her best to make things work. She looked at her watch and saw that she had less than an hour to get ready for dinner. She lifted her suitcase onto the bed and clicked it open. Then she heard the sound of a knock at the door.

Sam opened the door, revealing Jack standing in the corridor outside.

'I just came to see if you were okay. Do you have everything you need?'

She nodded. 'Everything's lovely. You never told me you had such a beautiful home.'

'I'm glad you like it.' His brows pulled together slightly. 'Are you sure you're up to having dinner with the family this evening? I know you've had a very long day.'

'Don't worry, I'm sure I'll be fine.'

He searched her face for a moment, then his expression relaxed. 'I'll come up and get you at eight. It'll take you a while to get used to the layout of the house.'

She nodded again. 'Thank you.'

He bent his head and kissed her gently on the mouth. 'I can't tell you how good it is to have you here at last,' he murmured. 'I've nearly gone crazy, waiting for you all these months. I never expected it to take so long.'

He had changed his clothes and she caught the familiar, tangy scent of his aftershave and the freshly laundered smell of his shirt. She looked up into his eyes and another feeling of unreality washed over her. 'I'm glad to be here too,' she whispered.

His eyes grew thoughtful. 'It's getting late. I'll leave you to get changed.'

The door closed behind him and Sam was left alone again. There was a long white bathrobe hanging on the back of the bedroom door that looked to be brand new. She quickly undressed and slipped it on. The material felt very soft and light against her skin, and she hugged herself at the sheer luxury of it. She picked up her small bag of toiletries and went out along the corridor.

The bathroom was very bright and clean and Sam immediately noticed the rows of the perfumed soaps and cosmetics and all the other little luxuries she had been deprived of in England for so many years.

She showered quickly and then went back to her room and made a start on unpacking her trunk and suitcase while her hair dried. When the suitcase was empty, she stepped back and swept her gaze over the few garments now hanging from the rail. After a few moments she pulled out a simple cream dress that she'd bought the previous summer. It was one of the nicest dresses that she had and she'd intended to keep it for a special occasion, but first impressions were important and for Jack's sake she wanted to look the best she could when she met his father.

She brushed her hair in the mirror above the dressing table, then made up her face with a little of the powder and rouge she still had remaining. She slipped on her sandals. They were practical and ugly, but she had no choice but to wear them. All her other summer shoes had worn out and they were the only ones she now owned.

She checked her watch. It was still only ten to eight, so she sat down on a chair near the window to wait. She watched the gardeners who were tending the lawns and flowerbeds and the trimly dressed maid who was sweeping the terrace near the pool.

She heard Jack's knock at the door and went across to open it. His eyes swept over her briefly and then he smiled. 'Ready?' he asked.

Butterflies fluttered in her stomach. 'Yes,' she said. 'I think so.'

The dining room was beautifully furnished in an elegant colonial style. A long dining table ran down the centre and a large crystal chandelier hung above it. The table had been set for five people at one end.

French windows stood open onto a terrace, towards the sunset, and a tall man with dark greying hair stood in front of them, looking out. On the dining table, the candles of a candelabra flickered in the light evening breeze, and the glasses and cutlery gleamed in their reflected light.

The man turned around as they came in.

'Good evening, Dad,' said Jack.

To Sam's relief, his father's face broke into a broad smile and he stepped forward and opened his arms in a gesture of welcome. 'So, you're finally here, young lady,' he chuckled. 'Well, we sure are glad to have you. Jack here was beginning to give up hope.'

Jack laughed. 'I guess I should warn you now, Sam. Don't believe anything Dad says.'

'I'm very glad to be here, Mr Webster,' she smiled.

'Please, call me Henry. Everyone else around here does.'

The sound of voices came from the corridor beyond the dining room and a few moments later Martha and Caroline glided into the room. They had changed for dinner and were both beautifully dressed in the latest styles. Caroline was wearing a deep red dress and her dark hair was piled up on top of her head. She was immaculately made up and her glossy red lipstick co-ordinated perfectly with her long, carefully manicured fingernails. With her blue eyes and honey-toned skin she was as almost as strikingly good-looking as her brother was.

'Ah, there you are,' said Henry, looking over at his wife and daughter. 'Jack was just introducing me to Sam.'

Martha smiled at her. 'I hope you found everything you needed.'

'Yes, thank you. Everything was perfect.'

'Well then,' said Henry, rubbing his hands together. 'Shall we eat?'

Henry sat down at the head of the table and Sam was placed next to Caroline, on his right. Jack sat down opposite her, next to his mother. She met his gaze through the flickering candlelight and he sent her an encouraging smile. A maid in a black and white outfit came in carrying a large china tureen. She put it down on the sideboard and served them with soup and freshly baked bread.

'So, Sam, what do you make of America so far?' asked Henry, breaking his bread over his soup bowl. 'Do you like what you see?'

Sam lowered her spoon and smiled. 'Yes,' she said. 'Yes, I do.'

'I guess it's all a bit different to what you're used to.'

For a brief moment, an image of the bombed-out streets of London came sharply into her mind. She hesitated, then realised that they were all looking at her expectantly. 'Yes, it is very different. Everything seems so bright and new.' She smiled across at Martha. 'You have a very beautiful home.'

Martha acknowledged her words with a gracious nod. 'Thank you,' she said. 'I hope you'll feel very comfortable here.'

It was getting late when the maid began serving them their dessert. It crossed Sam's mind that the abundant food that had been served could almost have fed a whole family in England for a week. She stared down at the apple pie that the maid had placed in front of her, marvelling at its thick golden crust of pastry and the large dollop of cream next to it. She took a small spoonful and for a moment delighted in the crispness of the crust and the sweetness of the apples as they melted in her mouth. She took a few more spoonfuls, but then the richness of pie became too much and she set down her spoon and fork, placing them neatly across the plate.

Martha glanced across at her. 'Is everything all right, Sam? You've hardly touched your food.'

'It's delicious, thank you, but I'm afraid I'm not used to eating quite so much.'

'It's only apple pie,' said Caroline. 'Don't you have that in England?'

'We used to, but food is scarce now. We have apples, of course, but things like butter and sugar are difficult to find.'

Martha's brows lifted. 'We know that you're still being rationed over there, but surely things are improving now. The war's been over for almost a year.'

Sam hesitated. 'Actually, things seem harder to get hold of now than ever.'

'Oh,' said Martha uncertainly. 'I'm very sorry to hear it.'

There was a short silence.

'I'm sure you're glad to be in America now,' said Caroline smoothly.

The maid came in to clear the plates and Sam peeked at Caroline, sitting in the chair beside her. There was something in her tone of voice that Sam couldn't quite fathom, and it occurred to her that she might in some way be questioning her motives for being there.

When she turned her head again, Jack caught her gaze. He smiled at her reassuringly and she told herself that she must have just been imagining things. She was exhausted after her long day and was probably being overly sensitive. To be fair to Caroline she had to give her the benefit of the doubt.

Martha folded her napkin and placed it next to her plate, then clasped her hands in front of her and rested her elbows on the edge of the table. 'We have a surprise for you, Sam. I'm sure that Jack won't mind me telling you about it. I've organised a party, to welcome you properly, and I've invited all our friends and neighbours. They're all dying to meet you. We always have a summer party, so we thought we might as well have it to coincide with your arrival.'

'How lovely,' said Sam. 'When will it be?'

Caroline studied the tips of her fingernails. 'Tomorrow night.'

'Tomorrow night?' repeated Sam, too surprised, for a moment, to conceal her rush of panic. She glanced quickly down at her dress.

Jack laughed. 'Don't worry, we'll get you something pretty to wear. I'll run you into town in the morning to do a little shopping.'

She shot him a grateful look through the flickering candlelight and he answered her with a thoughtful smile. She wondered if he was thinking about the last time that they'd been shopping together, in Brussels. It seemed to Sam as if that day had happened in a different life, to a different person. Did he feel that too?

After dinner, they went through to the living room. The curtains had been closed and a tray of coffee things stood waiting on a table. There were two cream-coloured sofas and several comfortable-looking armchairs. A large fireplace was the main feature of the room, and a richly coloured abstract painting hung above the mantelpiece.

Henry picked up a crystal decanter from a silver tray and poured a drink for Martha. 'What can I get you, young lady?' he asked, turning to Sam.

Jack was regarding her thoughtfully. 'Sam's had a very long day,' he told Henry, 'and she's going to have another big day tomorrow. I think we should let her go to bed.'

'Actually, I am rather tired,' admitted Sam, giving Jack another grateful look. As she thanked Martha for the meal and wished them goodnight, she felt him place his hand lightly in the small of her back. He guided her out into the hallway and they went up the staircase together.

He opened the door of her bedroom and switched on the light. He looked down into her eyes, gently brushed away a strand of hair that had fallen across her forehead, bent his head and kissed her lightly on the lips. 'You've had a very long day,' he murmured, drawing away from her. 'Get a good night's sleep and I'll see you at breakfast in the morning.'

'Good night, Jack' she whispered, stepping into the bedroom. She shut the door behind her and listened to the sound of his fading footsteps as he moved away along the corridor outside.

32. THE PARTY

Warm sunlight was streaming in through the windows of her room when Sam awoke the next morning. It was a few moments before she remembered where she was, but then it all came flooding back to her. She was really there at last. She turned her head and reached for the clock that stood on her bedside table, sitting up with a start when she saw the time. It was ten o'clock, and she knew that she'd missed breakfast.

She washed quickly, pulled on one of her cotton dresses and ran a comb through her hair, then ran downstairs to find Jack. She crossed the hall into the light-filled kitchen, but there was no one there apart from one of the pretty dark-haired maids. She went forwards into the room and saw a sealed envelope lying on top of the table. Her name was written across the front of it in Jack's familiar handwriting.

Caroline wafted into the room, stylishly dressed in a simple white shift. 'Good morning, Sam,' she said. 'I hope that you slept well.'

She nodded. 'Yes, thank you, I did. Actually, a little too well. I'm sorry to have missed breakfast.'

'Rita will fix you something to eat,' said Caroline, nodding towards the maid. 'But I'm afraid that you've missed Jack. He had to go in to the office today after all. It seems that there was something that couldn't wait, even for you.' She smiled sympathetically, but there was a trace of boredom in her voice. 'He wouldn't let us disturb you before he went, but he's left a note for you,' she added, gesturing to the table.

'Oh, I see,' said Sam lightly, careful to hide her disappointment. She turned away from Caroline and picked up the envelope from the table. She slit it open and found a fat wad of dollar bills and a single piece of folded notepaper wedged inside. She pulled out the note and read it quickly. Jack wrote that he was sorry that he wouldn't be able to take her shopping, but that Caroline would go with her instead. He also said that she was to buy whatever she needed with the money he'd enclosed.

'I've asked Harrison to bring the car round,' said Caroline. 'Do you think you could be ready in half an hour?'

The driver took them into town and left them standing on the kerb outside a tall department store at the end of a row of smart-looking shops. People laden with shopping bags were moving along the pavement and as she looked up and down the street Sam thought how well-dressed everyone seemed, and how vividly alive. She felt as if she'd arrived in some strange paradise where all the colours were sharp and bright, and where nothing had been touched by the destructive hand of war.

'Caroline!' A voice called.

Sam turned to see a slim, blonde girl in a yellow dress emerging from the revolving doors at the entrance to the department store. She noticed her smart high-heeled shoes and elegant hat, and felt dowdier than ever.

The girl was smiling as she came to greet them.

'How nice to see you, Eleanor,' said Caroline, returning her smile.

'It's nice to see you, too,' said Eleanor, 'although it's a bit of a surprise. Don't you need to get ready for the party tonight?'

Caroline laughed. 'That's why I'm here. I have an appointment at the beauty parlour in ten minutes.'

Eleanor nodded and smiled. Her gaze flickered over Sam and then she shot Caroline a questioning look.

'Sam, this is Eleanor Foster, a very good friend of mine. Our families have known each other for years,' said Caroline, making the introductions. 'And Eleanor, this is Jack's fiancée, Sam Mitchell.'

Sam noticed a subtle change in Eleanor's expression. Her eyes clouded over for a moment, but then, recovering herself, she smiled brightly. 'Did you have a good trip over?'

'Yes, thank you, I did,' said Sam.

Eleanor murmured another pleasantry, then turned to Caroline again, and Sam stood by as they exchanged some bits of news. Both of them looked to be in their early twenties, just as she was, but as she listened to them talking it struck her that their lives over the past few years couldn't have been more different from her own. She found herself thinking about the war, about all the rationings and hardships, all the bombings and all the days and nights spent in the air-raid shelters. She thought about all the wounded men she'd nursed in France and Belgium, and wondered if she'd ever find anything in common with the two young women standing before her now.

They heard the sound of a clock striking and Eleanor looked at her watch. 'Well, I'd better be going. I've a little shopping to do and I've arranged to meet Miriam for an ice cream later on.'

'I must go too,' said Caroline, 'but please tell Miriam how much we're all looking forward to seeing her at the party tonight.'

The two of them exchanged a final knowing glance, then Eleanor moved off along the street.

Caroline turned to Sam. 'I'll have to leave you by yourself now, I'm afraid. I've only got a minute or two before my appointment and the beauty parlour is two blocks down from here. I'll meet you back here at four, if that's all right. Harrison is coming to pick us up.' She nodded towards the store. 'The dress department is on the second floor. The elevator's on the left, just as you go in.'

Sam nodded. 'Thank you. There's no need to worry, I'm sure I'll be fine.'

Caroline joined the stream of shoppers flowing steadily past. Sam scanned the faces of the passers-by for another moment, then wove across the pavement to the entrance of the shop and pushed her way through the revolving doors.

'Good Morning, ma'am.'

An assistant in an elegant black dress greeted Sam as she stepped out of the lift.

She took another pace across the marble floor. Arrayed in front of her were racks of light flimsy blouses, pale-coloured slacks, and exquisite skirts and dresses. For a moment she was too astonished to speak.

The assistant looked puzzled. 'Can I help you, ma'am?'

'Yes,' laughed Sam, 'yes, I think you probably can. I'm looking for a dress.'

The assistant was young and she had an open, friendly face. 'Well, you've certainly come to the right place for that, ma'am. What sort of dress is it that you're looking for?'

'It's for a party, tonight. And I also need a few other things. I'd like a couple of summer dresses and some shoes and make-up. I've just arrived from England and I think my wardrobe is a little out-of-date.'

The girl smiled. 'I could tell by your accent that you weren't from these parts.' She looked Sam up and down appraisingly. 'From England, you say? My brother was a pilot stationed over there in the war and he's often told us how much you all went through.'

'Yes, it was rather hard,' murmured Sam.

'Well, I think you'll find everyone appreciates everything you people did for our boys while they were over there.' The girl tilted her head and her expression grew thoughtful. 'You say this party's tonight? Is it out at the Websters' place?'

'Yes, that's right.'

'In that case, I think we're going to have to find you something very special to wear indeed.'

The street was bathed in bright sunshine when Sam emerged from the store. There was another hour to go before she was due to meet Caroline, so she decided to risk making her own way along the street in the direction she'd seen Caroline go earlier. The beauty parlour couldn't be too hard to find, she thought.

Sam strolled along the street, her gaze lingering over all the wonderful goods arrayed in the windows of the shops she passed. She came to a café and paused for a moment to look in through the window. Chromium chairs surrounded gleaming metallic tables, and booths with upholstered seats lined a wall to one side. It was just like something she'd seen in an American film. Cakes were displayed beneath domed glass covers along a counter. When her gaze reached them, it suddenly seemed a very long time since breakfast.

A bell jangled above her head as Sam pushed open the door. She went across the black and white chequerboard floor and slipped into the booth at the very back. A waitress in a pink and white check uniform came over to take her order and a few minutes later she was tucking into the most delicious piece of chocolate cake she thought she'd ever eaten.

She heard the sound of people sitting down in the booth next to hers and was aware of the waitress taking their order. She realised that two women were sitting together, and she could hear their conversation clearly.

'So what was she like?'

'Oh, pretty, I suppose. In a pale, English sort of way.'

Sam thought that she recognised the voice. Wasn't it Eleanor's?

'I suppose some might call her beautiful,' the voice continued. 'But she isn't very glamorous. She seems to have no make-up or nail polish or pretty clothes. I was surprised, really. She doesn't have style, at least not the way that you do. I wouldn't have thought she was Jack's type at all.'

'So what does he see in her?'

'I really couldn't say. I guess he was alone in a foreign place and needed some company. You've read the articles in the newspapers, those English girls couldn't wait to get their hands on our guys while they were over there. You mustn't blame him.'

'I know, Eleanor, I've tried not to, but you know that we were almost engaged before he left. Why do you think he brought her over here? Why didn't he break it all off and come home to me?'

'Maybe he didn't think he could. You know what a great sense of duty he has. Perhaps things went further with her than he intended, and now he feels he has to do the honourable thing.'

'Did she really look like that sort of girl?'

'I don't know, Miriam. I guess she didn't really look the type, but a lot of things can happen when there's a war. We all know the kind of reputation some of those English girls had over there.'

Horrified by what she'd heard, Sam sat stock-still, her back pressed hard against the curved upholstery of the seat. Her face flushed a deep crimson. So there really was someone else after all. How naïve she'd been to believe that a man like Jack wasn't already involved with a woman. And was duty all he really felt for her? She knew from first-hand experience the depth of his integrity.

'Anyway, you'll see her at the party tonight,' she heard Eleanor continue. 'What did Caroline say about her?'

'Nothing really. How could she? The girl was standing by her side the whole time, so she couldn't say anything. But you know Caroline as well as I do. There's nothing she'd like more than to see you and Jack together again.'

Sam felt suddenly horribly exposed. Had she really come all the way to America just to make a fool of herself? It occurred to her how strange it was that Jack had left her with Caroline for the day, when she'd only just arrived. They'd been apart for nearly a year and surely if he really loved her he'd have made the time to be with her. For a moment her mind raced wildly. The wise thing to do would be to get a passage back to England as soon as she could. Wasn't that where she really belonged? But then her pride flared and the thought came to her that if she left she'd be running away from things, things she might never again find in her life. Her motivation for coming to America was one of genuine love, whatever the women behind her thought, and she had to give Jack a chance. She'd see how he behaved at the party that night before she took flight. She wasn't a fool. She would soon know if was really interested in this other woman; this Miriam.

Sam looked at her watch. Caroline would still be at the beauty parlour and she decided it was high time that she joined her there. She paid the waitress and waited until Caroline and Eleanor were deep in conversation again. She had bought several scarves at the department store and she fished one out of a bag and put it over her hair, tying it in a knot beneath her chin. She slipped out of the booth and her shoes tapped quickly across the tiled floor. She went out through the door and into the street without looking back, feeling confident that she hadn't been recognised.

The evening shadows were already lengthening when the taxi drew up outside the house. Sam had travelled back alone, having insisted that

Caroline shouldn't wait for her whilst she had her hair done at the salon.

There were caterers' vans stationed on the drive and men in waiter's outfits were carrying large trays of food into the house. Sam slid into the hall behind them, her arms laden with bags. She glanced through the open door to the sitting room and glimpsed the buffet tables laid out in the garden beyond. The members of a five-piece orchestra, smartly dressed in black and white tuxedos, were talking together on the terrace by the window. None of the family seemed to be about and no one noticed her as she quietly slipped up the stairs to her room.

Jack rapped his knuckles insistently against the ivory-coloured door.

'Sam, is everything okay? The first guests have arrived. Are you ready to go down?'

'I'll only be a couple more minutes,' he heard her call, speaking to him through the closed door. 'You go down and I'll join you when I'm ready.'

Jack frowned. There was a strain in her voice and he sensed that something was wrong. Was she mad at him for having left her alone all day? There'd been things he'd had to take care of, things that couldn't wait, but he wouldn't blame her for being angry. He'd asked Caroline to take care of her, but maybe that had been a mistake. She was only a year or so younger than Sam, but since he'd arrived home from Europe he'd found it hard to come to terms with the superficiality of his sister, whose only interests seemed to be gossip and fashion.

Jack thought about turning the handle and pushing his way into the room. It was what he longed to do. He stared at the back of the door and considered his options. He could hear the voices of people arriving in the hallway downstairs and realised that he'd run out of time. Tomorrow he'd explain everything, he told himself, but tonight there was a party to get through. A party his mother had insisted on giving, in spite of his protests. He'd told her in no uncertain terms that Sam would be feeling exhausted and disorientated when she arrived and that the last thing she'd want would be a party, but his mother had insisted on throwing one anyway.

His frown deepened. 'Okay then,' he said finally. 'I'll see you downstairs in a few minutes.'

Sam pressed her cheek against the door and listened until the sound of Jack's retreating footsteps had completely died away. She went then and looked out of her open window, at the unfolding scene below. Swags of white fairy lights had been draped between the garden trees and looped around the pool. There were tables and chairs on the terrace and lawn, and she could hear the soft murmur of people talking to one another and laughing. The buffet tables she'd seen earlier were laid with plates of meat and salads and canapés, and a bar had been set up that appeared to be amply stocked with beer and wine, and liquors and spirits. The small orchestra was playing at the edge of the terrace and already a few people were dancing. Others guests milled around on the lawn, making conversation and drinking cocktails.

She drew away from the window and stood in front of the mirror, looking at her reflection one last time. Her hair had been smoothed back and elaborately coiled at the nape of her neck and she'd applied her new make-up with the greatest of care. She was wearing a long narrow dress of black satin, strapless and cut low so that the creamy fullness of her breasts was plainly visible. The dress clung to her body like a second skin, tapering in at her waist and hugging the roundness of her hips. Never in her life before had she worn anything so sophisticated. Whatever happened, she thought, at least she could be confident that she was looking her best.

Sam stepped out from the living room through the open French windows that gave onto the terrace. She felt the caress of the balmy night air on her naked shoulders and looked about her at the sea of people that she didn't know.

She moved further out onto the terrace. More people were on the dance-floor now, swaying gently to the music beneath the fairy lights and the wide, star-studded sky.

Jack was standing on the lawn talking to a small group of guests. He lifted his gaze and saw her. He said something to excuse himself from the man he was speaking to, then pulled away from the group.

He began walking towards her. He looked tall and dark in his black and white evening suit and her heart fluttered as he approached. But then she saw a pretty, blonde girl in a long blue gown cut across his path and put her hand on his arm to gain his attention. He hesitated briefly, then stopped to speak to her. He gestured towards the terrace where Sam was standing and the girl turned her head and looked in her direction. She took Jack's arm, possessively, or so it seemed to Sam, and they started towards her together.

They stepped up onto the terrace. 'So you're Sam,' said the girl brightly, as they came up to her. 'We've all heard so much about you.'

Sam chanced a brief searching glance at Jack but she couldn't gauge what he was thinking. She turned to the girl again. 'Yes, that's right, I'm Sam,' she said, holding out her hand. 'How do you do?'

'Sam, this is Miriam,' said Jack. 'Miriam Foster.'

Miriam fluttered her eyelashes at Jack as he introduced her, then turned and briefly touched Sam's proffered hand. 'Delighted to meet you, I'm sure,' she murmured.

A waiter carrying a tray of tall stemmed glasses of champagne paused beside them and Jack handed each of them a glass.

They sipped their drinks.

'So how are you enjoying it here?' asked Miriam, after a few awkward moments. 'I guess it's all a little different to where you've come from.'

Sam smiled. 'From what I've seen of it so far, I like it very much.'

Miriam laid her hand on Jack's arm. 'I'm sure Jack here is looking after you very well,' she simpered. 'We're all very jealous of you, you know, Sam. We all think he's just divine.'

Sam's head began to ache. Had this girl really had a serious relationship with Jack? The way they were standing there, so close together, they certainly made an attractive couple. She loved him, and she wanted him to love her the same way in return, but only if she was truly the woman he wanted above all others.

She heard a familiar voice call out Jack's name and turned her head. Bill Crawford was approaching from the direction of the open French windows. A petite redhead was walking at his side. Sam saw Jack release his arm from Miriam's grasp. A look of relief flickered across his face. Was it guilt that made him look like that? Her mind raced in all directions.

'Bill,' said Jack. 'Glad you could make it.' He kissed the redhead lightly on the cheek. 'Hello, Maisie. It's good to see you.' He made the introductions and then he and Bill headed over to the bar to fetch some drinks.

Miriam frowned as she watched them go and then her gaze flickered back over Sam and Maisie. 'Well, I guess I'll see you later,' she said, turning on her heels and sauntering away towards another group of guests.

'I've been looking forward to meeting you for so long,' Maisie told Sam warmly, when they were alone. 'Bill told me what you did for him.'

Before she could frame her reply, Sam heard Caroline's voice raised in greeting.

'Maisie Crawford, when did you get here?' She stepped up onto the terrace from the lawn and gave Maisie a perfunctory kiss on the cheek. She arched an eyebrow and looked around. 'Is Bill not here yet?'

Maisie nodded in the direction of the bar. 'He's over with your brother, getting a drink. He'll be back to say hello in a minute.'

Caroline smiled. 'And have you been introduced to Sam?' she asked. There was the usual trace of boredom in her voice, but her fleeting look of reluctant admiration didn't escape Sam's notice. The time she'd spent shopping and at the beauty parlour had been worth it just for that, she thought.

'Jack introduced us. I was just about to thank her for what she did for Bill.'

'For Bill?' A look of puzzlement crossed Caroline's face.

Over her shoulder, Sam saw Jack and Bill step up onto the terrace. They were carrying drinks and sharing a joke and laughing about something.

Maisie looked at Caroline. 'She saved his leg when he was wounded in France,' she explained.

'Saved my life, I should say,' said Bill, coming up to them and handing a cocktail glass to his wife. 'We sure were lucky to have you over there, Sam.'

Sam flushed. 'I'm afraid Bill's exaggerating. Any of the nurses would have taken care of him, as he well knows.'

Bill shook his head. 'You're just being modest. There aren't many women who'd have had the guts to do what you did, and I'll always be grateful for it.'

Sam's colour deepened and she struggled for something to say.

'Maisie's very musical,' said Jack. 'She's promised to play the piano for us later.'

Sam shot him a look of gratitude for having turned the conversation to other things.

'Bill tells me that you have a beautiful voice,' said Maisie. 'Perhaps you'd let me accompany you one day.'

'That would be lovely,' murmured Sam, smiling shyly.

'You can come over any time. We don't live too far away. We moved here after Bill came back from Europe. He has a job with Mr Webster's company.'

The conversation moved to other things and Sam peeked sideways at Maisie. Perhaps it was possible that she might make friends here after all. Here was one woman at least who seemed to welcome her arrival. If only she could be certain that Jack really wanted and needed her, in the way that she wanted and needed him, then she knew that it would possible for her to be completely happy.

The opening notes of *Moonlight Serenade* carried towards them on the warm night air. She turned her head and Jack's gaze met hers. Beneath the soft lights, it was difficult to read his expression, but she saw that he was holding out his hand for her to take.

He guided her across the terrace and onto the dance-floor, then slipped his hand around her waist. Sam leaned her head against his shoulder. She pushed her doubts to the back of her mind and abandoned herself willingly to his embrace.

33. NEW BEGINNINGS

Sam wrapped a silk scarf around her hair and tied it in a knot beneath her chin. It was late morning and sunshine slanted in across her bedroom through the open window. People were clearing up after the party in the garden below, but inside the house Jack's parents and sister were still sleeping and everything was quiet.

She looked at her reflection in the mirror. She was wearing one of the outfits that she'd bought the previous day, a fitted light blue dress with a matching coloured cardigan. She thought of how Jack had admired her in it at breakfast. He'd knocked at her door and woken her just after nine and as they'd sat drinking coffee and eating toast at a little table on the terrace, he'd told her that he had a surprise for her and that they were going out for a drive.

She checked her appearance in the mirror one last time and then went downstairs to find him. The front door stood open and she saw a cream open-topped sports car waiting on the drive.

Jack came into the hallway and his gaze ran over her approvingly. 'Ready?' he asked.

'Yes,' she said. 'At least, I think so. It depends where you're planning to take me.'

He smiled. 'Don't worry, you'll soon see.'

They went outside together. Jack helped Sam into the passenger side of the car and she made herself comfortable on the soft leather seat.

The roads were wide and clear and the car cut smoothly along through the countryside. Sam gazed about her, wondering where they were going and feeling anxious again about everything that had happened the day before. She thought of the things that she'd overhead in the café and an image came into her mind of Miriam Foster walking across the lawn in a long blue gown beside Jack. She peeked at him sideways, but he was looking ahead, concentrating on the road, and it was difficult to read what he was thinking.

After they'd been going for ten minutes or so, houses began to appear. The car slowed and they turned into a long, tree-lined avenue. They passed several houses set well back from the road amid large, manicured gardens, then turned onto a drive.

They drew up outside a colonial-style house with a porticoed entrance. The white paintwork looked fresh and the windows sparkled in the sunshine.

They went together up the short pathway to the front door. Jack turned the key in the lock and the door swung open, revealing a bright, welcoming hallway with a wooden staircase and several doors leading off it. He took Sam's arm and led her to the back of the house and into a large kitchen-diner fitted out with brand new furniture. Everything looked very modern and clean and sunshine flooded into the room through double glass doors that looked out over a wooden veranda.

Jack opened one of the doors and they stepped outside together. Beyond the veranda was a large, lush-looking lawn and the whole garden was hidden by high hedges from the neighbouring houses.

'So what do you think?' he asked. 'Do you like it?'

'It's lovely.'

'I know it's not as grand as you're used to, but I thought it'd be a start.'

'A start?' She shot him another glance. She was so preoccupied with other things that she hadn't considered the possibility that the house was Jack's. 'Do you mean we're going to live here?'

He smiled when he saw her expression. 'Well, that was the idea. That is, if you'd like to.'

He was looking at her steadily, his eyes very blue and clear. Sam felt a sudden ache in the pit of her stomach. Was it duty or love that had made him bring her here?

His smile faded and his forehead creased. 'What is it, Sam?' he asked, his tone suddenly changed. 'Don't you like it?'

'I think it's perfect,' she said quietly.

He drew her around towards him, then gently tilted her chin with his hand so that she met his gaze. 'There was something worrying you last night, and it's worrying you again now. Please won't you tell me what it is?'

For a moment everything was quiet. His eyes looked strikingly blue against his tanned skin in the bright morning light. He gazed at her steadily, searching her face.

She hesitated. 'It's just…' Her lips twisted into a crooked smile. 'Are you quite sure that I'm the woman you really want?'

He stared at her blankly. 'What are you talking about, Sam? What do you mean?'

'I know you have a great sense of duty...'

'Duty?' he repeated. 'You think I brought you here out of duty?' For a moment he looked completely at a loss, but then his brows pulled together into a deep frown. 'I don't understand why you're talking like this. What happened yesterday? Did Caroline say something to you?' he demanded sharply.

'It wasn't Caroline. It was just something I overheard.'

'Something you overheard?'

She took a deep breath. 'Are you sure that it's really me that you want to marry?'

His expression hardened. 'I understand,' he said grimly. 'You've changed your mind.'

No, she thought despairingly, I haven't changed my mind. She shook her head. 'No, you're wrong, it isn't that. I wish we were married already. But ever since last summer, when you told me you thought we should wait before we got married, I've been wondering if this is what you really want. And then, yesterday, I overheard a conversation that made me think that perhaps I was really here because you felt some sort of obligation towards me.' Her lips quivered and she felt close to tears. The only thing of which she was certain was that she had to give him the opportunity to back out of their engagement, if that was what he wanted. But what would she do if he did?

'An obligation?' His brows lifted and he stared at her uncomprehendingly.

'Yes, an obligation.' She paused, then said quickly in a whisper, 'Because we've slept together.'

He looked utterly bewildered. 'And who is it that you think I really want to marry?'

There was a moment's silence.

'Miriam Foster,' she whispered.

A muscle twitched in Jack's cheek and for a moment he didn't say anything. Sam's heart went cold. Why didn't he deny it? She felt tears welling up in her eyes as she looked at him. She went to turn away from him but he caught her by the elbow, his eyes suddenly on fire.

'I don't know how much it is you know, but let me tell you this - Miriam Foster would stop at nothing to get what she wanted. There was a time, a long time ago, when I was under her spell, but she means nothing to me anymore, nothing at all. You're the woman I want to spend the rest of my life with, not her.' His grip on her arm tightened and he pulled her closer. 'I've made a lot of mistakes, and I know it. The biggest one was not marrying you in England last year, when I had the chance. I thought I was doing the decent thing, but I only wish you knew how much I regretted it afterwards. You could have been here months ago if you'd been my wife.

Instead, we've had to wait, and we're still waiting now.'

'But you've been so distant since I got here. And yesterday...'

'I know. Yesterday I left you all alone with Caroline, and that was another mistake. I didn't know you'd be running into Miriam Foster. The only reason I wasn't with you was because the sale was completing on this house and I needed to be in the office.'

He paused, but she didn't say anything. His words slowly sank in.

'Maybe I should have told you about this place sooner, but it's taken a lot of doing and I wanted it to be a surprise. My parents' house is swell, but I didn't think you'd want to start married life living with your in-laws. Living here we'll be close to the centre of town and it'll be easier for you to make new friends.'

She nodded mutely, still not quite believing.

'I've thought about all this long and hard. You're giving up a hell of a lot for me and I want to make everything as easy as possible. I know I may have seemed a little distant, but it's been the only way I've had to keep myself under control. Ever since you got here, I've had to fight to keep my hands off you. Last night, when I saw you in that dress, I thought I'd go out of my mind, I wanted you so much.' He lifted his hand and touched her cheek and when he spoke again his voice was soft, 'I've shared things with you that I'll never be able to forget. It was good to get home last October, but hardly anyone here can comprehend what we all went through. You know me, Sam, like no one else can or ever will. Marry me. All the papers are ready and we could do it today if you wanted. You only have to the say the word and we'll be husband and wife.'

She held his gaze for a long moment. How could she ever have doubted him? Why had she chosen to believe the idle gossip of jealous women and why hadn't she trusted what she knew deep in her heart to be true? She lifted her hands to his neck and pulled his face down close to hers. His arms tightened around her and his mouth covered hers, and for the first time since she'd arrived she felt the deep, raging fierceness of his need for her.

When at last he released her, she looked up at him shyly. 'Aren't you going to show me the rest of the house?'

He took her hand in his and led her up the stairs, then pushed open the door of the master bedroom and pulled her over to the bed. He followed her down onto the covers and his hands tangled in her hair as his mouth found hers once more.

'I love you, Sam,' he whispered. And she knew that nothing else mattered in the world.

ABOUT THE AUTHOR

Sally Anderson was born in Nottingham, England. She studied history at university and has always loved period dramas and historical fiction. A NIGHTINGALE SANG is her first novel.